DEATH
DESERVED

JØRN LIER HORST & THOMAS ENGER

TRANSLATED FROM THE NORWEGIAN
BY ANNE BRUCE

**ORENDA
BOOKS**

Orenda Books
16 Carson Road
West Dulwich
London SE21 8HU
www.orendabooks.co.uk

First published in the United Kingdom by Orenda Books, 2020
First published in Norwegian as *Nullpunkt* by Capitana Forlag, 2018
Copyright © Jørn Lier Horst & Thomas Enger, 2018
English translation copyright © Anne Bruce 2020
Published by agreement with Salomonsson Agency

A catalogue record for this book is available from the British Library.

ISBN 978-1-913193-00-3
eISBN 978-1-913193-01-0

This book has been translated with financial support from NORLA

Typeset in Garamond by typesetter.org.uk

Printed and bound by CPI Group (UK) Ltd, Croydon CR0 4YY

For sales and distribution, please contact info@orendabooks.co.uk or visit
www.orendabooks.co.uk.

ABOUT THE AUTHORS

Jørn Lier Horst and Thomas Enger are both internationally bestselling Norwegian authors. Jørn Lier Horst first rose to literary fame with his No. 1 bestselling William Wisting series. A former investigator in the Norwegian police, Horst imbues all his works with an unparalleled realism and suspense.

Thomas Enger is the journalist-turned-author behind the internationally acclaimed Henning Juul series. Enger's trademark is his dark, gritty voice paired with key social messages and tight plotting. Besides writing fiction for both adults and young adults, Enger also works as a music composer.

Death Deserved is Jørn Lier Horst and Thomas Enger's first co-written thriller.

Follow them on Twitter @LierHorst and @EngerThomas and their websites: jlhorst.com and thomasenger.com

ABOUT THE TRANSLATOR

Anne Bruce, who lives in Scotland, has a joint honours degree in Norwegian and English from Glasgow University. She has translated a number of books by Jørn Lier Horst, most recently *The Cabin*: both *The Caveman* and *The Katharina Code* won the prestigious Petrona Prize in the UK. She has also translated several novels by Anne Holt, the latest of which is *A Grave for Two*.

Follow her on Twitter @annembruce.

DEATH DESERVED

'Let's do it.'

(Gary Gilmore's last words before he was executed.)

SUNDAY 9 MAY 1999

The police radio crackled.

'0-1 seeking all available units for Agmund Bolts vei in Teisen.'

Alexander Blix glanced across at Gard Fosse. 'That's just round the corner,' he said.

Blix slammed his foot on the accelerator as Fosse picked up the mic from the dashboard.

'0-1, this is Fox 2-1,' Fosse relayed. 'We're in Tvetenveien, about one minute away.'

Blix switched on the blue light and sirens just as more crackling noises filled the car: *'Fox 2-1, 0-1 reading you. This is a possible shooting incident. There have previously been reports of domestic violence at the address.'*

Domestic violence, Blix thought. He'd been called out on a number of similar cases, but none where a shot had been fired.

He swung into Agmund Bolts vei at the end of the Østre Gravlund graveyard, stepped on the gas again and swept past several blocks of flats with balconies facing the street. Cars were parked on both sides of the road. Birch trees at regular intervals.

This was what they had trained for.

It was what they had been looking forward to – being first to arrive at a real crime scene. For a year they had been rookies, sitting in the back seats of patrol cars. Now they were in charge. Blix's hands clenched the steering wheel.

'Looks like it's up ahead,' Fosse said, pointing to a huddle of by-standers.

Blix braked sharply and stopped the car at an angle across the road. He turned off the engine and sirens, but left the blue light on.

'It came from in there,' a woman cried as Blix and Fosse leapt out of the car. She pointed at a small white house.

'Sounded like a high-calibre gun,' a man added.

'Has anyone come out since you heard the shots?' Blix asked. 'Or gone in?'

The woman shook her head.

'How many people live there?' Fosse asked.

'Four,' another woman answered. 'They've got two little girls, but I think only one's at home.'

Blix swore under his breath. 'OK,' he said. 'Go home and stay inside. And lock your doors.'

As the small crowd dispersed, Blix pushed the garden gate open. 'You take *that* side of the house, and I'll take the other one,' he told Fosse, pointing in both directions.

'You're not thinking of going in?' Fosse protested.

'A shot's been fired,' Blix replied. 'And there could be a little kid in there.'

'Safety first,' Fosse said, repeating their police college instructors' mantra. 'We have to wait for backup.'

Blix was familiar with the directive. The situation called for them to isolate and observe while waiting for reinforcements. But this was no college assignment.

'Backup could take ten minutes,' he said. 'And we don't know if we even *have* ten minutes.'

Moving to the car, he opened the boot, unlocked the gun safe and took out his service weapon, then loaded it with six cartridges and clicked the barrel into place.

'Seriously, we really have to—'

'Help the kid,' Blix interrupted, pushing past his colleague. 'If she's in there.'

He walked up to the front door and squinted through the thick glass window that occupied the top half of the door. Saw nothing.

He wheeled around to face Fosse. 'Are you just going to stand there?'

Fosse shifted his weight from one foot to the other. 'I don't like this,' he said.

'Neither do I,' Blix replied. 'But we have to do something.'

He moved around to the side of the house, where he stood on tiptoe, trying to peer in through the only window on the gable wall, but it was too high. He continued on, emerging into a small garden where snow was still piled up. The bushes were brown and scraggly. He spotted a rusty swing frame and a ramshackle veranda. Armchairs dotted with cushions. Empty, brown beer bottles on the veranda floor, and an ashtray overflowing with cigarette butts.

Blix stepped warily, fearing the sound of footsteps would signal his presence. The living room had picture windows, but the reflection made it difficult to see inside; he knew, though, that the huge expanse of glass left him exposed.

He turned around and made his way back to the front door. Fosse was now sitting in the car; Blix could hear that he was talking to the operations centre. Blix inserted his earphone and caught the operator saying that the nearest patrol car was twelve minutes away.

Blix took a breath, settled his shoulders. Tried the door.

It creaked as it swung open. Blix took two steps inside. Stopped. Listened. Heard nothing.

Or...

Was that a whimper? A sniffle? Someone saying 'shhh'?

He moved forwards, gun raised, leaving the door wide open behind him, hoping that Fosse would change his mind and follow.

A passageway led him further into the house. The floorboards were noisy. He peeked into the nearest room and quickly withdrew his head. A small toilet with a wash basin. He repeated the manoeuvre at the next room. No one there either. His breath quivered as he inhaled. He struggled to listen again, but could near nothing.

Bad sign.

The door to the kitchen was slightly ajar. Blix slowly nudged it open. It also creaked.

He let it swing wide.

A woman lay flat on her back, lifeless, her head turned to one side, so he could see her blank, staring eyes. A large pool of blood had collected on the floor beside her, a rag rug nearby beginning to soak it up.

He swallowed. Felt an insistent throbbing in his throat and chest.

He held his breath for a few seconds, then raised his gun and stepped inside the room, making sure to avoid treading in the blood. Crouching down, he checked the body for a pulse but found none. He stood up and spoke as softly as he could into the radio attached to his lapel.

'0-1, this is Fox 2-1 Alpha. A woman is dead, shot. I repeat: a woman is dead, shot.'

The radio made a slight crackling noise. As Blix stepped away from the woman, he caught a glimpse of the gaping hole in the centre of her ribcage.

'Copy 0-1.'

'Don't come any closer.'

The voice, hoarse and strained, came from further inside the house. Blix halted. He stretched out, trying to see around the doorframe and into the living room.

There, in front of a glass table, was a man with a gun in his hand. It was pointing at the blonde head of a girl who could not have been more than five years old. She was weeping silently. Sobbing. Shaking.

'Don't come any closer,' the man repeated. 'I'll shoot. I'll shoot both of you.' He shoved the pistol into the little girl's hair.

Blix hoped she hadn't seen the body in the kitchen. Hoped she hadn't seen the woman die.

'Relax,' Blix said – he could hear the tremble in his voice.

'Put the gun down,' the man said.

'Please, don't...'

'Put. The gun. Down.'

The man was probably in his late thirties, bearded, sweaty, with a shock of short, straggly hair. He took the gun away from the girl's head and turned it on Blix. No tremor. No nervousness. Just desperation.

The girl closed her eyes. Tears ran down her face.

'Don't do anything stupid,' Blix said – he was trying to call upon everything he had learned at college, what he should say, what he should do in a situation like this. But now he was in one, he could think of no sensible strategy. He was forced to improvise. Make an attempt to talk some sense into the man.

His mind drifted to Merete, waiting for him at home. She had never liked his choice of profession. She'd always warned him of the dangers he would have to confront.

He thought of Iselin, barely three months old.

Blix lowered his gun.

'What's your name?' he asked as he fought to control his breathing.

The man made no response.

'In only a couple of minutes, the whole house will be surrounded,' Blix went on. 'You won't get out of here.'

'They're mine!' the man wailed suddenly. 'Mine!'

'Yes, and you'll get to see them grow up,' Blix said, nodding. His eyes searched for a second child, but he only saw the girl.

'*No one* is going to take them from me,' the man said. 'Do you hear?'

'I hear you, but please – don't make things any worse than they are.'

'Put down your gun,' the man repeated with even more desperation in his voice. 'I won't tell you again. Get out of here! This is *my* home.'

Blix listened out for sirens. For Fosse.

'I can't do that,' he said, looking at the little girl again and trying hard to thrust aside thoughts of his own daughter. 'I can't leave,' he said. 'Not now when you—'

'You've got five seconds,' the man broke in.

Blix raised his eyes to look at him. Grubby white singlet, sweat stains on the stomach, curly chest hairs poking out.

'Please...'

'Five.'

He was not going to do it. These were just empty threats.

'Can't we just sit down and—'

'Four.'

Blix took a deep breath. Gulped.

'Let's talk about this...'

'Three.'

Blix gripped his gun even harder. 'Think of your daughter, think of what you're taking away from her.'

'Two.'

The guy looked completely mad, Blix thought. He raised his gun again.

'She's only, what, five years old?' Blix flexed his finger on the trigger. 'One.'

The guy is going to do it, Blix thought. *Bloody hell, he's really going to do it.*

And then a shot rang out.

1

There was a slight chill in the air. Blix tugged the lapels of his jacket together over his neck and trudged towards the police headquarters building. He glanced up at the nine floors of glass and steel, feeling his usual sense of humility. He swiped his pass, keyed in his code and went inside the building, which was already buzzing with life.

He reached the lift, thankful that he hadn't had to chat to any of his colleagues. On the sixth floor, he grabbed a cup of coffee before sitting down at his desk at the far corner of the spacious open-plan office.

As always he was the first one to arrive. Since turning forty, Blix had found that he'd started to wake up earlier and earlier – even before his alarm rang. But there was nothing to fill his time at home in his flat, and at the office at least he was sure of finding some coffee.

He slung his jacket over the back of his chair, stacked four used plates from the canteen, one on top of the other, and set them down on the empty desk next to his. Then he logged on and took a swig from his cup while waiting for his computer to fire up.

It had become a kind of ritual: every morning he visited the web pages for the *Worthy Winner* show. Today the faces of most of the contestants were crossed out. There were only four left in the house.

One of them was Iselin.

Everyone at the police station knew, but no one mentioned it. At least not to him.

Blix had been strongly against her participating in the programme, even though he hadn't actually been sure what it was all about. He'd wanted her to find a job or a place at college instead. Their argument had ended with Iselin making it clear that she didn't want to see him in the studio during the live transmissions.

He hadn't spoken to her since.

He clicked on the live feeds. Iselin was still asleep. The camera was in night mode and the greenish screen image had poor contrast, but he could see that she had thrown off her quilt during the night. In some strange way he felt closer to her now, looking at her through a camera lens, than he had done for many years.

For the first few weeks of the series, he'd remained unhappy about her being on TV and was pleased that she'd decided to use Merete's surname rather than his. But in the past few days he couldn't help feeling a certain pride that his daughter was regarded as someone worthy of winning the million-kroner prize money.

He clicked into the comments, where he found the usual smuttiness. Things he'd warned her about: viewers discussing her physical appearance, the things she said and the way she behaved. Most of these contributions were negative, but there were also a few cheering her on and giving her words of encouragement.

A movement nearby made Blix turn his head. Gard Fosse was standing on the other side of the desk with a folder tucked under his arm.

'A bit early in the morning for porn sites, isn't it?' he said, smirking.

Blix looked up at his superintendent lazily, before clicking on to the criminal records system and lifting his cup to his mouth.

'Good morning, boss,' he said, unsure whether or not his irony was obvious.

'I want you to look after the new start,' Fosse continued in a more formal tone.

Blix glanced up at him again. '*Me?*'

'She'll be here at nine o'clock,' Fosse replied, darting a look at the pile of dirty plates on the empty desk beside Blix; clearly that was where she was meant to sit. He opened the folder he was carrying. 'Sofia Kovic; twenty-six years old,' he read. 'Half Croatian. Graduated from police college five years ago as one of the best in her year. She's spent two years in Majorstua and three at Crime Prevention.'

Fosse held out the sheet containing these personal details; Blix reluctantly took it from him.

'Has she been brought in on a quota basis or something?' he asked.

'Best-qualified applicant,' Fosse told him. 'I expect you to give her a good reception. And another thing,' Fosse went on, leafing through the folder. 'I've arranged for you to go to the shooting range on Thursday.'

'Fine,' Blix muttered.

'You can't keep postponing it,' Fosse added. 'Your permit runs out next week.'

'I said it's fine.'

Fosse lingered for a few moments, gazing at Blix, before turning on his heel and heading into the corridor, in the direction of his grand office.

Blix followed him with his eyes. What different paths they had taken, he thought. They'd once been classmates and were then patrol partners. Best friends too, at one time.

He couldn't stop the film that now began playing inside his head. The call-out to Teisen. The blue light. The sirens. Everything that had gone wrong afterwards.

2

Emma Ramm let herself in, stowed her bike in the hallway and slipped off her shoes. She was exhausted from her ride, but she still managed to complete her exercise routine with some pushups. She went to the kitchen and filled a glass with water, taking a long sip as she picked up her phone and checked the American celebrity websites to see if anything noteworthy had happened overnight. TMZ had a story about a break-in at Mariah Carey's house in Bel Air. *People* magazine was reporting an apparent quarrel between Pink and Christina Aguilera; this was coverage she could lift. Before she put down her phone, she checked news.no and saw that her story about Vendela Kirsebom had pride of place on the front page.

Yet another day with people who'd gained fame for a variety of reasons. Some valid, others not.

How long could she bear working on all this? She dreamed of having something more substantial to sink her teeth into. Something that would show that she really was a competent journalist, not simply a celebrity blogger.

It was eight o'clock. She gulped down another glass of water and switched on the TV. The news headlines rolled across the screen. There had been another suicide bombing in Kabul. A gang fight in Malmö had ended with fatal consequences. New statistics showed unemployment in Spain was at an all-time high. And the weather forecast predicted a cold, clear day in Norway's capital city.

While Emma did some stretches, the hosts of *Good Morning, Norway* welcomed viewers back to another twenty minutes of easily digested output. One of them – a man with a round face, glasses and curly hair – leaned forwards restlessly. He glanced at his colleague before adjusting his glasses and saying: 'Well, viewers, this is what we *should* have been discussing for the next few minutes.' He held up a book Emma recognised immediately: *Forever Number One* by Sonja Nordstrøm. 'But the author, who should have been with us in the studio, seems to have been delayed.'

Emma smiled. This was typical of Nordstrøm: she always did exactly what suited her. Not for nothing did Anita Grønvold, Emma's boss at news.no, consistently call Nordstrøm a superbitch.

'So we'll have to wait a while before we hear more about the auto-biography that is already the talk of the town before it's even been published – even though no one has any idea exactly which beans Nordstrøm has chosen to spill.'

The other presenter now took over – a woman with long blonde hair, looking incredibly sharp and alert despite the early hour.

'Yes, there's been a great deal of secrecy surrounding this publication,' she said, her eyes searching for the right camera. 'There's no doubt that Sonja Nordstrøm has lived an exciting life. She's won everything that's possible to win in ... when you ... have done all the things she's done.'

Emma sniggered at the presenter's obvious ignorance, and filled her glass again.

'This is indeed a very special day for Sonja Nordstrøm,' the other presenter interjected. 'It's her fiftieth birthday, and she's decided to mark this milestone by publishing a book.'

'We can only hope she turns up,' the female presenter said with an exaggerated smile. 'In the meantime, we can welcome into the studio Petter Due-Eriksen, producer of this channel's hottest show – *Worthy Winner*.'

A burly man in his fifties sat down on the sofa, a microphone attached to a shirt that was rather too tight.

'Petter, we're nearing the end of the show now, aren't we? There are only four contestants left, and this evening they'll be whittled down to three, is that right?'

'Yes, now it really starts to get interesting.'

Emma turned down the volume and took off her training jacket. She had written about this new reality-show concept nearly every day, and was sick of the whole thing. Ten contestants were locked inside a house together with cameras everywhere. There was really nothing new to say about it.

She picked up her mobile and wondered whether to call Nordstrøm, but instantly gave up on the idea. The superbitch would never answer so early in the day. Anyway, Emma had an appointment with the woman's publisher in an hour.

Stripping off the rest of her clothes, she headed for the bathroom, carefully locking the door behind her, even though she lived on her own.

3

Soleane Publishing was located in Kristian Augusts gate, across from Café Amsterdam. There was no enormous, flamboyant sign above the entrance, just a small nameplate on the door that said the office opened at nine o'clock.

Emma checked the time on her mobile and sent a text message to Amund Zimmer, the head of the publishing house, saying she was waiting outside as arranged. Two minutes later, the door opened and an overweight man in his sixties appeared, a copy of *Forever Number One* in one hand and a phone in the other.

'Emma?' he asked.

She nodded.

'Apologies,' Zimmer said, waving his mobile as if it explained his tardiness.

'It's OK,' Emma assured him. 'I'm just glad to get my hands on a copy before it reaches the bookstores.'

'Here,' Zimmer said, handing her the book. 'Write something nice about it.'

'Do *you* know what she's up to today?' Emma asked, as he turned to go back inside. She pointed at the photo of Sonja Nordstrøm on the front of the book.

While Zimmer did seem prepared for the question, at the same time it clearly made him uncomfortable – as if he'd hoped she wouldn't ask. He ran his hand through the wisps of blond hair on his head and made a face. His mobile buzzed, and he checked it quickly, before saying: 'No.'

'No?'

He shook his head.

'You've no idea why Sonja Nordstrøm didn't show up on *Good Morning, Norway* today?'

'No. I haven't managed to get hold of her yet.'

'Is it ... normal for her not to turn up to appearances like that?'

Zimmer hoisted his shoulders and immediately let them drop again. 'Sonja Nordstrøm has always been something of a prima donna,' he said, 'but I can really only answer for what she's been like when *we've* had meetings with her. We've found her to be one hundred per cent professional. So it's a bit ... odd that she didn't appear for the broadcast earlier today. She's not the type to oversleep.'

Zimmer's phone started ringing again. He checked the screen, but once again decided to ignore it.

'What else do you have planned for her today?'

'Well...' he began, 'she should really be all over the place. TV in the morning, and then radio. There's a press conference here scheduled for noon' – he used his thumb to indicate over his shoulder – 'and we've got almost all the newspapers in the country signed up for that. And if I know the media, there'll probably be more radio or TV in the afternoon and evening, even though they haven't asked yet. We've requested she keep the whole day free, more or less, and she was OK with that; she was prepared to do it.'

His mobile stopped vibrating.

'She'll probably turn up eventually,' Emma said.

'Yes, I suppose so,' Zimmer said, with a fleeting smile. 'No doubt she will.'

His phone rang again.

'I have to dash inside again. It...' He raised his mobile in the air.

'Thanks for the book,' Emma said. 'I'm looking forward to reading it.'

'My pleasure.'

Zimmer let himself in, answering the call at the same time.

Emma stood deep in thought for several seconds. Then she located Sonja Nordstrøm's number and phoned her.

'*Hello, you've reached Sonja Nordstrøm. I can't take your call right n—*'

Emma hung up and spent a few moments pondering the situation: should she sit in her regular café and race through the book, or...?

A tram came jangling past. Number eighteen. Emma knew it went up to Ekeberg, where Sonja Nordstrøm lived. She broke into a run and caught up with it at the courthouse.

4

The brittle plastic splintered as Blix crushed the end of his pen between his teeth. He leaned back in his chair and looked down towards the other end of the room, where Gard Fosse stood with the new investigator, introducing her to Tine Abelvik and Nicolai Wibe – like him, two of the department's longest-serving detectives.

Blix found it unfathomable that Fosse had managed to manoeuvre his way to the top of the Violent Crime Unit without having a single genuine investigative gene in his body. Or maybe, he thought, spitting out a sliver of plastic, that was exactly why.

Sofia Kovic's southern European origins were easy to spot. She had brown, mid-length hair and dark eyes, and her skin tone was several shades darker than anyone else's in the department. Ten years ago she would have been unable to fulfil the minimum height requirement for entry to police college.

Fosse pointed across at Blix. Kovic tossed her head as they approached him, making her loose hair sit better. Blix put down his pen and picked some flakes of plastic from his tongue before getting to his feet to shake hands.

They exchanged pleasantries and Sofia Kovic smiled, revealing white teeth. 'I've heard about you,' she said.

Blix hadn't expected anything else. For ages now what had happened at Teisen nineteen years ago had been part of the police college syllabus. The episode had even been given a special name: *The Teisen Tragedy*.

'Blix is going to show you how we work in here,' Fosse told her. 'This will be your workstation.'

Kovic looked around. Blix said good morning to Abelvik and Wibe, then drew some case papers over to his side of the desk and moved the pile of dirty plates to the top of the filing cabinet.

Fosse exchanged a quick look with Blix. 'I'll leave you to it,' he said, turning on his heel.

With a stiff grin, Blix watched him exchange nods and pleasantries with people just arriving in the office.

'So,' he said, turning to Kovic, 'what made you want to work here?'

Kovic sat down. 'I think I can excel here,' she replied without hesitation. 'Do what I'm good at.'

'And what's that?'

'Collecting information, analysing cases, building appropriate hypotheses, thinking creatively, turning accepted truths on their head and finding alternative solutions.' Kovic paused. 'Investigate, in other words.'

Blix looked at her as he twirled his pen between his fingers. Her short speech sounded like something straight from a textbook. Something that would have impressed Fosse.

'It would be good if you managed to solve some cases too.' Blix put his pen back in his mouth.

Kovic put down the slim, transparent folder she'd received from the ICT department and switched on her computer. Waiting for it to start up, she checked her mobile, but immediately set it aside again.

'So what's it like having Fosse as your boss?' she asked.

Forthright, Blix thought. He swallowed the answer that was burning the tip of his tongue, and said instead: 'It's OK, no problems.'

'OK?'

'Yes,' Blix nodded, but did not deign to elaborate.

The truth was that he and Fosse had completely different approaches to police work. The simplest way to describe it was theory and practice. He followed his gut instinct, Fosse the book.

'He wants me to show you how we work here,' Blix said, reaching out to the papers on his desk and picking up a random bundle of case folders. He deposited them on her desk with a thump. 'This is how we work here,' he said, with an apologetic smile. 'One case at a time. Welcome to the madhouse.'

5

Emma got off at the stop near Jomfrubråten. She'd made good use of her tram ride, making a few phone calls to people she knew in the TV 2 building. She'd learned that a taxi had been ordered to collect Sonja Nordstrøm at 7.20 a.m. With a little determined digging, she'd even managed to find out the driver's name and phone number. Daniel Kvam. She'd called him straight away, but had only reached his voicemail.

For the last ten minutes of the tram journey, she'd thumbed through the first few chapters of *Forever Number One*, which had left her in no doubt that it would be explosive. Athletes, coaches and family members were told a few home truths, and Nordstrøm more or less accused one of her coaches of having sexually abused her.

Her phone rang just as she crossed Kongsveien.

'Hi, it's Daniel Kvam. You just phoned me?'

'Yes,' she said, and explained who she was. 'Thanks for returning my call. It's about a trip you had arranged for earlier today. You were to pick up Sonja Nordstrøm in Ekeberg at 7.20 a.m., is that right?'

'That's right enough,' Kvam said. 'But nothing came of it.'

Emma frowned.

'I waited outside her house for fifteen minutes, at least, but she never came out.'

'Didn't you phone her?'

'Yes, but it went straight to voicemail. I got out and rang her door-bell, but she still didn't appear, so in the end I drove off.'

Emma said thanks and hung up.

She was now standing outside Nordstrøm's magnificent villa, a house situated close to Kongsveien. It had to be at least 400 square metres of real estate, she reckoned, with a massive garage, painted white, adjacent. Building materials wrapped in plastic and remnants of packaging from renovation work were piled up in front of one garage door. Brown, compacted cardboard boxes.

The gate was open, which made Emma think Nordstrøm might have driven off somewhere earlier that day or the previous evening – that basically she'd done a bunk. A media circus such as Amund Zimmer had described would take the wind out of most people's sails, even if you were totally used to it.

Emma stepped on to the tarmac driveway leading down to the house. Stopping at the front door, she rang the doorbell and heard it chime inside.

No answer.

She tried one more time with the same result: no one came to open the door. Taking a few paces back, she peered at the windows on the upper storey, but there was no face peeking back at her from behind the curtains. She couldn't hear anything either.

She tried the doorbell once again. Still no sound from anyone inside. A flash of inspiration made her try the door handle, and she was taken aback to find the door unlocked. Emma let go of the handle but the door continued to glide slowly open. She took a step forwards. Poked her head ever so slightly into a spacious hallway with dark tiles on the floor.

Something on the floor further inside caused her to knit her brows. A coat stand lying on its side. She saw some shards of glass as well, scattered in front of a frame that must once have held a full-length mirror.

Emma stood still and called out: 'Sonja Nordstrøm?'

She listened, but there was no response.

The sound of her shoes on the tiled floor in the outer hallway resonated through the house.

'Hello!' she shouted again, noticing how shaky her voice had become. Her trepidation did not prevent her from venturing further inside, though, into a huge hall with floor tiles in a checkerboard pattern. She made sure not to trample on the fragments of glass from the full-length mirror.

A high ceiling, with the lights switched on, and a glittering chandelier. A staircase led to the upper storey.

Emma continued to call out to Nordstrøm, but still received no answer.

She looked into the kitchen, where everything was elegant – bright surfaces, cooker and fridge in brushed stainless steel. The dark tiles also covered the floor in here. A cupboard full of wine bottles. Fresh flowers on a colossal table. Two wine glasses on the worktop, just beside a copy of *Forever Number One*. Emma shouted Nordstrøm's name again, but heard nothing.

Or...

Yes, she *did* hear something.

She followed the sound out of the kitchen and into what appeared to be a living room. The TV was on, tuned into some sports channel or other. In the centre of the TV screen, a starting number was attached with a piece of tape. Number one.

Emma stood looking at it for a few seconds. *That's odd*, she thought, as she picked up the remote control to switch off the TV. Then, in a split second, felt how deathly still everything had become.

'Nordstrøm?'

Her voice hardly carried.

She made one more attempt, louder this time. Still no answer.

All of a sudden she did not want to be there. She had to get out. Fast.

She moved quickly. Her foot slid on the loose carpet in the hallway, but she managed to stay on her feet. She had to fight the urge to look back to see if anyone was watching or chasing her.

Once outside, she was able to breathe normally again. Closing the door behind her, she stood puzzling what to do next. A cat emerged from under a bush and disappeared around the corner of the house. Emma took out her phone and called Kasper.

Kasper Bjerringbo was a Danish journalist she had met at a seminar on digital journalism in Gothenburg a few months earlier. He had worked on Ritzau's crime reporting unit for years.

'Well, wonders will never cease,' Kasper said in a thick Danish accent.

'Hi, Kasper,' Emma said. 'Are you tied up?'

'Yes, at least I am now.'

Emma smiled, and felt her cheeks grow warm.

'Nice to hear from you,' Kasper said. 'It's been a while.'

'Yes, it has.'

'It ... we had fun, didn't we?'

She pictured his black curls, his captivating smile. His very fit, naked body.

'Yes we did,' she said. Until early in the morning, when tiredness had overcome her and she felt the urge to sneak back to her own bed.

'I need some help,' she said. 'Some advice.'

'What about?'

'Do you have any experience of ... disappearances?'

'Well, we have a pretty big case going in Denmark right now, in fact.'

'Oh?'

'Yes, a footballer who's been missing for just over a week – maybe you've read about him?'

Emma hadn't. She didn't pay much attention to football.

'Why were you wondering?' Kasper added.

Emma wasn't sure how much detail she should give him, so, without mentioning Nordstrøm by name, she told him about the missed appointment at TV 2 and about the house being empty, with the front door open.

'I think something might have happened to her,' she concluded.

Kasper was quiet for a few seconds. Emma pictured him sitting in his office, playing with his curls.

'Then you really have no choice. You have to contact the police,' he said. 'And you have to tell them you've been inside. If you withhold that kind of information, it might cause problems for you later.'

Emma looked up at the house, hoping she would see Nordstrøm's face in one of the windows. Kasper was right, of course.

'The police will almost certainly take it seriously, especially if we're talking about a famous person,' Kasper added.

'Thanks,' she said. 'I knew I could count on you.'

'You're welcome,' he replied, then paused for a moment. 'How are things with you otherwise?' he asked.

'Fine,' Emma said.

'You're not thinking of coming to Copenhagen anytime soon?' he added.

Emma smiled. 'I don't think so.'

'That's a pity,' Kasper said.

Yes, Emma said to herself. Maybe it was.

'I have to go now,' she said, thanking him again for his help.

For a brief moment, after the call ended, she closed her eyes and shook her head. *My God. Stupid, crazy behaviour.* Copenhagen and Kasper could actually be really enjoyable. At least until the question of where she should sleep arose.

The steady rumble of traffic from Kongsveien made her brush those thoughts away.

'OK,' she told herself, taking a deep breath. Then she dialled the number for the police.

6

The phone vibrated in Blix's pocket, and he fished it out. The display showed a number he had saved as 'TV-Eckhoff'. Eckhoff worked at the production company behind *Worthy Winner* and had been involved in developing the programme concept. During filming, he acted as a link between the participants and their families.

'Blix here,' he answered.

'It's Even Eckhoff,' the man at the other end said. 'Enter Entertainment.'

Blix pushed his chair out from his desk and turned away slightly. It was not often he felt uncomfortable talking to people, but there was something about Eckhoff's whole manner. His voice. As if he were absolutely determined to try to sell Blix something he didn't want.

'It's about the live broadcast tonight,' Eckhoff continued.

Blix pictured Iselin on the sofa with the programme presenter, and how the camera sometimes zoomed in on Merete and her new boyfriend. The two of them had been there for every live show. The production company was keen for the participants' family and friends to be present; they wanted to capture their reactions and emotions, but also have them there to console the competitors when they were voted off.

'I've spoken to Iselin,' Eckhoff continued. 'She'd really appreciate seeing you in the audience.'

'Has she said that?' Blix asked.

'Well, she said it was OK for me to ask you,' Eckhoff replied.

Blix felt touched. Of course, he was ready to take the hand Iselin was holding out to him, but he really didn't want to sit next to Merete and Jan-Egil.

'I'll see,' he said.

'We have to reserve seats in the auditorium, so it would be helpful if you could let me know as soon as possible.'

'OK,' Blix said. 'But I have to go now.'

He ended the call, pulled his chair up to his desk again and glanced at Kovic before busying himself with something on the computer.

A moment later, Gard Fosse appeared with a scrap of paper torn from a notebook in his hand and made a beeline across the office for Kovic and Blix. Blix could see how important he felt, and it irritated him.

'I want you to take a look at a missing person case,' Fosse said.

'Can't Crime Prevention take care of that?' Blix asked.

'They've asked us to look into it,' Fosse explained. 'They're working flat out on other things.'

'What about uniformed patrols?'

'The current response time for them is ninety minutes.'

He waved the paper in the air. 'A journalist phoned it in. The person who's gone missing is none other than Sonja Nordstrøm.' He paused. 'It won't look good if we sit on it.'

Kovic stood up and took the scrap of paper. 'Stupendous Sonja,' she remarked, looking enthusiastic.

'A journalist?' Blix protested. 'Shouldn't we receive a report from a family member before we rush out?'

'Nordstrøm has failed to turn up for both radio and TV interviews today, without notice,' Fosse said. 'The journalist is at her home now. She says the house is unlocked and she can't make contact with anyone inside. Off you go – check it out, and take it from there.'

Kovic had already slipped on her jacket. Fosse smiled ingratiatingly at her before wheeling around and moving on to the next delegated task of the day. Blix slowly rose to his feet – with a heavy sigh.

7

The police had told her to wait. At first Emma sat on the steps, but she felt ill at ease with her back to the empty house, so she moved to the wrought-iron bench beside the entrance.

She took her laptop from her bag and checked the online newspapers. They all carried something on the Nordstrøm autobiography.

'Took Drugs', was the title of the headline story in *VG*. It referred to Nordstrøm's worst rival throughout her career, Cecilie Krogsæther. The article was illustrated with a photo of her at the top of the podium at the Berlin Marathon, one year when Nordstrøm had not taken part. Nordstrøm's claims were elaborated upon in the article below: she had seen Krogsæther use hypodermic needles several times, and also cited her competitor's Czech doctor, who had apparently insinuated that Krogsæther didn't have clean blood in her veins.

Dagbladet's story was similar, but they had contacted Krogsæther's lawyer, who insisted that the allegations were absurd, and threatened consequences.

Cutting a little from both articles, Emma did a rewrite and edit. It was rare for her to take such shortcuts, but she knew Anita Grønvold was waiting for her to publish something.

It took her only a few minutes. At the end of the piece she added a promise that she would share with her readers more sensational snippets from Nordstrøm's autobiography as the day wore on. She pressed the *publish* button, then began to jot down the most important points in the sexual abuse accusations, at the same time reminding herself that she needed to talk to someone from the athletics world about who these might be levelled at, since the name of the coach was not given. The alleged assault had happened when Nordstrøm was only fifteen years old.

After that, Emma clicked onto her publisher's home page, where there was a video designed to attract readers. Following a series of cobbled-together images from Nordstrøm's career, accompanied by Vangelis' *Chariots of Fire*, a deep, histrionic male voice began to speak:

'At the age of four, Sonja Nordstrøm's father asked her a question: Do you want to be the best in the world? Yes, Sonja replied. Then you must listen to me, her father said. Yes, Sonja answered. Fourteen years later, Sonja Nordstrøm won her very first World Championship medal. A further twelve of these would follow, but success did not come without a price. In this outspoken autobiography, she tells of victory and loss, of friends and foes, and not least of difficult relationships with everyone who came close to her.'

New film clips followed – of Nordstrøm at the top of various podiums, celebrating, waving, but always with some reservation apparent in her face, as if she couldn't let herself really jump for joy.

None of the online newspapers had yet mentioned Nordstrøm's disappearance.

Emma cast a glance at the house before opening her desktop publishing program again and starting to draft a new article. The headline was a single word: *'Missing'*.

8

The wrought-iron gate facing the street was open and banging back and forth in the wind. Blix swung on to the pavement and parked alongside the fence.

Kovic checked the notes she had received from Fosse. 'The journalist's name is Emma Ramm,' she told him. 'She works at news.no.'

Blix's diaphragm contracted sharply. 'What did you say?' he asked in a cracked voice.

Kovic repeated the journalist's name and workplace.

Blix swallowed. Hard, several times over.

'Is something wrong?' Kovic asked.

Blix couldn't reply, and even found it difficult to meet Kovic's quizzical gaze.

'Hm?' was all he managed.

'I was just wondering if anything was up. You went pale all of a sudden.'

Blix was still unable to speak, instead gesturing that they should get out of the car.

He took some time to lever himself out of his seat. He had become hot, and once he'd finally emerged from the car, it was a relief to have the wind blowing in his face. He had to take a sidelong step to steady himself, grabbing the figurine on top of the gate, closing his hand around it so tightly that his knuckles blanched. At last he fixed his eyes on the girl seated on a bench outside the front entrance.

Blix felt his heart hammering inside his chest, and his armpits were sweating.

'Why don't you take the lead on this one?' he mumbled to Kovic, letting her go through the gate first.

Emma Ramm stood up and greeted Kovic, who then moved aside and introduced Blix.

He held out his hand, hoping Emma wouldn't notice how clammy it was.

'When did you get here?' Kovic asked.

'Forty minutes ago,' Emma answered. 'The door's unlocked, but she's not at home.'

Blix gazed at her. Her blonde, shoulder-length hair was arranged nicely. Her blue eyes were alert, her nose narrow and her cheekbones pronounced. She had very even, white teeth.

'Have you been inside?' asked Kovic.

'I looked in, yes,' Emma explained. 'There's a shattered mirror in the hallway.'

Kovic and Blix exchanged glances.

'So you can't be sure that she's not still here? Not one hundred per cent?' Kovic queried.

Emma's answer was slightly shamefaced: 'Not one hundred per cent, no.'

Blix cleared his throat. 'We'll go in.'

'Wait here,' Kovic said to Emma as she followed him.

Blix threw back his shoulders and tried to focus his thoughts on the job. Once inside the tiled hallway, he called out: 'Hello ... this is the police.'

Kovic pointed at the toppled coat stand and the broken mirror on the floor.

'Room by room,' Blix said.

They began to search the house. At every doorway they passed through, he was prepared to find Nordstrøm. In the bathroom with slit arteries; hanging by a rope from the chandelier in the living room; with an empty pill bottle by her side in the bed. But she was not there. Not on the ground floor nor the upper storey, and not in the basement either. Her car was still parked in the garage.

Blix went to check the tool shed while Kovic spoke to Emma Ramm in more detail. He made a circuit of the garden too, then took out his phone. He knew he should call Fosse, but couldn't bear to speak to him right now. Instead he keyed in Tine Abelvik's number and explained where he was and what they had seen.

'I've got a bad feeling about this one,' he said. 'Can you ask Ann-Mari Sara to come out here to take care of the technical side of things?' And before Abelvik managed to answer: 'And I'd like you and Wibe to start work internally. Trace Nordstrøm's phone, contact family members, do a survey of her circle of friends – the usual.'

'I'll see what I can manage,' Abelvik promised.

Blix rounded off the conversation and walked back to the front of the house.

'She wants an official comment,' Kovic said, nodding at Emma, who stood writing something on a notepad a few steps away.

She turned and approached them. 'For the article I'm writing,' Emma said waving the pad.

Blix stared at her. His thoughts crisscrossed, pressing forwards from the back of his head. It was difficult to grasp a single one. Instead he tried to push them away and concentrate on what was happening in the here and now.

'What's your assessment of the missing person case?' Emma asked.

'It's a bit early to say anything.' He cleared his throat and added: 'But we're making some preliminary inquiries.'

'What kind of inquiries?'

'Routine procedures,' he replied, unwilling to get embroiled in details.

'Investigations, then.'

Blix nodded.

'What was your name again?' she asked. 'Sorry, you told me earlier, but I didn't take it in properly.'

Blix hesitated. 'Alexander Blix,' he finally said.

Emma made a note of it. Nothing suggested that she recognised his name.

'With a k or an x?' she asked.

'With an x,' he said. 'Both names: Alexander and Blix.'

'I can quote you on that, then – that you've initiated an investigation?' she asked.

Blix met her gaze and noticed that it was full of life and dedication. Nothing more. Nothing to indicate that she knew who he was.

'Here,' he said, taking out his own notebook. He scribbled down his phone number and handed it to her. 'You can call me or ... make contact if you think of anything else.'

She thanked him, turned around and walked away. Blix stood watching her leave. When she was gone, he closed his eyes for a few seconds and focused on breathing. His cheeks were flushed and he felt sweat between his shoulder blades.

'What do we do now?' Kovic asked.

'Stay here until the technicians arrive,' he replied, without turning to face her. 'In the meantime we can make a few house-to-house inquiries in the neighbourhood. Ask if anyone has seen anything.'

9

Emma had almost reached the end of *Forever Number One*. After visiting Sonja Nordstrøm's home she had headed straight for her regular haunt – Kalle's Choice– a tiny little café on the corner of Sofies plass and Frydenlundgata. Many of the stories she had published had been written at the table in the far corner of the upper floor.

What struck her as she read was how Nordstrøm almost actively sought to destroy her own reputation. She scattered allegations here, there and everywhere, many of them crass and defamatory, which would certainly have personal consequences for her. Emma hoped Nordstrøm had proof of all the allegations she was making, and that the publishing house had performed a thorough legal risk assessment. If not, it could all end in court action.

Several media outlets had now got wind of Nordstrøm's disappearing act. Some of them had used Emma's quote from Alexander Blix, fortunately referring to her as the original source. The story was growing arms and legs, almost minute by minute: Emma spotted it on social media too. A lot of people were worried about what had happened to Nordstrøm, the national icon.

The question was: what now?

Emma leafed back to the beginning of the book. It had been written in collaboration with the sports journalist Stian Josefson – a man Emma knew had taken a severance package from *Aftenposten* a couple of years earlier, when even they had to slim down their workforce.

She decided to call him, glad that no one was sitting at the nearest tables.

The voice that answered sounded morose.

'I'm going to switch off my phone soon,' Josefson said. 'No, I haven't the foggiest where she is, and I've absolutely no comment to make about what's in the book. Got it?'

Emma realised he was about to hang up. 'I like the book,' she said swiftly. 'It's well written. I assume it was you rather than Nordstrøm who actually wrote it?'

Silence fell, momentarily.

'Well, yes. Thanks.'

Emma fiddled with the phone and switched on the recorder function.

'It must have been an interesting job?' she said, trying to pour as much sugar as possible into her voice. Her experience of celebrity journalism had taught her that flattery could make even the most buttoned-up person relax.

When Josefson did not reply immediately, she said: 'Can I ask you how you got the assignment? Was it the publishing house that contacted you, or did you already know Sonja Nordstrøm so well that you...?'

'It was my suggestion, in fact,' he said. 'My idea.'

'So you went to the publishing company and...'

'No, I worked on Sonja for months before she finally agreed. It was actually...' He suddenly seemed discouraged. 'What was it you wanted?'

'It almost sounds as if you regret it now?' Emma asked.

She heard him falter.

'A little,' he admitted. 'Mainly because of all the fuss. I hadn't expected that...' He paused again.

'That what?'

'Nothing,' he said in the end.

'Have you heard from Sonja today?' Emma asked after a few seconds.

'No.'

'You've no idea where she might be?'

'Not a scooby.'

'When did you speak to her last?'

'Last night.'

'How did she seem to you?'

'She was exactly the same as always. Apart from...'

He stopped again.

'Apart from what?'

'No, nothing.'

Emma heard noises in the background. Voices, a tumult. Josefson was outdoors.

'Did you discuss PR strategy in advance of the book launch?'

Josefson snorted. 'Do you think *I* had anything to do with that?'

He clearly intended to answer his own question, so she didn't reply.

'I was just a tool for her, like all the other people she used,' he went on. 'And for the publisher. They don't give a shit about my opinion.'

Emma doodled on her notepad hoping he would go on.

But he didn't.

'So you've absolutely no idea where she could be, then?'

'No. And it's no odds to me. I've done what I had to do. Now I don't have time to talk to you anymore.'

And he ended the call.

Emma sat staring at the phone for a few moments before putting it down. Stian Josefson was angry, she thought. Offended. It wasn't unusual for a co-writer with a role such as his to be overlooked once a book reached public attention.

Josefson's story was now her fourth instalment about Nordstrøm, though everything to do with the book was starting to pale into insignificance. What both she and her readers wanted answers to was the mystery surrounding her disappearance.

She took out the piece of paper with Alexander Blix's phone number on it and sat fiddling with it as she pondered whether it was too early to make contact. But he had given her carte blanche to do so, hadn't he?

She decided to send him a text message to start with, to avoid seeming too desperate or tiresome. She could call him later.

10

The house-to-house inquiries among the neighbours on the north side of the street didn't yield much. Most of them were not at home, but an elderly lady who lived two houses away was sure she had seen a man in a black car visit Nordstrøm on a number of occasions. Her grandchild, who ran a car showroom, drove the same kind of vehicle – a Volkswagen Tiguan. This was the only thing Blix had on his notepad when he returned to the house to meet Ann-Mari Sara.

The crime-scene technician reversed the large delivery van in through the gate and up towards the entrance. While her team kitted themselves out, he related what he and Kovic had observed during their superficial examination of the house.

'To me, it looks like an abduction,' he concluded.

Sara answered with a nod before she too donned one of the team's white, all-encompassing protective suits. She was known for being taciturn, but also thorough, systematic and focused. Blix enjoyed working with her.

His phone rang. It was a number he had stored as 'Journalist'. As Blix dismissed the call, Kovic arrived back from her own tour of the neighbourhood.

'We may have something,' she said with a nod in the direction of the nearest house. 'There was a car outside Nordstrøm's house late last night.'

'What kind of car?'

'The neighbour I spoke to only heard it – it was after he'd gone to bed. It arrived, the engine ran for a couple of minutes, and then it drove off.'

Blix's phone rang again. 'Journalist'. He switched off the ringer and left his phone to vibrate in his pocket.

'What time?' he asked.

'He was watching TV before he went to bed, and says it must have been just after the evening news on NRK. '

'What does that tell us?'

'I checked. The news ended at half past ten last night.'

Blix pivoted around, looked towards the gate and saw that two in-quisitive onlookers had turned up.

'Are there any toll booths in the vicinity?'

'I'll check that out,' Kovic said, making a note. 'Is there anything else for us here?'

'One thing,' Blix said.

He ascended the steps and called out to Ann-Mari Sara. She walked towards him, pulling down her mask.

'There's a copy of her book lying in the kitchen,' he said. 'I need it.'

Sara fixed her eyes on him. 'You want me to remove it from the crime scene?'

'I don't think anyone has smacked her on the head with it,' Blix answered.

Sara considered this for a second or two. 'Let me take some photos first,' she said, as she disappeared into the house again.

The phone in his jacket pocket vibrated again. Blix took it out and saw that he had received a number of messages as well. One of them was from 'TV-Eckhoff', wondering whether Blix had made up his mind about that evening's broadcast. He had. He would be there, but Sonja Nordstrøm might make it difficult.

He was about to send Eckhoff a reply when Ann-Mari Sara re-appeared with Nordstrøm's book in an evidence bag.

'You could have driven by a bookshop and bought one on your way back,' she said, handing him the bag.

'Well, now we've saved the force a few kroner,' Blix said with a smile as he took it from her.

The phone was relentless. 'Gard Fosse' this time. With a sigh, Blix slid his thumb towards the right.

'I hear you've initiated a full investigation,' his boss said.

'That's a privilege I still have in this job,' Blix replied sourly. For once there was no response.

'Sara has just arrived,' Blix informed him, glancing again at the gate where he now recognised the face of a journalist from *Dagsavisen*. 'Can you send a patrol car here too, to help us keep the rubberneckers away?'

A few seconds elapsed before Fosse answered: 'I'll see if we have anyone available,' he said, before coming up with what Blix knew was the real reason for his call. 'As far as the press is concerned, I'll take care of all that.'

Blix smiled. 'Of course,' he said, surprised that for once he had managed to keep the irony out of his voice. 'Was there anything else?'

The phone vibrated again.

'Keep me up to speed,' Fosse said, before ending the call.

Blix was left standing with the phone in his hand, flipping through the last few messages. One of them came from a number he hadn't saved:

Any news about Sonja Nordstrøm? Emma Ramm, news.no

Blix was about to ignore this too, but changed his mind and instead tapped in a speedy reply: *Not yet.*

'Here,' he said, handing the evidence bag with the book to Kovic. 'You can read it, see if it contains anything of interest to us.'

They headed back to the car and as he clambered inside, another message ticked in from the same number:

Forgot to tell you that her TV was left on. I switched it off. Didn't touch anything else.

Blix did not answer. But he saved her number. Under 'Emma'.

11

Blix laid aside his plate, wiped his mouth with the back of his hand and logged into the web pages of *Worthy Winner*, clicking through the various live cameras as he picked a crumb of food from between his teeth with his thumbnail. The slow connection meant it took some time for each video to open.

He found Iselin on a camera out in the garden. She was sitting on a bench with a blanket wrapped around her, staring into space. For a moment Blix thought the image had frozen, but then she raised her hand and rubbed her eyes.

Kovic flopped into her chair beside him.

'There's one toll station on Kongsveien and another on Sandstu-veien,' she said.

Blix closed the video feed.

'I've asked for a list of all the vehicles that passed through yesterday evening and during the night,' Kovic went on. 'They don't have photos of the cars, but I'm trying to do a survey of petrol stations and other CCTV footage in the area.'

Blix nodded. Kovic was a self-starter. She was not going to require much supervision, other than the purely practical – where they kept the office supplies and who you had to speak to if the coffee ran out. He wasn't often so fortunate.

'Look for a black Volkswagen Tiguan,' he said. 'She's had a visit from someone in that kind of car.'

Gard Fosse appeared at the other end of the room and pointed at them. 'We'll have a run-through in my office,' he called across.

Blix took a deep breath and rose to his feet, followed by Kovic.

Nicolai Wibe was already seated at the conference table in Fosse's office. He was a well-built man whose background was in undercover surveillance. A couple of years younger than Blix, he had a dishevelled appearance and down-to-earth demeanour. Police lawyer Pia Nøkleby, responsible for the legal aspects of the case, was also at the table.

'Abelvik will be here shortly,' Fosse explained, taking a seat behind the wide desk. 'What do we know?'

Blix took what had become his regular place – at the far end, nearest the door – and glanced up at his boss.

Blix relished his role as investigator. He was capable, and had no ambitions to climb further up the career ladder. Ranks and stripes had never been important to him. Nevertheless it stung him every time he was reminded that Gard Fosse had advanced further than he had.

'We know that Sonja Nordstrøm did not turn up as arranged at TV

2 earlier today,' Blix began. 'A taxi was booked to pick her up at 7.20 a.m., but left after waiting in vain for fifteen minutes.'

He looked at Kovic, who understood and took up the thread.

'The last person we know of, so far, who was in contact with her, was her publisher, who exchanged a few text messages with her last night: they were discussing their plans for today.'

She glanced down at her notes. 'Amund Zimmer is his name. He's coming in later to give a formal statement.'

The police lawyer jotted something down on a sheet of paper.

'Nordstrøm should have been on the radio too,' Blix continued, 'and at a press conference at the publishing house. I've tried to get hold of Stian Josefson, the journalist who co-wrote the book with her, but he's not answering his phone.'

Nøkleby nodded.

Wibe shoved a fresh portion of snuff under his upper lip.

'We're not getting any signal from her phone,' he said. 'So we can't trace her position.'

'Where was it last?' Nøkleby asked.

Wibe shrugged. 'I've set the wheels in motion to obtain historical telecoms data, but we probably won't have it until tomorrow.'

'I can take over that bit,' Kovic offered. 'I've done a lot of work on electronic traces.'

Wibe glanced at Blix, who nodded.

'Go ahead, then,' Wibe told Kovic. 'I'm happy to be shot of it.'

Tine Abelvik appeared at the door. She and Blix had worked together for eight years. An experienced detective, she still allowed herself to become emotionally involved in particular cases. Somehow, Blix thought, that made her better at her job.

'Sorry,' she said, sitting down. 'I got hold of the daughter, Liselotte. She lives in London. She doesn't seem to have much to do with her mother. They spoke on the phone last week, but nothing was said that could help us at all.'

Abelvik leafed through her notebook.

'Then I talked to the ex-husband. He's not been in contact with

Nordstrøm for ages. But he suggested that we check her summer cottage on Hvaler. She was in the habit of going there from time to time. I've asked the local police out there to check it.'

'Good,' Fosse said, with a nod.

'What else do we have?' Nøkleby asked.

Kovic gave an account of the door-to-door inquiries, mentioning the car that had seemingly left Nordstrøm's driveway at half past ten the previous night, but she was interrupted by the phone on Fosse's desk.

'I've asked Ann-Mari Sara to phone in,' he explained, putting the phone on loudspeaker.

'What do you have for us?' he asked.

'I don't think she left the house of her own free will,' Sara answered in her northern accent. 'There are signs of a struggle in the outer hallway, and her toothbrush hasn't been packed either. Her toiletry bag is in a cabinet in the bathroom. Her passport is lying in a drawer in the kitchen, and her handbag is in the living room; her purse and car keys are still in it.'

Blix's phone vibrated on the table in front of him. A call from 'Emma'. He snatched it up and stuffed it into his pocket to muffle its noise.

'Have you found Nordstrøm's mobile phone?' he asked.

'It's not here,' Sara said. 'And there's a rug missing.'

Fosse leaned towards the phone. 'A rug?'

'We can see that there was a rug on the floor in the hallway,' Sara informed him. 'Large enough to carry someone away in.'

'To move a body?' Wibe suggested.

'Yes, but we haven't found traces of physical violence. There's no blood here.'

'Could it have been on the rug?'

'Yes, I guess so, but from experience, lethal violence would have produced traceable spatter.'

'Anything else?' Fosse demanded.

'A man's been here,' Sara replied. 'There's semen on the bed sheets.'

'Recent?'

'Impossible to say. It could be from several men, for that matter. We won't know until it's analysed, but there could be a link with the wine glasses.'

'Explain.'

'There are two wine glasses and an empty bottle in the kitchen. She had a visitor.'

'Fingerprints?'

'Secured from both, but I won't have an answer for you on that today.'

'OK, then,' Fosse said, lifting his hand to the phone. 'We'll let you go on with your work.'

'One more thing,' Ann-Mari Sara said. 'Something I don't like.'

Fosse sat, his hand hovering over the phone, and raised his eyes to Blix. Neither of them was used to Sara expressing personal views.

'There's a starting number taped to the TV set.'

'A starting number?' Kovic queried.

Blix frowned. He hadn't noticed it either. Their rapid examination of the house had focused on searching for signs of life – or the opposite.

'It's from when Nordstrøm was running the Stockholm Marathon,' Sara went on. 'Her starting number was one.'

Silence filled the room for a second or two.

'How do you interpret that?' Blix asked.

'It's not easy to say,' Sara ventured. 'But it's a bizarre thing to do. It seems to me like someone was leaving a marker.'

'A message, is that what you're thinking?' Wibe probed. 'To us?'

'I don't know,' Sara answered. 'But a starting number indicates that something is about to start, doesn't it? Or it could mean the alternative – that something is over and done with, that you've reached your goal.'

No one said anything for a while.

'In any case,' Sara said, 'it's wrong of me to speculate. But now at least you know about it.'

Blix racked his brains to think what it might mean. A starting number, added to the possibility that something had happened to such a high-profile personality as Sonja Nordstrøm, made him sit bolt upright, impatient to get cracking. It had been a long time since he had felt such enthusiasm. He had missed the feeling.

12

The Nordstrøm case was the leading item on the news channel's four o'clock bulletin. A journalist stood outside the house reporting live.

Emma tucked her feet under herself as she curled up on the sofa, annoyed that she had neglected to take photos either outside or inside while she was up there. The thought quite simply hadn't entered her head. Maybe because there hadn't been any famous people to snap, as she was used to. Anita might even have dared to publish images of the interior of the house, at least if the police confirmed that no crime had actually taken place there. But so far they were being unforthcoming, according to the TV reporter.

The phone rang. It was him. The policeman.

'It's Emma,' she said, a touch too eagerly.

'Alexander Blix. You messaged me?'

'Yes, thanks for phoning back. We met at Sonja Nordstrøm's earlier today.'

'Yes, I remember.'

'I just wondered if there had been any developments in the case?'

'Nothing conclusive.'

Emma picked up a pen and flipped off the top with her front teeth. 'How are you organising the investigation?' she asked.

'You have to speak to Police Superintendent Gard Fosse. He's the one dealing with the press.'

'But you returned my call,' Emma protested.

'I thought you might have something more to tell me,' Blix mumbled, clearing his throat. 'Something that you'd remembered?'

'Oh, I see,' she said, slightly disappointed. She needed something she could use for her story. 'What do you get out of the starting number?' she asked. 'Is it some sort of message?'

'It's too early to have a clear idea about anything,' Blix answered.

'I expect you've had time to form a more exhaustive impression of what happened than me. I only popped my head round the door.'

He did not respond to that. Instead he asked:

'Did you touch anything while you were inside the house?'

'No,' she replied. 'Nothing except the TV remote control.'

'Right,' he said.

There was a short silence.

'I see you've interviewed Stian Josefson,' he said, clearing his voice again. 'Do you happen to know where he is?'

Emma was astounded that Blix had actually read her article.

'No,' she replied. 'I didn't interview him face-to-face.'

'You wrote that he had spoken to Nordstrøm yesterday.'

Emma moved the phone to her other ear. The seriousness in the policeman's tone made her wary.

'Yes?' she answered.

'You don't mention whether that was by phone or at her home. Did he say?'

Emma thought through the conversation, feeling foolish. That was a question she should have asked Josefson. 'No,' she replied, embarrassed. 'He broke off the conversation before we were finished,' she added. 'Is he a suspect?'

'We're charting Nordstrøm's movements in the past twenty-four hours,' the investigator continued.

'Can I quote you on that?' she asked.

'You need to speak to Gard Fosse about that sort of thing,' Blix told her.

'Fine,' she said.

'I can give you his direct number,' the investigator added. Emma thanked him; that would make things easier. 'You don't have to tell him you got it from me,' Blix went on.

'Is there anything in particular I should ask him about?' she queried, in the hope that the policeman would give her something more.

Emma sensed some hesitation before he said:

'You can ask him if Sonja Nordstrøm might have been kidnapped.'

13

Blix left police headquarters at 7.25 p.m., four hours after things had started to come to the boil in the department. Gard Fosse was standing in front of the main entrance, basking in the glow of a camera lamp. His grave expression hid what Blix knew was enjoyment.

The news that Sonja Nordstrøm may have been kidnapped had been given huge publicity within a short space of time. Nordstrøm had been world champion thirteen times in various middle and long distances. The international news agencies had started to phone in around five o'clock. Pia Nøkleby had been forced to send out a press release, but it hadn't been enough to keep the sports and crime journalists at bay.

The afternoon and evening had passed, and the detectives were no further forward. They had talked to people close to Nordstrøm and those she discussed in her book, but that hadn't produced any leads. The only one they hadn't tracked down was Stian Josefson, the man who had penned Nordstrøm's story.

There were no vacant parking spaces outside the TV building. Blix ended up parking three blocks away, just beside the square at Gullhaug Torg. He finally entered the building with only five minutes to spare before the show started.

He stood in the foyer, trying to find his bearings, but had no clue which direction to take. A young girl got up from a stool behind a desk. A radio transmitter hung from a strap over her chest, and she had an earplug in her right ear.

'Can I help you?' she asked.

'I'm to be in the audience for *Worthy Winner*,' Blix answered.

'The studio doors close ten minutes before the broadcast begins,' the girl told him.

'My daughter's one of the contestants,' Blix explained. 'Iselin Skaar. I'm her father, Alexander Blix.'

The girl gave him a sceptical look. After the divorce, Iselin had adopted her mother's name.

He considered using his police badge to gain entry, but decided on something else. 'Speak to Even Eckhoff,' he said. 'I think he's kept a seat for me.'

The girl glanced at the time before grabbing her chest mic and relaying the message. Her earplug crackled, but Blix failed to make out what was being said.

'Over and out,' the girl replied, as if she were part of a military operation.

'I'll escort you in,' she said, walking towards the nearest door.

It was pitch dark inside. As Eckhoff approached, his foot became entangled in a cable, but he managed to extricate himself and limped towards Blix. He was wearing a navy-blue suit, an open-neck white shirt and an earplug in one ear. He also held a clipboard in his hand.

'That's brilliant, you managed to make it,' he said, shaking Blix's hand. 'I think you'll like today's test.'

The tests were ethical and moral dilemmas the contestants were faced with either before they entered the house, or during their stay. The way the participants responded, and how their choices chimed with the public's ethical principles, were reflected in votes for the contestant the viewers felt most worthy of winning the prize money.

Eckhoff claimed to be the one who had dreamed up the various tests the programme concept was based on. Blix was reminded of how strongly he disliked people who had an urge to call attention to themselves. In that sense, Eckhoff reminded him of Fosse.

'I kept a seat for you,' Eckhoff said. 'Come with me.'

Eckhoff advanced between the rows of seats in the auditorium. Blix caught sight of an empty seat beside Merete. She spotted him and enthusiastically waved him over. Blix thanked Eckhoff for his assistance, and began to make his way along the row, mumbling apologies to everyone he passed.

'Ten seconds!' yelled one of the operators down on the floor.

Merete stood up and gave Blix a quick hug. Blix held out his hand to Jan-Egil, Merete's new boyfriend, who remained seated, but shook his hand with an indifferent smile.

'Five seconds!'

Someone with sizeable earphones on his head held a hand in the air and counted down, finger by finger. Then the reality show's familiar theme music began to play over the loudspeaker system. Screens suspended from the ceiling showed the introductory titles. The programme presenter got ready in front of one of the cameras. A man encouraged the audience to cheer and applaud, and the screens showed the camera drifting across their faces.

Then the studio manager gesticulated towards the presenter, giving the go-ahead.

'Good evening, everyone, and welcome to *Worthy Winner*! I'm Tore Berg Tollersrud. We now have four contestants left in the house. In the course of this evening, they'll go down to three!'

The audience cheered on cue and held up homemade placards.

'Let's meet the contestants!' Tollersrud yelled.

For nine weeks, Iselin and the other participants had stayed in the specially built house, fully equipped with the most up-to-date and high-end conveniences. Twenty-six cameras and forty-eight microphones were installed around the house and in the area outside, where the contestants could exercise or just have a smoke, if they wanted to. Through the web pages of *Worthy Winner*, viewers could take out a subscription that gave them access to all these cameras, following whichever one they wanted at any particular time.

An exit led from the house into the studio where the live broadcasts were filmed. The sliding door moved up and the four remaining contestants emerged on to the stage one by one as the presenter introduced them. Iselin was number three. She was wearing the blue dress she had worn for the first live transmission.

On her way to the sofa where the other contestants were sitting, she glanced up at the audience. Blix shot one hand in the air and waved, but she did not seem to notice him. He listened to the applause and cheers, but it was difficult to judge her popularity compared to that of the others.

Tollersrud started with some general questions for the housemates, but soon Iselin was in the firing line, as he quizzed her about the past week.

'We've been following you closely,' the presenter said, 'and we've noticed that you've kept yourself to yourself a lot of the time.'

'We've been cooped up together for weeks on end,' Iselin answered. 'There aren't many of us left now, so this is the first time there's been a chance to spend some time on my own.'

The audience laughed.

'So you're ready for another week?'

'I'm ready,' Iselin assured him.

Blix felt his mobile phone vibrate in his inside pocket. He took it out as discreetly as possible. It was Tine Abelvik.

'Can't you put that away for now?' Merete whispered sharply. Blix flicked away the call and put his phone back.

Tollersrud had finished with the introductions and turned to face the camera. 'So now we're ready for this week's test, folks! To find out which of the participants is a worthy winner, we, as you know, have been following them for a while with a hidden camera to discover who they really are – when they don't know they're on TV.'

Blix glanced across at Eckhoff, who was standing at the side of the stage, smiling. His shaved head glistened in the blaze of the spotlights.

'Around three weeks ago, before you entered the house, you each found a five-hundred-kroner note,' Tollersrud went on, turning towards the four on the sofa.

The contestants looked at one another. Some began to laugh, and one hid his head in his hands. Iselin nodded thoughtfully.

'You no doubt remember what you did yourself, but tonight the audience will see it too.'

Berg Tollersrud addressed himself to the nearest contestant. 'Arild, what do you think about that?'

Arild was a smallholder from Hjartdal. Blix thought of him only as The Farmer.

'No, I'm not really sure, I—'

'Where did you find the five-hundred-kroner note?'

The Farmer placed one hand on his thigh. 'Right beside my car outside the store where I usually do my shopping.'

'What did you do with it?'

Even from where Blix was sitting, he could see that The Farmer was blushing furiously.

'Well, I ... didn't have time to try to find out who it belonged to.'

'I'm not condemning you, Arild,' Berg said, with a smile. 'Far from it. There's no right or wrong answer here.'

Blix's inside pocket buzzed again. He ignored it.

'Let's see!' the presenter continued.

The large screens now showed how the hidden cameras had been set up. Then The Farmer came on the scene, driving an old red Nissan, and parked. A bald man walked in front of his car and dropped a 500-kroner note on the tarmac. Blix smiled as he recognised Eckhoff. He was walking a bit stiffly, like amateur actors usually do when they know the cameras are on them.

It did not look as if The Farmer had noticed Eckhoff dropping the money, but when he spotted the banknote on the ground, he was quick to pick it up and stuff it into his own pocket. When he looked around, it was obvious that this wasn't to see who might have lost it, but to make sure no one had seen what he had done.

The item ended with laughter and applause from the audience.

Blix felt his phone once more. Text message this time. He hooked it out without looking at Merete. It was from Abelvik: *Sonja Nordstrøm's phone has just been switched on.*

Blix raised his eyes from the screen before leaning in again to write: *Where is she?*

He was aware of Merete's gaze on him, and tried to ignore both her look and the poke of her elbow.

Another text message: *Where are you? Need you here.*

Blix looked over at his ex-wife and inclined his head towards her to whisper: 'I need to take a phone call.'

Merete looked at him with raised eyebrows. 'Now, this minute?'

Blix nodded and got to his feet.

'Are you coming back?'

Blix didn't answer, but began to edge towards the end of the row, apologising again and again.

'Stay where you are, we'll be right back,' Tore Berg Tollersrud announced onstage. It was a timely pause as some people stood up, making things easier for Blix. Down on stage he saw Iselin get up from the sofa and gaze out into the auditorium. For a brief second, their eyes met.

Blix waved, but Iselin did not wave back. She just looked at him. Blix tried to signal that he would be back and that he just had to take a phone call. But Iselin was looking at something else.

Outside, it was growing dark. He keyed in Abelvik's number. 'What's going on?' he asked.

'Things are a bit up in the air, to be honest. Sonja Nordstrøm's phone is on, but it's not moving.'

'Where is it, then?'

'Gamlebyen Graveyard.'

Blix took a few seconds to have a think.

'Is anyone heading out there?' he asked, starting to walk towards his own car.

'Wibe's on his way there with Ann-Mari Sara. Kovic and I are just getting into our car.'

'Have you tried to phone her?'

'Who?'

'Nordstrøm.'

'Of course. She's not answering.'

Blix picked up his pace. 'We should get an ambulance out there too,' he said. 'If Nordstrøm is there, she might need medical assistance.'

'Kovic has given advance warning to A&E,' Abelvik explained.

Blix wheeled around to face the TV building and thought of Iselin. Swore to himself.

'OK, then,' he said. 'Let's meet at the northern entrance.'

14

Blix parked behind a police patrol car. Tine Abelvik, Nicolai Wibe and Sofia Kovic stood at the graveyard entrance, and Ann-Mari Sara was making her way towards them with two flashlights.

The air was cold and raw. As he approached the group, Blix pulled his jacket flaps together at the neck.

Abelvik brandished a phone at him. 'We have her positioned here,' she told Blix. 'But with no more than two hundred metres precision, so we'll have to cover a pretty extensive area.'

Sara handed him a flashlight.

'Kovic comes with me,' he said, pointing in one direction. 'The others go that way.'

The grass between the gravestones was damp. In the distance Blix could hear the roar of traffic on the E18 motorway. Lights twinkled in the buildings above the Ekeberg cliffs.

Blix and Kovic chose a path each between the gravestones, and began to trudge along, side by side, about twenty metres apart, scanning the terrain, shining their flashlights in between the tombs and the trees.

From somewhere behind them, Abelvik called out Blix's name. He wheeled around and sprinted over the wet grass, Kovic following close behind.

'Over here!' Abelvik shouted. She was standing in the doorway of a tool shed.

'Is it Nordstrøm?' Blix asked.

Abelvik shook her head. 'It's a man,' she answered from inside the hut.

Blix shone his flashlight inside the hut. The man was lying on his side, moving his arm slowly. He looked to be in his sixties and wore workman's clothes. His face was smeared with blood. He was struggling to say something, but couldn't get it out.

Abelvik sat down next to him, put an arm on his shoulder and said something soothing to him.

'The ambulance will be here in three minutes,' Wibe said, putting his mobile back in his pocket.

'OK,' Blix said, looking around at the same time. 'Sara, you stay here. Check whether he has any ID on him. The rest of us will go on searching for Nordstrøm.'

He pivoted around to face Abelvik. 'You're sure her phone's somewhere in here?'

Abelvik checked her phone again, nodding. 'We're almost on top of it.'

They spread out for a fresh search. Behind them blue light pulsed over the gravestones.

'Call her,' Blix said. 'Then we can follow the sound.'

Wibe took out his phone again. 'What's her number?' he asked.

Abelvik produced her notebook. He punched in the numbers she gave him and pressed the dial button; a ringtone sounded.

They stood gazing at one another. The noise came from a spot towards the middle of the graveyard.

'Bloody hell,' Wibe gasped.

The sound grew louder with every step they took. Blix sped up, sweeping the flashlight beam to and fro. He cast a glance over his shoulder and saw that the paramedics had arrived at the tool shed.

The ringtone came from somewhere directly to his right. A clearing. He swerved towards it, rounding a tombstone, and saw before him an open grave.

He managed to stop just half a metre from the edge. He leaned forwards and peered down into it.

There was only a mobile phone. A gold-coloured iPhone.

And then the ringing stopped.

15

The flashing light of the ambulance cast flitting, edgy shadows over Gamlebyen Graveyard. It acted as a magnet for people out jogging or taking a walk in the chilly autumn-evening air. Blix had posted uniformed police at the cemetery's entrances to ensure no intruders gained access.

Blix checked his mobile. Gard Fosse had called twice, Merete three times. She had sent him several text messages as well. Blix didn't read them, but he phoned his boss and gave him a brief update on the situation.

'What does it mean?' Fosse demanded. 'Nordstrøm's phone found in an open grave?'

'I don't know,' Blix admitted.

Fosse sighed. 'We keep this to ourselves until we know more.'

Blix glanced again at the onlookers lining the graveyard walls. A camera flash suggested that one or two journalists were out there too.

Abelvik approached him. 'It's the caretaker,' she explained, indicating the ambulance, where Wibe was seated beside the stretcher, taking a statement from the injured man. 'Børre Simonsen. He lives near here and had just popped in to pull a tarpaulin over a grave that had been prepared for tomorrow, because rain is forecast overnight. While he was doing it, he was attacked and struck down.'

Blix headed for the ambulance, stood a couple of paces behind Wibe and listened to the conversation.

'I noticed him earlier in the day,' the caretaker was explaining in a shaky voice. 'He stood watching when we were digging the grave.'

Wibe noticed Blix behind him. 'This is my boss, Chief Inspector Blix,' he told Simonsen. Then turned to Blix. 'Mr Simonsen was just telling me a guy was hanging about the graveyard – looked like a drug addict, apparently.' He turned back to the caretaker.

'Could you give us a description of the guy?' he asked.

Børre Simonsen seemed to search his memory. 'He was about my height, just over six feet tall, and he had maybe a few weeks of beard growth. I'd guess he was in his early thirties. But – it's impossible to tell with people like that.'

Wibe made some more notes. 'Any other distinguishing marks? Scars, crooked nose...?'

Simonsen mulled this over. 'He had mid-length, slightly straggly hair. Hardly any teeth, I think. That's not uncommon among druggies.'

Once again he needed a moment or two to reflect.

'And then I think he had a burn mark. Here. On his cheek.' Simonsen lifted his hand to his own left cheek.

'A burn mark? Or do you mean a birth mark?'

'I'm not entirely sure. But it was red, at any rate.'

'You're certain it was on this side of his face?' Wibe pressed him.

'Yes,' Simonsen answered. 'Maybe about the size of a five-kroner coin.'

Wibe jotted this down. As he did so, he raised his eyebrows to Blix, as if to ask if he wanted to throw in any questions.

'Did you see if he had a phone?' Blix asked.

'A phone? No, it...' Yet again Simonsen scoured his memory banks for a response. 'He didn't have one out, at least. Maybe he had one in his jacket pocket, I've no idea.'

'Have you seen him here before? Here in the graveyard?'

Simonsen shook his head.

'No one who's been in the habit of hiding in the tool shed or stealing anything from in there?' Blix pointed at the hut behind them.

'No, it's never happened before.'

Blix thanked him and gave Wibe a nod before traipsing through the gloom of the cemetery towards the open grave.

Ann-Mari Sara had donned a whole-body protective suit and was climbing down into the grave with the help of an aluminium ladder.

The display on the phone lit up when she retrieved it.

'It's full of unanswered calls and messages,' she said, slipping the phone into a transparent evidence bag.

'How long do you need to check it?' Blix asked.

'A bit difficult to tell,' Sara replied. 'But we should have most of the answers by the time you're at work again in the morning.'

'Anything else?' Blix added.

Sara looked up at the heap of earth beside the grave. 'There are some good footprints there,' she said. 'Some of them probably from the care-taker, but there are traces of more than one person.'

Sara clambered out again. Blix took her hand and helped her up.

'From whoever threw the phone in there?' he asked.

'Probably.'

Kovic and Abelvik appeared out of the darkness.

'A witness observed a man coming out of the graveyard around 7.30 p.m.,' Kovic said. 'That could be our suspect.'

'There are a couple of journalists out there,' Abelvik added. 'Should I tell them to ring Fosse?'

Blix shook his head. 'Officially, at present, this has nothing to do with Nordstrøm,' he said. 'I'll talk to them. Say the usual – looking for witnesses – but tone it down a little. Then we'll meet back at HQ in half an hour.'

16

The computer ran faster in the evening than during office hours.

Blix tapped in the address for *Worthy Winner*. This time it was The Farmer who had left the house. Iselin was still there. It dawned on him, perhaps for the first time, that his daughter might in fact win the whole shebang. One million kroner. That would be quite a start to adult life.

He glanced up. The investigators were assembling around a confer-ence table in the middle of the open-plan office. The entire room was organised to facilitate day-to-day investigative tasks, but also equipped to allow major cases to be led from here. The walls were lined with whiteboards and a number of flat screen TVs. A digital clock showed the time as 22.43.

Blix closed down the *Worthy Winner* website, got to his feet and brought his notes across to his usual place at the end of the table.

'It's been more than twenty-four hours since anyone heard anything from Sonja Nordstrøm,' he began. 'The local police on Hvaler have been out to inspect her cottage, and it looks to have been untouched for a good while. There's no activity on her credit cards. The data crime unit is trying to hack into her computer and email account. Ann-Mari Sara is working on her mobile phone, primarily with regard to DNA and fingerprints. It's chock-a-block with calls and messages, but we need her pin code to access them.'

Fosse stood at the other end of the table with a ring binder clutched to his chest. Blix assumed his boss would soon get on his soapbox.

'We must try to find the junkie from the graveyard,' he went on, looking ahead.

'I've a few contacts in those circles,' Wibe said. 'They're night birds, so I can get a move on with that as soon as we're finished here.'

'Great,' Blix said.

Fosse stepped forwards. 'Has anyone read her book yet?' he asked.

Blix made eye contact with Kovic. He knew she'd made a start, but she didn't say anything.

'I have,' Fosse went on. 'Not from cover to cover, but I've read the most important points and skimmed through today's newspaper coverage of it. There are quite a few people who might have good reason to want to get even with Sonja Nordstrøm.'

He crossed to the whiteboard and grabbed a green marker pen. This was direct interference in Blix's role, but he refrained from making any comment.

The pen scraped across the board as Fosse wrote *Cecilie Krogsæther* in clumsy letters.

'They were the worst of enemies while they were competitors,' he said. 'In the book, Nordstrøm alleges she took drugs.'

'That skinny waif couldn't possibly have done any harm to Nordstrøm,' Wibe interjected.

'No, but maybe someone who liked her and didn't like Nordstrøm blackening her name is behind ... whatever has happened.'

'Not very many people knew the contents of the autobiography before it was published today,' Kovic pointed out.

'All the same,' Fosse said firmly. 'Krogsæther or people with connections to her have to be eliminated from the case. The same applies to Morten Forsmo.'

'Who's that?' Abelvik queried.

'Sonja Nordstrøm's long-term coach,' Fosse said. 'Even if it doesn't say specifically that he's the one who sexually assaulted her, it's not difficult to work it out. Having such an allegation thrown into your face in public may well bring thoughts of revenge to the surface.'

'But the same counter argument also applies,' Kovic said. 'How could he have known in advance that—'

'He could have found out about it somehow,' Fosse broke in. 'Heard rumours, what do I know? The point is that he has to be ruled in or out of the case. He's been struggling with money and alcohol problems for a while too, according to what I just read in *VG Nett*,' he went on, making a note of Forsmo's name beneath that of Krogsæther.

Blix disliked seeing Fosse at the whiteboard, full of self-importance as he delivered his lecture. The information he was spouting was banal, things they had already covered. He was simply stealing their time. But he was the boss.

'And then there's Arne Rakvåg,' Fosse ploughed on. 'Nordstrøm's ex-husband. She criticises his drinking in the book, and discusses what many would probably call his lack of a sex drive.'

'Good God, did she write about *that* too?' Abelvik groaned.

'Sex sells, you know,' Fosse said, flinging out his arms demonstratively, before consulting the notes in his ring binder. 'Or it may be that someone in SNS Sportswear is trying to put some pressure on her.'

He added *SNS Sportswear* below *Rakvåg*.

'Rumours have been circulating for some time that Nordstrøm plans to sell her interest in the company. That would dramatically affect the share price, since Sonja Nordstrøm *is* SNS Sportswear.'

'So people with shares will lose money,' Abelvik commented.

Fosse nodded.

'Certain members of the finance industry have close ties with hit men,' he went on. 'There could be something along those lines going on here.'

'Or else it may be as simple as someone wanting money from her,' Kovic suggested. 'They've abducted her and are trying to pressure her into paying for her freedom.'

Fosse gave a patronising smile. 'Then they would have taken her daughter instead,' he said. 'It's not so easy for a kidnapped person to rustle up the money for their own ransom.'

Fosse surveyed the assembled officers before approaching the table and laying down the pen, as if to underscore that he had said his piece. Then he left the room.

Blix ran his hand through his hair, aware that all eyes were now on him.

'Something else is going on here,' he said.

'What's that?' Abelvik asked.

'I don't know,' he said. 'But everything seems very stage-managed. Twenty-four hours after Sonja Nordstrøm disappears, her mobile phone is activated so that we find it – in an empty grave. If the motive lies with something in the book, it wouldn't have been necessary to stage something like that.'

Wibe nodded in agreement.

'It's meant to convey some kind of meaning,' Blix concluded. 'A message.'

'Exactly what Ann-Mari Sara implied about the starting number at her house too,' Kovic said.

Silence reigned for a while until Wibe said with a sigh: 'There's some sick bastard running around, playing us for fools.'

The same thought had occurred to Blix.

17

The recording of the previous day's live show was made available online overnight. Blix spooled through it while he ate his breakfast, fast-for-warding to the part with Iselin and the 500-kroner note. The video was from CCTV cameras in a grocery store. The initial images were from diagonally above, as Iselin picked up a shopping basket and entered the store.

A different camera angle showed how a 500-kroner note had been dropped just before Iselin turned into an aisle. She picked it up and looked around, but could see no one else in the vicinity. She walked on to the next row of shelves, where there were several customers, but she didn't make contact with any of them. Instead she placed a couple of items in her basket and headed for the checkout.

The faces of the shop assistant and the other customers were blurred out. The recording had no sound, but Blix saw Iselin put her purchases on the conveyor belt as she said something to the young lad at the till and pointed further into the store before handing over the banknote. The boy took it, stashed it beside the till and then rang up her items. The recording ended with Iselin paying and leaving the store.

Blix smiled with satisfaction. Back in the studio, Tore Berg Tollers-rud turned to Iselin: 'In retrospect, Iselin, are you sure you did the right thing?'

She shifted position on the sofa before replying: 'Well, at the time it felt like the right thing to do.'

Tollersrud put his forefinger to his chin, as if considering whether or not her answer was acceptable.

'Let's see what happened afterwards.'

The film clip restarted; the boy at the checkout served one customer, and then another, but as soon as he had a few minutes free, he looked around furtively, picked up the banknote and tucked it into his own pocket.

Tollersrud reappeared. 'What do you think, Iselin – are you still certain you did the right thing?'

Iselin seemed to weigh this up. 'Yes,' she said. 'I can't help it if the guy at the checkout was an idiot.'

One of the other competitors laughed. Tollersrud smiled.

'What about the rest of you?' he went on. 'Do you think Iselin dealt with it well?'

When none of them held up a hand, the presenter challenged the guy at the end of the sofa, who sat leaning forwards with a confident smirk on his face.

'I think it was both right and wrong,' he said. The strapline at the foot of the screen stated that he was Toralf Schanke, thirty-one years of age and a joiner.

'How's that?'

'Right, because you shouldn't take someone else's property. Wrong, because it passed on the dilemma to another person instead.'

Blix left the film clip and clicked on to Iselin's profile. He read some of the comments she had received from viewers the previous evening. The online bullies filled him with anger. Writing such nasty things about Iselin without even knowing her. He wanted to find them, one by one, and take them to task.

Blix moved on to a live image of his daughter lying asleep beneath a sky-blue quilt. Her left foot jutted out, and the pale sheet was crumpled, as if she'd had a restless night.

He watched her for a few more moments, and his thoughts strayed to Emma. Wondering if he should say something to her, he decided it might be best to let things lie.

18

Emma skipped up the stairs to the open-plan office with huge screens and clean, white surfaces. Several other bloggers were in situ, but Emma didn't feel much like conversation so early in the morning and contented herself with nodding to one or two of them.

Emma could barely count on one hand how many times she'd actually been on the news.no premises, but today there was no way to avoid it. Anita had called her in for a meeting.

She found her boss at the coffee machine.

'Excellent effort yesterday,' Anita said as she poured herself a cup. 'Now we just have to give it even more gas.'

A fleeting smile before she inquired, with a look, whether Emma would like a cup too. She shook her head.

'Let's go in to see Henrik, then.'

Anita gestured with her head to the nearby conference room, where a man sat waiting for them, totally engrossed in his mobile phone. Henrik Wollan was the crime journalist at news.no. Emma had studied for her journalism degree with him, and they had started at news.no around the same time.

'I wanted to bring you two together here because Sonja Nordstrøm's disappearance has turned into a criminal case,' Anita said. 'And because I'm keen for Emma to go on covering it.' She sipped at her coffee.

Wollan leaned forwards across the table and said: 'With all due respect, Anita, Emma has zero experience of covering crime stories. Isn't it better if she continues to write about her celebrities—?'

'No,' Anita interrupted, looking up at them both. 'Emma can contribute a different perspective precisely *because* she hasn't covered crime stories before. And after all, she was the one who broke the story. I want the two of you to cooperate.' She repeated the word with emphasis on each individual syllable: 'Co-op-er-ate. Anyway, Sonja Nordstrøm *is* a celebrity.'

Emma felt herself grow in stature, even though she didn't relish the thought of having to share information with a self-righteous guy like Wollan. Ever since their student days he had held his own abilities in high esteem, and every time he published a new blog with a touch of news interest, the article was plastered all over social media, usually accompanied by poorly disguised braggadocio. Emma had never completely understood why Anita had employed him, apart from that he was tabloid right to his fingertips.

'Now,' Anita said. 'Let me hear your thoughts on this story and how we should cover it.'

19

Blix helped himself to his morning cup of coffee and then sat down and fired up his computer. No new instructions had been left for him or messages regarding the Nordstrøm case, which was still officially coded as *Missing woman over eighteen years old*.

Kovic appeared beside him. 'I've received the list of calls from her phone,' she said, dropping into her chair. Her fingers raced across the keyboard as she logged on to her computer, opened her email program and a file attachment from Telenor's contact centre.

Blix rolled his chair towards her. The large Excel file contained raw data that could have done with some formatting to make it clearer, but he was quickly able to make sense of the columns and rows of telecoms traffic.

Kovic removed the data use and they were left with an overview of incoming and outgoing calls and messages. Then she drew a red line to make a division between before and after Sonja Nordstrøm disappeared.

On Sunday, 7th October at 21.54, she had received a text message, and after that things had gone remarkably quiet for nearly twenty-four hours – until the phone was switched on and turned up in the Gamlebyen Graveyard.

'Who is it?' Blix asked and pointed at the final text message.

Kovic looked up the number: Amund Zimmer, Soleane Publishing House.

'Her publisher,' Blix commented. 'The time corresponds roughly with what he said himself when we interviewed him.'

Below the red line there was a long list of incoming text messages, all registered in the first minute after 20.00 hours, when the phone was turned on. There were also individual calls, but no length of conversation was recorded. These had probably been diverted to voicemail after ringing out.

One phone number stood out. It had a foreign prefix: +45 – Denmark. The columns for time and date showed that this was the number that had called when they'd found the phone in the grave.

Blix put his finger on the computer screen. 'Can you find the owner?' he asked.

Kovic opened a Danish net page for tracing individuals. The number produced no hits. She tried a couple of other similar online sites, but the searches were fruitless.

'Unlisted number,' she said. 'I can send a request to the Danish police for help to identify it, but that could take time. We might have to complete an official application.'

Blix nodded. Electronic tracking was an excellent tool, but unearthing information was often a complicated process.

'Do that,' he said, trundling his seat back to his own desk.

20

Even though Emma had to work with Wollan, it didn't mean she had to sit beside him. Once the meeting was over, she took her bike to Kalle's Choice and was soon ensconced at her regular table.

With a tall, hot latté before her, she noticed with pleasure that a number of overseas Internet pages had referred to the first story she had written about Sonja Nordstrøm's possible kidnap. She'd never experienced that before. Even though it was gratifying, at the same time she felt she didn't really deserve it. She wouldn't have had a story at all without the hints Alex Blix had given her – and when Emma phoned Gard Fosse's direct number, he couldn't exclude the possibility that Nordstrøm had been kidnapped. It was enough for Emma to make a headline.

She drank down the sweet coffee, musing on Blix. There was something about him she could not put into words. A kind of shyness about his manner. Something that whetted her curiosity.

She used her tongue to remove some milky foam from her upper lip, and logged into a media archive she subscribed to. Tapping his name in, she used the various search tools to exclude everything to do with Sonja Nordstrøm, hoping to discover what other cases Blix had worked on lately. The most recent result was a story published on *Aftenposten*'s online pages late the previous evening: 'Witnesses Sought after Attack in Graveyard'.

She clicked on the article and found a photo of Blix, taken in front of the entrance to Gamlebyen Graveyard. A caretaker had been attacked at around 8.00 p.m., and the police were looking for witnesses. It didn't say much more, other than that the entire graveyard had been cordoned off while police examined the scene. Another photograph showed three patrol cars and a total of seven uniformed police officers. The accompanying caption emphasised that this had been a major police call-out.

Emma raised her eyes from the screen for a few seconds. Blix led the investigation into the Nordstrøm case, which was in its initial stages, and according to Gard Fosse had top priority. That didn't chime with Blix being sent out to cover an assault case. Emma packed up her belongings and abandoned her half-empty coffee cup.

Her bike ride from west to east Oslo made her cheeks sting with cold. The graveyard was quiet. She dismounted and wheeled her bike along the paths, scanning the gravestones as she passed. There were a couple of other people in the cemetery, visiting to remember their loved ones, she presumed, and she felt a stab of conscience. It was a while since she had visited her parents' graves. They were in different graveyards, which made them awkward to visit. Fortunately, her mother had been laid to rest in the same one as her grandfather, Olav, but even so it was a long time since Emma had tended their graves.

The caretaker had apparently been attacked in a tool shed, and after a brief search she found it. As she propped her bike against its wall, her mobile vibrated inside her jacket pocket. When she saw that it was a text message from Kasper Bjerringbo, butterflies began to flap in her stomach. He was congratulating her on her coverage of the Nordstrøm case. Emma smiled to herself and sent a quick thank-you.

Now it was time to investigate. No one was inside the tool shed right now, but she saw that a hosepipe was attached to a tap on its wall and stretched around to the rear. Following it, she came across an older man, who had laid down the hose with the water still pouring out, forming a puddle in a thicket where plants were growing wild. He carried a green plastic watering can in his hand and was using it to water the flowers at one of the gravestones.

The man looked startled when Emma approached. 'Oh!' he exclaimed, quickly followed by a somewhat shamefaced, 'Sorry.'

'I should apologise for scaring you,' she said.

'Not at all,' the man replied, moving his free hand to the small of his back. 'You just took me by surprise, that's all.'

The man, who looked to be in his early sixties, smiled at her, and when he drew himself up to his full height, she saw he had stitches above one eye. His nose also seemed slightly red.

'That's maybe not so strange,' Emma said, 'after what happened here yesterday.'

She was pleased with her own comment, as he could think it was aimed at him directly, but it could also simply refer to the attack reported in the media.

'Yes...' he said, lowering his eyes.

Emma took a few steps closer. 'Were you the one who was attacked?' she asked as gently as she could.

He looked up at her. 'Yes, it ... was me.'

'And you're back at work already?' she said, sounding impressed. 'I'd have taken the chance of some time off while I was at it.' Emma forced a smile and a chuckle.

'There aren't many other staff here, apart from me,' he said. 'So...'

'If only all employees were like you.'

The man smiled. 'Can I help you with anything?' he asked.

'Yes, maybe,' she said. 'I'm Emma Ramm, and I work for news.no. I'm a journalist.'

'I don't want to end up in a newspaper,' he rushed to say.

'You don't need to, either,' Emma said. 'I was just wondering why there was such a large police presence here last night?'

'Yes, there were lots of them,' the man said. 'But it probably wasn't because of me.'

'No?'

The caretaker shook his head. 'It was something about a lady they were looking for.'

Emma didn't know if she could hide her elation. 'A lady?' she repeated, taking another step nearer.

'Yes, but all they found was her phone, lying somewhere in the graveyard.'

Emma gave this some thought. It couldn't possibly be about anyone but Sonja Nordstrøm. In that case, this was certainly a dramatic development. The police had been searching for her among the gravestones. And in the end they found her phone – but not Nordstrøm herself.

'Was there anything else you wanted to know?' he asked. 'I arrived a bit late today, and we've a burial in a couple of hours.'

Emma mulled this over. 'I don't think so,' she said. 'Thanks a million for your help.'

21

Nicolai Wibe tossed a newspaper on to the conference table.

'I found him,' he said, as he approached Blix.

'Found who?'

'The junkie in the graveyard.'

'How's that? Where is he?'

'Long story,' Wibe said, half turning away. 'He's down in the basement. Starting to get the shakes and keen to get out as fast as possible. I haven't taken a formal statement yet because I thought you might want to be present. It's an interesting tale.'

Blix got to his feet and glanced at the time. Half an hour to go before the morning meeting.

'What's his name?' he asked, skirting the row of desks.

'Geir Abrahamsen. Geia to his friends.'

The lift took them down to the basement, where their shoes echoed along the corridor of cells. The duty officer rattled his keys and opened the cell for them. A pale man glanced up from the mattress at the far end. Blix had no doubt he was the right person – the red mark on his cheek was conspicuous. The man tried to stand up, but his legs were wobbly, and as Blix hunkered down and spoke his name, Geia slumped back. The stench of alcohol hit Blix full in the face.

'Tell us about the man with the money,' Wibe said.

Geia opened his mouth, as if to protest. Blix saw that the caretaker at Gamlebyen Graveyard had been correct: there were hardly any teeth left in the man's mouth. 'Tell us what you said to me before,' Wibe encouraged him. 'Tell us what happened.'

The look on Geia's face was tortured. 'Yesterday morning,' he began, scratching his cheek with dirty fingers. 'A guy came over to me and said I could earn some dough if I did him a favour.'

Blix shifted his weight from one foot to the other. His knees were playing up.

'He gave me a phone that he wanted me to switch on at eight o'clock on the dot. I was to drop it in one of the graves at the Gamlebyen Graveyard – without being seen. I was planning on doing it, but then I panicked when that caretaker turned up, so ... I had to...' He shook his head. 'I got ten thousand kroner for it,' he said quickly, making eye contact with Blix. 'Do you know how much money that is to me? Plus promises of more if I just did exactly what he said. But...' He looked down and then looked up again, searching for the cell door. 'He also said that... ' Once again he scratched his cheek, on the red mark. '...That if I didn't do exactly what he told me, that he would find me and ... get me.'

Blix raised an eyebrow. 'Get you? Did he say that?'

'Yes.'

Geia nodded quickly. 'I'd no doubt he meant it.'

'This man,' Blix said, now on tenterhooks. 'What did he look like – do you remember?'

Geia shook his head. 'All I remember is he was wearing a hoodie. And he was very careful not to let me see his face.'

'How tall was he?'

Geia gave this some thought and looked up at Blix. 'About the same as you, maybe.'

Blix was six feet tall.

'Colour of his eyes?'

'I didn't see.'

'What did he sound like? What was his voice like?'

Another pause.

Blix waited impatiently for a response. 'Was it light, deep, harsh, soft...?'

'It was ... quiet.'

'What do you mean?'

'Quiet. It was quiet. Cold. Kept an even tone, if you know what I mean. Exactly the same tone of voice.'

Blix mulled this over as he stored Geia's information into his memory banks.

'Any facial features you noticed?'

'I never saw it,' Geia said, before adding: 'His face, I mean. Please. I don't want to get mixed up in anything. OK? I...'

As Blix stood up, his knee joints clicked.

'You said he'd promised you more if you did as he said. Did he say anything about when he would come back? When you would meet him again?'

Geia shook his head and tried to stand up too. This time he managed it, only just.

'Can I get out now?' he asked.

Blix looked at Wibe and pulled him back a few metres.

'Go through the formalities with him,' Blix whispered, 'and then let him go. He has to tell us at once if he's contacted again. And this time he has to be careful to see what this guy in the hoodie looks like.'

Wibe nodded.

Geia gave a deep sigh.

Blix left the cell, and as soon as he was out of the stuffy basement corridor, his phone buzzed:

Hello again. Gard Fosse isn't returning my calls ... I've just chatted to Borre Simonsen at Gamlebyen Graveyard. I have a good story I'd like to publish. Ring or text me when you have a minute. Regards, Emma Ramm, news.no

22

The owner of Kalle's Choice was called Karl Oskar Hegerfors, and he was from Sweden. He stood behind the counter serving an old man with a walking stick. Hegerfors smiled at Emma as he handed a double macchiato and a cinnamon bun to the old man.

'*Tjäna, grabben,*' Emma said after the man with the walking stick had moved away.

'*Tjäna, tjejen,*' Kalle replied. 'How's your left leg today?' he then asked, in Swedish. Emma stopped and raised her eyebrow. 'I'm fed up asking you about the weather or suchlike,' the Swede went on, 'so today I thought I'd ask you about your left leg.'

Emma looked down at it in consternation.

'Is there something wrong with my left leg?'

'You tell me.'

Kalle knocked some coffee grains from an espresso press. The tapping penetrated straight through Emma's skull.

'There's nothing wrong with it,' she said, taking a step closer to the counter. 'Can I have an orange juice, a glass of water and a Greek salad, please?'

'OJ, GW and GS,' Hegerfors jotted down on a notepad in front of him. 'You don't want to try anything new, then?'

'New things are dangerous.'

He smiled and looked up at her. With only a pinch of benevolence,

Emma could place him in the category 'attractive'; he had short dark hair and was just tall enough – seven or eight centimetres taller than she was – and he always pushed his shoulders back a little and had good posture into the bargain.

'You look stressed out, my girl,' he said.

'Indeed I am, my boy. And hungry too.'

Her phone gave off a message signal. The text was from Blix. He had taken his time answering her message about Gamlebyen Graveyard, but here it was at last.

Where are you? was all it said.

'I'm a slave to your command,' Kalle said, giving a deep bow as he backed into the kitchen.

Emma smiled.

Kalle's Choice, Sofies plass. Why do you ask? she typed, before heading for her usual seat on the first floor. Once she was there, she took out her laptop.

As she'd pedalled back from the graveyard, Emma had planned her story about Nordstrøm's mobile phone. Now it was just a matter of writing it out and getting a comment or confirmation from the police.

Soon Kalle arrived with the food.

'When are you going to reward me for my efforts?' he asked.

'When you become a rich man with a house in the Stockholm archipelago,' Emma said with a smile, as she speared a cube of feta cheese with her fork. Hegerfors turned around with another theatrical bow. Emma smiled again and checked her phone. No reply from Blix.

Her phone rang while she sat holding it in her hand. It was Irene, her sister.

'Hi,' Emma said. 'You'll have to be quick; I'm a bit busy right now.'

'OK,' her sister answered. 'I was just wondering if you could look after Martine today?'

'Today?' Emma replied, slightly crestfallen.

'I know it's short notice, but ... I've been asked to take an extra night duty, and ... well, I wouldn't ask if it wasn't important.'

Emma glanced at the half-finished story on her computer screen. It wasn't exactly convenient to look after a five-year-old girl – today of all days. But she knew Irene didn't earn a huge amount as a nurse. She rented a two-bedroom flat in Sagene, but with rents as high as they were, things weren't easy financially. Emma had offered to let them rent one of her rooms for a notional sum, but even though the offer had clearly been tempting, her sister had been too proud to accept.

'OK, then,' Emma said. 'But I might have to do some work.'

'Martine's well used to that, isn't she?'

'Yes, I suppose,' Emma said. 'She's used to pancakes, at any rate. So that's what we'll have today too.'

'Just don't let her eat too much sugar,' Irene said. 'She sprinkles it on pancakes if she gets half a chance.'

'Just like you did when you were a little girl.'

'I still do.'

'Me too.'

They both laughed.

'Thanks so much, Emma,' her sister said in the end, and Emma could hear how tired Irene was. One more night duty, on top of all the others she took as often as the chance arose.

'And you'll pick her up from nursery too, then, won't you?'

Emma looked at the time. That gave her a few more working hours. 'Yes, of course.'

'Thanks again, Emma. You're a star.'

They rang off.

A movement on the stairs made Emma raise her eyes. Alexander Blix was approaching her.

'Hello, Emma,' he said.

'Hello,' she said, taken aback.

'Can I sit down for a couple of seconds?' He pointed at a chair on the opposite side of her table.

'Yes, of course,' she said after a brief hesitation. She drew her laptop closer to her side of the table and closed the screen.

Blix sat down.

'Have you found her?' Emma asked.

He shook his head.

'But you've found her phone?'

The policeman paused for a moment before nodding. One corner of his mouth rose in a tentative smile. First he wanted to know what had led her to the graveyard and the caretaker. While Emma explained, he rubbed one hand over the bristles that had begun to sprout on his chin.

'Well thought through,' he said, an impressed look on his face.

Emma accepted the compliment with a smile.

While Blix explained what had led the police to the cemetery, Emma opened her laptop again.

'Who switched it on?' she asked, writing at the same time.

'I can't answer that,' Blix replied. 'But what I *can* say is that we don't think it was Nordstrøm.'

'What more can you tell me?'

Blix hesitated.

Emma lifted her fingers from the keyboard, and put her hands up, showing she wasn't going to type what he might tell her. 'I can keep it out of the story if you prefer.'

'Her phone was found in an open grave,' he said finally.

Emma's eyes widened.

Blix leaned across the table. 'But you can't quote me on any of that,' he said. 'I shouldn't really be here. The two of us shouldn't even be talking to each other, but there's something I—'

His phone rang, interrupting him. He looked both discouraged and anxious, then looked away and plucked his mobile from his jacket pocket. He seemed to consider turning it off, but then changed his mind.

'Sorry,' he said. 'I need to take this.' He answered the call. 'Yes, Blix here?'

Emma went on writing as he talked. Keeping what she had already included about the police source, but changing the headline.

'Where, then?' Blix inquired into his phone.

He stood up with a serious expression on his face. Turned halfway around, and then back again.

'OK,' he said. 'Thanks. I'm on my way.' He hung up. Stared straight ahead.

'What is it?' Emma asked, getting to her feet too.

'I ... don't entirely know,' Blix began, meeting Emma's gaze. He seemed to reconsider rapidly, then said: 'You can't write about any of this, Emma. Not yet. But a dead body's been found close to Sonja Nordstrøm's summer cottage.'

Emma sat gawping for a few seconds.

'Is it her, then, or what?'

'It's too early to answer that,' he said. 'But I have to run. Don't write about this latest development either. Understood?' He placed one hand on the back of the chair. 'Can I rely on you not to?' he asked, his tone more severe.

Emma nodded, tentatively at first, then more insistently.

Blix disappeared down the stairs.

Emma sat down again and moved her bowl of salad to the neighbouring table. A corpse found. At Sonja Nordstrøm's cottage.

Oh. My. God.

A quick Internet search told her that the cottage was located on Hvaler, an archipelago south of the Oslo Fjord and close to the Swedish border. Google informed her that it was 108 kilometres away, and that driving there would take one hour and twenty-nine minutes.

She looked at the time. The nursery closed at half past four. It was doable, but there was a chance she might not make it. Should she call her sister and ask to borrow her car, and then get someone else to look after Martine? But she knew Irene didn't have anyone else to turn to at such short notice.

One more possibility existed. Wollan. She didn't like him or the way he put stories together. He usually drew hasty conclusions and exaggerated his descriptions, but Anita wouldn't be happy if the chance of being first out of the blocks to report Sonja Nordstrøm's death slipped through their fingers.

She picked up her phone and turned it over in her hand. To Wollan, journalism was generally all about clicks and ratings. If some piece of information or aspect of a story diminished its sensationalism he usually left it out. Emma was reluctant to let him spoil the Nordstrøm story like that, but her respect for Anita forced the decision upon her. She keyed in his number and, in a few hurried sentences, told Wollan what she knew.

'So Sonja Nordstrøm's dead?' he asked.

'We don't know that for sure.'

'But who else could it be?' he added, not expecting an answer. 'Are you on your way out there?'

Emma explained why she couldn't go.

'OK, then, I'll do it.' He made it sound as if he was doing her a favour. 'Have you published anything yet?' was his next question.

'I need to get official confirmation first.'

'Hello?' he said. 'You're sitting on a scoop here. If you're certain of your information, then obviously you should publish it.'

'That would destroy my relationship with my source.'

'Your source...?' he said with a touch of sarcasm. 'You've been working on crime for exactly one day, and you've already got a source?'

Emma had no reply. She regretted involving him, but there was no going back on that now.

'Don't give it another thought,' Wollan went on. 'I'll put it out; that way you avoid any problems.'

'It's not been verified yet...' Emma began.

'Call me if you find out anything more,' Wollan said. Emma didn't get as far as voicing her objection before he rang off.

23

The traffic ahead of him veered to one side when Blix turned on the sirens and blue light. He wound his way from the city centre up on to the motorway. Exit signs with the names of the various towns around the capital whizzed by: Kolbotn, Ski, Ås, Vestby, Moss and Rygge. As he approached Fredrikstad, he phoned Gard Fosse.

'Are you far away?' Fosse asked.

'Maybe twenty minutes or so,' he answered. 'Is there any news?'

'Only that the media have got wind of us finding Nordstrøm's phone,' Fosse snorted. 'Call me as soon as you know any more.'

Blix flicked off the blue light and dropped his speed as he opened his phone browser and clicked into news.no.

'Nordstrøm's Phone Found in Open Grave'.

He scanned the phone screen as he drove, reading a sentence or two at a time. According to what news.no had learned, Sonja Nordstrøm's phone had been used on Sunday evening. A police source indicated it had been located in an open grave.

He tossed his phone on to the seat beside him and picked up speed again. Of course she'd published it, he thought, pounding the steering wheel with his fist.

The first sign for Hvaler appeared. Ten minutes later, Blix was drawing up behind a row of police patrol cars. No reporters seemed to be on the scene yet, but that wouldn't last long.

As he stepped out of his car, he was met by a biting blast of sea air. The sky had clouded over. If they were unlucky, it might start raining during the afternoon. Blix hoped the Hvaler police had made good progress with their crime-scene work.

He greeted a uniformed policewoman and skirted around to the rear of Sonja Nordstrøm's cottage. He introduced himself to another officer and asked for directions.

'Just follow that path,' the officer told him.

Blix made his way along a narrow footpath lined with low bushes and sparse trees, which sheltered him from the worst of the squalls. He was careful where he put his feet: roots and twigs protruded here and there. Soon he reached a smooth expanse of rock. A number of police officers were huddled several metres from a rowing boat, which was moored beside the rock, bobbing lethargically on the waves. One of the crime-scene technicians was holding on to a rope that was attached to the boat, while another took photographs.

Blix nodded to them all and introduced himself to the local officer in charge. He seemed flustered, somehow, as if he'd made a mistake that Blix hadn't yet discovered.

'We were here yesterday,' he explained. 'At your request. The boat-house was locked then, and the boat was safely inside.'

'So it's Sonja Nordstrøm's boat?'

'Yes.'

Blix took a step closer to the craft and peered down. The body lay on its stomach, with the face turned sideways towards Blix.

'A man?' he said, looking back at the local officer, who responded with a nod.

Blix crouched down. There was something familiar about the dead man's ashen face. He had short, fair hair and blue eyes.

'Do you have any idea who it is?' Blix asked, turning to face the local officer.

'My lad at home's a fan,' he said, sighing, as he pointed at the corpse. The man was wearing a football top with the number seven on the back.

'It's Jeppe Sørensen,' he went on. 'The Danish football player, from the national team. I think he's been missing for a week or so.'

Blix wasn't particularly interested in football, but he'd heard that Sørensen was AWOL.

'He was supposed to sign a professional contract with Borussia Dortmund a while back,' the officer added. 'But then he suffered a knee injury. It destroyed his career. There's been speculation that he fell into a depression because of it. And when he disappeared people even suggested he'd taken his own life, but ... we can knock that theory on the head now at least.'

Blix watched the crime-scene officers continuing their work for a moment. On a rocky foreland fifty metres away, a man appeared, holding a camera. The first journalist, Blix thought, turning his back on him slightly.

'He's cold,' one of the technicians shouted from the boat.

'What do you mean?' the local officer asked.

'This isn't normal rigor mortis,' the technician explained. 'He's frozen, and has just begun to thaw out.'

Blix took a deep breath and then exhaled slowly.

One of the crime-scene officers supervised as the local police officers lifted Jeppe Sørensen on to a body bag. They zipped it up and then brought him on to the rock before four men carried him away from the scene.

Blix dipped his head and followed in their wake, a gust of wind sweeping in from the sea, propelling him forwards.

24

'Auntie Emma!'

Martine leapt up from the playroom floor at Svingen nursery. Emma had been leaning against the doorframe for the past minute or two, watching her niece as she sat in a circle with three other children – two girls and a boy – playing with toy figures. Emma couldn't make out what they were meant to represent. Now Martine was rushing towards her. Her face had erupted into a grin displaying her tiny teeth – at least, the ones she hadn't lost yet. She hurled herself into Emma's arms.

Emma picked up her niece and held her for a few moments, hugging her close. 'Hi, sweetheart,' she whispered into her ear. 'Oh, I've missed you.'

'Am I coming to your place today?' Martine demanded expectantly, pulling back a little.

'Well … OK, then,' Emma replied and set her down.

Martine jumped for joy. 'Can we have pancakes?' she asked.

'I thought we would have fish today instead.'

Martine's smile of anticipation vanished immediately.

'Fish, carrots and potatoes – isn't that your favourite?'

Martine was about to protest.

'I'm only joking; of course we'll have pancakes.'

Martine was jubilant again.

'Are you ready to go?'

She agreed excitedly. Emma signalled to one of the staff members, received a nod of acknowledgement and they headed out to the cloakroom to fetch Martine's belongings.

They'd barely entered Emma's flat when Martine kicked off her shoes and ran inside. She knew exactly where Emma's iPad was and had learned the code into the bargain, so it wasn't long before she was engrossed in one of the fifty or so games her aunt had allowed her to download.

Emma had only just managed to throw together the pancake mixture when the phone rang. She picked it up with some trepidation.

'Hi, Emma,' Kasper Bjerringbo began – she could hear from his voice that something serious had happened. 'Have you heard?'

'Heard what?'

'You remember that footballer I told you about? Jeppe Sørensen?'

'Yes?' Emma said.

'He's been found dead. Murdered. In Sonja Nordstrøm's boat.'

Emma needed a second or two to digest this information.

'What the hell are you saying?'

'Auntie,' Martine yelled from the living room. 'You're not allowed to swear.'

'They found him a couple of hours ago,' Kasper went on. 'Lying in Sonja Nordstrøm's boat. I just received a tip-off from one of my police sources.'

Emma swallowed hard. 'What on earth has a footballer got to do with Sonja Nordstrøm?'

'I've no idea. But you should maybe write a story about this yourself. That report you guys have splashed with is pretty speculative.'

Emma picked up her laptop and fired up the screen.

'Hang on a second,' she said, waiting impatiently for her computer to find the network. Then she clicked into news.no. Henrik Wollan had already published something.

'Body Found'.

That was all it said, in big, fat block capitals, above a picture of the Hvaler archipelago and a white body bag being carried across the flat rocks on the shore. Inserted below it was a photo of Sonja Nordstrøm.

'Good grief,' Emma said under her breath as she scrolled down and noticed that Wollan had included her by-line too. She skimmed through the brief article he'd written. The police at the crime scene refused to make any comment about cause of death or the sex of the victim, but the way the story was angled gave a clear indication that this was Sonja Nordstrøm encased in the body bag.

'I'll write something myself – get it sorted out,' Emma said. 'Can you send me a link or a text with a summary of what you have on the footballer?'

'Give me a couple of minutes, and I'll see what I can find.'

'Brilliant, thanks for letting me know.'

'My pleasure.'

'Have the relatives been informed yet?'

'Eh?'

'In Denmark – have the footballer's relatives been informed?'

'I don't know. Let me check.'

'OK. Terrific. Thanks.'

They wrapped up the call.

Before she started writing, she rang Blix. She wanted another source to confirm the discovery, preferably a Norwegian one. It rang for a long time. *Bloody hell*, Emma said to herself, *pick up the phone*. But it just went on ringing.

She sent Blix a text asking if Jeppe Sørensen was the body they had found. While she waited for a reply, she began to write. It only took a few minutes to set up a new story with a headline and introduction, and a line in the body of the text to tell readers that more was to follow. She nudged the mouse's cursor up to the 'publish' button, and felt a tingling in her fingertips as she pressed it.

Her phone buzzed. Kasper: *Relatives informed.*

Excellent, she could go ahead and publish; she trusted Kasper.

Emma decided that she didn't have time to phone Anita before going into news.no's desktop publishing program and removing Wollan's story from the top of the front page. She didn't give two hoots that it was neither her job nor her privilege to do so.

She couldn't recall the last time she'd felt so elated. It was almost uncomfortable to have to admit it, but her whole body was trembling, as if what she was doing was fun. She typed as fast as her fingers allowed, clicking into her email and opening the four links Kasper had just sent, but she didn't get as far as reading any of them before her phone rang again.

'Hi, Anita.'

'What the fuck's going on?'

Emma explained what she knew about the discovery of the body.

'And you're absolutely certain of this?'

'I'm working on finding a source to confirm it, but I've no reason to doubt the source I already have.'

'Shit,' Anita said. 'This is just...'

For once it seemed that Anita was lost for words. Emma went on writing while her boss collected herself.

'OK,' Anita said at last, 'just give it full throttle and I'll delete that other story.'

Emma pictured Wollan's face, burning with anger, when the facts of the matter were made known to him. But this was no time to gloat. It was time to write and in the next ten minutes she hammered out 842 words about Jeppe Sørensen, taking chunks of Kasper's reports and translating them into Norwegian.

'Auntie, will we be eating soon?' Martine shouted through from the living room.

'Not long now, darling,' Emma replied. 'I'll start cooking very soon.'

Emma was no longer hungry, though. All she wanted was to drive to Hvaler, speak to Blix and try to find a few more sources to interrogate. But she'd promised Martine pancakes, so instead she had to get moving with the frying pan.

As she poured out the lovely thick batter, she wondered what her next steps with the story should be. She had little doubt that this would blow the whole of Scandinavia to kingdom come. Not to mention the whole of Europe. Sonja Nordstrøm and Jeppe Sørensen were both famous sports personalities, and that was the only connection between them she could discern.

But something very odd was going on here, she thought, as she flipped the first pancake. Something really weird.

25

'Everybody.' Gard Fosse clapped his hands three times in succession.

The whole room turned to their boss as he pointed at a TV screen showing a woman with dark, mid-length hair, who was staring straight at them.

'This is Lone Cramer,' said Fosse. 'She works in the Danish National Homicide Section. Did I get that right?' Fosse asked, turning to face her with a genial smile.

'Perfect,' Cramer said, clearing her throat.

'She is central to the Danish investigation into Jeppe Sørensen's disappearance,' Fosse went on. 'She's going to give us a brief summary.'

Typical of Fosse, Blix thought, to turn on the charm when detectives from abroad were taking part in a videoconference. It was never more noticeable than when the on-screen officer was female.

The Danish investigator sat up straight and cleared her throat again. 'The last known sighting of Jeppe Sørensen was made by his live-in partner just before eight o'clock on the evening of the twenty-ninth of September,' she began.

Cramer spoke quickly, making no allowances for the fact that her listeners were Norwegian. Blix had to concentrate to understand it all.

'Sørensen went out to meet a pal of his in Nørrebro, so he took the lift down to his car in the underground garage. The car never left the building.'

Cramer went on to give an account of the steps taken by the investigators: examination of CCTV cameras, credit-card check, survey of taxis and public transport. None of it yielded anything relevant.

'His phone has been switched off from the time he disappeared,' she added, glancing down at her papers. 'But an hour ago we were notified by the phone operator that his mobile was activated last night at eight o'clock, and that it was located in Oslo.'

Blix sat bolt upright. 'Do you have his phone number to hand?' he asked, riffling through his notes.

Lone Cramer read the number aloud.

Blix got to his feet and took a step towards the TV screen. 'That's the number Sonja Nordstrøm's phone was called from last night,' he said. 'At the graveyard.'

The gravity of what he said sank in around the table. Blix gave Cramer a quick summary of the Nordstrøm case.

'So someone has kept Jeppe Sørensen's mobile ever since he disappeared,' Kovic commented. 'And they've chosen to use it to call Sonja Nordstrøm's phone at the very moment we were in the graveyard. That's sick.'

Silence fell around the table.

'Our hypothesis until now has been that Jeppe Sørensen took his own life,' Lone Cramer said. 'He was depressed because of his injury. He thought his career was over. And there was nothing to suggest any kind of crime had been committed down in the garage. No sign of a struggle, traces of blood or anything like that. Nothing whatsoever.'

Blix put his hand in the air. 'We've found burn marks on his neck that suggest he was knocked out with an electroshock weapon,' he said. 'And our pathologist thinks he was probably strangled after that. This could mean the garage is, in fact, a possible crime scene.'

Cramer nodded in agreement.

'But the only thing that links Sonja Nordstrøm and Jeppe Sørensen, apart from the phone call, is that both are sports celebrities who have been abducted,' Blix went on. 'Or have you come up with anything else?'

Cramer shook her head. 'Sonja Nordstrøm's name doesn't figure in any way in our investigation,' she said. 'I just checked to confirm.'

Kovic stood up. 'I need to take this,' she said, holding up her vibrating phone.

'Who was this friend he was supposed to meet?' Blix asked, staring hard at Cramer.

'Dennis Carlsen,' Cramer replied. 'An estate agent. He was observed in a café at the time in question. But he's been eliminated from the case.'

They exchanged several more practical details then ended the video-conference with the Danish detective.

Their discussion continued, however.

'It's one thing to attack Jeppe Sørensen,' Tine Abelvik remarked. 'It's another thing entirely to transport him across the border to Norway, and then keep him in deep freeze for a week or so before putting him in a boat that belongs to our missing person.'

'We don't know if that's what happened,' Wibe objected. 'We don't know when he was killed, or when he was frozen.'

'No, maybe not, but all the same we must be talking about a pretty unhinged person. He pays a drug addict ten thousand kroner to put Nordstrøm's phone in a graveyard at a particular time. Why not do it himself?'

'Maybe he couldn't,' Blix said. 'Maybe he was busy with something else right then.'

The comment was left hanging in the air.

'We've one thing we can do,' Blix ploughed on. 'Nordstrøm's boat was in the boathouse as late as yesterday, and there are very few roads leading out there. You have to pass a toll booth to get over to Kråkerøy and on out to Hvaler, unless you travel by boat, of course.'

'I can check the toll stations,' Abelvik volunteered.

'Coordinate with Kovic,' Blix said. 'She's already started to chart the vehicles that passed the toll stations in the vicinity of Nordstrøm's house the evening she went missing. Cross-check the lists and see if the same vehicle has been in both locations.'

Abelvik made a note.

'And compare them with border crossings,' Blix added before turning to face Wibe.

'How's the search for the man with the hoodie going?'

'We've found a few surveillance cameras that may have caught him, either before or after Geia was recruited to carry out that phone stunt in the graveyard, but so far they haven't come up with anything. We've got undercover cops on Geia's coat tails to see if Hoodie Man makes contact again, but I'm not too optimistic.'

Kovic reappeared and interrupted them.

'I've got something,' she said, still brandishing her phone. 'I've gone through Nordstrøm's phone traffic. The person she's had most contact with in recent weeks is Stian Josefson.'

'The journalist who wrote the book with her,' Blix explained to the group.

'It wouldn't be out of the ordinary, except I can't get in touch with him. His phone is switched off. The call I just had was from his wife. Josefson hasn't been home since the evening Nordstrøm disappeared. According to his wife Josefson and Nordstrøm had an appointment that evening.'

'The two wine glasses,' Wibe said, moving forwards in his seat. 'This is starting to get interesting.'

'There's more,' Kovic said. 'Norway played Denmark in an international football match two and a half years ago. *Aftenposten* ran an extensive spread on Jeppe Sørensen in the run-up to that. Guess who wrote the article?'

Kovic turned her mobile to show them the newspaper report she had dredged up. From a distance Blix couldn't see anything other than the headline: 'Playmaker and Playboy'.

'Stian Josefson,' Kovic announced. 'There are photographs in the article suggesting he visited Jeppe Sørensen's home and interviewed him there. And there's more: Josefson was on a business trip to Copenhagen the night Jeppe Sørensen went missing. He returned home late on the thirtieth of September, according to his wife.'

Gard Fosse, who hadn't contributed anything for some time, now clapped his hands.

'Excellent. Bloody brilliant!'

'How did he travel on this business trip?' Abelvik asked. 'Car, ferry, plane?'

Kovic smiled. 'He was writing a story about Danish furniture, about how popular it is in Norway. His wife claims he was supposed to buy a cabinet for them, so he drove his own car.'

'What make?'

'A Volkswagen Tiguan. What's interesting is that he came home empty-handed. He didn't buy a cabinet. One of the neighbours saw a black Tiguan in front of Nordstrøm's house. That adds up. He's been at her house a lot while they've been working on the book.'

'Maybe the semen in the bed is his too,' Wibe suggested.

Kovic gave a little shrug, as if she wasn't clear whether this was meant as a joke.

'Does his wife have any idea what has become of her husband?' Fosse asked. 'Now, I mean?'

Kovic shook her head.

Abelvik shifted in her seat. 'If Josefson has visited Jeppe Sørensen at home in Copenhagen, it's not implausible that he knows where the garage is situated,' she said.

Kovic nodded. 'After all, they knew each other, in a sense. Sørensen would probably have been happy to chat with Josefson, if he made contact.'

They sat around the table tossing ideas back and forth like this until Gard Fosse signalled an end to the meeting.

'There's one issue I must raise,' he said, letting his gaze slide slowly around the room. 'The discoveries of both the body and phone very quickly ended up in the media. News.no was first to break both stories.'

His eyes continued to wander until they reached Blix. Blix crossed his legs under the table. He had two missed calls and one unanswered message from Emma on the phone in his pocket.

'The journalist at Nordstrøm's house, the one who reported her missing, works for them,' Kovic interjected. 'They're probably following the case closely.'

'They refer to police sources,' Fosse continued.

'That's what they always say,' Wibe said dismissively.

'I'd just like to remind you all that no one is to speak to anyone outside this investigation group about this case. Not friends, not family

– not even other colleagues. And of course no one who works in the press.'

Blix struggled to breathe normally. He tried to return Fosse's searching look with a nonchalant expression, but wasn't sure how successful he had been.

26

Calle Seeberg wasn't happy to be outdoors. In Norway 'outside' was normally synonymous with 'freezing', and you always had to check the weather forecast before heading out for a hike, then dig out equipment, sometimes even buy new gear. To cut a long story short, there was too much palaver involved in trekking. Seeberg couldn't remember the last time he had been out in a field or forest, or up a mountain. If it were up to him, he would stay indoors where he didn't have far to walk to the fridge, the sofa and the remote control.

But it wasn't up to him anymore. His doctor had said: 'Calle, if you want to pass the age of fifty-five, if you want to give away your daughter at her wedding someday, you have to get out and exercise. And by that I don't mean sauntering to and from the shops or work. The best thing would be for you to start doing some running. Start small, by all means – you mustn't give your body too much of a shock. But your lungs do need you to stub out those cigarettes – that's the first thing you need to do. And your arteries are calling out for you to get moving. Exercise three times a week, at least. And you have to eat something other than pizza and potato crisps.'

It was no secret to anyone who knew Seeberg well that he had smoked and drunk to excess in the course of more than three decades in the media industry. This had cost him two marriages, at least one job and – in his doctor's opinion – perhaps fifteen years of his life. Now it was a matter of damage limitation. Of course he wanted to live. Wanted to give away his daughter, continue to work for Radio 4; wanted to take the population's pulse by raising current topics in his morning broadcasts and play devil's advocate to the punters who phoned in – not because he necessarily disagreed with them, but because he was keen for them to clarify their own arguments. This was a journalistic method that enraged many of his callers, but it was great radio – no one could complain about that.

The worst aspect of feeling age creeping up on him was that he had started to become forgetful, fortunately not in an Alzheimer's kind of way, but he often forgot what he had done with his keys and glasses, names of old friends or acquaintances, and politicians he had interviewed. Actors he had seen in films also disappeared totally from his memory banks from time to time. His doctor had told him this could also be a signal that his body needed a change.

Change.

Moving from one state to another.

It was easy to say, even easy to make a start, but not so easy to carry through over a period of time. He'd succeeded in cutting down on his daily quota of cigarettes. The amount of alcohol consumed over a week was not what it used to be either, and he was also trying to eat a bit more healthily. Broccoli and other vegetables instead of deep-fried side dishes.

However, progress was slow, and even though he'd dropped eight kilos in the past four months, it was still difficult to breathe when he walked upstairs, and running never got any easier – his legs were just as heavy, his chest just as tight. There were times when he wondered whether Grandpa Seeberg might not be the only one in the family to die of a heart attack.

So in addition to being a talk show host on Radio 4, Calle Seeberg was engaged in change – even though every fibre of his being fought against it. Because many people knew his face, and since exercise called into question the image he'd created for himself, he confined his training sessions to the hours of darkness, so that as few people as possible would see him wearing incongruous clothes. Now, because it was autumn, he could also wrap himself up and wear caps that made him even less recognisable. Nevertheless, he sometimes encountered astonished, open-mouthed looks from people coming in the opposite direction, and was aware of how ridiculous he looked as his 105 kilos pounded the pavement. He was painfully aware that he became redder in the face than a garden gnome when he ran, and even though he kept his pace slow, the noise he produced was loud.

The footpath along the Akerselva river was lit by streetlights spaced ten to fifteen metres apart. Calle Seeberg never ran further than the waterfall at Gjerdrums vei. This was a natural place to stop and catch his breath; the incline had been gradual all the way from Grünerløkka, and he had started to look forward to the considerably easier homeward stretch. On some late-autumn evenings, an eerie haze rose from the black water under the bridge, and in the soft lamplight the mist seemed golden, as if someone down there was exhaling gold dust.

One evening, Calle Seeberg stood watching this unusual sight when he heard a snap in the bushes beside the stone building nearby, where art classes were held on the upper floor. He had heard the same noise a couple of days earlier, and from the same place, too: a twig being trampled on? But no one was lurking in the shrubbery when he squinted at it; he had done the same the previous time – and spotted no one then either.

On two occasions in the past week he'd noticed a man out jogging at the same time as him. There was nothing odd about that; many people had regular exercise routines, but this person had kept exactly the same distance from him both times – fifty metres or so behind. He'd been wearing dark training kit, and a hood pulled up over his head. The reason the man had stuck in Calle Seeberg's mind was that he seemed to limp a little as he ran.

Seeberg knew that celebrities often acquired stalkers. It was part of the package. A degree of attention had never bothered him, but when he started to feel something niggle in his body, an antipathy such as now, that was something else entirely.

The man was nowhere to be seen today, and Calle Seeberg wasn't in the habit of being scared, so he decided to follow his usual procedure before setting off on his journey home. But when he ran through the gloomy thicket on his way into Nydalen, beneath the unlit bridge, he could have sworn that he heard movement behind him, even through his own deafening panting.

Another snap from among the trees, and his pulse jumped to a level that made him feel his heart beating in his chest – an intense, rhythmic hammering. And when he heard the sound of footsteps just behind him, he had to force himself not to turn around. Instead he straightened his back a little and tried to pick up speed.

Fortunately the terrain sloped down a little at this point so it was easy to increase momentum, but of course that would apply to whoever was behind him too. He had a strong feeling he wasn't moving fast enough. His thigh muscles began to stiffen and his chest felt like it was tied in knots. Luckily it wasn't far to the well-lit stretch of Nydalen's numerous brick buildings and media offices.

When he emerged near the power station, he heard the rhythm of music – an insistent bass. It took him a minute to realise it came from the headphones on a woman who was running past him with disturbing ease, as if there was no weight in her legs at all.

Calle Seeberg reduced his speed a little and began to breathe with less effort, annoyed at himself for having let fear get under his skin. When he wheeled around, he saw nothing but the dark brown path he had just run along, and the faint outline of trees and branches stirring ever so slightly in the feeble evening breeze.

He completed the rest of his homeward journey faster than usual and turned around from time to time – but saw nothing of a limping man in a hoodie. When he reached the bridge below the Oslo National Academy of the Arts – the one with all the hearts and padlocks attached – he was relieved that it would be a few days until his next training run.

Soon Calle Seeberg was letting himself into the lobby of his apartment building in Fossveien. He took the stairs up to the third floor with slow, heavy steps. He was just about to enter his apartment when he discovered that the door was ajar.

Had he forgotten to lock it when he went out?

Seeberg tried to cast his mind back, but he couldn't recall whether he'd done so or not. It was something he did without giving it any thought. Gingerly, he pulled the door open. Everything was as normal in the hallway. His shoes were in their usual place.

But – didn't it smell slightly different in here?

Yes, it did. He felt it tickle his nose. He was reacting to something or other, an allergic response. As if someone had brought a dog into his home.

Hesitantly, he stepped inside.

'Hello?' he shouted, noticing at once that he'd been holding his breath for several seconds. He continued on. Stopped. Listened. A door banged somewhere in the distance. Outside, at street level, he heard the noise of hard skateboard wheels on the tarmac.

Then all was quiet again.

No, he could hear nothing from inside. But all the same he moved warily, not even bothering to remove his shoes. He checked the home office, where Liv Tonje usually spent the night, on the odd occasion she managed to break free after fifteen years or so in her mother's tight bonds. He glanced into the spare bedroom, which was really more of a lumber-room now. There was no one in the kitchen. No one in the bedroom. There was no one in the bathroom either, even though the strange smell was more pungent in there.

What was causing it?

He decided to take an allergy pill right away, just in case. It took next to nothing for him to have a reaction. He shook out two tablets from the medicine bottle and washed them down with a quick mouthful of water from the tap, before dashing out into the hallway and shutting the front door emphatically. Then he sat down at the kitchen table and lit a cigarette. After all, he'd earned one, hadn't he?

27

Two other contestants were left, in addition to Iselin. Blix let the cursor glide over their profiles. Toralf Schanke and Jonas Sakshaug. According to the popularity barometer, Sakshaug stood a good chance. A restaurant chef, he'd managed to engage viewers by sharing a number of his favourite recipes, and asked for theirs in return. The best of these might be included in a cookery book he was about to publish, he'd promised in his profile.

Closing down the website, Blix logged into the case-management program and saw that the Nordstrøm investigation had been hidden from everyone except those actively involved in it. This was standard practice in high-profile cases.

He took out his phone. The last message from Emma remained unanswered. She wanted him to corroborate that the body found on Hvaler was that of Jeppe Sørensen. The message was now a few hours old, and in the meantime the discovery had been officially confirmed.

He weighed up whether or not to send her a reply, but decided to leave it. Then he deleted the entire message log, and went into his call list and deleted that too.

Kovic was crossing the room towards him. 'Stian Josefson is in Denmark,' she said excitedly, waving a sheaf of papers. 'He bought a ticket on the quayside yesterday afternoon, and took the DFDS Seaways ferry to Copenhagen at sixteen-thirty. He was spending loads on his credit card in one of the bars on-board all evening. I've tried to call him, but his phone's still not turned on.'

'So if he was on board the Danish ferry last night...' Blix thought aloud.

'He can't have been on Hvaler at the same time, putting Jeppe Sørensen in Sonja Nordstrøm's boat.'

Blix drummed his fingers on the desk. 'His car, though, passed the border between Sweden and Norway on the thirtieth of September, after he'd been in Denmark. It also passed Sandstuveien – the closest toll station to Nordstrøm's house when you travel from the border – at twenty twenty-one. That's an hour and a half before she sent her last text message that night.'

He swore inwardly. The trail that had seemed so promising only an hour ago already looked like a dead end. 'Is there anything else to pick up from the toll stations?' he asked. 'Have we collected all the registration numbers?'

'We're still waiting for data from Østfold,' Kovic answered. 'We're checking the vehicles from the toll booths in Kongsveien and Sandstuveien against criminal records and people from Nordstrøm's circle, but there are loads of leased and company cars. It's time-consuming.'

'What about Wibe's video project?'

'He's busy working his way through all the CCTV images from the area around Akerselva,' she told him. 'A café at the foot of Markveien has cameras pointing out towards Eventyrbrua. With a bit of luck he'll find a man in a hoodie making his way down below the bridge where Geia was hanging about.'

'OK,' Blix nodded, though he didn't have much faith this would lead to anything. 'Thanks, I'll follow up on Denmark.'

Blix ferreted out the number for Lone Cramer of the Danish police.

'The man who was last to see Sonja Nordstrøm alive is in Denmark now,' he told her almost as soon as she'd picked up, and went on to give her a speedy resumé of the facts. 'We need help to track him down.'

'Send over everything you have on him,' Cramer said. 'Then I'll send out an all-points warning.'

Blix thanked her.

'What do we do if we find him?'

'Let me know,' Blix said. 'And I'll be on the first flight.'

28

Usually Emma rose at quarter to six in the morning to exercise before the working day began, but with Martine visiting she could afford to allow herself another whole hour before she got up. She awoke at her normal time, but it was still a rare treat simply to lie there relaxing as she gazed at her sleeping niece. Few things in the world were more peaceful and carefree than the face of a little child in the Land of Nod.

Just after seven o'clock Emma gave the teddy bear Martine had clutched all night a slight tug. Slowly and surely she began to let go and open her eyes.

'Good morning, sweetie,' Emma said.

Martine grunted under the quilt and took in a long slow breath through her nose.

'Did you sleep well?' Emma asked.

'Mm,' Martine said, with a yawn.

'I've got an important question for you.'

Martine blinked repeatedly before hauling herself up.

'What would you prefer for breakfast – a smoothie or some dry old slices of bread?'

The youngster wrinkled her brow with displeasure. 'Smoothie, of course. With blueberries.'

Smiling, Emma stroked the girl's cheek, burning hot after a night's sleep.

'Blueberries it is, then. Run into the bathroom now, get yourself washed and tidied, and I'll get it made.'

'OK.' Martine pushed the quilt away and leapt out of bed. All at once she was as wide awake as if it were the middle of the day. Emma watched her niece scamper through to the bathroom, singing a Disney song they'd heard on TV the night before.

Emma got up herself and was about to make the bed when a strand of hair on Martine's pillow brought her up short. It was fairly long, and brown, and there could be no doubt that it came from her niece. Emma folded back more of the quilt so that the rest of the pillow was visible. Several more strands of hair, the same colour, had collected on the sheet. Emma quickly lifted the pillow and saw more hairs there too – Martine was always such a restless sleeper.

No, Emma told herself. *It can't be…*

She removed the quilt completely, but found no more strands of hair. *Please,* Emma said inwardly, *not…*

Martine came back.

'Aren't you going to make me a smoothie, then?' she demanded, sounding precocious and almost critical.

Emma didn't answer at first. Then: 'Yes, of course...' She looked fleetingly at Martine's hair, partly combed. Had this happened before? Did Irene know about it? Did they know at nursery?

Emma perched on the edge of the bed as Martine hunkered down on the floor to get dressed.

'Come here a minute,' Emma said in a gentle voice.

'What is it?'

'Just ... come here a minute.'

Jumping up, Martine approached Emma and sat down at her side. Emma stroked the nape of her neck and studied her niece's scalp surreptitiously. She could see some light patches there.

Fuck.

Fuck, fuck, fuck.

'What are you doing?' Martine asked.

Emma pulled her close. 'I just haven't had my morning cuddle yet,' she said, kissing the top of her head. 'Aunties need morning hugs, don't you know.'

'And children need smoothies.'

Emma blinked repeatedly. 'So they do. With blueberries.'

*

After they'd had their breakfast and prepared a packed lunch, Emma cycled her niece to nursery. The autumn weather was glorious today too, with clear air and blue skies.

At nursery, after Martine had said good morning to the adults, Emma lingered to watch her niece play with the other children. Happy-go-lucky. As if she had no idea at all about her hair.

Maybe she didn't, Emma thought, all the time wondering whether she should say anything, or ask someone.

After a prolonged goodbye-hug from Martine, Emma went outside and tried to turn her thoughts to something else. The police were having a press conference at ten o'clock, so she had time for a visit to Kalle's Choice first, where she could read up on all the other media coverage of Nordstrøm's vanishing act and the discovery of Jeppe Sørensen's body.

But it seemed like nothing new had occurred overnight. All the new stories were attempts to say something fresh with the old information.

At a quarter to ten, Emma was parking her bike outside the police station. She'd never felt like an 'ordinary' or 'proper' journalist, as she'd only ever written about celebrities, so it was a kick to be leading the pack in the Nordstrøm disappearance. When she entered the press room, she couldn't help but notice that she was being scrutinised by several of the other reporters. She didn't say hello to anyone, though, but she did notice Henrik Wollan glowering at her.

The press turnout was enormous – there were at least a hundred people present: TV, press and online reporters and photographers, radio journalists and the usual writers. A man in a black hoodie jostled her, murmuring a brief apology. She saw journalists she only knew by face and name but that she both liked and respected. Nora Klemetsen from *Aftenposten* was there. Petter Stanghelle from *VG*. Line Wisting, whose podcast Emma had listened to frequently when she was out cycling. They were all here.

Kasper Bjerringbo too.

Emma spotted him in the throng of people, engaged in enthusiastic conversation with another reporter. He caught sight of her mid-sentence. Stopped and smiled. Emma took a deep breath and felt a sharp tingling in her chest. She smiled back, with glowing cheeks.

Four months had gone by since the seminar in Gothenburg. When he'd asked her, as she was rushing out of his hotel room at five o' clock in the morning, why she didn't want to stay and sleep beside him, she hadn't been able to bring herself to answer. She never did, when men asked.

Now Kasper listened dispassionately to what his colleague had to say, before excusing himself and starting to weave his way through the crowd. Emma felt the hammering in her chest grow louder and faster.

Kasper was slightly taller than her. His short, curly hair hardly moved when he walked and he wore round glasses, which made him look intelligent. Four months ago his face had been smooth-shaven, almost boyish, but now he sported a beard, which he must have been growing for a few weeks. It suited him. My God, how it suited him.

When he stopped right in front of her, the smile didn't leave his face. There was something magnetic about him; she couldn't explain it in any other way. And when he took another step towards her and opened his arms, she let it happen – and ended up in his embrace again, just as she had on the dance floor that night in Gothenburg. This time, though, it was not a lingering one, just a brief hello.

'So lovely to see you again,' he said. 'Even though the circumstances are not so pleasant.'

'Hi, Kasper,' she said. 'Did you arrive today?'

He shook his head. 'I've been in Norway for a few days,' he replied. 'My aunt's moving back to Denmark and I've been helping her. We're a small family.'

'So you were in Norway when I spoke to you on the phone yesterday?'

He responded with a burst of quick, nervous laughter. They were surrounded by a buzz of voices.

'The removal lorry left today,' he said instead of answering her question. 'So for the rest of the month I have a big, empty apartment in Slemdal all to myself.'

Something in the way he said this made it sound like an invitation.

'It's not completely empty, though,' he added. 'There are a few items left that I'll take back down with me. A double bed, among other things.'

Emma made no comment, and was grateful when the awkward pause between them was interrupted by a side door opening beside the podium. Gard Fosse entered the room with a woman Emma knew to be the police prosecutor, Pia Nøkleby. Fosse was two heads taller than her, and despite the seriousness of the situation they looked rather comical as they walked in side-by-side.

'I hope we can talk afterwards?' Kasper said, indicating that he had to get back to his photographer.

Emma nodded, though she felt the look she gave him failed to express how much she wanted that.

'You're looking good, Emma Ramm.' He backed away as he spoke, smiling all the while.

'You too,' she said, feeling herself blush.

The police lawyer gently tapped the microphone, and a hush fell on the room, even the last few garrulous reporters falling silent. Her chat with Kasper meant Emma was too late to find a seat, so she remained on her feet beside the wall at one side.

'Good morning. Thanks for coming.' Pia Nøkleby cleared her throat. She was a woman in her early forties with short brown hair. Slightly too much make-up, Emma noted. Her lipstick was bright red.

'You all know why we've invited you here this morning. Our discovery of the body out at Sonja Nordstrøm's summer cottage yesterday afternoon has naturally raised her disappearance to an entirely new level, and I'd just like to reassure everyone here, and the general public at home, that we're doing all we can to find her and to get to the bottom of this case. I'll hand over now to Police Superintendent Gard Fosse.'

Sitting up straight, Fosse appeared to enjoy having everyone's eyes on him for a few moments. Then he leaned closer to the microphone and said: 'We can confirm that Sonja Nordstrøm is now officially a missing person, and that she may be the victim of a crime. I can't elaborate on our specific reasons for saying that here and now, but the discoveries we've made both in Nordstrøm's home and at her cottage mean that we're now actively asking for help from the public.'

He coughed softly into his hand, before continuing.

'To be explicit, we're interested in all possible sightings, especially of vehicles at and around Nordstrøm's residence on Sunday evening. We're also looking for similar observations on Hvaler, where Nordstrøm has a summer cottage, the following evening.'

That very moment, a mobile phone began to ring. The ringtone was an old-fashioned dance-band tune, a melody that Emma had often heard on the radio. The phone continued ringing, and people started to look around for the phone's owner. But the tune did not stop.

Fosse glared around the room in irritation, not continuing with his speech.

Finally, Emma saw one of the reporters bend down and pick something up from the floor. It was the ringing phone. The reporter pressed a button and the sound stopped.

'Thank you,' Fosse said. 'Please switch off the sound on your phones while we're busy here, to avoid any further disturbance.'

But the reporter who'd picked up the phone held it up in the air, and looked around, apparently searching for its owner – no one came forward. The reporter shrugged and returned the phone to the floor.

'It's only natural to ask ourselves if Sonja Nordstrøm and Jeppe Sørensen had anything to do with each other,' Fosse went on with renewed vigour in his voice. 'This is one of the things we'll be looking at more closely in the hours and days to come. We're also working with the Danish police on this, and we've sent one of our investigators to Copenhagen.'

Emma took notes. A Norwegian detective going to Denmark was the only new piece of information so far. Maybe it was Blix, she thought, since he wasn't present. Sofia Kovic, the other investigator Emma had met at Nordstrøm's house, was here though, watching the press conference from the sidelines.

Gard Fosse continued talking about the importance of giving the police space to investigate the case on a broad front, both technically and tactically, and he repeated Nøkleby's assurance that all available resources were being employed to get to the bottom of this case.

The conference was then opened up to questions from the room, and Petter Stanghelle of *VG* led off. He asked a question Fosse was unwilling to answer. Emma had a number of queries, but decided that she had a better chance of having them answered if she took them to Blix.

29

Copenhagen had been their city – Blix and Merete's favourite place; this was where they loved to go when they wanted some extra-special time together. They'd been here several times, even after Iselin had come into the world, sometimes by car, but as a rule they had flown. Copenhagen had been like a second home to them, the only city apart from Oslo where they both felt completely at home. The feeling enveloped them the minute they came upon Vesterbrogade, passing cafés and stores and strolling along Værnedamsvej – that short little street chock-a-block with restaurants and small fascinating shops. Blix hadn't been to Copenhagen since his final break with Merete, but right now, as the plane's wheels touched down and taxied smoothly to its parking spot at Kastrup airport, he felt how much he missed those times, that life. The company. The sense of belonging to something. A family. A future.

Blix tried to shake off these thoughts. He had a job to do, and as soon as he exited the arrivals hall, he flagged down a cab that took him to the Danish Police HQ in the heart of the city.

Stian Josefson had not been difficult to find; he'd used his credit card in one of Copenhagen's many watering holes at 10.38 the previous night – this one in Strøget, the city's pedestrianised shopping street. Armed with a description of him, two officers on Lone Cramer's staff had brought him in. Because of the condition Josefson was in, however, and the resistance he had put up when the policemen had genially asked him to accompany them, they had felt obliged to let him spend the night in the drunk tank, where he lay, still fast asleep, when Lone Cramer escorted Blix inside.

'You're welcome to take him back with you to Norway,' Cramer said. 'Even though he clearly lavishes money on our bars.'

'I'll see what I can do,' Blix replied.

He stepped into the cell and pulled the door closed behind him. The sound made Josefson open his eyes, and at the sight of Blix he nearly jumped out of his skin. He sat bolt upright, too quickly it seemed, as the movement caused him to pull a face and touch his temples.

Blix tried to wave away the stench of drink, urine and sweat.

'Good morning,' he said. 'Or ... I guess it's nearly lunchtime by now.'

'Who are you?' Josefson asked. 'And what the fuck are you doing here?' He looked around, as if unsure where he was.

'You're in a police station in Copenhagen,' Blix explained. 'I'm Alexander Blix, and I'm here because Sonja Nordstrøm is missing, and because we suspect that some kind of crime has been committed against her.'

Josefson sat up straight, at once adopting a more alert expression. 'What's happened?' he asked in a submissive, cracked voice.

'That's what we're trying to find out. Do you need to splash some water on your face?'

Blix looked at the hungover man before him. Three days' worth of stubble. Crumpled, white shirt with a splat of mustard in the middle of his chest. A pair of jeans with what looked like a recent tear on one knee. Blood had dried around the gash.

'Yes, that ... might be a good idea.'

Blix gestured in the direction of the hand basin. Manoeuvring himself up into a standing position, Josefson staggered across the room and turned on the tap. He belched discreetly, and put his hands under water, then rinsed his face and massaged his eyelids a little before turning off the tap and drying himself with a paper towel that lay beside the basin.

'Better?' Blix inquired.

'A bit,' Josefson agreed.

Blix produced a digital recorder and explained to Josefson the formalities associated with providing a police statement.

'Are you willing to give a formal statement?' he asked.

'I've nothing to hide,' Josefson answered, looking obstinately at the recording device.

'Is it true you'd arranged to visit Sonja Nordstrøm on Sunday evening?' Blix began.

'Yes, I … I was there. I was to drop off a copy of our book to her. There had been so much secrecy about it that neither Sonja nor I were to receive any copies until the evening before the official launch to the general public.'

'What time were you at her house?'

Josefson gave this some consideration. 'About eight o'clock, probably. It was around that time when I arrived.'

'How long did you stay?'

His glance veered off to the left. 'A couple of hours, maybe.'

'That's a long time just to hand over a book?'

Josefson met Blix's penetrating gaze. There was a long, lingering pause, before he finally let his head sink as he said: 'Sonja and I … we were more than just partners in crime.'

'You were lovers.'

'Yes.'

He waited for a moment before adding: '*Were* is also the right way to put it. She said she didn't want to meet on that basis any longer.' It came out with a touch of bitterness, as well as perhaps a trace of sadness, Blix wasn't entirely certain. 'We were attracted to each other while we were working on the book, our shared project. There were quite a few long and intense working days. One thing … led to another, and…'

He looked away for a second or two.

'But then she didn't want to have anything more to do with me, so…'

'Why didn't she?'

'Good question,' Josefson said. 'I wondered about that too. She just said we'd got what we wanted from our collaboration, and then she told me to leave.'

'Was that how she expressed it?'

'Virtually. That was what she meant, at least.'

Blix gave this some thought before launching into his next question.

'The crime-scene technicians have found … traces of sex in her bed,' he said. 'Did you have sex that evening?'

Josefson hesitated a little before nodding his head. 'It was probably what we might call in good Norwegian a farewell fuck,' he said with an acerbic undertone.

'Did she end things with you first, or did she do that afterwards?'

'Afterwards,' he said. 'At first she behaved exactly as usual, but then it was as if she just flicked off a switch and went completely frigid. From one minute to the next. While we lay in bed. It was ... brutal.'

'Did you lose your temper with her?'

Josefson looked up at Blix. 'You can bet your boots I did.'

'Were you so angry that you—'

Josefson interrupted him with a brusque hand gesture. 'I know where you're going with that, and I realise why you're here,' he said. 'But no matter how angry I got, I could never have laid a finger on her. I adored Sonja Nordstrøm. The past nine months are the best I've had in my life.'

Blix noticed Josefson glance down at his wedding ring.

'I didn't want to go home to Kristine afterwards and pretend nothing had happened. I just couldn't bear to do that.'

'So you went boozing. You did a runner and took the ferry to Denmark.'

Josefson nodded sheepishly.

Blix had him give a full account of his departure times and ticket purchase. Until now, the man in front of him had been the only common denominator between Sonja Nordstrøm and Jeppe Sørensen, but the ferry trip gave him a cast-iron alibi: he couldn't have been whoever it was that put Jeppe Sørensen in Sonja Nordstrøm's boat.

'Where's your car?' Blix asked.

'My car?'

'You own a black Volkswagen Tiguan,' Blix reminded him.

Josefson cleared his throat. 'It's parked on the quayside at Hjortneskaia.'

Blix jotted this down.

'You come to Copenhagen quite frequently, as far as I understand?' he went on.

'Yes, I ... like it here.'

'I can appreciate that. I believe you interviewed Jeppe Sørensen some time back?'

Mention of the Dane's name made Stian Josefson frown, but his reaction was too muted to suggest that he'd heard the news about the discovery of his corpse.

'Yes?'

'You've also interviewed Sonja Nordstrøm in great depth during the past nine months – do you know whether she had anything to do with Jeppe Sørensen?'

Josefson shook his head.

'You're sure?'

'We never talked about him, at any rate. She wasn't interested in football. Why do you ask?'

Blix told him what had already been splashed all over the media.

'That's the weirdest thing I've ever heard,' Josefson commented. His face had taken on a thoughtful expression.

Blix went on: 'Of course, a lot of people don't come out well from this book of yours, but apart from that – do you know if anyone might have had reason to do something to her?'

'To kill her, you mean?'

Blix gave no response, simply waited while Josefson mulled this over.

'No,' was the conclusion he finally reached. 'I can't think of a single person.'

30

She lay on her side and tried to relax – as far as that was possible with her hands tied behind her back. They were bleeding from the attempts she had made to free herself.

How long had she been here now?

She had no idea – she had no watch. To begin with, she'd made an effort to count the hours, but she couldn't concentrate – her thoughts were confused by the fear of what he intended to do to her. Now she was just trying to breathe as evenly and quietly as possible, in and out through her nostrils, while she waited. And waited. And waited.

What was she waiting for, exactly?

How long would she have to stay here?

What was his plan?

These were the same questions she had asked herself time and again. He had not raped or assaulted her. The only thing he had demanded of her was to stand up, lie down, and open her mouth. Put her hands behind her back. Keep quiet. Not to resist. 'Because that won't help in the slightest.'

She couldn't recall the last time she had wept. She had never done so in public, and to be honest rarely in private either, not even classic weepies had any effect on her. But in the past few days the tears had come all the time, unbidden, needing no prompt from her thoughts. The sofa cushion she was lying on was sodden.

It surprised her that, whenever she struggled to get free, she no longer felt any pain. Not in her hands anyway. Maybe her brain wasn't registering it anymore. Perhaps the cold in this cabin had numbed her senses. Put all her impulses on hold.

She'd started to wonder whether there was someone she'd unwittingly hurt at some point. She was no angel, which was no secret – the newspapers never tired of saying so – but she had never gone in for tormenting people.

She thought about her blanket. The one she usually threw over herself when she stretched out on the sofa at home. She would never have imagined it possible to miss something as trivial as a blanket so much. She longed to wrap it around her. Inhale the scents of the fabric, drink a cup of tea and just watch something innocuous on TV. Something that didn't matter.

She had no memory of how she had arrived here; all she remembered was the ambush. He had worn black gloves. A hood on his head. Some kind of electrical apparatus in his hand. He'd held it up to her throat and the last thing she had seen were blue sparks reflected in the paintwork of the car beside him.

When she came round, she was in this cabin. He had been standing in front of her, watching her flounder and blink, struggling to understand. She had feverishly tried to loosen her bonds, but had only discovered how hard and tight the knots were.

A noise made her raise her head. Was it a vehicle? Someone coming to save her from this dreadful nightmare? Hope gripped her for the first time in hours. Maybe she would be able to get out of here. Perhaps her nightmare was over.

She could hear the car engine coming closer and closer. She tried to haul herself up; using the muscles in her diaphragm that she had exercised so often she managed to scramble into a sitting position. The exertion made her dizzy for a few seconds. The taut gag over her mouth made it difficult to breathe, and her body couldn't get enough oxygen however much she tried.

The car was close now and finally stopped outside. She heard a door open. And another. Footsteps on the ground. Keys rattling. Steps coming nearer; she couldn't hear whether there was one person or several. Her breath grew ragged again.

The door opened.

It felt as if a heavy lump fell from her throat to the pit of her stomach. She began to sob, to cry. She didn't see his face, but it was definitely him. She recognised the black gloves. The hood. She began to hyperventilate. She had to force herself to blink repeatedly to see clearly through her tears.

A cold blast came in through the open door. Beneath her flimsy clothes she felt goose bumps appear on her skin. He stepped inside the room and paused a moment. He was carrying a loudspeaker, which he set down on the floor. He gave her a long, cold stare, then he wheeled around and exited again, without closing the door. She heard his footsteps growing more distant and then disappearing; then, after a moment, they began to approach again.

Yet another loudspeaker was put down. Once again he stared at her before vanishing again. Not long afterwards, he returned, this time with an amplifier and a remote control. A white extension lead. Two plastic bags, one from a clothes outlet she recognised and the other from a bookshop. He placed everything on the floor, before beginning to join it all together.

She looked on with mounting terror as he linked all the cables.

He shut the door. Switched on the equipment and the various units, then fiddled with a few buttons before producing an iPod from his jacket pocket, attaching it too, and making some intricate thumb movements. Music wafted out of the speakers – a song. There was something familiar about it, but she couldn't bring to mind what it was. Once the male vocalist had sung one or two verses, the man stopped the music and nodded in satisfaction. The room was silent again.

He turned on his heel and approached her with short, slow steps. 'Get up,' he said.

Hesitating, she planted her bare feet gingerly on the ice-cold floor. Discovered that she could still feel pain. He stood right beside her, and stared deep into her eyes. His were blue. Glacial.

Then he took hold of her trousers and began to unbutton them.

No! she screamed internally, as she tried to wriggle away. *No. Please, not…*

'Take it easy,' he said. 'I've no intention of raping you.'

His cool, controlled tone made her stop, and he went on removing her trousers. She tried to ask him what he wanted, but the words disappeared into the cloth covering her mouth.

Soon her trousers were off; he had to lift her legs to complete the operation. Then he grabbed hold of her panties. Began to pull them slowly down her hips to her thighs. She smothered a gasp and closed her eyes as fresh tears coursed down her cheeks. He knelt down, pulling at her underwear, his face only a few centimetres from her crotch. She held her breath, afraid that she might at any moment feel his lips or tongue, but it didn't happen. Instead he hoisted her feet and unhooked the panties, taking them off and laying them down beside her trousers.

The fine downy hairs on her thighs stood on end. With every second that passed, she expected him to put an icy finger inside her, wrench her around and force himself on her. Instead he picked up the plastic bag from the clothes outlet and took out a bikini.

'I bought this for you,' he said. 'I think it'll fit.'

He held it up. Leopard print. It resembled one she had worn the last time she went swimming on the sandy beach at Huk.

He bit off the sales tag, bent down and pulled on the bikini bottom, slowly and carefully, lifting it over her hips. The stitched seams of his leather glove scratched her skin. The bottom was a bit too big for her, but the elastic at the waist held it in place. It felt good not to be completely naked.

He stood up and looked at her.

'Sexy,' he said. 'Sex Y.'

She understood what he meant, just not what he wanted.

He smiled again at his own comment. All at once he became serious again. 'Sit down.'

She did as he said. 'A bit further over,' he instructed, nodding his head, closer to the corner and the TV set, which hadn't been on in all the time she'd spent there.

'That's perfect,' he said once she had obeyed his order. 'Thanks.'

He was holding the bikini top in his hand. 'I think I'll wait and put this on you afterwards.'

Afterwards? she wondered. *After what?*

'If I free your arms, you'll only try to escape. I don't want to have to fight you.'

He put the bikini top on the sofa beside her. Picked up the other bag and took out a book. He set it aside and approached her with the empty bag. So close to her now that she could feel his moist breath on her flesh; smell it too – fetid, sickening.

He put his hands behind her head and removed the gag. She gasped a breath through her open mouth. Her lips and throat were dry as dust.

'Do you have any regrets?' he asked.

She stared at him. Tried to ask what he meant, but her first attempt at speech was futile.

'Regrets?' she eventually managed to stammer.

'About your conduct.'

She had no idea what he was talking about. 'I haven't done anything special.'

This was clearly not the answer he was hoping for. His eyes drilled into hers. She was the one who cast her gaze down in the end, struggling to think of something else to say; but all the pleas she had formulated in her head as she waited, all the strategies she had concocted, seemed to evaporate.

'You're going to be ever so famous now,' he said. 'A real legend.'

She looked up at him again with wide, open eyes, with no inkling of what he meant. Not until he pulled the bag he was holding over her head. And shut out all the air.

31

Blix didn't like flying, not because he was scared, but because he was no longer contactable. During an ongoing investigation, the forced isolation of a flight was even worse than usual.

Fifty-four minutes after taking off from Kastrup, the captain lowered the wheels on to Norwegian soil at Oslo Gardermoen airport and reversed the engines. The 737 aircraft was still roaring when Blix deactivated flight mode on his mobile phone. Only a few seconds later the text messages began to tick in.

The first was an express message from the operations centre at police headquarters: *Woman's body found in holiday cabin in Nordmarka.*

The next one, from Kovic, was worded in much the same way.

Blix called her.

'I've just landed,' he said. 'Is it Nordstrøm?' The latter in a whisper, so that the passenger one seat away couldn't catch the name.

'Don't know,' Kovic answered. 'We're on our way out there now.'

'What more can you tell me?'

'It was two mushroom pickers who reported it. The cabin door was wide open with music playing at full blast.'

'Music?'

'The same song on repeat. Full volume.'

The plane stopped and the seatbelt light was extinguished. Blix quickly unbuckled his. 'OK,' he said. 'I'm on my way.'

Blue light was sweeping over the spruce trees when, just over an hour later, Blix parked behind a group of four police patrol vehicles and two ambulances. Red-and-white crime-scene tape stretched around the cabin where the body had been found, mainly to keep the press at a distance. So far out in Nordmarka, there was little chance that intruders would encroach, but officers were strategically placed, just in case.

Blix showed his ID to one of them before making his way under the tape. The smell of autumn swirled in the air around him. Wet trees, damp heather. It was already late afternoon, and the air around him glimmered a dull blue.

Wibe approached and immediately announced: 'It's not Nordstrøm.'

Blix frowned. 'Who is it, then?' he asked – his thoughts racing to the slim bundle of missing-persons cases they had worked on in the past few months.

Wibe opened his mouth to reply, but then closed it. 'You really have to go in and see for yourself,' he said at last.

Halting outside the entrance, Blix glanced at the door. The door-frame was splintered around the lock. 'Have you found a crowbar or something similar nearby?' he asked as he climbed the steps.

'Don't think so,' Wibe responded from behind him.

Blix snatched a pair of foot protectors from a box on the floor and pulled them over his shoes before heading inside. Squeezing past the large loudspeakers in the hallway, making sure not to touch them, he nodded to Kovic and moved further inside the cabin, where he cleared his throat noisily, so that Ann-Mari Sara, crouched over the cadaver, could stand up and step aside.

A dead woman was seated on the sofa.

She had a plastic bag pulled over her head. Drawn together around her neck with tape. A hole had been torn in the white plastic to expose parts of her face.

She was far younger than Sonja Nordstrøm. The blonde hair protruding from the plastic was tangled. Dull. And she was wearing only a bikini. But what made Blix catch his breath and take another step closer was the book perched on the dead woman's lap.

Forever Number One.

The questions piled up inside his head.

'Who is it?' was the first thing he could say.

'Jessica Flatebø,' Kovic replied.

For the next few seconds Blix just stood staring at his colleague. 'The reality star,' he then said, mostly to himself. At the same time his mind flashed to Iselin.

'She's easily recognisable,' Kovic added. 'See – the enormous tattoo on her arm.'

Blix looked: an eagle or a falcon.

'How long has she been sitting here?'

'It's impossible to say for certain,' Sara answered. 'But it can't have been more than a few hours. Rigor mortis has only just started to set in.'

'But she's been missing for six days,' Kovic interjected.

Jessica Flatebø, Blix thought. Who'd been on the receiving end of a social-media smear campaign that had gone on so long, the speculation was she had gone to ground. Either that or she'd quite simply been unable to stand any more – had been bullied into taking her own life.

'But the book only came out the day before yesterday,' Blix pointed out, using his hand to indicate the copy on Flatebø's knee. 'If she's been here all that time, she's been left here on her own for a while at least – so that the perpetrator could buy the book somewhere.'

'But he killed her only a few hours ago and maybe turned the music up full blast afterwards?'

Wibe appeared in the room. 'This is just *absolutely*—'

'Do we have any clues?' Blix broke in, addressing Sara.

'Two sets of footprints,' Sara replied. 'Sizes thirty-eight and forty-three.'

'Male and female,' Kovic added.

'What about the cause of death?'

'No obvious external injuries to speak of, so taking that bag around her head into consideration...'

'Suffocation,' Kovic concluded.

'Even though the bag's been ripped open?' Wibe was sceptical.

'She's hardly done it herself,' Sara said. 'Her hands are tied behind her back.'

'So the killer must have torn it open after she was dead, then,' Blix said, 'to expose her face to us or something.'

'To make it look like she's reading the book?' Wibe frowned.

'Is that what she's doing?' Kovic speculated. 'To me, it looks as if she's watching TV.'

Blix tilted his head and studied the dead girl's eyes. Kovic was right: they were directed straight at the TV.

Blix's gaze flitted to the unnaturally voluptuous breasts, wedged into a bikini top that was slightly too small. In the photos he had seen of Jessica Flatebø, she had always been scantily clad. The focus had been on flesh. And it was always clear how willing she had been to be pictured in the minimum of clothing, especially in front of the TV cameras. It had secured her a career of sorts, for good or ill.

Kovic stood behind Blix, leafing through her notes. 'She was wearing jeans, a denim jacket and a white top when she went missing,' she said. 'And red trainers.'

Kovic surveyed the room as if she expected to see them somewhere.

'We haven't found anything like that here,' Sara told her.

'We'll have to go through everything she did that day one more time,' Wibe said. 'Talk to everyone she had contact with.'

'What else do we know about her?' Blix queried.

Kovic thumbed through her notes again. 'She's twenty-one years old,' she began. 'Originally from Vestfossen. Lived in Bøler. She was in the last series of *Paradise Hotel*.'

'Did she have a regular job?'

Blix took a few steps to one side, got down on his haunches and studied the corpse from a different angle.

'I don't think so,' Kovic answered behind his back. 'She had a blog that she updated fairly regularly – Sex Y – until she stopped all of a sudden last week. No farewell instalment. She had just over a hundred and seventeen thousand followers on Instagram. Apparently there's money to be earned from that, or so I've heard. From advertisers and suchlike.'

Blix got to his feet again and scanned the rest of the room. The cabin was small and sparsely furnished. In addition to the sofa Jessica Flatebø was sitting on there was a coffee table and two armchairs. Mice had nibbled the cushions. A couple of simple landscape paintings and a yellowed map of the Nordmarka forest region hung on the walls. A variety of trinkets and ornaments were displayed on the dusty window ledges, which were sprinkled with dead insects. The kitchen area consisted of only a few cabinets, a worktop and a hotplate, with a small fridge.

'Who owns the cabin?' he asked.

'The original owners died three years ago, only a few weeks apart,' Kovic explained. 'They hadn't used it for the last few years of their lives. They had two children, but neither lives in this part of the country, though they've kept some heating on to prevent the pipes from freezing in winter.'

Wibe, pulling on a pair of gloves, had moved into the hallway to inspect the music equipment. 'An old iPod,' he said, as he picked up the player.

'Don't touch anything!' Ann-Mari Sara instructed.

At that moment, old-fashioned dance-band music thundered out of the loudspeakers. Blix was startled.

'Turn that off!' he shouted.

Wibe fumbled with the iPod, but ended up resorting to yanking out the cable.

Silence descended. Kovic stood with her mouth open.

'Fucking idiot,' Sara raged.

Blix gave Wibe a stern look then looked across at Kovic, whose eyes were wide with alarm.

'That music,' she said. 'No one mentioned it was that particular song.'

'What about it?' Wibe asked, clearing his throat, still slightly embarrassed by his blunder.

'The press conference,' Kovic said, but stopped herself – as if she needed a few more seconds to prepare what she was going to say. 'You weren't there, but a phone rang while Fosse ... the ringtone was...' She nodded at the stereo unit. 'It was the same tune as you just played here.'

'I don't understand what you mean,' said Blix. 'Tell me again.'

Kovic recounted what had happened at the press conference.

'So, whose phone was it?' Blix asked.

'No idea; no one seemed willing to claim it.'

'Where's that phone now?' Blix motioned to Kovic that they should step outside.

'I don't know,' she said, moving out of the room. 'No one's come back for it as far as I know.'

'Call Fosse,' Blix said swiftly. 'Or Nøkleby, or anyone at all – just somebody who was there – someone with responsibility for the press room.'

Kovic already had her phone to her ear.

Blix led the way back to the car. *This is all linked*, he thought. Nordstrøm's disappearance; her phone, switched on at 8.00 p.m. on the dot and laid inside an open grave. Jeppe Sørensen, strangled, deep frozen and then left at Nordstrøm's summer cottage – so that anyone could stumble upon him. Another phone ringing at the police press conference about Sørensen's murder; the ringtone identical to the melody used to alert casual passers-by to find yet another dead body. A body with a copy of Nordstrøm's book on her lap.

And still there was not a single trace of Nordstrøm. That in itself was disquieting. But what worried Blix the most was that someone seemed to be directing what was happening. And so far that person had complete control over events. They'd wanted them to find Jessica Flatebø exactly like this.

Kovic finished her call. 'They have the phone at the station,' she said eagerly. 'It was just left lying there.'

'Good,' Blix said. 'I'll bet a hundred kroner it belongs to Jeppe Sørensen.'

32

Emma browsed through her blog archive, alarmed at how many times she had written about Jessica Flatebø – mainly before her disappearance, but there had also been a number of articles during the six days that had elapsed since she went missing. Stories about Flatebø always attracted a lot of readers, generally because they were about her latest capers on social media, and were often illustrated with a photo, the main focus being either her lips, plunging neckline, backside or legs.

Flatebø had become a phenomenon: overnight, seemingly, everyone had known who she was, mainly because she had entered *Paradise Hotel* with an insatiable appetite for both sexes, but also because of her model looks and notoriously unrestrained behaviour – whether the cameras were on her or not. It had been a winning combination, getting clicks from both women and men, who would have liked to find themselves the targets of her sexual appetite, but also from the morally righteous contingent, who just *had* to see what she had got up to this time.

Younger readers, on the other hand, apparently looked up to Flatebø for everything she did. In their eyes she was cool, funny, exciting and inspirational. Far too many wanted to be like her one day. It was their comments that had made Emma regret having given Flatebø an even broader platform.

When it was reported that she may have disappeared of her own free will, people immediately began to suggest suicide, so Emma had been given strict instructions to give the story a wide berth, since Anita didn't want news.no to profit from a personal tragedy, no matter how well known the person might be.

However, the Oslo Police had now issued a bulletin saying a dead body had been discovered in Nordmarka, and that 'it is suspected that Flatebø was the victim of a crime'. The pendulum had swung back, and Anita had asked Emma to assemble as much material as she could, and was happy for her to recirculate old articles as well.

Emma had considered sending a message to Alex Blix to ask whether he knew anything about Flatebø, but decided against it. He probably had more than enough on his plate with Nordstrøm and Sørensen. What's more, she didn't want to give him the impression that she was trying to exploit him. She found some comfort in the fact that none of the other media outlets had broken any stories about it either.

It was nearly seven o'clock when her mobile phone buzzed.

It was Kasper: *I need a guide to Oslo's restaurant scene.*

Emma gave a fleeting smile before answering: *Have you tried Yellow Pages?*

She waited on tenterhooks for his response.

Too many to choose from. Need a good recommendation. And preferably a blonde, beautiful woman to share a meal with. ☺

Emma hugged her mobile phone for a few seconds. Even though a lot might still take place in the course of the evening, she *did* have to eat.

Three quarters of an hour later she stepped into Villa Paradiso in Grünerløkka, taken aback by how nervous she felt. On other dates she'd had in the past few years, her expectations and conditions had been crystal clear in advance. A drink or five, food, maybe sex – at his place or some other neutral location – if he behaved himself and fulfilled all her other criteria. Now she had no idea what she wanted. But she was pretty sure what he had in mind.

As usual the restaurant was packed to the rafters, but Kasper had arrived early and bagged a table for two in the far corner of the ground floor. He stood up and waved as Emma spotted him. They greeted each other with a tentative hug. Kasper smelled fabulous – shampoo and toothpaste. Smelling good was criterion number one.

'Brilliant that you have time for a bite of food,' he began.

'In fact, I'm not entirely sure of that,' Emma answered. 'I might have to get up and run at some point.' She held up her mobile phone.

'You're pretty good at that, as I recollect. Or was it cycling you did?'

Emma nodded and gave him a smile.

'In Copenhagen we understand bike lovers very well,' he said. 'No one cycles as much as we do, as you know.'

He smiled broadly as he pulled out a chair.

'So gallant,' Emma remarked.

'Yes, you'd think a poor guy from Denmark was trying to impress someone.'

Emma smiled again. Humour – criterion number two.

'How's he doing?' Kasper asked as he sat down.

'It's really too early to draw conclusions.'

All around them the air was filled with the hum of voices. Outside the window, people sauntered in and out of Olaf Ryes plass, a small, circular park in the heart of Grünerløkka. The restaurant's wood-fired pizza oven gave off an enticing aroma.

The waitress, a short woman with close-cropped, raven-black hair, arrived with the menus. Kasper ordered a beer, Emma a glass of dry white wine. Kasper asked Emma to recommend something from the selection of pizzas.

'The one with four cheeses is pretty good,' she said.

Kasper took her at her word, while she chose a Margherita.

'So...' Kasper said once the waitress had left with the menus '...how are things with you?'

Emma had no desire to talk about her life, so she replied merely with 'fine' and turned the question back on him.

'Things are ... "fine" with me too.'

'Do you have any good material on Jeppe Sørensen for tomorrow?'

'Not really,' he answered genially. Emma had the feeling he was reluctant to give anything away, now that they were essentially competitors.

The waitress returned with their drinks. Kasper gave the woman a smile too. Polite – criterion number three.

He raised his glass eagerly and said: 'What about you? Have you any hot topics ready for the morning?'

Emma shook her head. 'We don't let things lie in my line of business,' she said. 'We publish as soon as we get hold of something.'

'So what's the latest?'

Emma told him about Jessica Flatebø. Kasper hadn't heard of her, but spoke in a resigned tone about a similar celebrity blogger in Denmark. Both young girls who had nothing to offer apart from their looks.

He took a gulp of beer from his glass and leaned slightly towards her. 'How have you been since ... Gothenburg?'

Emma quickly looked up at him, aware that her cheeks were burning. 'Well, there's been a lot on at work and loads of...'

'Cycling?'

'Yes,' she said, grateful to him for giving her something to laugh at.

'Have you...?' He paused for a moment before completing the question. 'Have you thought about *me* during all that time?'

Emma took a sip of her wine to buy herself a moment or two. She shot him a look over the rim of her glass, noticing that he didn't seem nervous about what her answer might be. On the contrary: he was self-assured, but not in an unpleasant way. Criterion number four: she liked men who exuded confidence.

Emma didn't know how honest she should be. A 'yes' would put more significance on their affair than she was willing to admit. A 'no' would seem dismissive.

'As I said, there's been a lot of...'

She couldn't find the right words to round off her sentence. She could have said her grandmother, Martine, work. She could have said Emma, but she wasn't prepared to open up to him about herself just yet.

'Well, *I*, at least, have been thinking about *you*,' Kasper said, in a quiet, warm voice. Emma had hoped he wouldn't – that they wouldn't – arrive at this, at *Gothenburg*, at such an early stage in the evening. 'I've been wondering what you thought about ... *us*.'

Emma refused to meet his eyes. 'I haven't thought much about it, in fact,' was all she said. 'You went to Copenhagen, and I went home.' She lifted her gaze, briefly, and saw that he'd been hoping for a different response.

'Do you want to know what I thought?' he said after a lengthy pause.

'I'm not really sure,' Emma answered, after a few seconds hesitation.

'I thought it was a wonderful evening. A wonderful night. With a girl I'd love to get to know a bit better.'

'Isn't that what you're doing right now?'

'I don't know,' he said. 'Am I?'

Emma would have liked the opportunity to let her eyes wander, but she was sitting with her back to the rest of the restaurant. All she could see was Kasper.

They sipped their drinks without a word.

'So what do you think might be the connection between Sonja Nordstrøm and Jeppe Sørensen?' he asked.

Emma was pleased he had changed the subject. 'Other than being superstars in their homelands and involved in sport?' she asked, pondering this for a few moments. 'I don't really know,' she added. 'I haven't a clue.'

'Jeppe was down in the dumps, psychologically,' Kasper said. 'But there was nothing of that kind in Nordstrøm's case, was there? Was she suffering some sort of depression because her career was over?'

Emma shook her head. 'It's been a long time since Nordstrøm quit competitive sports, and she's never been the kind to let things get her down. Quite the opposite: whenever she's had problems, she's just worked her way through them. Moved on without a backward glance.'

'You've been reading her book.'

'Yes.'

'I must get round to doing that too.'

'I've got a copy at home,' Emma said, but regretted it immediately. She didn't want to open that door. Definitely didn't want to open the door to her own home – it would be too difficult to get Kasper to leave afterwards. Especially as she possibly wouldn't want him to.

'And why should the perpetrator go after famous people with depression, anyway?' she continued. 'That makes no sense.'

'I can only agree with you there,' Kasper said.

But he'd given Emma something to think about. For a killer, it could be a smart move to find a victim whose mental problems were already well known. Missing-persons cases often turned out to be suicides, and even though the police and friends would conduct a search, they wouldn't necessarily do it in the expectation that anything criminal had happened. And the media would more or less take a back seat, making it easier for a perpetrator to slip through the net.

In the case of Jeppe Sørensen, however, there was little doubt that everyone would find out that he'd been murdered. This made Emma wonder how Jessica Flatebø had been found – was it in the same obvious way as Sørensen? Jessica too had struggled with her mental health in the past few months.

33

'Will he be finished anytime soon?'

As Blix gathered up his dirty plates and cutlery, he glanced out into the corridor towards the video room. Øyvind Krohn, the Violent Crime Unit's ICT expert and photo analyst, had been called back to work to trawl through the CCTV footage of the room where the police press conference had been held.

'I don't think it'll take too long,' Kovic said.

Blix took the dirty dishes upstairs to the deserted canteen, where he sorted the plates and cutlery into the baskets at the kitchen sink before taking out his phone and opening the latest exchange of messages with Emma. She'd asked if there was a connection linking Nordstrøm, Sørensen and Flatebø. All he'd answered was *Yes*. She'd not asked any further questions. Not yet at least.

Despite Fosse's explicit warnings, Blix couldn't supress the urge to help her in some way. Feed her some titbits, something that couldn't be traced back to him. The information that Sonja Nordstrøm's book had been found with Flatebø's body was a rumour already circulating in the police station. In fact, the first patrol to arrive on the scene had assumed it was Sonja sitting there. Lots of people knew about the book being at the scene, including the paramedics who had been inside before the police.

He was starting to write a new message to her when his phone rang in his hands. It was Kovic.

'Krohn's ready,' she said.

'Coming,' Blix replied and disconnected.

He deleted what he had begun to write. As he did so, he told himself that he was acting unprofessionally. Which is why he also deleted his most recent messages to and from Emma.

Krohn sat hunched over the keyboard in the video room, flanked by Wibe, who made room for Blix as he approached.

'It all seems so well planned,' Wibe commented. 'That the phone is lying where it is, that it starts ringing just there and then, playing that particular tune. It's not by chance; just as it wasn't by chance that Nordstrøm's mobile was found where it was and at that exact point in time.'

Blix agreed. 'The phone left in the press conference has to belong to Jeppe Sørensen. It was there as part of the plan. Which is precisely why I'm not expecting the technicians to come across anything on it – unless there's something the perpetrator wants us to find.'

Krohn turned up the volume on the computer. Gard Fosse's voice could be clearly heard; he was lecturing about the discoveries the police had made and how they needed the public's help. Then the music began to play. Fosse stopped. Blix leaned closer to the screen.

'Go back,' he said. 'And zoom in on the area where the phone is situated.'

Krohn followed Blix's instructions, rewinding one minute back in time, and then playing the recording again.

'Where is it lying, exactly?' Kovic asked.

'It's impossible to see,' Krohn said. 'But it looks as if that woman picks it up from the floor.'

He used the cursor to circle one of the journalists.

The next minute passed without them spotting anything notable.

'OK – rewind it all the way back to the beginning,' Blix said. 'Before there was anyone in the room at all.'

Krohn moved the play button and wound back until people were starting to arrive. First they saw a man in uniform setting out name markers and glasses of water on the podium. Then the reporters entered. Some sat right at the front, whereas others were busy setting up cameras and microphones. Minute by minute, the rows filled up.

Emma appeared on the far edge of the screen. She stood chatting to a man with round glasses and short, curly hair. The sight of her made him slide his hand into his pocket and curl it around his phone.

His gaze moved back to the middle of the room where the phone was found. Men and women, large and small, were milling around. Soon all the seats were occupied.

'I can't see anyone leaving a phone on the floor,' Wibe said.

'Me neither,' Kovic added.

'Try another angle,' Blix told Krohn.

A few clicks and keystrokes later, the images from another camera in the room appeared on the screen. It was a bird's eye view, looking from the ceiling on to people's heads, but there were so many bodies in the room it was impossible to see what was going on at their feet.

The recording was now nearing the start of the press conference. Blix scanned the centre rows, hoping he might recognise some of the faces. Pia Nøkleby launched into her introductory remarks and then handed over to Gard Fosse. Blix followed every movement as Fosse spoke. The audience seemed to be giving him their full attention, but it was impossible to get a clear view of every single face.

Then the tune began to play. At first, everyone was silent. Then, eyes darting, they were looking around in bafflement, until one woman bent down and picked up the ringing phone. She pressed something and the music stopped. Fosse thanked her. The woman scanned the room in confusion, holding the phone aloft, before putting the phone back down again.

'Someone sitting close by must have put it there,' Blix said. 'Move closer in on each one of them.'

Krohn paused the recording and zoomed in. First on the woman who had picked up the phone, and then on the man beside her, a tall burly guy.

'Lars Rovell,' Blix said. 'Works for the *Stavanger Aftenblad*, in their Oslo office. Take the next one.'

Krohn marked out another square area just behind Rovell. A slim woman with a high ponytail: Blix did not know her.

'Just go on,' he said to Krohn. 'And the rest of you: if you wanted to leave a mobile phone on the floor in a room full of people, without anyone noticing it – what would you have done?'

'Crouched down and pretended to tie my shoelaces,' Kovic suggested.

'Just held it in my hand and then dropped it on the floor,' Wibe proposed. 'Coughed at the same time, maybe, to muffle the sound; the floor's carpeted after all.'

'But we don't see anyone bending down,' Blix said. 'And nobody coughing either. At least not in the few minutes just before it starts.'

Krohn continued to zoom in on the people around Rovell and the woman who had switched off the mobile phone.

Blix himself had a suggestion. He thought it through one more time before sharing his idea with the others. 'I would have put the phone down as soon as I took my seat,' he began. 'Long before the press conference began. Once the press conference was in full swing, while people were engrossed in what was being said, I would have shoved or kicked the phone either to the side or forwards.'

'One more time?' Krohn offered, ready to rewind again.

'No, let it run,' Blix told him.

The recording played on. Fosse explained that they were cooperating with the Danish police force and had sent an investigator to Copenhagen. The audience were all sitting and standing in the same places, apart from a few photographers who were moving about to find other angles and better pictures.

Blix glanced at Emma again. She was standing at the back of the room, near the door, jotting something down.

'Wait,' he said. 'Freeze.'

Immediately behind Emma, someone had appeared, a hood pulled up over his head. Blix pointed at the screen.

'Isn't that outfit a bit unusual for a journalist?' he asked.

Krohn zoomed in, marked off the area and trained in on the face partly covered by the hood. The image was grainy at first, but then it came into focus.

Blix's mouth dropped open.

The man's eyes were not directed at what was happening on stage, so it was not easy to make out his features.

But Blix knew them all the same.

He had seen them before.

'God Almighty,' he said under his breath.

'What?' Wibe asked. 'Who is it?'

Blix did not answer.

'Get hold of Gard Fosse,' he said instead. 'Get hold of everyone. We need to meet right now.'

34

Emma had drunk one glass more than she'd intended, but she felt far from intoxicated as Kasper settled the bill and simultaneously asked where she lived.

'It's quite a way from here,' she said. 'I think I'll take a taxi.'

A group of smokers stood outside the restaurant. It had started to rain a little. Cold, drizzly drops.

Emma turned to face him. 'Thanks for a lovely meal,' she said.

'My pleasure.'

He stood looking at her, as if weighing up his next words with great care. 'Thanks for everything,' he said in the end, and took a step closer to give her a hug.

Emma let it happen. Kasper held her close and for a bit longer than the usual clinch, his grip telling her this was what he wanted. She noticed it too, in the way his cheek slid slowly away from hers, but remained close, in the way his beard discreetly rasped on her skin, en route to her mouth.

She took a determined stride away from him. Her thoughts strayed to the brief message she had received from Blix. There *was* a connection linking Nordstrøm, Sørensen and Flatebø. She longed to go home and find out more.

That's what she told herself at least.

'Shall I see you home?' Kasper suggested. 'Or maybe *you* could come home with *me*?' He gave a sheepish smile. 'I could do with the company,' he added.

Insistent – yet another characteristic Emma valued.

'I don't think so,' she said, however. 'I need to work.'

Kasper eyed her for a few moments, before saying: 'OK ... we can maybe meet up tomorrow?'

Not insistent – a personal trait Emma sometimes really disliked.

'I guess we will,' she finally answered.

And so they parted.

Emma decided to walk. After a few hundred metres or so she took out her phone and wrote a text to Blix: *How does it all link together?*

She ambled onwards with the phone in her hand, but Blix didn't reply. Eventually she put her phone back in her bag and took the road up Telthusbakken – a long, steep slope that set her thigh muscles on fire.

On her way on to Bjerregaards gate she had the distinct feeling that someone had been walking the same route as her for some time. She turned to take a look and glimpsed a dark hooded figure on the other side of the street. It was impossible to make out his face, though.

Emma picked up speed. The lighting in Bjerregaards gate was barely adequate, but the closer she came to Ullevålsveien, the more shops and eateries there were, and there was more traffic too. Once on Ullevålsveien itself, she dashed between a night bus and a cyclist, across the two lanes, and increased her pace on the other side. She turned around again at the Underwater Pub. This time she saw nothing of the shadowy figure in the hoodie.

It had happened before, men following her. Once her gut feeling had been so strong that she had dived into a late-night convenience store in Seilduksgata and waited until the person behind her had walked past. Only a few days later, she had read in the newspaper that a girl with blonde hair, around her own age, had been raped somewhere close by.

Five minutes later she was home in Falbes gate, where she hastily let herself in and could breathe more easily. She soaked up the stillness in her flat before allowing her thoughts to return to Kasper and what he might think about her. She wished she had handled the evening better.

She checked her phone. Still no response from Blix. It was now nearly eleven o'clock. She probably wouldn't hear anything from him tonight.

In the bathroom she spotted long, brown strands of hair in the basin. Emma's mind turned to her niece, and to what lay ahead of her – if Emma's assumptions proved correct.

She stripped off all her clothes. Ran her fingers slowly through her own hair as she gazed at herself in the mirror. It never ceased to surprise her how real it felt.

Casually, she began to loosen the hair from her scalp. Centimetre by centimetre, with one hand, as she opened the cabinet beneath the basin with the other.

This was where she kept all her wigs.

They were all approximately the same length, but in slightly different shades.

Taking her time, she lifted that day's wig off her completely bald head and placed it on the stand before raising her eyes to the mirror again. She ran her hand over her smooth scalp, thinking of Martine. She didn't know whether her own mother had suffered from the same condition. It was not directly hereditary, the doctors had explained, even though it was not unusual for several members of the same family to be affected.

She lingered for a while, and then puffed out her cheeks and gave a heavy sigh at her own reflection, before resolutely removing her make-up and then creeping under her quilt.

35

'Thanks for turning out so late at night. We may well have made a breakthrough.'

Blix was holding a long pointer in his hand. He tapped the photo-montage projected on the board in front of him.

'This is Walter Georg Dahlmann.'

The onscreen image divided in two. On the left, a head-and-shoulders shot of a man in his mid-twenties who looked tired and angry. On the right, the same man, only fifteen years older and even more unkempt.

Gard Fosse appeared in the doorway. With arms folded, he leaned against the frame.

'He's forty-three years old now,' Blix went on, 'and he's originally from Dalen in Telemark. He had two tours to Afghanistan and after the last one he was diagnosed with post-traumatic stress disorder. In 2004, Dahlmann was' – Blix rapped the stick on the left-hand side of the picture – 'sentenced to sixteen years imprisonment for killing his ex-girlfriend, Maria Lenth, and her new boyfriend, Simen Veum. Some of you might remember Simen well; he worked here, on the fourth floor. He was twenty-seven. A nice guy; I worked with him a few times.'

Several heads nodded in the room.

'Dahlmann finished his sentence three months ago. We don't know what he's been up to since then, but we do know he was here during today's press conference.'

Blix picked up a remote control and clicked it rapidly a few times, making Dahlmann's movements through the press conference venue earlier that day appear on the board.

'Nicolai Wibe has also gone through all the videos from the area around the Eventyrbrua bridge on the day Geir Abrahamsen – Geia –

received ten thousand kroner for activating Sonja Nordstrøm's mobile phone and tossing it into an open grave. This guy' – Blix clicked on a grainy CCTV image, taken from a distance – 'is not a hundred per cent match for Walter Georg Dahlmann, but it's the same type of hoodie. Same colour. He's also got the same build, and looks around the same height. Krohn and his team are working on obtaining a positive ID for us. This guy walks down under the bridge where Geia was loitering, and comes out again barely seven minutes later – something that agrees with the timescale Geia has given us.'

Blix gazed out over his assembled troops; his reasoning seemed to have been received well. 'We don't know if it definitely was Dahlmann who planted the phone at the press conference, but it's natural to draw that conclusion. He doesn't have press credentials, and he doesn't work for any media outlet.'

'So bring him in, then,' Fosse's voice boomed from the back of the room. 'Find out what he was doing there. And see what he has to say for himself.'

'That's our next step, obviously,' Blix said, raising his eyes to Fosse. 'As soon as we find out where he is.'

'You don't know?' the superintendent continued – his words sounded like a complaint.

'When he was released, he gave his grandmother's address,' Kovic explained. 'But he hasn't been there. I've spoken to his mother, and she has no idea where he is, and she doesn't have a phone number for him either. But she thought he might be in Oslo or Drammen. Possibly Kongsberg; he had some friends there, apparently.'

'Does he have a car at his disposal?'

'Not as far as we know.'

Fosse had no further questions, but to Blix it looked as if his boss was deep in thought.

'Before she was killed, Maria Lenth had made quite a name for herself: she had written two books that had received a good deal of attention, and was on the way up. She'd been on TV a couple of times too. Had a lot of press coverage.'

Blix clicked on a picture of Lenth – a beautiful woman with long brown hair.

'She'd been with Dahlmann for three years before she dumped him, apparently because she had become scared of him; he'd shown violent tendencies on a number of occasions. Just over six weeks later, she and Veum were killed.' Blix used his hand to smother a cough. 'Dahlmann tried to do a runner but was arrested following a two-day hunt in the Østland region. He pleaded self-defence: he claimed that Simen Veum and Maria Lenth had tried to kill *him*.'

'What was his story?' asked Wibe, seated near the centre of the room.

Blix nodded to Kovic, who stepped forwards and faced the group.

'Dahlmann alleged that Lenth had emptied a joint bank account they held. He said he paid her a visit and demanded his money back.'

Blix navigated to one of the current photos of Dahlmann.

'But Lenth refused,' Kovic went on. 'And in the ensuing argument, in which Dahlmann apparently behaved in an extremely threatening manner, Veum drew a gun. Dahlmann managed to disarm him, but in the turmoil Maria Lenth attacked him with a kitchen knife. It ended with her getting her throat cut. And Veum died four days later from his stab wounds.'

Kovic gave Blix a fleeting glance and he responded with an encouraging nod.

'After the killings, Dahlmann panicked. Maria Lenth was a well-known person and in a relationship with a police officer. Dahlmann thought no one would believe *his* side of the story. And he was right,' Kovic added. 'He said that was why he tried to flee.'

Kovic took a gulp of water from a glass on the table before her.

'That's good,' Fosse commented. The others turned towards him. 'We have a suspect. But what on earth does Walter Georg Dahlmann have to do with Sonja Nordstrøm, Jeppe Sørensen and Jessica Flatebø?'

'That's what we have to try to find out,' Blix replied.

'And why go into the press conference and show us his face?' asked Abelvik. 'He must have known we'd check the surveillance cameras?'

'Good question,' Blix said. 'So far everything suggests he doesn't behave recklessly. Maybe he wants us to see him.'

Gard Fosse moved forwards.

'So now he's completely freaked out,' Wibe suggested. 'This stress condition from Afghanistan – the screws are all loose, is that it?'

'I'm not so sure,' Blix said. 'This seems planned to me.'

Fosse was now at the front, standing beside Blix and Kovic. 'Let's not give a damn about the psychology until we actually know for certain that this is the right man,' he said. 'The first priority is to find him. Get him into an interview room. Then we'll need something to build on. This Geia guy has spoken to him, hasn't he? Get him in for a photo line-up.'

'There are people out there looking for him as we speak,' Blix said.

'Excellent,' Fosse said. 'Then we'll implement an all-out search first thing tomorrow.'

He pivoted round and was on his way out when he came to a sudden halt. 'And we'll keep the fact that we have a specific suspect within these four walls. Understood?' He scanned the room with a frown and then left.

36

Ragnar Ole Theodorsen was, as always, running late. There was always something stealing his time, whether it was a delayed taxi, a neighbour who 'just wanted a word', or a phone call arriving at an inconvenient moment.

Today, though, it had been a song, which was suddenly at his fingertips. He'd been listening to the radio, and then one of the melodies they played, a chord change, had put him on the track. He hadn't copied anything – just let it inspire him; and once he had just over eight bars that sounded good, he'd felt he definitely had something. It wouldn't necessarily be The Big Tune that would act as his pension, but it always brought him a childish pleasure to believe that it might, for a few seconds at least. He hadn't managed to record it, time had run away from him, but he would do that as soon as he got back.

Theodorsen didn't have a mobile number for the journalist he was supposed to meet; otherwise he would have texted to say he'd been delayed. Well, he said to himself. It's part of being a star, isn't it? You were allowed to be late.

He repeated the word 'star' to himself and shook his head with a smile. There wasn't much glamour about what he did these days. Twenty years ago they'd played to packed houses everywhere they went. Now they were lucky if a hundred punters forked out for tickets. But who was he to complain? It was miles better than a nine-to-five. It beat any other job too, being able to travel the length and breadth of the country, playing your own music to audiences, and selling an album or two. He had enough to get by.

It wasn't so often these days that the press showed any interest in what they were doing, so their management had given strict instructions to him and the other members of the Fabulous Five: they had to say yes to all requests. This was why Ragnar Ole Theodorsen alighted from the tram at Stortorvet, in a downpour, twelve minutes late. As a rule all five of them were interviewed together, but this journalist had insisted that he was the only one of interest on this occasion. 'You're the brains of the Fabulous Five. You're the one who writes all the songs.' It hadn't been easy to argue against that.

Theodorsen walked into the Samson bakery and café, took off his glasses and surveyed the premises. At the far end he saw a hand flapping in the air. Theodorsen nodded to an assistant and stepped inside. He was met by one or two looks, but no one seemed to recognise him. The person who had waved at him got to his feet and shifted the rain jacket that was slung over his chair.

'Sorry I'm late,' Theodorsen said.

'I'm just happy you could come,' the journalist said. 'I ordered a large pot of coffee. Would you like anything else? A bun or a cake?'

'Coffee's more than sufficient,' Theodorsen said as he sat down. 'Thanks anyway.'

He picked up a napkin from the table and began to clean his glasses. He put them back on as the journalist turned over a cup and began to pour.

'There's milk and sugar here too, if you want some.'

The light voice sounded slightly lethargic.

'Thanks.'

Theodorsen took a mouthful of coffee and gazed at the journalist's shock of hair. It looked a little ... off centre? Was it a wig?

'The Fabulous Five,' the journalist said. 'You've been in the game for a few years now. Does it get easier or more difficult, do you think?'

Theodorsen mulled this over. It was a good question, one he had pondered a great deal recently. 'A bit of both,' he answered. 'It's easier to be on tour, because we've done that for so long. It's almost like going to the loo, if you know what I mean. Goodness, don't quote me on that.' He burst out laughing. 'What I'm trying to say is that we just go ahead and do it, without a moment's thought. It's no longer so strenuous either. But it's more difficult to come up with good tunes than it was before. Maybe that's got something to do with age. After all, I'm fifty-seven now.'

He laughed again, but the journalist just looked at him coldly. There was no note pad with a list of questions on the table. No tape recorder, either.

'What's it like being famous?'

Theodorsen smiled. 'Well ... I don't feel really famous, to be honest. I can walk about freely in the city streets. It's worse in rural areas, in fact, when we're on tour. Sometimes a lot of people crowd round asking for selfies and suchlike. Especially the ladies.'

He tried another burst of laughter. But there was still no response. Theodorsen found this strange and felt slightly uncomfortable. He took another slurp of coffee and racked his brains for something else to say.

'It was fun for as long as it lasted. Being famous, I mean. Loads of attention.'

'Did you feel you deserved it?'

Theodorsen squinted at the questioner. 'In some ways ... I think it's always deserved in one way or another. You strike a chord with people somehow. Mean something to them. And I think we did that. Thirty years ago, anyway, when we started out.' He chuckled again. 'But I like to think we do still mean something to people. At least to the ones who turn up to our concerts. There must be some reason they do that.'

The journalist waited, just looking at him. Waiting for more.

'We write old-fashioned dance-band music. It's not rocket science. Not the world's most advanced form of music either.'

'There are some people who write a song with only four chords, and yet they become world superstars. Earning millions.'

'Yes ... well, if you think of it like that, then maybe it's not really deserved. But ... it has something to do with the whole package. What you sell in addition to the music.'

'Have *you* anything more to sell?'

'Other than my handsome appearance, you mean?'

Once again he attempted to raise a laugh, but it fell on stony ground.

'What I think people like about us is that we are ourselves. Honest. Unaffected. We don't try to be anybody else.'

'So fame is no longer a driving force for you?'

Theodorsen gave this some thought. 'Don't get me wrong, I do miss those early days, when people stood waiting for the tour bus to arrive, going crazy when we got out. It would really be great to relive some of that. And stay at swankier hotels than we do now.'

He smiled. Took another gulp of coffee, waiting for the next question, which he hoped would be about their forthcoming tour, or the album they were going to record around New Year.

Instead the journalist asked: 'Did you know that one of your songs was played at a murder scene recently?'

Theodorsen looked up at the journalist.

'Someone found a dead girl in a cabin up in Nordmarka. "Angel", that song of yours, was playing on repeat.'

Theodorsen swallowed hard a couple of times. 'No, I ... didn't know that.'

'What do you think about it?'

'What do I think about it? Well, I ... don't really know. It's...' He cast around for words for a moment or two.

'Do you mean that ... Jessica something or other?'

A mere nod in response.

'I read about her in the newspaper, of course, but I'd no idea that ... I haven't seen any mention of "Angel" in either *VG* or *Dagbladet*.'

'It's not general knowledge yet.'

'I see. So why—?'

'When it is – do you think it will make your song popular again?'

Theodorsen smacked his lips and put down his coffee cup. The porcelain rattled. 'No, I shouldn't think so ... After all, it's not really important to the whole story.'

'It's not so unusual, you know,' the journalist said. 'Artists who die becoming hugely popular again.'

'I haven't thought much about that, to be perfectly honest.'

*

Ten minutes later, the interview was over.

The journalist pulled a cap on his head, stood up and shrugged on the rain jacket.

It had been a bizarre meeting – all that chat about fame. Theodorsen was uneasy about what sort of angle the journalist intended to take.

'When will this appear in print?' he asked.

'It's not up to me,' the journalist answered. 'But I imagine it will hit the headlines soon.'

'Do you? That's ... terrific.'

There were fewer people than usual in the café. The heavy rain, Theodorsen thought, as he turned to face the journalist.

'Do you want to take any photos?'

'All right,' the journalist replied, pulling his jacket hood over his cap. 'Do you think you could stand over there?' He pointed outside, to the stairway leading down into Stortinget subway station.

'Over there?' Theodorsen queried. 'Right in front of the stairs?'

'Yes, that'd be perfect.'

Theodorsen had been on many strange photo assignments over the years, so this didn't surprise him too much. He had learned just to do as he was asked; that way it was done and dusted all the sooner. He was keen to rush home to his new song. So he went outside to the staircase, struck a pose and waited for the journalist to take out his camera, probably just his mobile.

'You'll be really famous after this,' the journalist promised, thrusting his hand inside his rain jacket.

Theodorsen was about to smile, but instead his lips, parted slightly, froze in an expression of astonishment.

Then he heard two *pops*, in rapid succession, before he felt something in his chest, a sharp pain penetrating deeper and deeper. He couldn't breathe, no matter how hard he tried. He touched his chest; his hands were quickly coloured red, and when he lifted his eyes again, smoke was still oozing from the barrel of the pistol – now aimed at his head.

And when he saw the flash from the muzzle, he thought of the song that had been at his fingertips that morning. At this precise moment the chords escaped him, and the words too: he couldn't recapture a single stanza. He only knew that he was no longer on his feet and was falling backwards. Towards the stairs. Towards eternity.

37

The first news alert arrived at 8.14 p.m. *NTB*, *VG* and *TV 2* were all reporting that someone had been shot and killed close to Stortinget subway station. On social media the victim's identity was already circulating. The rumours of yet another celebrity murder had Emma scurrying through the rain.

She tried to manoeuvre through the onlookers who had gathered around the police cordon. She wanted to catch Blix's eye, but couldn't find him among all the uniforms.

The entire subway station was taped off, and Emma assumed that all the trains had been halted too.

She tried to remember everything she knew about Ragnar Ole Theodorsen. It wasn't much, she quickly realised, but she was aware he was the singer in the Fabulous Five, a dance band that had released a big hit quite a few years ago. She tried to recall how it went, but couldn't: there was too much of a din around her. Rain hammering on the ground, pattering on umbrellas.

But the name suddenly came to her. 'Angel'. And that unlocked the melody. She'd actually heard it somewhere recently.

At the police press conference only yesterday.

At that exact moment she spotted Blix ducking under the police tape. He was accompanied by a number of officers, among them the detective Emma had met at Nordstrøm's house.

Emma took out her phone. She had sent him a message early that morning, desperate to learn more about Jessica Flatebø's murder, but he hadn't yet answered. It didn't stop her from trying again.

ANGEL at yesterday's PC. The man who wrote ANGEL killed today. Connection? Comment? I'm by the Stortinget station entrance.

She followed him with her gaze, hoping he would see her or hear her message, but he moved down the steps, presumably to where Theodorsen's body still lay.

She sent another text: *I'm sure I'm not the only reporter who remembers that. Thinking about an article.*

For the next few minutes, nothing happened, but shortly Blix emerged again. He exchanged a few words with a colleague before checking his mobile and raising his eyes, as if scanning his surroundings. Then he caught Emma's eye and shook his head. Emma was unsure how to interpret this, so she tried to respond with a look of surprise. Blix looked down at his phone again and tapped in a few words.

Emma's phone buzzed.

Can't talk now. Will call later.

Emma keyed in a reply: *When?*

Blix, engaged in conversation, immediately disappeared down the stairs again. At that same instant, she spotted Henrik Wollan, standing beside several other representatives of the Norwegian press. He looked back at her with an icy stare. She decided to go home as she needed a change of dry clothes. Not least a dry wig.

38

'Where is Dahlmann? Have we tracked him down yet?' Gard Fosse barked.

Blix, seated beside Ragnar Ole Theodorsen's corpse, looked calmly up at his boss. The nearest they'd come to Dahlmann was a seven-day-old ATM withdrawal in the city centre. The photo from the CCTV camera was worse than the one they already had.

'Have we anything to go on here?' Fosse demanded, looking around. 'He was shot in broad daylight in a very public place. Surely someone must have seen something?'

Blix got to his feet and muttered his thanks to Ann-Mari Sara who continued her examination of the body.

'A man in a dark rain jacket and cap,' Wibe read aloud from his notebook. 'He disappeared down into the subway station. Very few people noticed him in the commotion, unfortunately. There are a number of possible escape routes from here, in every direction. Every single subway line leads into Stortinget. The perpetrator could be anywhere in the city within minutes.'

Abelvik came up the steps carrying a large, grey paper evidence bag. 'His rain jacket,' she said. 'It was lying in one of the rubbish bins beside the ticket barriers.'

'There must be cameras here?' Fosse scanned the area.

'Krohn has gone to collect the footage,' Kovic replied. 'But they've been vandalised a lot recently. Spray paint.'

Fosse turned towards the stairs. 'Do we have anything we can give the press? Apart from a dark rain jacket?'

'Black cap, dark trousers, blue Wellington boots,' Wibe answered. 'About six feet tall.'

Fosse stood contemplating the corpse, before wheeling around to face Blix. 'This is urgent,' he hissed through gritted teeth. 'Who knows what this madman will think of next?'

Blix had the feeling his boss held him personally responsible for the homicides, and for there being so little to go on.

'We don't know for certain that this was Dahlmann,' he said.

They began to ascend the stairs.

'Maybe we should be more open about the connections?' Blix suggested. 'After all, spreading information can produce information.'

'But we don't know anything!'

'People could draw conclusions for themselves,' Blix added. 'Someone who was at the press conference yesterday and heard the ring tone, for instance.'

Fosse simply shook his head.

'We do have a suspect,' Blix reminded him. 'What about publicising our search for Dahlmann?'

They emerged on to the square.

'He shouldn't know we're pursuing him,' Fosse said, surveying the scene before crossing to the waiting press corps.

Blix couldn't see Emma among them. He took out his phone, opened her last message and wrote:

Talk to Unni Sarenbrant and Berit Norberg, the mushroom pickers who found Jessica Flatebø. Ask them what kind of music was playing at the crime scene.

He paused for a moment before pressing 'send'. He was not giving her information from the case, just nudging her in the right direction. That much he could do for her.

39

Calle Seeberg was on all fours. He couldn't fathom how there could be anything more to throw up, but his body obviously thought there was.

He let the waves ebb and flow. All he really wanted to do was lie down, but he was due to be on air again in ten minutes, and he had to be ready.

Eventually it felt as if his body had completely emptied itself out. He had no idea how he would find the strength to get up, go into the studio and lead another half-hour of current-affairs chat. He couldn't even remember whether he was due any guests.

He blinked. His eyes felt dry and sore. His head was aching. He tried to struggle to his feet. Couldn't do it. Good God, he said to himself, what had happened to his body? It must be some kind of allergic reaction. He'd experienced it before, but never as horrendous as this.

Still on all fours, he tried to think whether he might have ingested something he had no tolerance for. He had eaten dinner last night, pizza. Nothing out of the ordinary about that. He had knocked back a beer and munched a few leftover potato crisps. There had been nothing wrong with his body then, other than that his allergy tablets hadn't had any effect; his eyes had been itchy and his nose stuffy for some reason or other. It had been harder to breathe than usual too, which made him take two more allergy pills.

Calle Seeberg made another effort. This time he succeeded in pulling himself up to his full height. He clung to the wash hand basin, turned on the tap and let the water run until it was really cold. Only now did he realise how hot he felt; and when he raised his eyes to peer at himself in the mirror he saw that he was pouring with sweat.

Christ, what did he look like? His face white, his eyes red, as if he had taken a shower in baking powder.

Seeberg rinsed his hands and face, took a few mouthfuls of water and spat it out again. He only just managed to do it all. How the hell would he be able to speak?

He put both hands in the basin and took several deep breaths, but it gave him a pain in the chest again. He tried to summon some energy, but he knew he didn't possess it. Should he do what he'd never done before in his entire career? Should he leave work and go home?

But who would take over for him then? They had no one who could step in at such short notice.

Seeberg washed his hands again and dried them off. Struggled to pull himself together. Just one more half-hour and he could take a taxi home, or go to A&E. He hazarded a guess that his body was reacting to his new diet. But he hadn't lost that much weight. He'd maybe smoked a packet of fags less each week. Nothing to cause such an effect on his body. The more he thought about it, the more certain he became that he must have consumed something or other.

On his way back to his desk he turned over in his mind what he had eaten in the past twenty-four hours. A totally ordinary breakfast: four slices of rye bread with butter and Jarlsberg cheese. A glass of fruit juice. Coffee. He'd drunk a glass of water as well, before brushing his teeth.

Seeberg was aware of bumping into something on his way back to his desk, but he didn't see what. He noticed some kind of movement in his peripheral vision, voices in adverts, jingles being played, and ending. He swayed and had to clutch the room dividers as he moved towards his own place.

His full 105 kilos crashed down on the seat. He grabbed hold of the armrests and held on tight. In a moment or so the blurred desk came into focus again, and he saw, lying on top of it, a letter with his name on it. It bore no stamp.

'Are you feeling OK, Calle?'

It was his producer talking, shouting, somewhere in the room. Seeberg raised his thumb in the air, because he was unable to speak. He grasped the envelope, but laid it down again: there was no urgency; he could read it later.

'Are you sure? You look white as a ghost.'

The producer again. Maybe. He gave her another thumbs-up. Took a deep breath and braced himself.

Seven hundred thousand listeners a day. He couldn't let them down.

Just one last half-hour, he said to himself, like a mantra, as he stood up and tottered towards the studio. Only a few final minutes.

40

Emma was busy pinning photos on the wall in her living room, even though she felt daft doing so. As if she were in a bad movie. But there was actually a point to it. It gave her oversight, and it was what all investigators did.

The printer spat out a picture of Jeppe Sørensen in his Danish football strip. Emma hung it beside the front cover of *Forever Number One*, Sonja Nordstrøm's book. She'd also found a photo from Jessica Flatebø's blog, and she placed it beside Sørensen. And finally on the provisional timeline – a picture of Ragnar Ole Theodorsen on stage in front of the other members of the Fabulous Five.

His name had been released to the media now. The live broadcasts from the subway station entrance had ended, but *Nyhetskanalen*, the news channel, which was on in Emma's living room, was transmitting the same images over and over again.

The phone rang. It was Blix.

'Hi,' she said, pleased to be speaking to him at last.

'Hi,' he answered.

Emma did not understand why he was helping her, especially since Wollan had trumpeted some of the information she'd received in confidence. But she couldn't bring herself to ask. Didn't want to spoil anything.

'I spoke to the mushroom ladies,' she said, to show him she'd discovered what linked the cases. 'They told me about the music.'

'Did they say anything about the book?' Blix asked.

'What book?'

'*Forever Number One*,' Blix explained. 'It was in the cabin.'

'Oh,' was all Emma said, glancing up at the pictures on her wall. 'Do you have any other leads on her?'

'Not currently.'

Silence hung between them for a while.

'What do you think's happened to her?' she asked.

'I think she's been killed too. I think she'll turn up dead somewhere or other very soon. With a message.'

'A message?'

Blix sighed. 'I don't know. What happened today, and yesterday, to some extent seems to be a very clear statement. He's not afraid to show himself. Some of my colleagues are saying he's a raving lunatic, and he may well be, on some level. But to me he seems ice cold and calculating. A man with loads of self-confidence.'

'Is that his message, then? That he's no intention of hiding away?'

'Maybe. But I'm not thinking of that kind of message. More that it's a new piece of the jigsaw puzzle. One tiny crumb in a long line that he wants us to spot, and follow.'

There was another pause and Emma looked up at the pictures again. Her gaze flitted from Nordstrøm to her book. Then to the photos of Jeppe Sørensen and Jessica Flatebø. And on to Ragnar Ole Theodorsen, who had been shot, so that he had fallen ... down the stairs.

She studied each image again.

No, it couldn't possibly be about that, she thought. But then she retraced her way through the train of thought once more.

'OK, so please don't interrupt what I'm about to say,' she ventured. 'Just listen to the whole of my reasoning. OK?'

'OK.'

Emma moved closer to her wall of pictures.

'Sonja Nordstrøm disappears,' she said, pointing at the letters that formed the word 'ONE' on the book's dustcover. 'The Norwegian media go bananas, and they all follow the developments. And then – *bang* – Jeppe Sorensen is found on her boat.'

She moved her finger from ONE to the number seven on his football strip.

'It's impossible not to link Jeppe's murder to Sonja Nordstrøm's disappearance, which is why the whole of Norway's media attended the press conference yesterday, where a mobile phone suddenly started to ring. It rings long enough for everyone who has ever listened to the radio in the past twenty years to realise the ringtone is "Angel", the song by the Fabulous Five, composed by Ragnar Ole Theodorsen.' She paused for breath, certain now of Blix's full attention. 'The same song was played from a cabin in the forest to entice someone to stumble upon Jessica Flatebø.'

She lifted her finger from the number seven to Flatebø's blog and the logo at the top. *Sex Y.*

'The following day the frontman in the Fabulous Five is also killed.' Emma's finger shifted to the drum kit and the letters that comprised the band's name.

'It's a countdown,' she said.

'What did you say?'

'It's a bloody countdown.'

'What are you talking about?'

'Just think about it,' Emma told him. 'Forever *One.* Jeppe Sørensen always played with the number *seven* on his back. Jessica Flatebø was contestant number *six* in *Paradise Hotel*, and she played on *sex* and the number *six* in every possible context, including in her blog. She'd also been missing for six days before she was found. And the Fabulous *Five*...'

Emma did not conclude her hypothesis, certain that Blix had managed to follow her argument.

'But that doesn't add up,' Blix said.

'Why not?'

'One-seven-six-five. That's not a countdown.'

'Maybe not. Unless you exclude Sonja Nordstrøm – she's the only one who hasn't turned up dead yet. And it all started with her. She fired the starting shot. The first. There was even a starting number hung up in her home. Number one.'

There was silence at the other end of the line.

'You talked about messages,' Emma ploughed on. 'Are there any other connections between the victims apart from the ones the perpetrator has given you?'

It took time for Blix to answer.

'So you're saying that the next victim will be someone who has a link to the number four in some way?' he said, his voice filled with doubt. 'And then one with number three and number two? And then Sonja Nordstrøm will turn up dead, as forever number one, and then it's all over? The perpetrator will have reached his target?'

Emma heard how far-fetched it sounded when he said it aloud.

'I don't know,' she said with a sigh. 'It was just a theory.'

Again the line went quiet. Emma studied the pictures again. It was all a bit too crazy to be correct.

On the TV she could see, for the third time now, a reporter having a serious conversation with Gard Fosse. The volume was already low, but now she turned the sound off. Her eyes were drawn to the strapline at the foot of the screen: BREAKING NEWS. At the same time she heard her mobile phone ping. An express message from *VG Nett*'s news service.

'Shit,' she said.

'What is it?'

'Are you watching TV?'

'Not right now. What's going on?'

Emma walked a few steps closer to the set.

'Calle Seeberg. The radio chat show host, you know? He's dead.'

'Oh fuck.'

Emma read the whole of the text running across the screen. 'It says he collapsed during a live broadcast today,' she said, looking up at the wall again. The pictures. The numbers.

'Do you know what radio station he worked for?' she asked as a cold shiver ran through her body.

'No?'

'Radio 4.'

41

The Radio 4 studio was located in Lille Grensen, the street running diagonally through Akersgata and Karl Johans gate – only a stone's throw from Stortinget subway station. It took Blix no more than a couple of minutes to cover the distance from the steps where Ragnar Ole Theodorsen had been shot.

He met Kovic outside the entrance.

'Why are we here?' she asked.

'I'm not certain it's anything important. Just come in with me, and I'll fill you in later.'

The receptionist needed no explanation as to why they were there, and the radio station staff didn't seemed surprised when Blix and Kovic entered the editorial room on the first floor. People just stopped talking. Dried their tears.

Blix approached the first person he came across, a young man who didn't look more than twenty. His eyes were bloodshot.

'Who can I talk to?' Blix asked, showing his ID badge. The young man pointed to a short female in her mid-forties. She was still sobbing when Blix introduced himself.

'Victoria Løke,' she said. 'I'm Calle's producer. Or at least – I *was*.'

Blix introduced Kovic before going on to ask: 'Do you know what happened to him?'

She shook her head and shrugged. 'He just collapsed.'

'All of a sudden?'

'Yes.'

'No sign beforehand that he was in any pain?'

'He didn't seem too well earlier,' Løke said. 'He was a bit distant, maybe. Unfocused. And just before he died he was speaking more slowly than usual. He seemed short of breath.'

Kovic looked at Blix with puzzlement in her eyes.

'Who has he been in contact with today?' he asked.

'Apart from all of us working here, you mean?'

'Yes?'

'Well, there were a couple of guests. A professor of sociology and a parliamentarian. Just a normal working day.'

Blix nodded. 'Do you have any surveillance cameras here?' he asked, hoping there might be footage of Seeberg as he collapsed, or – best of all – just before.

'Not in the editorial room.'

'What about the studio?'

'We've got a couple of web cams, but we only use them if we have special guests. Someone who's going to sing a song, for example, live on air. Then we film it and put it out on the Internet. But we haven't done any filming today.'

'But the actual radio recording, Seeberg's last broadcast – you must have that?'

'All our broadcasts are stored on hard disk. We send out all our shows as podcasts afterwards, but we haven't done that this time, of course.'

'Can you show us the studio where he was sitting?'

She nodded and showed them to an open door. In the studio they saw three chairs around a table. Three microphones and three sets of headphones. Løke indicated the seat behind the computer screen.

Blix went inside and looked around. A notepad, transmission schedules, two ballpoint pens, a coffee cup and a glass of water. That was all. Scattered on the floor was paraphernalia left behind by the paramedics who had performed CPR. A pair of single-use gloves and the paper packaging that must have been around the sterile equipment.

'Can you close off this room until we've examined it more thoroughly?'

'Yes, yes of course.'

'And I'd like to hear that last recording you have of him.'

Løke nodded and ushered them into her own office, where she sat down and searched through a folder.

'Here it is,' she said, starting to play a sound file and turning up the volume.

Calle Seeberg's well-known voice filled the room. There was something different about him, though. He welcomed the listeners back and told his audience, slowly and in a listless voice, what he wanted to talk about for the next half-hour. Then he tried to introduce Highasakite. He needed three attempts, and laughed it off by saying what an incredibly difficult name it was for a Norwegian band, but there was nothing breezy or cheerful about his words, and he was obviously having breathing difficulties. His chest was wheezy.

The song began. Løke fast-forwarded until it was finished.

'This is when it happens,' she said.

Blix concentrated. Normally Seeberg would have repeated the name of the tune listeners had just heard, but now it sounded as if he was only stuttering, as if he couldn't get out a single word. Then he began to make a gurgling noise before something hit the table surface with a bang. Followed by the sound of a chair toppling and then the thump of Calle Seeberg's heavy body as it landed on the floor.

For a second all was silence and then someone shouted his name. Other sounds filled the room. The patter of feet and chairs being scraped aside. Victoria Løke grimaced as if she couldn't bear to hear any more.

'*Lay him on his back,*' someone said.

'*He's not breathing!*' a woman shrieked. '*Call an ambulance!*'

Swearing.

'*Calle! Can you hear me?*'

'*We're still on air.*'

More swearing. Then music began to play. Løke turned down the sound.

'It's absolutely dreadful,' she said. 'Fortunately, I didn't see it, I only heard it. I ran into the studio when I realised what had happened.' She shook her head. 'It's the worst thing I've ever experienced.'

'Did you try to revive him?'

'Yes, of course,' she said indignantly. 'For ages. We kept going right up until the paramedics arrived.'

The song continued to play in the background.'

'We've heard enough, thank you,' Blix said.

'He couldn't breathe,' Kovic commented when the room was quiet again.

'That's how it sounded, anyway,' Blix agreed. 'Can you show me his workstation?'

'Of course.'

Løke led them back out into the editorial room and towards a desk partly enclosed by two-metre-high dividers. The desktop was strewn with papers, notepads and cables. Pile upon pile of documents, books and magazines. Two cups of cold coffee. Blix took note of a photograph of a girl who, in the photo at least, couldn't be more than fourteen years old. He had a similar photo of Iselin on his desk.

People had bad turns all the time, Blix thought, his thoughts straying to Emma's countdown theory. Even radio hosts could just drop dead.

His eyes came to rest on a white envelope with Calle Seeberg's name handwritten on it. Blix picked it up. Turned it over and saw that Seeberg hadn't opened it. There was no stamp on the front either. Blix squeezed the envelope. There was something inside it: it felt like a photograph.

'Fan letter?' Blix asked, turning to Løke.

'Not inconceivable,' Løke told him. 'He still gets a lot of fan mail.'

'Physical, though? People don't just send an email or a text message?'

'*Most* people, perhaps. A few are still old-fashioned.'

Blix turned over the envelope again. No sender's name on the reverse.

'It arrived by courier earlier today,' a woman at the desk opposite volunteered.

Blix lifted his head to look at her. A woman in her mid-twenties wearing a headset.

'How long ago was that?' Blix asked.

'Er, a couple of hours, maybe. No, wait. It's less than that. I'd just been out on a job when I heard the courier say he had an envelope to deliver to Calle Seeberg. I brought it up with me from reception.'

Blix's brow furrowed. He opened the envelope and took out the photo.

And gasped.

It was a number four.

In grey tones and black and white. The number four was in the middle, with a white circle around it. On the sides of the photo, grey squares. It looked like a still from the countdown at the start of an old, silent film.

'Where did the courier come from?' he asked, aware at once of a slight quiver in his voice.

The woman shrugged. 'I don't think he was wearing a uniform,' she said. 'You'll have to ask at reception.'

'What did he look like?' he went on. 'What was he wearing?'

The woman gave this some thought. 'A black rain jacket,' she said at last.

Blix glanced at Kovic.

'And a grey cap. I didn't see him very well, because he had a hood pulled over his head.'

'Over a cap?'

'Yes.'

Blix peered down at the picture with the number four on it, regretting that he wasn't wearing gloves.

'Thanks,' he said, nodding at the woman with the headset and returning the photo to the envelope.

He turned to face Kovic. 'I think Calle Seeberg is another number in a sequence,' he said, recognising that she was brimming with questions.

Before she had a chance to say anything, he addressed himself to Løke again. 'The CCTV footage from reception,' he said. 'I need to see it. Right now.'

42

Blix approached Abelvik as she sat at her desk with damp hair, eating a sandwich.

'Have you seen Fosse?' Blix asked. 'He's not in his office.'

'I think he's gone to the gym,' Abelvik said, her mouth full of cheese.

'Now?' Blix asked, looking at the time. 'With all that's going on?'

Giving a shrug, Abelvik swallowed and took another bite.

'Do you have an address for Dahlmann yet?' Blix asked.

'Not yet. But I'm going to phone his best pal in just a minute.'

She glanced down at her wristwatch. 'He's on a flight back from Amsterdam,' she added.

'OK, great.'

Blix took the lift down to the basement gym, where he found Gard Fosse on one of the three treadmills. It looked as if he'd been working out for a while: perspiration was running down his blotchy face.

'Blasted doctors,' Fosse said as Blix approached. 'Insisting we have to exercise to prolong our lives. I'm sure it does the exact opposite. It can't possibly be good for you to keep doing this sort of stuff.'

Fosse was dressed in a pair of tight-fitting shorts and a white singlet. His paunch wobbled beneath the flimsy material, and his feet were dragging wearily on the rough treadmill belt. He had covered a distance of 4.78 kilometres and it had taken him twenty-six minutes to do so.

'How's it going with the new girl?' Fosse asked.

'Kovic is doing well,' Blix replied. 'Do you know that Calle Seeberg is dead?'

'The radio chat show guy?' Fosse panted.

Blix nodded and Fosse shook his head, grabbing the towel draped over the treadmill display and wiping his face.

'He collapsed in the studio.'

'And so?'

Blix moved closer and showed the picture he'd brought with him.

'This is Walter Georg Dahlmann, caught on a CCTV camera in the Radio 4 building just this morning,' he said.

Fosse went on running for a few more seconds, then abruptly stopped the rollers with a swipe of his hand, as if the alarm button in the centre of the control panel were an insect he intended to kill. With the sound of the rollers fading away, Fosse's frantic breathing sounded even louder.

'He delivered an envelope with this photograph inside, for Calle Seeberg's attention,' Blix continued, holding out the number four.

Fosse dried his sweat again. 'How did he die?' he asked.

'Circulatory failure, most likely. It's a bit early to say.'

'But we suspect he's been murdered too?' Fosse queried.

Blix nodded. 'Some form of poisoning.'

'In the letter? Powder, or something?'

Blix shook his head. 'But I think I know what's going on here,' he added. 'And what might happen, looking ahead.'

Fosse met Blix's gaze in the mirror in front of him. Dried himself again.

Blix spent the next few minutes going through the high-profile cases they were working on, explaining how each victim could be linked to a number.

Fosse picked up a water bottle and unscrewed the lid. He took long greedy gulps from it before squinting sceptically at Blix.

'I didn't believe any of it either until Calle Seeberg dropped down dead during his show today,' Blix went on. 'But it can't be denied that he worked at Radio 4.' Blix placed extra emphasis on the number four. 'And he is – was – perhaps the most prominent celebrity they have. This is somebody who is killing famous people, and it's happening in descending order.'

Fosse stepped off the treadmill and took a seat on a bench close by.

'Why would Dahlmann deliver a number four to Seeberg unless that particular number signifies something?' Blix ploughed on. 'It's obviously a number from a countdown series into the bargain.'

'But a countdown to what?' Fosse asked. 'What's the point of it all?'

'I don't know that yet.'

Fosse downed more water. 'Who, then, is number three?' he demanded.

'I don't know that either. We just have to hope we can stop this before it gets to that stage.'

Fosse needed a few more minutes thinking time.

'What are your next steps, then?'

'The radio studio's been cordoned off,' Blix explained. 'Ann-Mari Sara has sent a few technicians to examine the scene. I've asked Pia Nøkleby to request a post mortem, and then we'll pay a visit to Calle Seeberg's home to see if there's anything in his flat to indicate how he was poisoned.'

Fosse got to his feet and headed for the dumbbells. Blix noticed that he still looked dubious.

'Fine,' Fosse said, slinging his towel over a chair. 'But we'll keep this close to our chests. The same applies to the numbers. As things stand, it's nothing but a wild guess.'

Fosse picked up a dumbbell marked with the number ten. 'Our first priority is to find Dahlmann.'

He lifted his eyes to his own reflection. 'And since Dahlmann was obviously daring enough to attend our press conference yesterday, it could be that he'll do the same today. Then it'll pay dividends *not* to have disclosed his name earlier.'

Fosse shifted his eyes from himself to Blix, apparently feeling pleased with himself. 'If we had done, we'd never have had that opportunity.'

Blix wanted to point out that there would be no such opportunity, since Dahlmann certainly wouldn't show himself. Not now. He wasn't stupid; he knew the likelihood was too great that they were on to him.

'Tell everyone, make sure they keep their eyes peeled, and that they're ready for action as soon as they catch sight of him,' Fosse continued in a brash manner, before lifting the dumbbell and performing a biceps repetition.

Blix was tempted to tell him he was doing the exercise the wrong way, but decided to leave him to it.

43

A communications adviser welcomed the assembled journalists to the press conference, then handed over to Police Superintendent Gard Fosse.

His cheeks were flushed. He poured himself a glass of water before delivering a chronological account of the facts and circumstances.

'We are searching for a named suspect in connection with Ragnar Ole Theodorsen's murder,' he went on. 'A forty-three-year-old male is the subject of an intensive police search.'

This statement unleashed a salvo of camera flashes. Fosse sat posing for a few seconds before going on to speak in general terms about the police working hard, both technically and tactically, to hunt down the person in question. He then said the police were seeking tip-offs from the public and he held up a still image of a man with a black hood on his head, looking down. The picture had been taken by one of the surveillance cameras inside the subway station.

'We don't know which route he took after shooting Theodorsen,' Fosse added. 'Which is why we need help from the public.'

When the room was opened to questions, Emma was one of the first to raise her hand. She was sitting close to the front this time, in the hope of being seen, but the first questions went, as usual, to the biggest media players. But none of them posed the question Emma was keen to hear an answer to, so she kept shooting her hand up. Only when the session was nearing its end did she get a chance to speak.

She cleared her throat and stood up. 'Emma Ramm, news.no.'

She felt nervous. The press conference was being broadcast live, and she had never liked asking questions in public.

'Calle Seeberg also died today,' she ventured. 'Do you regard his death as linked to the murder of Ragnar Ole Theodorsen and the other recent celebrity killings in the Østland area?'

Fosse regarded her for a few seconds, fixing his eyes on her in a way that suggested he knew who she was, or at least would remember her next time.

'The murder of Ragnar Ole Theodorsen is the focus of this press conference,' Fosse said slowly, as if to gain time to formulate his answer. 'But I can confirm that police are making routine inquiries into the death of Calle Seeberg. These have certainly been demanding days for the investigators in Oslo Police District. We are also looking into the murder of Jessica Flatebø and cooperating with the Danish police with the homicide of Jeppe Sørensen.'

'But are you investigating the connections between them?' Emma demanded.

'All of these inquiries are in their initial stages,' Fosse answered, shifting position in his chair. 'This involves the exchange of experience and expertise.'

Several journalists in the room now turned to face Emma.

'Does that include the Nordstrøm case?' she asked.

'Yes,' Fosse confirmed. 'But there is little point speculating about what may or may not have happened, not least out of consideration for the family and friends of these victims, and especially in a public forum, as you are doing now.'

Gulping, Emma gathered her thoughts quickly. She saw that Fosse was about to hand the floor to someone else.

'There's an arrow from Sonja Nordstrøm to Jeppe Sørensen,' she said. 'You said so yourself yesterday. And there's another arrow leading from that press conference to Jessica Flatebø. I'm thinking, of course, of the music played on a mobile phone in here – "Angel", composed by Ragnar Ole Theodorsen. The same song was played in the doorway of the cabin where Jessica Flatebø was found. And this morning Theodorsen himself was shot and killed.'

The room became eerily silent. For a moment it felt as if only Emma and Fosse were present in the room.

'They are all famous people who have no other obvious connection to one another,' she continued. 'The same can be said of Calle Seeberg, who died earlier today in – as far as I understand – unusual circumstances. Hence my question.'

A journalist further back coughed as Fosse exchanged glances with Pia Nøkleby.

'As I said, it's not part of our brief to speculate at this stage in our investigation.'

Fosse rose to his feet with a nod to the PR manager.

'Thanks for coming,' the communications adviser said, taking a few steps to the front of the podium. 'Unfortunately there won't be an opportunity for one-to-one interviews at this stage.'

Fosse picked up the sheets of paper in front of him and before he left his place, he shot another quick look at Emma. She stood watching as he disappeared out through a side door.

'We'll keep you updated as soon as we have made progress in the investigation,' the adviser continued.

The assembled journalists packed up their gear and began to file out. Emma stayed where she was, her laptop on her knee, and added Fosse's comments about a connection between the murders and the news story she'd already written. She omitted the fact that the killings seemed to have been committed in a numerical sequence. She would include that in her follow-up story, which she'd not quite finished yet.

Kasper Bjerringbo approached her. Emma hadn't realised he was here. No hug this time. No thanks for a good time. She wondered whether he was disappointed that there had been no more than dinner the previous night.

'Are you sure it was a good idea to share your theory with the rest of the world?' he asked.

Emma pressed 'publish' before looking up. 'I'm not afraid of competition,' she answered.

'It's not the competition I was thinking of,' Kasper said. 'It's the people out there. The ones watching and listening. Maybe it'll put the frighteners on them.'

'Well,' Emma replied. 'Maybe it should.'

'Maybe it's not up to you to decide that?'

Emma felt her irritation rising to the surface.

'Are you going to write about these arrows in that blog of yours?'

His tone sounded mocking, so she said nothing but 'I don't know' in return and walked past him, following the crowd of reporters out into the daylight. Only when she felt the fresh air on her face did she realise how hot she was.

44

The text message from Fosse arrived only fifteen minutes after the press conference finished. Blix was seated in the canteen with a cold hamburger sandwich and Kovic for company. The superintendent wanted a chat with him straight away, in his office. Blix said he would come as soon as he had finished eating.

Fosse responded: *This minute.*

'Uh huh?' Blix said to himself.

'What is it?' On the opposite side of the table, Kovic had just started tucking into a chicken salad.

'No idea,' Blix replied, rolling his eyes. 'But it seems I'll need to run. If I'm held up, check how Abelvik's getting on with Dahlmann. She was about to speak to his best friend.'

'OK.'

Blix took the rest of his sandwich with him and descended the stairs to the floor below. He managed to gobble down the last mouthful as he reached his boss's office. Fosse was sitting behind his desk.

'What's all the urgency?' Blix asked.

'Sit down.'

Blix resisted the order for a moment, but then drew a chair nearer to the desk.

Fosse looked at him and waited an age before saying: 'Emma Ramm.'

He stood up and began to pace to and fro behind his desk. Blix licked the last few crumbs from his lips while he waited for his boss to continue.

'She's never worked on crime news before, not until very recently, but she suddenly leads the news agenda in front of a pack of baying crime reporters. And at the press conference today she was audacious enough to question me along almost the same lines you pitched to me down in the gym.' Fosse stopped and pivoted around to face Blix.

Blix slumped into his seat.

'She wrote her first story as a crime journalist after she'd met you at

Sonja Nordstrøm's home.' Fosse began to stride back and forth again. 'I've gone through the other stories she's written since then too. She's come up with news from so-called "anonymous police sources" more than once.'

Blix didn't know what to say.

Once again Fosse stopped in his tracks. 'You were the one who leaked the information that Nordstrøm's phone was found at Gamle-byen Graveyard,' he said, his eyes boring into Blix.

'No,' Blix answered, shaking his head at the same time. This was actually true: Emma had found out about the phone on her own initiative.

But Fosse pounced on him again before Blix had a chance to clarify. 'I'm not stupid, even though I know you sometimes think so. I also know that one of her colleagues was the first reporter to turn up out at Nordstrøm's summer cottage the day Jeppe Sørensen was found. Long before all the others. What happened – couldn't she go herself?'

Blix had a protest on the tip of his tongue, but he couldn't spit it out.

'You don't think I know who she is?'

Blix sat bolt upright, aware of a sharp shudder in his gut.

'You owe her nothing, Alex.'

Not even now did Blix manage to force out a single word.

'I've pointed out several times in this case how important it is for us to keep information to ourselves,' Fosse went on. 'It could cause direct damage to the investigation.'

Fosse paused, stopped again and this time rested his hand on the back of his chair.

He leaned forwards, breathing noisily. 'It's of no interest to me how this has come about, but I can't risk leaks,' he added. 'I can't control the press and I can't take Emma Ramm off the case. But I can remove you.'

Blix looked up at him again. 'What are you saying?'

Fosse waited for a few seconds before replying.

'I'd rather not suspend you, because that will just lead to a lot of internal upheaval, and put you in an awkward position with the others.

But it would seem strange if you're still here but no longer working on a case you've led from the start. So ... you've earned a considerable number of days in lieu, Alex; I suggest you take a week off to start with, with immediate effect.'

Blix cleared his throat. He felt his irritation bubbling up, but managed to control his temper. 'I can cut off all con—'

Fosse raised a hand. 'Does she know who *you* are?'

Blix did not answer.

'You haven't told her?'

'No.'

Fosse finally sat down. Pulled himself closer to his desk with a resolute motion. 'I need competent investigators on this case, you're well aware of that. This means I can't have you in the building while we work on these celebrity murders. Have I made myself clear?'

Blix did not respond, simply waited for a few moments before pushing back his chair and getting to his feet. He looked down at his boss, feeling his blood boil. Initially he'd intended just to turn and leave, but he simply couldn't do that.

'Typical,' he said.

'What is?'

'This has always been your problem, Gard.' Blix struggled to control the tremble in his voice. 'You've always hidden behind rules and regulations. Protocols. That's probably why you've landed in this beautiful office.'

Blix pointed at the walls, at the photos of Fosse pictured with the justice minister, the prime minister, and the chief of police. 'This lets you avoid doing anything out in the real world, where you just might have to tackle things differently. Where you'll find situations you can't deal with by looking something up in a book. You've never had the slightest clue about practical police work.'

Blix grabbed his chair with both hands, so hard that his knuckles whitened. 'And you're about to demonstrate that again, by removing one of the best investigators you've got from a case where you need all the help you can get. Simply because the correct, formal procedures haven't been followed. You know as well as I do that the investigation hasn't been damaged by me discussing the case with Emma Ramm. On the contrary, in fact; but you don't give a shit about that. As far as you're concerned, principles trump everything.'

Fosse was about to answer but Blix had no intention of being stopped.

'Days off in lieu?' he snorted. 'I don't give a damn what you tell the others in the unit. I've no problem about explaining why I'm off the case, or standing up for what I've done. You can do it in the public arena if you like, after all that's where you shine. I couldn't care less. But I do care about stopping a crazy murderer who has killed God knows how many people in the past few weeks, and who still hasn't finished his project. That should be your priority too.'

There was more Blix wanted to say, but he stopped and stamped out of the office, slamming the door behind him.

The toilets were three metres down the corridor. Blix went in, turned on the tap at the basin and splashed cold water on his face. His outburst had inflamed his cheeks. He took a deep breath and tried to calm down.

He faced his own reflection in the mirror.

You don't think I know who she is?

Blix tore off some paper towel, dried himself and headed out. In the corridor, he bumped into Kovic.

'There you are,' she said enthusiastically. 'We have an address for Dahlmann. The emergency response team have been alerted. Shall we go?'

Shaking his head, Blix marched past her. Kovic turned and stared at him.

'Has something happened? Is something wrong?'

'I just need to take care of some personal business,' Blix replied. 'It might take a few days.'

'Days?' Kovic asked in disbelief. 'But...'

She said nothing more. And although Blix didn't see them, he felt her eyes on the back of his neck.

'I'll phone you later,' she called after him.

Blix didn't reply.

45

The possibility that one and the same perpetrator lay behind all the celebrity murders was now the focus of all news coverage, but no one mentioned the fact that a news blogger at news.no was the one who had first pointed out the links. Instead, the media had dredged up expert comments from previous police investigators and brought in various specialists in psychology. The expression 'serial killer' was used in headlines, but none of the media outlets had so far referred to any numerical connections.

Emma had finished writing her article detailing how each victim represented a number, and how they had been killed in descending numeric order, as in a countdown. However, she still felt something was lacking – something to give the story substance.

She hoped Blix would have it.

He had sent her a text message and asked if they could meet up at Kalle's Choice. She had no idea what he wanted to talk to her about, and when he eventually trudged upstairs to the first floor of the café with a cardboard beaker of coffee in his hand, his whole demeanour, with his heavy, but purposeful footsteps, only confused her even more.

'Hello,' he said. His face was pale, his eyes dark.

'Hi,' Emma replied, drawing her mobile and the tall latté glass nearer.

Blix sat down and plonked his phone on the table. 'How are things?' he asked, as he looked up at her with a tentative smile.

'They're fine, so far,' she answered. 'I'm trying to write about the numbers, but it's difficult to do so in a convincing way.'

Emma hoped he would take the bait, but he didn't. Instead he took a mouthful of coffee and sat twirling the beaker around. Staring at it at the same time.

'And then there are some numbers missing,' he said in the end.

Emma leaned back a little and studied the policeman in front of her. 'Do you mean you're investigating more murders?' she asked. 'That there have already been victims number ten, nine and eight?'

'We don't have any active cases to suggest that,' Blix said, shaking his head. 'But it's entirely possible that other well-known people have been killed, without it being discovered yet.' He lifted his gaze and looked at her. 'Celebrities are your department,' he went on. 'Are there any you know of who've died suddenly and unexpectedly in the recent past?'

Emma mulled this over, but couldn't think of anyone. Not in Norway at least.

A pause followed.

'Was that why you wanted to talk to me?' she asked.

Blix waited for a few seconds. Then he shook his head. 'Emma,' he began, and something in his tone had changed; it had grown more serious. 'I have something I ... have to tell you,' he continued. 'Something I think you ought to know.'

Blix curled his hands around the beaker and hesitated for a few more seconds.

Eventually he said: 'In 1999...' He seemed unable to continue without hesitating. 'Sunday, the ninth of May, nineteen ninety-nine, to be precise.'

Emma opened her mouth, but couldn't say anything. At the mention of that date her stomach had abruptly twisted itself into a knot.

'I was a relative rookie at that time,' Blix went on. 'I was driving on patrol with Gard Fosse. That Sunday ... it was a cold spring day. There wasn't very much to do. Not until...'

Blix seemed to focus on something on the tabletop. Emma shifted her weight in her chair. Knew somehow what was to come.

'The report was relayed over the police radio at fourteen twenty-three, just before we were to drive back. An alert about a domestic incident. In Teisen.'

Fleetingly, he looked up at her. And Emma saw it in his eyes, what she had begun to feel anxious about.

He went on talking, but she didn't look at him. She felt something open up inside her. A wound she thought had healed long ago.

Now she understood why this was so difficult for Blix to talk about.

Why he'd been behaving so strangely towards her.

Why he was helping her.

He was the one who had killed her father.

46

They sat on either side of the table, without moving a muscle. What had happened on that fateful day in May 1999 passed once again through Blix's mind's eye.

'I had no choice,' he said, longing to put his hand over Emma's. Instead he clutched the beaker of coffee.

'He was going to shoot,' Blix went on. 'It was only a matter of half a second, maybe not even that. I had to act.'

Emma closed her eyes. Tears were trickling down her face.

'He would have killed you, Emma. Me too, maybe.'

The cardboard gave way in his tight grip, and coffee splashed over the rim on to the fingers of his hand. Blix moved the beaker to his other hand, shook off the spilled drops and placed the beaker back on the table. Wiped himself with a napkin.

'You might be wondering why I'm telling you this now,' he said. 'I ... wasn't sure whether I should say anything, but after we met...' He exhaled loudly. 'I made a decision there and then that led to immense consequences, both for you and for me. I killed a man, you lost your parents. Nobody knows how things would have gone if I'd never set foot in that house.'

Emma blinked.

'But I ... felt a certain responsibility for you in the years that followed. I had an urge to know how things worked out for you. I was aware that your grandparents had taken responsibility for you and your sister, but that wasn't enough for me. So I met your grandfather too, from time to time, for as long as he lived.'

Emma glanced up at him.

'That's why I know you've had a tough time, Emma. That you acted up a lot. I've always felt that was partly my fault. When we met at Sonja Nordstrøm's house that day, I was unsure whether you knew who I was. Whether your grandfather had told you about me, and whether you blamed me, were angry with me. But I realised you didn't know anything. After all, you were so little then. And your grandparents had spared you the details.'

He paused. Lifted the cardboard beaker, saw the coffee stains below it. He wiped them away and placed the beaker on the napkin.

'And maybe it would have been best to continue like that,' he added. 'But for me to be able to look you in the eye, I really had to tell you about it. I think you deserve to know. My father left when I was eight years old, and I never found out why.'

He looked up at her, struggling to read the expression on her face: was she furious, shocked, sad, or did she not feel anything at all? But her look was blank; an occasional tear rolled down her cheek.

'So ... if there's anything you're curious about, just ask. I'm not sure I can give you all the answers, but ... you can call me whenever you like.'

Blix waited for an answer, a response. A sentence. Anything at all. Emma just went on staring straight ahead.

Blix stood up.

'I'll leave you in peace. Ring me if you want to ... chat about it. Or ... if you want to talk about something else.'

Before he left, he took a picture from his inside pocket. He'd taken a copy before he came out.

'This was lying on Calle Seeberg's desk this morning,' he said, as he placed an A4 sheet on the table before her.

Emma raised her eyes to him and Blix saw both astonishment and elation in them.

'You can't mention you got this from me,' he said, pointing at the number four. 'But you can use it to support your number theory.'

47

Blix took a step out into the bitterly cold night. Contradictory emotions were tugging at him. Relief because he'd finally managed to share the truth with Emma. Disquiet because he had no clear impression of what she thought about it. Anger because he'd been excluded from the investigation, when the rest of the force were out searching for Walter Georg Dahlmann. This was a job Blix had really wanted to see through, especially now that he was sure Dahlmann had a major project on the go, something that could only lead to more dead bodies – if no one succeeded in stopping him. Blix was sure the investigation would be in a weaker position without him.

He drove home and let himself in. Usually he spent as little time as possible in his flat, quite simply because he didn't like being there. The stairway was always filthy, and the flat was small and cramped. His furniture was old and the worse for wear. He had no outdoor area where he could relax. It was no surprise that Iselin never wanted to visit him here, especially now that she could compare it to that palace belonging to Merete's new partner.

Blix fetched a beer from the fridge and opened his computer, which was on the kitchen table. On the *Worthy Winner* home page it stated that the contestants had been given the task of writing an opinion piece on a topic of interest to them. The response from viewers at home, and the interest generated by the articles, would form a big part of the decision about who progressed further in the game.

Noticing that his daughter had already delivered her contribution, Blix clicked into it. She had written about climate change. That it might be a good idea to introduce a single-child policy again, all around the world, to curb population growth. There were insufficient resources on the globe to feed everyone, Iselin wrote, and it was difficult enough as things were already.

This was a controversial initiative, one that Blix was taken aback to discover was in his daughter's thoughts. He had never considered her to be particularly interested in social and political matters. At least she had never discussed such problems with him. It made him feel depressed. The things in her life that he had let slip through his fingers, because he hadn't been able to make things work with Merete. Because he'd been too much of a workaholic and hadn't been able to let go of the past.

The opinion piece had provoked an avalanche of comments, some positive, many contemptuous. Who did innocent, little Iselin think she was, having opinions on such a thorny subject when she hadn't yet lived on earth for twenty years?

The production company had also put together an article about the close relationship developing between Iselin and Toralf Schanke. It had started as early as the first week, Blix read, but had remained on a fairly casual level. Both still dismissed the idea that there was anything between them.

His phone drew him out of the reality world. It was Kovic. He considered just letting it ring, but he was too inquisitive; he couldn't stop himself from answering.

'Hello,' he said, aware how exhausted he sounded. 'Did you find Dahlmann?' He straightened up a little.

'We found the basement flat he's been living in since his release,' Kovic explained. 'A visitor from the Red Cross arranged it for him. But he wasn't there.'

'Did you find anything else?'

'Not in the flat, but on the slope behind a shared parking area we found a Persian rug with blood on it. I'll be surprised if it doesn't turn out to belong to Nordstrøm – both the blood and the rug.'

'What about the other victims?' Blix asked. 'Anything to link him with them?'

'Not yet. Wibe's in charge now. He and Abelvik are going through the flat more thoroughly with Sara.'

'Any idea where he is?'

'No, but we've spoken to the neighbours. One of them saw him early this morning, so we're going to lie low in case he comes back some time this evening. If he sees our vehicles, we'll only scare him off.'

Blix took a brief swig from his can. Everything seemed under control.

'But that wasn't really why I called you,' she said. 'How are you doing?'

Blix was in two minds about how honest he should be. He ended up following Fosse's line. 'I'm fine,' he answered. 'It's just that I need time to sort out some personal business.'

He was taken aback to find this didn't feel like a lie, although the silence on the line suggested Kovic wasn't convinced.

'Tell me if there's anything I can do,' she offered.

'You can keep me posted about Dahlmann,' Blix said. 'That will be more than enough.'

48

Although Emma had a key to her sister's flat in Halvor Schous gate, she always rang the doorbell – even when she'd been invited over or had let her know in advance that she was coming.

It was Martine who answered. 'Auntie!' she shouted gleefully through the intercom.

Emma's heart melted. With slightly heavier footsteps than usual, she trod upstairs to her sister's flat.

Martine stood waiting at the door.

'My little sweetheart,' Emma said, sweeping her niece off her feet and hugging her hard – as she always did. Only she was more careful this time when she ran her fingers over her hair.

Martine ushered Emma into the flat.

'Hi, sis,' Irene said as she shuffled towards her sister. It crossed Emma's mind that she looked far older than last time they'd met. She was wearing black woollen socks, a pair of baggy grey joggers and a white top. Her face was ashen and her hair loose, with split ends.

They greeted each other with a hug.

'Do you have any wine?' Emma asked.

'I'm sure there's some in the fridge – essential supplies,' Irene replied. 'What's up?'

Emma hesitated. 'Let's wait until Martine has gone to bed,' she said. 'Then I'll tell you everything.'

An hour later Emma had read a chapter of a popular children's book about a detective agency, Martine had turned out her light, and Irene had opened a bottle of white wine. They sat in the kitchen, where Emma related everything Blix had told her.

When she'd finished, her sister was silent.

'Did you know?' Emma asked finally.

'Know what?'

'Who shot Dad? What happened that day?'

'I knew what happened,' Irene said, 'I was never very interested in who'd done it.'

Emma took a mouthful of wine. 'Was it Grandpa who told you?'

Irene picked a potato crisp from the dish she had set out. 'Yes, but he didn't say very much,' she said as it crunched between her teeth. 'He did everything he could to shield us from the truth. That can't have been easy for him either.'

Emma's phone buzzed. A text from Kasper. Although she drew it towards her, she didn't read the message.

'I think Dad was angry because Mum wanted to leave him. Because he drank too much or something. Take us with her, and just go.'

This was what Emma had always thought too.

'In a way I'm glad I was at Helene's that day,' Irene went on. 'At the same time, I'm sorry I wasn't there with you.'

Emma opened Kasper's message. He wondered if she'd like to have a drink with him somewhere. She didn't answer.

While Irene refilled their glasses, Emma checked the article she had published. Anita had placed it at the top of the news.no home page and it had generated a lot of views already. In the comments section, a lively discussion was in progress about the identity of the next potential victim. Most of the comments attempted to inject some humour. Someone called Jesper Lillevik thought Arne Treholt – the espionage-convicted politician – could be a candidate because 'three' was part of his surname, while Ulf Andersen joked that he was in big trouble now, since he'd been number three in the district tennis championships in 1998. Emma had also tried to hazard a guess herself, but hadn't come up with any possibilities.

'I miss Grandpa,' Irene said, sitting down again.

'I do too,' Emma said.

The wine just grew better and better the longer the evening wore on.

'Do you want to sleep here tonight?' Irene asked after a while. 'I can make up a bed for you on the sofa.'

'No thanks. I must get home. There's a lot on at work just now, so I ... need a good night's sleep. Thanks for the wine.'

*

Emma wasn't in the habit of cycling after she'd had a drink, so she felt far from safe in the traffic. But at last she was home. She left her bike in the hallway, kicked off her shoes, but then she stopped short.

On the floor lay a sheet of paper, folded in two; it had obviously been pushed under the door. Emma crouched down to pick it up and then unfolded it.

It was a drawing.

At the top of the page there were three crosses drawn side by side in pencil. Underneath them, a clock with hands. According to the sketch, it was three o'clock.

The drawing was signed in the bottom right corner, but Emma couldn't decipher what it said. The only thing she could make out with any certainty was a capital D at the beginning of the surname.

49

Blix stood in the bathroom, ready for bed, when the phone rang. With his toothbrush still in his mouth, he padded out to the kitchen, more to check the identity of the caller than answer them. It was almost midnight; he was usually in bed long before this. When he saw that it was from Emma, he spat out toothpaste into the kitchen sink and answered with a watery 'hello'.

'Did I wake you?' she asked.

'No, not at all,' he said, swallowing a couple of times. 'I was up. What is it?'

Emma hesitated for several seconds.

'I think I've received a message,' she said.

Blix wiped his mouth. 'What do you mean?'

Emma told him about the sheet of paper with three crosses and a clock drawn on it.

'Can you think of anyone who'd send you something like that?' Blix answered pensively.

'Well ... I'm not really sure, but it's a bit odd, don't you think? Calle Seeberg had a number four delivered to him just before he died.' Emma paused for a moment before she continued. 'But I'm not exactly a celebrity, so I don't really fit the pattern.'

'But you're scared all the same.'

When she didn't answer immediately, Blix put his toothbrush down on the worktop and said: 'Stay at home, and don't let anyone in. I'm on my way.'

Since he'd drunk a couple of beers, Blix hailed a taxi. Quarter of an hour later he stood outside Emma's block of flats in Falbes gate, surrounded by office buildings, apartment complexes, garages and tarmac. No parking spaces close by. The narrow streets were dimly lit. It would be easy to loiter in the shadows, if you were so minded.

Blix located Emma's doorbell and pressed it firmly. She answered one second later, as if she were standing with her hand on the intercom, waiting for him to ring. The door hummed as she let him in.

There were twenty-four flats in the building, spread over eight floors. Emma lived on the third. Blix saw that the lift was on the seventh, and decided to take the stairs.

Everything around him smelled sterile and modern. The building seemed brand new, with not a single scratch on the railings or walls.

Before he knocked on Emma's door, he checked that he was alone on the landing. He bent down a little to allow Emma a glimpse of him through the spyhole.

Ushering him in without a word, she closed the door quickly behind him and locked it.

'Hi,' he said finally.

'Hi,' she echoed.

They stood gazing at each other for several seconds, then Blix hung up his jacket and left his shoes beside a black bike with *WHITE* embossed in grey script on the carbon frame. Here and there, the wheel rims were flecked with pink.

'You didn't need to come, you know,' Emma told him. 'It's probably just someone fooling around.'

'Who would that be?'

She shrugged.

'Where's the drawing?' he asked.

'In here.'

She led the way into the living room. The sheet of paper lay unfolded on the coffee table between the sofa and the TV.

'Have you touched it?' he asked.

'Yes, of course, I had to.'

Blix sat down, leaning forwards on his elbows. His first thought was that this hadn't been drawn with a gentle touch. The circle had a jagged edge, and there was quite a distance between some of the numbers, but less space between others. The crosses were also of varying sizes. The sketch had been scribbled on the spur of the moment, and it looked as if the surface the drawer had leant on had been neither smooth nor firm.

'Dahlmann,' he said.

'Hm?'

Emma, who by now was seated on the sofa beside Blix, leaned in closer. 'Walter Georg Dahlmann,' he said. 'He's drawn this. It's his signature.'

'Who is he?' she asked.

Blix leaned back, but did not answer immediately.

'When were you here last?' he asked instead.

Emma thought about this. 'Early this morning.'

'Are there no CCTV cameras here?'

'We've talked about getting some, but we haven't got round to it yet.'

Silence again.

'Who is Dahlmann?' Emma asked again.

Blix folded his hands together. He told her about Dahlmann's background, the two people he'd killed and his prison sentence. How angry he still was at 'the System', as he called it, after he was released.

'He used the example of O.J. Simpson,' Blix added. Then remembered Emma's age. 'Simpson was a major celebrity in the USA, and was acquitted of murdering his wife and her friend. Many people thought Simpson escaped prison because of his status. Dahlmann felt the roles were reversed in his case. No one believed his story, because a famous person had lost her life.'

'So he creates another story now. Like some kind of revenge on "the System". On celebrities.'

Blix spread his arms expansively. 'At least he's had plenty of time to make his plans,' he said. 'And it's no secret that many people can't cope with imprisonment. It does something to them.'

Emma tucked her legs under her. 'Why did he come to my door, do you think?'

Blix was unsure what answer to give. 'Many people who commit murder with a specific plan in mind are obsessed about how their actions are perceived, especially by the media. He may have seen what you've written. You've just today broken the story about the numbers. This could be meant as a kind of acknowledgement of you, or else it...' He paused for a moment before going on. '...It could of course be a warning.'

Emma stared thoughtfully into the middle distance.

'Three crosses, three o'clock? It's a pretty obvious signal,' Blix said.

'Signalling what, though – that three people are going to be killed?'

'At any rate, that someone is going to die.'

'Three o'clock.'

Blix looked at the time. It had gone midnight.

'When, though?' Emma continued. 'Tonight? Tomorrow?'

'It's impossible to say from the drawing. But I don't think he intends to go after you, Emma. It would be the most natural thing in the world for you to take every possible precaution. But this,' Blix said, pointing at the sketch, 'I interpret more as a warning about what's to come. To someone other than you,' he rushed to add. 'And it could happen at any time. On any day at all, for that matter.'

Emma did not seem convinced. 'Do you think he wants me to do anything with this?' she asked.

'I don't know. But it's crystal clear: if you write about this, it will be headline news. At the very least he assumes that you'll inform the police; you can't not. So he's raising the game another notch; and that may well be what he's after – even more attention. But that will make it even more difficult for him to carry out his plan.'

'How do you mean?'

'He's chosen fairly high-profile victims so far. Today's murder was even more sensational because he committed it in a public place, in broad daylight. He's not hiding, in other words. So he has no plans to operate in secret now. Presumably he's brimming with self-confidence, since we haven't managed to catch him yet, and he sees no point in scaling things down and going into hiding. Quite the opposite.'

'Maybe he *wants* us to be afraid,' she said. 'Or perhaps he just wants *me* to be.'

Another lengthy silence ensued.

'I'll have to show this to the others,' Blix said, feeling a stab of humiliation. 'Hear what *they* think about it. And you should let your boss know.'

Emma nodded.

'You ought to have protection,' Blix went on.

'What do you mean?'

'You can't be left on your own now, Emma. Not tonight at three o'clock, or tomorrow around that time. You shouldn't be alone at all, in fact.'

She shook her head. 'I don't want someone looking over my shoulder all the time. It's out of the question. I can look after myself.'

'I don't doubt it,' Blix said. 'But just to be on the safe side.'

'I'm not a celebrity, Blix.'

'No, but you write about them. You contribute towards making people famous. That could be enough to justify killing you. In Dahlmann's eyes, anyway.'

Blix saw her consider this.

'But what does the number three symbolise anyway? As far as I'm concerned? I don't work at TV3 or the P3 radio station...' She struggled to come up with other alternatives, but couldn't find any.

'I don't know,' Blix said. 'Not yet at least.'

'Who would watch over me, then?' she asked after a pause. 'You?'

Blix mulled this over. 'I don't have anything else to do, so...'

'What do you mean?' Emma said. 'You must have plenty to do, with everything that's going on.'

'I...' Blix lowered his gaze and, with a sigh, told her about the leave of absence he'd been forced to take.

'Because of me?' she asked.

Blix shook his head. 'Because of *me*,' he answered. 'I was careless. Unprofessional.'

'Sorry,' she said all the same, tucking some of her loose, blonde hair around one ear.

'If there's anyone who should apologise, it's me,' Blix told her.

'What do you mean?'

Blix returned the look she gave him, but didn't say anything.

'Do you think I blame you for killing my father?' Emma asked.

'I don't know. Do you?'

'My father was a scumbag,' she said. 'He murdered my mother and you saved my life. I should thank you; you did us all a favour. Apart ... from Mum, of course, she...' Her voice tapered off, and she stared out at something indefinable outside the living-room window. It was a long time before she spoke again.

'I remember very little about my mother. I can recall her scent. What she looked like, of course. Her voice. But I don't recollect anything in particular that she did. What sort of food she liked and so on. What she liked to do. I remember nothing of what happened that day.'

She looked down at her fingers. Rubbed something off one of her nails.

'I've never tried to find out either, because I don't want to know what Mum looked like after...' She stopped herself. 'I don't want to know what she was doing on the last day of her life. Except, of course, for quarrelling with my father.'

Blix did not utter a word. He understood she intended to continue, now that she was in full flow.

She angled her head towards him. 'What was she wearing that day? Do you remember?'

Blix turned this over in his mind. 'She was dressed in blue trousers and a thick, brown knitted sweater.'

That made Emma smile a little.

'It was cold that day,' Blix added. 'In fact, it was snowing a little.'

'What else?' Emma asked. 'Shoes? Socks?'

'Slippers.'

'That's right,' Emma said, nodding. 'She always wore slippers, I re-member that. Big, grey slippers.' She laughed, a short burst of laughter.

Blix smiled with her.

'She was shot in the stomach?' Emma said tentatively.

Blix nodded.

'So, there was a lot of blood, then.'

'Yes ... there was.'

Emma seemed to think this over for a few seconds.

'Do you know if ... Can you say anything else about her?'

Blix mused on this.

'She'd baked buns that day,' he replied. 'The aroma filled the whole house. The tray was on the kitchen worktop.'

Emma smiled. 'Anything else?'

'I think she liked to read,' Blix went on. 'There were loads of books in your house. On a table in the living room and on the bedside table at her side of the bed.'

'Do you remember what she was reading?'

Blix nodded. He remembered it mainly because Merete had been reading the same book.

'It was a book by Karin Fossum. *Eva's Eye*.'

Once again Emma smiled. 'I've read that,' she said. 'It's good.'

'I think she read to you and your sister as well,' Blix continued. 'You had a lot of children's books. Astrid Lindgren and Anne-Cath Vestly.'

Emma looked at him with moist eyes.

'And she read magazines. *Se og Hør*, I seem to remember.'

'Maybe that's where I get my interest in celebrities from,' Emma said, trying to smile.

Blix waited for a moment.

'Do you want me to go on?' he soon asked.

Emma gazed at him again. This time with a genuine smile. 'Do you have any family?' she asked.

'I'm divorced,' Blix explained. 'I've a daughter about your age. Iselin.'

'What does she do?'

Blix shifted slightly in his seat. 'Right now she's on a TV programme.'

Emma sat up straight. '*Worthy Winner*?' she asked. 'Is *that* Iselin your daughter?'

He nodded.

'I've written a lot about that programme,' Emma went on.

Blix nodded again, noticing how it affected her mood when she talked about something else.

'I know,' he said, realising he felt better too, talking about something different. Something harmless.

50

Blix didn't know when he fell asleep, but it was some time after three o'clock. Kovic had called in a couple of hours earlier. She had taken Emma's fingerprints and took the drawing away with her. The looks she had given, to Emma and Blix in turn, had been bewildered and incredulous, which was why he decided to invite her to the Kaffebrenneriet café in Grønlandsleiret at 9.00 the next morning. It was only a stone's throw from police headquarters, but there were seldom any employees in there at that time, and he would be able to explain everything to her, undisturbed.

Kovic was punctual.

'What's actually going on?' she asked, sitting down on a stool on the other side of the high table where Blix was seated. 'Have you been taken off the case, or what?'

He waited for a moment, unsure how to express himself.

'You'll have heard about the Teisen tragedy at police college?' he said, even though he knew the answer.

'They've recreated the situation on a shooting simulator,' Kovic replied. 'All the students have to go through it. Most fire a shot. It's justified according to the weapon regulations. The subject under discussion is whether it was right to enter the house.'

Blix nodded and took a swig of his coffee. Rotated the cup in his hands.

'Emma Ramm is the little girl who was there,' he said. 'She was called something else then. She took her grandparents' name afterwards.'

Kovic's mouth dropped open, but she didn't say anything.

'I shot and killed her father,' Blix said to be certain that Kovic had understood. 'Fosse believes that the Teisen tragedy and my emotional attachment to Emma makes me unsuitable to go on working on this case,' he said. 'We've agreed I should take a few days leave.'

Kovic ruminated for a few seconds.

'So Fosse thinks you're the leak?'

Blix couldn't bring himself to confirm this. But he was pleased she'd immediately drawn the right conclusion.

'But we need you,' she protested.

'I don't disagree with you there,' Blix said, lifting his cup to his mouth. 'But the decision's been taken.'

They sat in silence for some time, watching life pass by on the pavement outside.

'Have you found Dahlmann?' he asked, putting down his cup.

Kovic shook her head. 'The technicians are busy checking the drawing for possible fingerprints. DNA. Handwriting analysis.'

'What does Fosse say?' Blix asked, sensing his anger from the previous day's meeting in his boss's office flaring up again. 'Is he taking it seriously?'

Kovic raised her coffee cup and swallowed a mouthful.

'Yes,' she said. 'We're preparing ourselves for something to happen at three o'clock.'

Blix glanced at the time. Fewer than six hours left.

51

Emma entered Anita Grønvold's office and closed the door behind her, even though no one else was nearby.

It made a frown appear on her editor's forehead. 'What's up?' she asked.

'I don't entirely know,' Emma answered, sitting down. 'I received an anonymous letter yesterday.'

She produced her laptop from her bag. Anita sat motionless, waiting for her to continue. Emma dug out the picture she'd taken of the sheet of paper with the sketch of the clock face and the three crosses.

Anita had a coughing fit that forced tears to her eyes. She swore and took a swig of coffee from a cup on her desk.

'Bloody hell,' she said with her eyes fixed on the screen. 'Is it from the killer?'

'Either that or someone's pulling my leg.'

Anita looked up at her. 'Who might that be?'

'Wollan, maybe,' Emma suggested, peering out through the glass window at the spot where Wollan normally sat. 'He probably doesn't like playing second fiddle.'

Anita shook her head. 'That's not his style,' she said. 'Though he can be pretty childish at times. Where's the original?'

'The police collected it last night,' Emma said.

Anita seemed about to unleash a reprimand, to tell Emma she should have phoned her first.

'Well, I'm glad you took a photo of it. What are the police saying?'

'They think Dahlmann wrote it,' Emma explained.

'Dahlmann?' Anita repeated.

'Walter Georg Dahlmann.'

Anita's eyes grew big and round. 'The double murderer from Dalen?'

'You know of him?'

'Yes, for fuck's sake. It's a few years ago now but everybody remembers him, don't they? Wollan did a major write-up about him a year ago, in connection with a retrial application.' Anita stood up. 'Does anyone else have this?' she demanded.

'No, but we can't write about it.'

'What on earth do you mean?'

'Not yet at least,' Emma said. 'My source has already been taken off the case. I don't want to create even more problems for him.'

'Bloody hell, Emma. We've got the scoop of the year here!'

'I know,' Emma said, nodding. 'But it's complicated.'

Anita sat down again. 'Are you sleeping with him?'

The question gave Emma quite a jolt. 'Eh?'

'Are you sleeping with your source?'

'No, no, it's not like that. It's more complicated. Anyway, the whole story has come very close to home now.'

Anita cursed again. 'Do they think you're number three?' she asked. 'That you're the next victim?'

'No, not really,' Emma replied, packing away her laptop.

Anita grabbed her coffee cup but discovered it was empty. 'But we *must* have first dibs on this,' she said, putting down her cup. 'You have to make sure of that. And you'll have to speak to Wollan so he can prepare a story about Dahlmann. He's got lots of background info on him.'

Emma nodded without really knowing how she could ensure exclusive rights. She really had enough on her plate dealing with her own fears. It made no sense for Walter Georg Dahlmann to come after her, given that he'd warned her about what was going to happen. But it was impossible to rid herself of the anxiety.

Getting to her feet again, Anita headed for the coffee machine and took a clean cup.

'Phone a psychologist,' she said.

Emma looked blankly at her.

'We must have something in print,' Anita went on, as she inserted a coffee capsule. 'Get a psychologist to say something about what kind of man the police are searching for. After all, you have the solution now. You can actually make something sensible out of it, something that fits Dahlmann.'

The coffee machine had finished. Anita handed her the cup.

'But you're going nowhere until after three o'clock.'

52

The reek of gunpowder hung like a cloud in the air.

Blix followed the shooting instructor's orders – emptied his gun and checked it before pulling the ear protectors down around his neck and squinting at the target at the opposite end of the room. It looked like an excellent collection of shots.

At police college he'd loved to shoot. He liked to feel the interplay between his body and the mechanics of the gun, but the real reason he enjoyed it so much was because he was so expert at it. He was really good at hitting the target.

What had happened at Teisen had taken all that joy from him. Putting his finger on the trigger brought back vivid memories of what had happened. The jerky movement of Emma's father's head as the bullet penetrated his skull. The blood, the backwards fall, how he hit the coffee table, how Emma slid out of his grasp. Her eyes afterwards, full of tears, horror and fear.

He could have requested to be excused from using a gun on active duty, but it was part and parcel of being a policeman. The annual accreditation test was never something he looked forward to, though.

After the shooting at Teisen Blix had tucked his gun into the waistband at the back of his trousers, stepped across to the little girl and swept her up into his arms. With a firm hand on the back of her neck, he had walked her out of the living room, making sure her back was to the corpse, so she wouldn't see her father's blank, dead eyes. If he thought about it long enough, he could still feel Emma's breath and heartbeat.

At the annual shooting training a few years later, a colleague had asked what he recalled best about the incident, what had made the greatest impact. 'Apart from all of it?' Blix had replied, brushing off the subject. He had actually thought it was the silence afterwards. After he had fired the shot, and after both he and the girl had gone quiet. That brief second of absolute, total silence. It was impossible to describe, because it was so replete with emotions. Adrenaline. Questions. A dread that still held him in its grip.

The shooting instructor told him to fill the magazine with six shots. Blix plucked six brass cartridges from a box in front of him and weighed them in his hand before squeezing them into place in the magazine. The resistance in the spring gradually increased as he filled the gun.

'Ear protectors on!' the instructor commanded, letting his eyes run along the row of shooters.

'Magazine in! Load your weapon!'

A series of metallic clicks followed as the line of officers locked their magazines in place. Blix went through the loading motions and inserted a cartridge in the chamber. Then he secured his weapon and stood ready to fire. Tried to forget. Tried to focus.

'When the shooters are ready, five standing shots at the centre of the target! Thirty seconds! Fire!'

Blix raised his gun, aimed it at the target and focused on the black bullseye. He took off the safety catch and breathed in through his nose and out through his mouth before releasing the first shot. The next ones followed in rapid succession.

The practice was not only about hitting the bullseye, but also about having control over the number of shots fired. There were six in the magazine, and after the practice there should be one cartridge left in the chamber.

Three, two, one, he counted to himself. Each shot wrenched his wrist, but he kept a firm grip on the half-kilo or so of deadly power. Around him the cartridge shells tumbled to the floor.

He secured his gun and stood waiting for further orders from the instructor.

Three, two, one, he thought again, and pictured in his mind's eye the three crosses on the message Emma had received. It sounded a lot, three more people, on top of the others already killed.

'All fired?' the shooting instructor yelled.

Consent by silence.

'Empty your weapons, prepare for inspection!'

Blix drew the slide back and caught the last cartridge as it was ejected from the chamber.

So far Dahlmann had taken a sports star, a footballer, a reality celebrity, a vocalist in a band and a radio chat show host, Blix thought, as he held his gun and cartridge ready for inspection. Two women and three men. There was no indication of who Dahlmann might target next, what line of business that person might work in. Or maybe that was part of his plan. Maybe he wanted to take everyone by surprise once again. Blix was as baffled as everyone else.

The instructor walked past, nodded in approval and crossed off something on a form.

'Get ready for the next exercise!'

Blix filled the magazine. Pictured the three crosses again. How clumsily they were drawn. Different sizes, lopsided lines. There was no doubt they indicated three deaths.

The cross was the principal symbol of Christianity, he thought. Signifying Jesus Christ, the crucifixion and resurrection, the salvation of believers, death and the church.

'The church,' he said aloud, realising he had seized on a significant thread. It excited him. There were several Christian celebrities. Musicians, preachers, politicians; but the one that came to mind first was Hans Fredrik Hansteen. The celebrity televangelist with his own TV channel.

Blix didn't catch the instruction that was called out. Only a few months ago, he had watched a documentary that shone a negative spotlight on Pastor Hansteen, suggesting that he had become 'rich on God'. The faithful had donated large sums of money over the years, ostensibly to obtain God's forgiveness. In the past two decades almost 450 million kroner had ended up in the bank account of Hansteen's congregation.

'Ear protectors on!'

Blix returned his gun to his holster and took out his phone. He tapped the pastor's name into a search engine. The top result led him straight to the church's home page, *www.treenighetskirken.no*. The Trinity Church.

'The trinity,' Blix said aloud to himself. 'Three.'

'Blix?' the instructor's voice sounded stern.

Blix quickly looked at his watch. 'Sorry,' he said. 'I have to run.'

He donned his jacket on the way out and called Gard Fosse's number as he clambered into his car.

Fosse did not answer.

The tyres gripped the road. He tried Kovic and got a response.

'Quick,' he panted. 'Send a patrol car to Hans Fredrik Hansteen's house.'

'Why—?'

Blix cut her off. 'I think Hansteen could be number three,' he shouted and rang off to avoid wasting time on explanations.

He looked at his watch.

It was 14.51.

53

Pastor Hans Fredrik Hansteen stared at the red light, which today represented his congregation. He had no idea how many viewers were watching right now, but it would be a large number. Thousands of family members.

He curled his hand around the wireless mic and stretched the other hand out. 'You know me,' he said. 'You know I'm not trying to trick you. But I also know that God loves a cheerful giver. And remember – what you give, you're not giving to me or to us here at the Trinity Church, but to the Lord.'

He looked into the camera with a smile. Waited for the red light to go out. When it finally did, his face fell back into its natural, relaxed folds, and he tried to breathe normally; it was difficult to hold in your paunch and talk at the same time.

Leaving the studio he noticed the wall clock; it was 2.20 p.m. Finished for the day. The broadcast schedule for the remainder of the day comprised reprises of old evangelical meetings and miracle conferences. People loved those programmes, despite having seen them lots of times before. Maybe it was the music. The atmosphere. Or the message. Possibly all three. As long as the account numbers ran across the screen, it didn't matter too much.

Hans Fredrik Hansteen's thoughts turned to Michael J. Masterson, the apostle from the USA who was expected tomorrow. Hansteen didn't have time to meet him in person at the airport, but he would send a limousine. It wasn't often he had a visit from someone who had brought people back from the dead, although Hansteen was slightly sceptical about that.

Justine gave him a smile as he entered the front office. 'Did it go well?' she asked.

Justine de Laet had come all the way from Belgium to work for him. He loved her smile. He loved most things about her, to be honest, as long as God didn't hear of it or manage to read his thoughts.

'It did indeed,' he said, smiling back. 'Do I have anything else on today?'

'You have a meeting at home at quarter to three.'

Hansteen screwed up his face, unable to recall what this was about.

'That donor, you know? The one who wanted to meet you personally. There was some mention of half a million, I think.'

'Ah,' Hansteen said. 'Of course. I'd completely forgotten.' How could he forget half a million kroner?

'It's just as well I've got you,' he said, beaming.

Justine had learned Norwegian after arriving in the country. If Hansteen didn't already have a wife and two grown-up children, he would have offered her one of the rooms in his house. It would have been nice to have some company now that the rest of the family – that is to say his wife – was in Spain.

Picking up his jacket, mobile and car keys, Hansteen wished Justine a lovely day in the spirit of God, before dashing out to his car. He was actually running late. Fortunately it wasn't far from Fornebu to Ris, but you never could trust the traffic. He didn't have an electric car either, so he wasn't permitted to use the public transport lanes. But he had enough horsepower to help him. His car, a Mercedes GLS 350d, was a top-of-the-range model, and the biggest one available, so everyone else would just have to move out of his way. A servant of God was on the road.

The most eccentric and generous donors preferred, as a rule, to keep their names private. Hansteen had nothing against meeting them in person, though, so that he could offer his thanks and have a chat. That was all many of them wanted in return for their generosity – personal contact, a handshake, the feeling of being seen and heard. As if Hansteen were God himself and possessed restorative powers.

As he swung into Trosterudveien, he knew he was a few minutes late, but that could be excused in a man of his stature. He parked outside the house but saw no other vehicles there. Maybe he was early? No, the appointment had definitely been made for a quarter to three. A rather odd time of day to meet anyone when he came to think of it.

Hansteen stepped out and looked around. No one waiting for him on the steps. He let himself in. Tossing his keys aside, he hung up his jacket and checked his phone. No messages. He laid it down on the worktop.

The house was quiet now that he was the only one living here. Usually he relished it. Now, though, he had a strange sense that there was someone else present. There had been some trouble with the alarm system in the past few days, so he wasn't completely certain that it was working properly. Only a few days ago it had gone off while he was at work, but the security company hadn't found anything untoward when they came out to check.

He entered the living room where the big wooden clock ticked steadily.

Hansteen stopped.

There was a man sitting in the garden.

He was wearing a navy suit, black shoes, had his legs crossed, and held a briefcase on his lap. Hansteen went out on to the veranda, leaving the door open behind him. The man turned his head towards him and got up with a smile. One leg dragged slightly as he came to meet him.

54

'Apologies for making myself at home like this. I was early so I just had a look around. It's so incredibly beautiful here.'

Hansteen strolled down to the lawn, which was still damp after the previous day's rain. He wasn't keen on people entering his property without his permission, but he wasn't in a position to get worked up about it. Half a million was a lot of money. He couldn't – wouldn't – let that slip through his fingers.

The man moved his briefcase from his right hand to his left and they shook hands.

'The ways of the Lord are indeed mysterious,' he said.

Hansteen did not understand what he meant, not in this particular situation at least, but it was just one of those things people said – without really knowing its import.

The man in front of him did not appear to be an eccentric. More ... Hansteen didn't honestly know. An estate agent, perhaps. His suit was on the small side, or maybe it was just the way he was wearing it. As if it were uncomfortable or he was unused to having it on.

'Hans Fredrik Hansteen,' the man said. 'In the most distinguished flesh. It's fantastic to meet someone who serves the Lord as you do.'

'The pleasure's all mine.'

Hansteen pulled back his hand. It had been a heavy-duty handshake.

'So ... how's life in the Trinity Church these days?'

'Yes ... it's fine, thanks.'

'You've had some negative publicity recently, I seem to recall?'

'Yes...' Hansteen said, hesitantly. 'Extremely undeserved, if I may say so. Dishonest journalism. Not a word about all the people we help to live worthy lives in the spirit of God.'

'Sensation,' said the man. 'That's what the media's after.'

'That's certainly true. Would you like to come inside? I don't have my jacket on, and...'

'I'm short of time,' the man interrupted, looking at his watch, then raising his eyes and smiling stiffly. 'Anyway, it's a fine day. I don't often have the opportunity to be out in God's wonderful fresh air.'

Although Hansteen hesitated a little, he nodded, and they moved to the bench where the man had been sitting. Above their heads a magpie darted from one tree to the next. A plane on its way to land at Oslo Gardermoen airport disturbed the silence.

'So who are you, actually?' Hansteen asked as they sat down. 'You were quite ... vague on the phone, my secretary said?'

The man put his briefcase aside and crossed his legs, steepling his fingers. 'I prefer to remain very private.'

'I understand that,' Hansteen said – trying his best to be obliging. 'But now I'm the only person here. I can keep a secret.'

'Yes, because you're an honest and upright man, aren't you?'

Did he detect a trace of irony in his voice? Hansteen was uncertain, but he nodded all the same and assured the man that everything they discussed would remain between the two of them.

'You can depend on God's servant,' he added – an argument that normally worked with his congregation.

The man simply laughed and looked at him as if he'd said something crazy.

Hansteen thought this a bizarre reaction, but perhaps, if they talked a little longer, he'd come to understand more about this mysterious man.

'You don't get out very much, you said.' Hansteen clasped his hands and turned to face the stranger. 'Do you work in an office? Or at home?'

'I work all over the place.' The man showed no sign that he was going to explain further.

'I'm sure God would like to know who he's receiving so much money from?'

'I *am* God.'

Hansteen smiled at first. Then he grew more serious. 'What do you mean by that?'

'I have power over life and death. Isn't that what God does?'

Hansteen shifted in his seat. The bench was hard and cold. 'I suppose you could look at it like that. But what do you mean, more specifically? Are you an author or something?'

This made the man laugh. 'No. But it's not a bad guess.'

Hansteen waited for an explanation, but it didn't come.

He looked at the time. 'I understand you don't want to say anything. I respect that. So shall we get this over and done with?' He pointed at the man's briefcase and clapped his hands, resisting a sudden impulse to rub his hands together.

But the man made no move to open the case. Instead he looked at his wristwatch. 'It's not three o'clock yet,' he said.

A cold gust swept across the garden, chilling the back of Hansteen's neck. 'Does that matter?' he asked.

'Oh yes,' the man replied. 'It's of great consequence.'

'I don't understand ...'

'No, that's not surprising,' he said. 'But then you've never understood that you've swindled a lot of gullible people either. Or maybe you've understood it, but just didn't give a damn. Because you've grown rich yourself. Just look at the house you live in.' He pointed at it. 'Your winter cottage in Norefjell too, which is almost as large. Your summer house in Alicante, where your wife is right now.'

Usually Hansteen had no problem fending off personal attacks, but he hadn't expected this onslaught. Not only that – he felt a creeping sense of discomfort. This man knew Ulla Marie was in Spain. And he didn't like the look he was giving him, nor the aggressive tone that had crept into his voice.

'Tell me,' the man said. 'How many people have you fooled in the past twenty years?'

Hansteen's lips fell apart. 'Fooled ...? I haven't fooled anyone.'

'Maybe you've lost count. If you ever count at all. But I do. I'm very fond of numbers.'

Hansteen couldn't understand why this man had wanted to meet him, if it was just to come out with nonsense and baseless accusations. *The money*, he said to himself, like a mantra. *Remember the money*.

'Let me tell you something about what we do,' he said, using his TV voice, the one so many people said they liked so much. 'We build schools in countries that are far worse off than we are. In Ethiopia, for instance, we've just dug toilets at one of the schools, we've purchased school clothing for the youngsters, pencils and rubbers and ... other school materials. There's going to be a canteen there eventually.'

He tried to force a smile, he was so desperate for the man to see and appreciate all the goodness in what he did.

'But it's obvious – we have a huge number of sponsors, and unfortunately we've found it necessary to take a small administration fee.'

He rounded off with another smile, but this sales pitch, which he had delivered so often in the past, did not seem to have any effect.

'I've watched your fundraising campaigns,' the man said. 'On TV. Only ten per cent of the money you collect goes to the projects you like to boast about. The rest ends up in your own pocket.'

'Those figures are not correct,' Hansteen replied, shaking his head.

'Oh yes they are.'

He gazed at the man in front of him. Agreeing to this meeting was obviously a mistake. He felt cold. He was about to get to his feet when the man laid a hand on his arm to hold him back. His grip was firm.

'It's not yet three o'clock,' the man insisted.

'Yes, you said that already,' Hansteen replied, aware he was starting to get annoyed. 'What in God's holy name does the time of day have to do with this?'

He received no answer.

'And why did you want to meet me if you only wanted to—'

'As a matter of fact,' the man broke in as he stood up himself. 'It takes a bit of time to get everything ready, so maybe we're as well to begin after all.'

Perplexed, Hansteen sat watching the man as he picked up his briefcase and opened it with two sharp clicks. A shudder ran through Hansteen's body when the man took out a length of rope and handed it to him.

Hansteen automatically accepted it. 'What ... is this?' he asked.

'I've been lying to you,' the man said, taking out a square device – a little like a mobile phone. 'You're not going to receive half a million from me.'

'But...'

'How does that feel?' he asked. 'Being lied to? It's not good, is it?'

Hansteen sat there staring at the man, struggling to gather his thoughts.

'Are you angry? Disappointed? Sorry?'

Hansteen looked at the rope. Felt the fibres on his fingers, dry and cold.

'I'm going back inside,' he said, standing up. 'This...'

But the man was in front of him, blocking his path. Hansteen tried to edge past, but the man moved across.

'Do you want to shout for help?' His voice was chilled and controlled.

Hansteen met his cold gaze.

'Where's your God now, when you need him most?'

Hansteen swallowed hard and felt how dry his throat was. How cold he was, all over. He struggled to say something, but no sound emerged. He wanted to pray, but none of the words was distinct. He felt a strong desire to phone Ulla Marie, an indescribable longing to hear her voice one more time.

The next moment, the man took a step closer. Hansteen didn't have time to react before he heard a buzzing sound, as if something was giving off sparks. Just as he was about to ask what in heaven's name was going on, it was as if his entire body were shaking and closing down. He couldn't utter a word. He fell to one side, towards the bench. And when he struck it, it felt as if the sky, bright blue today, tore asunder above him.

55

Blix ended up in a traffic jam near Røa, and even using the blue light it was a slow business weaving his way through.

Hansteen was not answering his phone, but a secretary answered at his office. She informed him that the pastor had a private meeting at his home at quarter to three. There was a name in the appointments book: Dahlmann.

Blix glanced at the dashboard. It was already 15.04.

Swearing with frustration, he pummelled the steering wheel.

Killing someone took time, though. It took time to make an escape too. Blix kept his eyes peeled as he drove up past the grand houses and gardens in one of Oslo's most fashionable residential areas. He passed a woman with a pram as well as a jogger. A man in a tight-fitting suit carrying a briefcase with a placard from an estate agency chain tucked under his arm, turned and gazed after him.

His phone rang. It was Kovic.

'Haven't you been removed from the case?' she said.

'That's not important right now. Where are you all?'

'Just beside Ullevål stadium. What about you?'

'I'm almost there. Are there any patrol cars ahead of me?'

'Yes, there should be.'

Then there may still be hope, Blix thought, as he disconnected the call. Several hundred metres further along, he spotted the rear of a police patrol car. Swinging his car up on to the pavement, he jumped out. Found Hansteen's number in his phone log and tried again.

Outside the entrance to the pastor's huge house, he met a uniformed officer.

'Should we go in?' he asked.

Blix strode past him without responding. Pushed at the door and found it open. He heard a phone ringing inside and rushed towards the sound. It was on the kitchen worktop. But there was no Hansteen.

Blix dismissed the call and shouted Hansteen's name. No answer. He walked into the living room and called out again, but still no sign of life.

'Blix,' said the officer who'd followed him inside. He stood at the living-room window, pointing outside.

At the foot of the garden, they saw Pastor Hansteen hanging from a tree.

'Fuck,' Blix swore, and they rushed outside.

With the aid of the young officer, he managed to bring Hansteen down from the tree. They laid him out and began to try to resuscitate him, but they soon realised that it was futile. He'd been dead for several minutes.

Kovic, Wibe and Abelvik arrived just as they stopped.

'It takes a strong man to lift such a heavy body up into a tree,' Wibe commented. 'How much did he weigh – a hundred and twenty kilos?'

'Something like that,' Blix said, as he wiped the sweat from his forehead. 'He's still warm. Dahlmann can't have got far. We need to spread out. Call in as many officers as we can. He could be anywhere at all. In a neighbour's house, a kennel...'

'Nordmarka forest is right on the doorstep,' Abelvik said. 'There are footpaths leading to Sognsvann lake.'

'We have to get someone out there, have them move towards us from that side,' Blix said. 'Look out for someone who appears strong. And look for someone who...'

Blix stopped himself. His journey to Ris was running through his head.

'Fuck,' he said to himself. There had been something about that man in a suit he'd encountered along the road. Something he'd subconsciously latched on to. There had been something about his bearing or the way he walked. He could easily have been Dahlmann.

'What is it?' Kovic queried.

'I spotted a guy as I drove here. An estate agent. There was something familiar about him. The timing fits really well. He was walking on his own. Looked pretty stocky and strong; his suit was too small for him.'

'Is Dahlmann strong and stocky?' Wibe asked.

Blix pondered this for a few seconds. 'Difficult to say from the recent photos we have, but I don't really think so.'

'And he's not an estate agent either?'

'No, but he could have been in disguise. He looked as if he was on his way to the subway station. I'll go there.'

Blix turned towards the street.

'There's only one line at that stop,' he yelled as he set off. 'Call Ruter's head office and get them to stop all their trains to and from Ris. And make a start on door-to-door inquiries.'

Behind the steering wheel again, he focused his mind on the man he had spotted. It couldn't have been Dahlmann, could it? He could have disappeared in any direction, not only via the subway. But whether or not he was right, he didn't have a single second to lose.

56

The clocks on the wall in the news.no editorial office showed the time in Tokyo, New York, London and Oslo. Beside the row of clocks were TV screens showing live footage from CNN and other international news channels, as well as the web pages of the major newspapers.

The Oslo clock showed twelve minutes to four. Emma shifted her gaze to the wide door leading into the corridor. Anita had locked it at ten to three. And soon an hour would have passed since Dahlmann's appointed time. But nothing had happened. The police Twitter account had not been updated, and none of the major media outlets had reported anything of significance.

Emma tried to concentrate on the interview she'd conducted with a psychology professor, and managed to write the final paragraphs. She'd laid out to him her whole hypothesis, explaining that everything seemed painstakingly directed by a man with a plan. The aim of the interview had been to encourage the psychologist to come up with something about what the subsequent plan might involve. The most useable quote Emma had gleaned was that the perpetrator might have a yearning to become a celebrity himself. 'This reminds me a little of Gary Gilmore,' the psychologist had said, 'who in a sense acquired the status he craved once he'd become a double murderer. He appeared to get a kick out of knowing that people would remember his name forever.'

The professor thought the police were pursuing an obvious psychopath, that the person concerned in all probability harboured delusions, either about himself or about the world he inhabited.

She'd also spoken to a retired police investigator, someone who was often approached for comment on current cases, but all he could contribute was a 'deep anxiety about the outcome'.

Nevertheless, there was enough to run a story, and Emma used the fresh quotes to regurgitate much of what she'd written the previous day, bringing her countdown theory into focus once again. She uploaded the article and brought it to Anita Grønvold's attention.

Then she concentrated again on her lists.

She had searched the newspaper text archives and come up with a list of well-known people who could somehow be linked with the number three, and a similar list for the number two. The list for two was far longer and contained many high-profile programme presenters on TV 2.

The list had grown unmanageably long, so she'd begun to look at eight, nine and ten instead. People who, according to the countdown theory, must already be dead. Timewise, she had restricted her searches to the weeks prior to the disappearance of the Danish footballer. Jeppe Sørensen was number seven, and with the exception of Sonja Nordstrøm, everything pointed to the killer operating in chronological order. This had given her one possible hit for the number nine.

Mona Kleven.

Only *Aftenposten* had written about her death. It emerged that the forty-five-year-old union leader had died in a subway accident at Sinsen the previous Friday. Reading between the lines of the brief report, it was regarded as a suicide.

Kleven had initially come to attention as 'the Miracle Baby', when she was the only survivor of a plane accident in the seventies. As a teenager, she had found the spotlight again after being involved in a dramatic train crash that also claimed a number of fatalities. Later she became a familiar face as the chief employee representative of a major trade union, but then she had contracted a serious form of cancer. A national newspaper ran an in-depth interview with her once she had recovered. It described how, throughout her life, she'd been haunted by accidents. She'd broken two bones in a riding accident in her twenties, and she'd also survived a diving accident. They portrayed her as a woman with nine lives – an epithet that had stuck to her during her very public battle to regain leadership of the trade union.

A sudden noise made Emma raise her head. Someone was yanking hard at the door. The door handle waggled up and down several times, followed by furious knocking, before the door was opened from the inside.

'Have we started locking the door or what?' an irritated Henrik Wollan demanded when he entered, wrenching off his jacket. Emma had no chance to say anything before Anita emerged from her cubicle.

'Ruter has just announced that the police have stopped all traffic on line one, and there's police activity at Ris subway station,' she said, phone in hand.

'What kind of activity?' Wollan asked.

Anita did not reply, her eyes glued to her phone.

'Several messages on Twitter about major police mobilisation in Trosterudveien,' she went on.

Emma glanced at the newspaper websites on the big screens. The front page of *VG* had just been updated: 'LATEST: Suspicious Death in Ris'.

'Get into a taxi,' Anita said, pointing at Wollan.

'But I just arrived,' he protested.

'And now you're going out again,' Anita ordered, making a get-out gesture with her hand, before turning to Emma: 'You post a short version.'

Wollan gave a loud sigh as he shrugged on his jacket again. Emma bent over her keyboard to see what the other media sources were saying. *VG Nett* had two lines: the police confirmed that they had been called out to a suspicious death in Ris, and that the operation was ongoing.

Emma called Ruter's customer service centre, and while she was on hold, she began to hammer out the story. A young man answered almost immediately and Emma introduced herself.

'Why is line one at a standstill?' she asked.

'You'll have to ask the police about that,' he replied. 'All I know is that they've stopped four trains and no one is allowed to get off until the police have searched them all.'

'Thanks,' Emma said, and hung up.

This was all she needed to add an edge to her story. She published it with a promise that news.no would be back with more details.

She considered contacting some of the people who were tweeting about the police operation, but instead headed to the phone directory and looked up Trosterudveien.

The list of residents was lengthy. She scanned through them, on the lookout for famous names. On the third page, one turned up, and the pieces of the puzzle fell into place.

Hans Fredrik Hansteen, the celebrity pastor.

The Trinity Church.

Three.

57

All the coaches that had left Ris station between 3.05 and 3.40 p.m. were halted and all the passengers held up until the police had scoured every carriage. On line one this involved two trains in both directions. One of them had been stopped between Stortinget and Jernbanetorget, and had already been searched. The others were several hundred metres ahead of Blix, between Steinerud and Frøen stations, while the final two had come to a halt at Vettakollen and Lillevann. Patrol cars were on their way.

The train driver opened the doors once Blix had shown his police badge. Just as he was about to start searching through the carriages, his phone rang.

'No trace of Dahlmann yet,' Kovic reported breathlessly. 'We'll soon have covered half of Trosterudveien. A lot of cars have been coming and going in the area. We're trying to check them all.'

'Look at the toll stations in the vicinity as well,' Blix said, scanning the occupants of the carriage, who were staring wide-eyed at him. 'With a bit of luck we'll get a match with one of the cars we've identified near the other crime scenes.'

'We'll be lucky if he's used the same vehicle for everything he's done,' Kovic replied.

'Check it out all the same,' Blix told her and rang off, then prodded a young man in a suit, sitting half-asleep. He wasn't either Dahlmann or the man Blix had spotted.

A passenger asked what was going on. Another wanted to know if there was a terrorist threat.

'No,' Blix answered. 'We're just looking for someone.'

Six men in suits were on board. None of them resembled the man Blix had passed in his car.

At the end of the train he jumped down on to the track again and phoned Hans Fredrik Hansteen's secretary.

At first she refused to believe what had happened, and then she burst into tears.

'The man Hansteen was supposed to meet at his house,' Blix continued after a pause. 'Dahlmann. Do you know who he is?'

The secretary sniffed, struggling to compose herself. 'No,' she replied tearfully. 'He just called and said he wanted to meet Hans Fredrik face to face. Today.'

'How long ago was that?'

She sniffed again and took some time to reflect.

'I think it could have been Monday.'

'Can you find out exactly when? It would help us a great deal if we could have the precise time and a phone number.'

Blix heard her leafing through a book or a sheaf of notes.

'I don't think I can be any more specific. But I'm pretty sure he phoned on Monday.'

Blix tried to get more details from her, but the call was one of many. He made a mental note to ask for the Trinity Church's phone lists, and drew the conversation to a close.

His next phone call was to Gard Fosse. The tone at the other end was cold and dismissive.

Blix made no comment about his outburst the previous day, instead getting straight to the point. He gave an account of what had taken place and the progress made in the investigation before explaining how he had realised Hansteen would be Dahlmann's next victim.

'I was maybe only ten minutes too late,' he concluded.

When Fosse gave no immediate response, Blix went on: 'You can't keep me out of this case, Gard. Not now. You need me, and you know that.'

'What about Emma Ramm?'

'What about her?' Blix retorted. 'None of what I've given her has harmed the investigation. And if I hadn't spoken to her, we wouldn't have come as close as we did today.'

Before Fosse managed to get a word in, Blix continued: 'You need as many people as possible right now. What if he kills again before you're able to catch him? The chances of us doing that are far greater if I'm involved.'

Once again Fosse took time to think.

Blix exhaled loudly. 'You can suspend me once all this is over,' he said. 'God knows you and I haven't always agreed on ... things, but set that aside, for once, and let me get on with my job.'

Fosse finally responded with a sigh: 'OK. Finish up at Ris when you think you can, and we'll have a run-through here at the station afterwards.'

'Thanks,' was Blix's terse response.

58

Anita had Wollan on loudspeaker. She came out to Emma with the phone in her hand.

'Nobody here is willing to say much right now,' Wollan reported. 'But it *is* the pastor who is dead.'

Emma was longing to ask if Wollan was sure this time, but managed to hold back.

'It's like a war zone here,' Wollan continued, and then provided an animated description of large-scale activity, with police dogs, patrol cars and helicopters in the air. Wollan reckoned there were at least twenty-five uniformed officers in the neighbourhood.

'We'll publish the name as soon as we know that the family have been informed,' Anita instructed.

'I'll keep you posted,' Wollan said.

With that, the conversation ended.

Emma took out her own phone. She didn't know where Blix was, but assumed he was being kept in the loop.

Hans Fredrik Hansteen = number 3? she wrote in a text message.

While she waited for an answer, she embarked on an article in which she recounted Hansteen's purported role in the perpetrator's project. But how did this fit into the bigger picture? she thought. Sonja Nordstrøm had not turned up or been found as yet, but Emma was certain the athletics star who had written an autobiography called *Forever Number One*, was indeed number one in Dahlmann's countdown. Which meant he planned another victim before that.

Her phone rang, interrupting her thoughts. Blix's name flashed at her.

'Is it the pastor?' she asked, without even saying hello. 'Is he number three?'

'Yes, it is,' said Blix. 'I'm sorry I didn't call you right away. But you don't need to worry anymore.'

'Have his next of kin been notified?'

'They have, yes,' he said. 'We're going to issue a public bulletin stating that Dahlmann is a wanted man sometime this afternoon.'

'We?' she repeated. 'Does that mean you're back on the case?'

'Yes, but Fosse's still the one who'll make the statement,' he said. 'He's taken me back on sufferance.'

'Do you have any theories about who'll be the next victim?' she asked.

'Not yet.'

Opening the folder in which she'd collected references to Mona Kleven, Emma explained how she'd found her name.

'The woman with nine lives?' Blix asked.

'She died last Friday,' Emma told him. 'Fell in front of a subway train. It was reported as an accident.'

At the other end she heard someone shout for Blix.

'I'll look into it,' he said. 'I have to run.'

59

Blix had his eyes fixed on the computer screen. Iselin was sitting beside Toralf Schanke, the joiner from Tinn. The distance between them on the sofa had diminished each time he had seen them together. He didn't have the sound on, but their conversation seemed carefree. Even cheerful.

'Great to have you back,' Kovic announced as she flopped on to the chair beside him. 'I'm glad Fosse came to his senses.'

Blix clicked on another window and responded with a brief nod.

'You'll have to bring me up to speed,' he said. 'What else is new, apart from the dead pastor?'

Kovic produced two reports from the pile of papers on her desk and handed them to him. 'Calle Seeberg was poisoned, and Jeppe Sørensen was strangled,' she told him.

Blix skimmed through the first post-mortem report: the Danish footballer's air passages had been blocked when a millimetre-thick cord tightened around his neck. The images illustrated the conclusion.

Blix turned to the report on Seeberg.

'That's possibly the more interesting one,' Kovic commented.

Blix read the description of how traces of digoxin had been found in the radio host's blood.

'Digoxin is a medication for heart patients,' Kovic informed him. 'Seeberg didn't have heart trouble, but he did take Aerius, an antihistamine for allergy sufferers. Digoxin is easy to confuse with Aerius,' Kovic said. 'Digoxin tablets were found in the plastic bottle that contained Seeberg's allergy pills.'

Blix glanced at a photo of a clump of hair sitting beneath the shoe rack in the hallway of Seeberg's home. According to Sara's report, the hair came from an Alsatian dog.

'So someone swapped his medicine and planted dog hairs to trigger an allergic reaction?'

'It all points to that,' Kovic said. 'It doesn't take much for the dose to be fatal.'

Bloody hell, Blix thought. So Seeberg, entirely unwittingly, had taken the poison that had killed him.

'What about Sonja Nordstrøm? Any news of her?'

Kovic shook her head. 'Nothing, except that everyone she vilifies in her book has been eliminated from our inquiries.'

Blix flicked through the forensic papers on Calle Seeberg one more time. 'So unnecessary,' he said.

'What do you mean?'

'Dahlmann could just have shot him, couldn't he? Or attacked him in an underground car park, the same as the football player. The same applies to Nordstrøm. He'd no need to abduct her. He could just have shot her at the appointed time.' Blix waved the papers in the air. 'This is innovative.'

'It must be part of his plan,' Kovic said. 'To exercise control and attract attention. Demonstrate how brilliant he is.'

Blix nodded thoughtfully.

'What do we actually have on Dahlmann?' he asked. 'Is he really capable of devising and implementing such a plan?'

He looked up from the papers though he didn't really expect an answer. Wibe was heading towards them.

'That didn't help much,' he said, flinging down a bundle of photographs. The picture of Dahlmann slid out and sailed across the desk.

Wibe had hauled Geir Abrahamsen in for a photo line-up to see if he could identify Dahlmann as the man who had paid him to drop Sonja Nordstrøm's phone in Gamlebyen Graveyard.

'He couldn't pick him out.'

'That's no surprise,' Kovic said. 'He could barely describe the man he met.'

Fosse appeared behind Wibe and clapped his hands to catch everyone's attention. The investigators gathered around him.

'We've just issued a wanted notice for Walter Georg Dahlmann,' he told them, 'in the hope that Dahlmann's friends and acquaintances will come forward and tell us where he's hiding.' He made eye contact with each of them, one by one. 'In addition, it's important that people take their own precautions,' he added.

He then handed over to the leader of the uniformed section, who gave an account of the various security measures implemented in the TV 2 offices in Oslo and Bergen, among other places.

'So, we know who the killer is,' Fosse went on. 'It's just a matter of finding him. Until that happens, all holidays, leave and time off are withdrawn.'

With that, Fosse left the room. Once he was gone, Tine Abelvik approached Blix's desk.

'I don't understand how it's possible for Dahlmann to keep escaping the way he does,' she said.

'I'm actually not convinced Dahlmann's the person we're looking for,' Blix told her, aware all eyes were now directed at him.

'What do you mean?' Wibe asked.

'I'm not sure he's the man I saw making his way from Hansteen's property.'

He turned to face Kovic. 'Can you dig out the CCTV footage taken at the Stortinget subway station after Ragnar Ole Theodorsen's murder, and the pictures of Dahlmann in the Radio 4 building that same day?' he asked.

Kovic located these and displayed the images side by side on the screen.

'Look at the figure on the left,' Blix said, pointing at the picture taken at the subway station. 'There we have a man wearing a cap with a hood drawn over his head – so we can't see his face, obviously. He doesn't look up in any of the pictures we have of him inside the subway station. Not a single time. Which makes it impossible for us to ascertain, with one hundred per cent certainty, that this is Walter Georg Dahlmann.'

Blix looked at the others before gesturing towards the next image.

'Look at the difference,' he said. 'In this photo, taken in the Radio 4 building, we see someone making no attempt to hide his identity. The same is true at the press conference the day after Jeppe Sørensen's body was found.'

'That could be because he hadn't committed any crime on those occasions,' Wibe suggested. 'It's a different kettle of fish when you've just killed someone. At the press conference, all he was doing was leaving a mobile phone, and at Radio 4 he was delivering a photo.'

Blix placed his finger on the Radio 4 picture. 'That photo was taken only a few hours after Theodorsen was shot. Does this look like a man on the run?'

The chair rocked as Kovic leant back in it. 'Do you mean there are two of them involved?' she asked, her voice filled with doubt.

'We can't rule that out,' Blix said. 'It would explain why Geir Abrahamsen couldn't pick out his picture in the photo line-up. And why didn't Dahlmann just drop the phone into the grave himself, since he obviously doesn't have a problem with walking into a press conference the next day and doing something fairly similar?'

Blix allowed his argument to sink in.

'From the very beginning I've had the feeling that someone is coordinating all this. Deciding exactly when the various pieces of the jigsaw are presented to us,' he went on. 'Whether it's a phone, a dead body, a song or a drawing, there's someone in complete control.'

'So, someone gave Geir Abrahamsen instructions and paid him for his trouble? And they're doing the same with Walter Georg Dahlmann?' Kovic suggested.

'It's an idea I think we should bear in mind,' Blix said, then looked at Wibe. 'You were the one who thought the perpetrator was playing a complex game with us. Wouldn't you say that it simply makes it too easy for us that Dahlmann, all of a sudden, makes an appointment with a famous pastor and then more or less confesses in a drawing he pushes through a crack in Emma Ramm's door? If it's Dahlmann who's doing all this, then it almost seems as if he *wants* us to nab him.'

'At any rate, Dahlmann's the key to it all,' Abelvik said. 'If he's going along with something, he can tell us who he's in cahoots with.'

There was silence for a few seconds.

'We know Dahlmann's not at home,' Wibe said. 'We know he doesn't use a credit card, mobile phone or email – or at least he hasn't in the past few days. Since he showed himself at Radio 4, he's gone to ground.'

'Someone knows something,' Abelvik insisted. 'We'll talk to everyone he served time with and everyone who visited him in prison. It's only a matter of time before we get something more on him.'

Kovic's computer emitted a message alert. She sat up slightly, studying the text in front of her, and then opened one of the files attached before peering more closely at it.

'I've asked an analyst I worked with in Majorstua to take a look at the toll stations,' she explained. 'She's searched for vehicles used in the vicinity of the various crime scenes. It looks as if there's a match: a car that passed a toll booth close to Sonja Nordstrøm's house on Sunday evening also passed the toll station near Kråkerøy the following night.'

She looked up. 'Kråkerøy is just beside Hvaler, where Jeppe Sørensen was found,' she added.

'Whose car is it?' Wibe asked. 'Who was driving?'

'There are no images taken at the toll booth,' Kovic replied, squinting at the screen. 'But it seems the car, an Audi, belongs to a man called Thor Willy Opsahl.'

Once again silence fell.

'Who the hell is that?' Wibe demanded.

'I've no idea,' Kovic said. 'But he lives in Holmenkollen. I suggest we pay him a visit ASAP.'

60

Usually Emma walked or cycled everywhere in Oslo, no matter what time of day or night, but this evening she took a taxi home and asked the driver to wait until she'd let herself in.

Once inside her flat, she made sure she was alone, and only then did she manage to relax and breathe normally again. When she finally sat down on the sofa, with her laptop on her knee, she was furious at herself for allowing fear to take such a grip on her.

What was it she'd actually been so afraid of?

Dahlmann, of course. That he still had some kind of plan for her. But when she tried to examine this rationally, she could find no reason for him to do so. He had used her to sound a warning about Pastor Hansteen. Why should she be of any importance to him after that?

Dahlmann's face looked out at her from every web page. Speculation was rife in the comments sections and on social media. The hash tag *#whowillbenumbertwo* had begun to trend.

A message alert sounded on her phone. She hoped it was Blix, but instead it was Kasper asking if she'd like to accompany him to the cinema.

So far it had been easy to fend off his advances, and her job had demanded all her attention in recent days. And right now there were also some very good reasons why she was reluctant to venture outside.

When they'd met in Gothenburg, they had chatted about work, primarily hers. Kasper couldn't stand celebrities, especially ones who could scarcely sing but became famous and filthy rich regardless, because they had a professional PR machine around them. Worst of all were the ones whose only achievement was an appearance on a reality programme and who subsequently milked their fifteen minutes of fame for all it was worth.

At first she'd thought Kasper was merely trying to provoke her. At any rate, he had wondered why she wrote about these people, and why it was so important for the public to know the most intimate details of a well-known person's life. 'Maybe because people like to dream,' Emma had answered. 'Maybe they yearn for a different life. Maybe they dream of being celebrities themselves.'

'I'd prefer to live in a world free from celebrities,' was Kasper's response. 'People are not worth more just because they're famous or good at playing football.'

These thoughts drew her back to the case and to Jeppe Sørensen. She glanced at the wall where she'd hung up pictures of the dead celebrities. The Danish footballer stood out in the row of victims, quite simply because he was Danish. All the others were Norwegian.

Why had Dahlmann gone to Denmark to find one of his victims? Surely he could have homed in on a well-known Norwegian number seven player. Emma wondered whether to discuss the question with Kasper, but let it be. She put down her phone without answering, and instead looked up Wollan's big story on Dahlmann in the news.no archives. The article was comprehensive, and – Emma reluctantly had to admit – well written. Wollan had really gone into depth, and had explained why Dahlmann – yet again – had requested a retrial. It was obvious Dahlmann was someone who interested Wollan, but Emma could not spot any reference to Denmark in the piece, or to any of the other victims.

She was about to close down her computer when an email notification appeared at the top right-hand corner of the screen. The subject heading was 'Sonja Nordstrøm RIP?', which encouraged Emma to click on the email. The sender was countdown@countdown.com.

Dahlmann, she thought, feeling her pulse start to race. *He must be making contact again.*

There was no text in the email, only a link – and a picture.

She clicked first on the image, fearing the worst – that this time it would be a photo of Nordstrøm, dead.

It took only a couple of seconds for the file to open. Initially Emma was unsure what she was looking at. The image was grainy and poorly lit; it reminded her of a screen grab. Then details began to emerge.

It was someone in a nightgown, sitting with their feet tucked up beneath their body. The feet were slender, dirty. Female. The fingers, also filthy, were folded in front of her legs – as if to keep hold of them. It was impossible to make out the woman's face, because her head was bowed. As if she were praying, or sobbing.

Or dead.

Emma was reluctant to click on the link, but couldn't resist doing so. An Internet window opened up. It took many long seconds for the page to download, centimetre by centimetre. Emma gripped her laptop tightly.

Black screen.

Then ... a digital clock in the top right-hand corner. The seconds were ticking. Emma looked at her own watch. The clock on the screen was showing the actual time.

Then a light came on.

That was when Emma realised she was looking at a live image.

From a real place, a real room.

And as the contours of the place became clearer, she got to her feet, took a step back and clasped a hand to her mouth.

61

Blix glanced up at the green light as they passed the toll station on the ring road near Ullevål stadium.

'Is this one of the ones he clocked in at?' he asked.

'Yes,' Kovic replied at his side and peered down at her papers. 'His car was first recorded at Sandstuveien, not far from Sonja Nordstrøm's address. Time: twenty-two forty-seven. Then he passed through here a quarter of an hour later. The next day, that is Monday night, he passed the toll booth we've just driven through, at one oh five – before he was tracked on the E6 on the other side of the city seventeen minutes later. And then he was at Kråkerøy almost exactly an hour later.'

She thumbed through the pages. 'It takes no more than twenty to twenty-five minutes to drive on out to Hvaler, where Nordstrøm has a summer cottage, in the middle of the night at least. Then he takes the same route back again towards the city around one hour and twenty minutes later.'

'More than enough time to dump Jeppe Sørensen in Nordstrøm's boat and make his way back.'

'Exactly.'

Kovic's phone rang, and she put an earphone in her ear and answered. All she said was 'yes' and 'no' while taking notes. Blix manoeuvred speedily through the traffic.

'OK, thanks very much.' Kovic pressed a button on the dangling hands-free set. 'Thor Willy Opsahl is forty-two,' she told him, looking down at her notes. 'Originally from Asker. No family. Clean sheet, apart from six points on his driving licence.'

'Any connection to Dahlmann?' Blix asked.

'No, but it's possible this is about something else,' Kovic replied hesitantly. 'Thor Willy Opsahl is better known by the name Viking Willy.'

Blix turned off from Sørkedalsveien and accelerated up Holmenkollveien, checking all the while in his mirror that Wibe and Abelvik were directly behind them.

'He won a hundred and eighty-four million kroner in the Viking lottery last year,' Kovic continued. 'He was the only ticket holder with six correct numbers.'

Blix remembered the newspaper reports. Usually lottery millionaires tried to remain anonymous, but Opsahl had not shunned publicity.

'It's over there,' Kovic told him, indicating the direction.

Blix turned into a one-way street flanked by old houses with extensive gardens. Opsahl's villa was situated almost at the very end of the cul-de-sac. Painted white, it had a black tiled roof that glinted in the lights from the neighbouring houses. A garage as large as a normal house had been built beside it, with a silver Audi Q8 parked outside. Blix pointed at the registration number, a personalised number plate with a specially chosen combination of letters and numbers.

'AFTER 8,' he read aloud. 'Does that match the lists from the toll company?'

'It's automatically converted to the ordinary registration number on the list,' Kovic explained, but she then stopped abruptly, as if something important had suddenly occurred to her. 'Eight was the decisive number when he won,' she said in a soft voice. 'Six other people had exactly the same numbers, minus the eight. So that was the number that made him wealthy. I remember it now.'

They stepped out of the car and peered up at the house. An exterior lamp lit up the façade around the entrance.

'He refused to share the jackpot with anyone,' Kovic said. 'One or two newspapers dubbed him the greedy bastard of the year.'

Blix's phone rang. He saw it was Emma calling, but he had no time to speak to her now.

'Number eight,' he said as he approached the Audi.

Wibe and Abelvik had now parked and were already beside him. Wibe switched on a flashlight and directed the beam in through the side window.

A copy of *Forever Number One* lay on the driving seat.

'Get hold of Ann-Mari Sara,' Blix said, glancing up at the house again. 'This is a crime scene.'

Wibe skirted around the car, shining the flashlight inside. 'It's empty,' he said. 'But there's something on the seat beside the book.'

'Is it locked?' Kovic asked.

Blix produced a pair of disposable gloves before touching the driver's door. It opened easily.

'It's a garage door opener,' he said, picking up the tiny remote control from the seat.

He looked at the others before pointing it at the garage door and pressing the button. Slowly the garage door began to slide open. The light inside came on automatically.

Thor Willy Opsahl was hanging from one of the beams on the ceiling in the middle of the garage. His feet only just touched the floor. There was nothing nearby he could have climbed on to manage this by himself. Suicide was out of the question.

The four detectives hovered outside the open door.

'How long do you think he's been hanging there?' Blix asked, staring at the blue-black face.

'More than a week,' Wibe reckoned. 'The body's about to detach from the head.'

Blix nodded. More than a week placed the homicide chronologically prior to the murder of the Danish footballer.

'His car was last used early on Tuesday morning,' Kovic pointed out. 'At any rate, it's not recorded at any toll station after that.'

'Dahlmann must have been driving around in it,' Wibe said. 'While Viking Willy's been hanging in the garage.'

'So he's been strung up here for more than a week, and no one's missed him?' Abelvik asked.

'He had no job or family,' Kovic explained. 'No one who *would* miss him.'

'It's so fucking devious,' Wibe said. 'Calculated and cunning.'

Blix nodded, but this description did not fit the Dahlmann he knew, which only reinforced his suspicion that Dahlmann, too, was a pawn in this game.

His phone rang again. It was Emma, for the second time.

'I have to take this,' he said brusquely and drew back slightly.

The others stood talking among themselves. When Blix was sure no one could overhear him, he answered the call.

'She's alive!' Emma shouted.

'Alive?'

'Sonja Nordstrøm,' Emma clarified. Her voice was shaking at the other end. 'I've received an email with a link to a web camera that shows live footage. I'm sitting here watching her right now!'

'What the hell are you telling me?' He couldn't help raising his voice, and he saw Kovic look over.

'She's alive, Blix. Sonja Nordstrøm.'

Blix shifted the phone to his other ear. 'Describe what you can see.'

'She's sitting on the floor,' Emma told him. 'A concrete floor, I think – it's not easy to make it out. She's in a small room. It looks like a dungeon or a cell or ... I don't really know. In any case, she's alive.'

'What's she doing?' Blix asked.

'Nothing,' Emma replied. 'She's just sitting there. There's a plate of food on the floor. Slices of bread. She's only eaten half of one.'

Blix used his free hand to rub his face. He watched Kovic approach with a quizzical look on her face.

'That email you received – does it say it's from Dahlmann?'

'No, it's not signed ... but ... wait a minute.'

'Wait for what?'

'Just ... wait a minute. I've got another email from the same sender.'

'What? What does it say?'

Emma did not answer immediately.

'Who...?'

'My computer screen's frozen,' she said. 'It's running a bit slow.'

Blix waited. And waited.

'Oh bloody hell,' Emma said. 'This is just not happening.'

'What is it?'

He heard Emma take a deep breath. Then she said: 'He says that I have to publish the link on news.no. And that I must do it before twelve noon tomorrow, Saturday. If not...'

'If not what?'

'If not, Sonja Nordstrøm will die.'

62

Sonja Nordstrøm was still seated on the floor. She made a slight movement with her head, and ran a hand slowly over her knee.

Emma checked the time and stood up. Eight minutes had gone by since she'd phoned Blix. Her heart felt like a drum beneath her sweater. She could only imagine what it must be like for Nordstrøm.

Blix arrived just after eleven. He was accompanied by the same investigator who'd been here the previous evening – Kovic. Emma had first met her outside Nordstrøm's house in Ekeberg.

'Let's see it,' Blix said, marching in without taking off his shoes. Emma showed them into the kitchen where her computer was still on the worktop. The live images were in full screen mode.

'Shit,' Sofia Kovic said, craning forwards towards the worktop. 'She really *is* alive.'

Blix merely stared wordlessly at the screen.

'Show me the emails,' he said. Emma squeezed between the two investigators and selected the email program.

'He didn't sign the second email either,' Emma told them, making space so that Blix could operate the machine. 'But there's no doubt it's from Dahlmann, surely?'

Kovic glanced at Blix, who gave no answer.

'What shall we do?' Emma asked.

'I've called for the top IT folk,' Blix said. 'We'll have to take the computer with us to the police station and examine it there. See if we can manage to trace where this was sent from.'

'I didn't mean with the computer,' Emma interjected. 'With Nordstrøm. We'll have to do as he says, won't we? We can't risk anything happening to her, now we have proof she's alive?'

When Blix did not give an immediate response, she went on: 'Well – if it gets out that we didn't bother following his instructions, and then that leads to her murder...'

'What if he kills her anyway?' Blix interrupted her. 'On live video. With everyone watching. We can't let him do that either.'

Emma had no good answer to that.

'What *I* can't fathom is why he doesn't just broadcast the link himself,' Kovic said. 'Use a comments section on a blog or something like that. You can remain anonymous there too.'

'He's making us share responsibility,' Blix said. 'And landing us in a hell of a predicament at the same time. If we publish, we're giving in to a terrorist, and we have no guarantee whatsoever that he won't kill her anyway or come up with further demands. And if we don't do as he says, Nordstrøm dies.'

'Terrorist?' Kovic repeated.

'Yes, that's exactly what he is, don't you think? He's stirring up fear. Throughout the city. Across the entire country.'

'And it's policy never to accede to terrorists,' Emma said.

Blix crossed to Emma's kitchen sink and turned on the tap. He rinsed his hands and rubbed them quickly over his face while they were still wet. He shut off the tap with a little too much force.

'This is his finale,' he said. 'It all kicked off with Nordstrøm, and it's going to end with Nordstrøm. The circle will be closed. That's the master plan.' He pivoted towards them. 'And he wants everyone to watch.'

'Then ... he must have taken number two already?' Kovic speculated. 'Since he's ready to kill Nordstrøm as soon as twelve noon tomorrow?'

'Maybe,' Blix said. 'Or else it's imminent. Or maybe it doesn't matter to the killer anymore what order the bodies are found in, now that the countdown plan has been revealed.'

Emma saw from his demeanour that something else had happened.

'Have you looked into Mona Kleven's death, then?' she asked. 'Number nine?'

Blix looked at Kovic.

'The woman with nine lives,' he clarified. 'There's no CCTV at the subway station where she died, but a great deal to suggest she did not jump or fall.'

Emma absorbed this information.

'We found number eight instead,' Blix went on. 'Just before you called.'

Kovic looked as if something was on the tip of her tongue, but she kept it to herself.

'Who was it?' Emma asked.

In two short sentences, Blix explained before heading for the door.

'But now it's a matter of finding out how we can save Sonja Nordstrøm's life,' he said.

63

Blix stood by the window, looking down at the entrance. A man carrying a bag in each hand was on his way out.

'He uses Tor.'

Blix turned around. Øyvind Krohn sat hunched over Emma's laptop, which was linked to one of Krohn's own computers. Blix was unable to follow the numbers, columns and letters flickering on the screen.

'Who or what is Tor?' asked Emma.

Krohn flashed a smile. 'It's a browser people use when they want to remain anonymous on the Internet,' he said. 'You just download the Tor program and install it on your computer; it has a pre-uploaded browser.

Then you use Tor instead of Chrome or Firefox or whatever you normally use. So when you open a new window, your IP address is concealed.'

Krohn turned his head ever so slightly to make sure everyone in the room was following this. 'In fact, Tor was originally developed by the American navy,' he added. 'Edward Snowden published everything he'd collected via Tor.'

'But how does it *really* work?' said Emma.

Krohn turned to face the computers and continued his work. 'The Tor network hides your identity by moving your Internet traffic over a number of Tor servers, which are actually computers belonging to other people. In addition Tor encrypts and re-encrypts the Tor traffic, something an ordinary Internet connection cannot do.'

'Layer upon layer of packaging,' Emma said.

'Correct. In the end these thoroughly encrypted packages of data are sent out at random via the various servers. For us, that's only *one* problem.'

'What's the other?' Blix demanded.

'That it's a Me2b video. It's almost the same as YouTube. The same set-up anyway.'

Kovic was standing beside Blix. 'What does that mean?' she asked impatiently.

'It means that it's going to take time to find out which computer the feed is run from. Another thing is the encrypted labyrinth we have to negotiate our way through. Me2b is just as obsessed with privacy protection as YouTube and Facebook and all the other big companies. We can't hack in to find out by ourselves. We have to talk to someone at Me2b and get *them* to find the stream's original IP for us.'

Krohn looked at the time.

'It's the middle of the night in Norway and evening in the USA, so it certainly won't be easy. People have left work. Plus they're miserly about personal security.'

'Even though we're talking about saving a life?' Kovic asked.

'Personal privacy is personal privacy,' Krohn told her. 'We have the same discussions here in Norway. Where do we set the limit on the information we can extract about people's computer use without their knowledge?'

'When they do something criminal,' Kovic insisted.

'You won't get any opposition from me on that point,' Krohn said. 'But it's obvious that others won't be so—'

'Let's concentrate on this right now,' Blix broke in. 'We don't have many hours left. Are you saying there's nothing you can do to find out where this feed comes from?'

Krohn stopped tapping the keys. He whirled his seat around and looked up at Blix, Kovic and Emma.

'We have a few things we can have a crack at, of course. But it won't be done in a flash, and we probably can't do very much without help from the USA. But I have a channel into Me2b I can try. I just hope I can get hold of her.'

Blix looked at his watch. Less than eleven hours to go until the dead-line expired.

'But can't just anyone access this feed, since it's been put out on Me2b?' he asked.

'It's a so-called unlisted link, and the person who uploaded it has invited only one user. An email address.' He turned towards Emma. 'Yours.'

Blix ruminated for a few seconds.

'So the link can only be followed up if you're logged on as Emma?'

'Yes,' Krohn answered. 'But we can send on the link if we choose to post it.'

Blix nodded and said: 'OK. We'll stay here all night. Give us a shout if you find out anything.'

64

Before they had arrived at the police station, Blix had called both Gard Fosse and Pia Nøkleby to explain the situation. They had both come in straight away.

Fosse's eyes opened wide when he saw that Emma was also present. Blix had left her at his desk for the moment.

Blix dashed towards his boss to prevent a public argument.

'What the fuck are you up to?' Fosse whispered.

'Dahlmann,' Blix began, also sotto voce, 'or whoever it is who's running the show here, has used Emma twice to pass on vital information. Either he has a bigger plan for her, something that makes it natural for us to want to look after her, or else there's a possibility he'll contact her again. In either case she's essential to the progress of the investigation.'

Fosse ran his hand over his head, with a sigh.

'This has nothing to do with Teisen,' Blix said. 'You know that yourself.'

The superintendent put his hands by his side. Deep in thought for a few seconds.

'OK. But she can't sit here listening to everything we say. You'll have to find somewhere else for her.'

Blix accepted this. And when he installed her on the sofa in a spare office she made no protest.

'Try to get some sleep,' he suggested.

Emma shook her head and produced a tablet from her bag. 'I need to hand in an article,' she said.

'You can't write about this,' Blix objected.

Emma gave him an indulgent look. 'I do know that,' she replied. 'But I have to put out something about Viking Willy and that you're looking into Mona Kleven's death. Number eight and number nine.'

Blix surveyed the room. 'That's fine,' he said. 'But there's no need to inform your readers you're working from inside the police station.'

He closed the door behind him and returned to the others. Fosse had taken a seat at the head of the conference table.

'The chief of police has called in the top brass for a crisis meeting,' he announced. 'I'm seeing him and the public prosecutor in fifteen minutes. They want our advice. What do you all think? What action should we take?'

'Go live with the link,' Abelvik suggested. 'Enough people have died in the last few days. We don't need another death on our consciences.'

'It won't be on our consciences, though,' Wibe said. 'We're not the ones who'll be killing her. It's not our fault, either, that we have a crazy murderer on the loose here in the city.'

'A lot of people would disagree with that,' Abelvik protested. 'It's our job to stop people like him, and we haven't managed to do that. Now we have the chance to prevent another life being lost, and we should seize the opportunity.'

Fosse looked at Blix. 'What are the chances of finding her before noon tomorrow?'

'I don't know any more than you do,' Blix replied. 'It's a bit like looking for a needle in a haystack, if I've understood Krohn correctly. Of course, we may have a real stroke of luck, but we should make plans in case Krohn and his team don't come up trumps.'

Blix sat in his own chair, while Fosse stood in the centre of the floor. The others had sat down at their desks around the room.

'Maybe he's bluffing,' Kovic suggested.

'There's nothing so far to indicate he won't go through with what he's threatening to do,' Blix said.

Fosse coughed into his palm. 'The chief of police will never comply with a madman's demands,' he concluded. 'I agree with Wibe, and what I'm about to say may sound cynical, but to my mind Sonja Nordstrøm was already dead on the second day with no sign of life. I've no intention of letting a murderer have his bloody finale with the whole world watching. We're not broadcasting that link.'

'We run the risk of him broadcasting it himself regardless,' Abelvik pointed out.

'Yes we do,' Fosse said. 'But *we* have no influence over that, unless we can locate him.'

Fosse looked at his watch.

'We've ten hours at our disposal,' he said. 'And the clock is ticking. There must be something *we* can do, wouldn't you say?'

65

Blix was too restless to sit inside the police station looking over Krohn's shoulder. Kovic felt the same.

They took a patrol car and drove up to Nydalen to pay a visit to a pizza restaurant there.

The phone call to the Trinity Church had been made at 11.47 on Monday morning – almost a week ago now. It had been traced to the restaurant in Gullhaug Torg. The waiter who'd let the perpetrator use the restaurant phone had been tracked down, but could only recollect that the man had tossed a few coins into the tips jar on the counter before asking if he could make a quick call. He couldn't give any description. The technicians had also been to the restaurant but their search had proved fruitless.

It was easier to find parking round here in the middle of the night rather than when he'd come to see Iselin in the TV studio, which was just around the corner. An enormous production bus was now parked outside the anonymous building where his daughter was housed. The Justice Department was situated only a stone's throw further back, and there were various commercial premises in the area.

'What are you hoping to find?' Kovic asked.

Blix gave a shrug. 'I just wanted to look around,' he said. 'Try to envisage him as he walks into the restaurant. See where he might have come from, and where he went afterwards.'

They sauntered up to the restaurant. Blix cupped his hands against the glass of the door and peered inside. He could see the phone on the wall at the end of the counter; it would be out of earshot for a busy waiter.

Two customers who'd also been in the restaurant when the call was made had been traced through their bankcard details. Neither of them could recall a customer using the phone.

'It was a calculated risk,' Kovic said. 'He knew we would trace the phone call and made sure he didn't do anything to make himself memorable.'

Blix turned around and surveyed the area. Apart from a taxi pulling out, the area was deserted, but 11.47 a.m. was lunchtime for most people. There could have been hundreds of witnesses seeing the man entering and leaving the pizza restaurant. There were also several schools in Nydalen, and a new block of flats was nearby, not to mention the busy subway station.

'Also, he must have known there was no CCTV coverage here,' Kovic added.

Blix stood staring at the subway station entrance. 'What's the next stop?' he asked.

Kovic gave this some thought. 'Ullevål and Blindern,' she said, using a head movement to indicate west. 'Storo and Sinsen to the east.'

'The woman with nine lives,' Blix said, 'Mona Kleven. She was knocked down by the train at Sinsen, two stops from here.'

'And after the shooting at Stortinget station, the perpetrator also disappeared into the subway,' Kovic nodded. 'He probably did the same after killing the pastor. It's a kind of common denominator.'

Blix turned to face the TV headquarters again, where his daughter was being filmed 24/7.

'If he uses the subway,' Blix said, 'maybe we can track him using CCTV footage. See where he gets on, and where he gets off. Link it up with his use of Viking Willy's Audi. We can circle in and come a bit closer to where he hides out. Where he's keeping Nordstrøm.'

'Time-consuming,' Kovic commented, looking at her watch. 'And we can't make a start on it until the right people are at work.'

'But it's worth a try,' Blix said. 'Even if it doesn't yield results before noon, it could still be useful.'

66

A feeling of not being alone jerked Emma from her doze. Startled, she sat bolt upright on the sofa.

Kovic stood in front of her. Emma brought her hands to her head to check her wig was still in place.

'I didn't mean to scare you,' the detective said. 'Here. I brought you some food.'

Emma cleared her throat and nodded, needing a few seconds to compose herself. Kovic held a steaming cup in her hands as well as a plate with two slices of bread.

'We don't have much in the way of provisions here on a Saturday morning, but I took a chance that you like liver paté.'

She smiled gently as she placed the food and coffee down on a small table in front of the sofa.

'Thanks,' Emma said. 'That's very kind of you.'

She felt as if she'd been out on a drinking spree. Her body ached all over and her eyes were swollen.

'What time is it?' she asked, stretching out.

'Soon be eight,' Kovic said.

Emma had no idea when she had fallen asleep, but it couldn't have been long ago.

'How did it go last night?' she asked, taking hold of the coffee cup.

'I can't say much,' Kovic answered. 'But there's no news to tell.'

Nodding, Emma took a swig of coffee, surprised at how good it actually tasted.

'I don't suppose you would've been here if you'd found her in the course of the night,' she said, studying the slices of bread. 'Or Dahlmann, for that matter.'

Kovic smiled again, her eyes betraying her exhaustion.

Emma took a bite of one of the slices of bread; Kovic had placed a sliver of cucumber on top.

The investigator looked lost in thought for a few moments before she ventured: 'Blix told me about ... the two of you. What happened at Teisen.'

Emma stopped chewing for a second or two, but then resumed.

'*My* father died when I was eleven,' Kovic went on. 'An accident at work. He fell from a ladder and hit his head on a rock.'

She shook her head slightly. Emma had no idea what to say.

'He ... I adored him,' Kovic continued. 'Every evening he used to take me down to the harbour at Trogir to swim. It was always the highlight of the day. Just him and me. And the water. The fish.'

She gave a dreamy smile. 'Sometimes he brought something nice for us to enjoy afterwards too. Some fruit or ... something.'

'He sounds like a great dad,' Emma said, swallowing.

'He certainly was.'

Emma wondered where Kovic was heading with this conversation.

'Statistics show that many people who have a hard time in life, whether they're criminals or junkies or whatever, do so because they're missing one or both parents. But you've done well. I've done well. Sometimes I wonder why things went so well for people like us, while others never climb out of the gutter.'

She seemed to ponder her own question for a moment. 'Maybe it's just down to luck,' she said. 'Or maybe it's as simple as some people being born strong while others don't have it in them.'

Emma thought about this for a few moments.

'For me, everything changed when my grandfather died,' she said. 'He had hidden the fact that my grandmother had begun to suffer from dementia, but it became really clear afterwards, of course, when there was only my grandmother left to look after my sister and me. I realised that everything was no longer just about me.'

She paused for a second.

'I could easily have ended up in the gutter if it hadn't been for my grandfather having a heart attack.'

Kovic waited a little before saying: 'Isn't it strange that a death can both break you down but also build you up?'

Emma had never thought of it in this way before, but didn't take long to answer. 'Yes, that's true.'

The next minute, Blix came into the office. His movements suggested great haste. First he said hello to Emma, and then he addressed Kovic. 'I need you. Right now.'

Kovic got to her feet.

'Has something happened?' Emma asked.

Blix didn't reply.

Seconds later both investigators had dashed out of the office.

67

'Good news from Krohn,' Blix said to Kovic over his shoulder. 'He got hold of his contact in Me2b, who has managed to get us an address. The live link is being sent from a farm outside Nannestad.'

'Where's that?'

'Not far from Jessheim.'

Kovic had to jog to keep up with him. 'Is he sure?' she asked.

'As sure as he can be,' Blix said. 'Plus we've got good circumstantial evidence. I'll explain in the car.'

'Shouldn't the emergency squad or whoever deal with this?' Kovic asked.

'We're keeping a low profile,' Blix told her. 'Anyway, we don't have time to waste asking them.'

Seconds later they were on their way.

The tiredness that had washed over Blix at daybreak had been blown away. All night long he had been checking tip-offs and poring over case papers, searching for any tiny detail they might have overlooked or not given enough attention. He had been on the point of losing hope.

Now it was back again.

'What circumstantial evidence are we talking about?' Kovic asked on the way down to the garage.

'The farm is owned by a man in his eighties,' Blix began. 'But it's his grandson who lives there now. He went to school with Walter Georg Dahlmann.'

'Shit,' Kovic said. 'There just has to be a connection.'

Blix nodded as he settled in behind the steering wheel. Kovic fastened her seatbelt as the car shot out of the garage.

It was nearly 9.00 a.m. now, but there were few cars on the road. Grey weather, but no rain.

'We can't do this on our own,' Kovic said.

'A patrol from Romerike will meet us,' Blix explained, handing her a note with the address of Jekkestad farm. 'Wibe and Abelvik are following in an unmarked car.'

Kovic keyed the address into the GPS, which calculated it would take thirty-seven minutes to reach the farm. Blix planned to cut that time down drastically.

'What's his name?' Kovic asked. 'The schoolmate.'

'Bjørn Helge Bergan.'

'Criminal record?'

'Yes, but nothing major. Drugs, mostly.'

'Do you think he's there?'

'His mobile phone is, anyway,' Blix told her, gripping the wheel more tightly. 'A farm is actually the perfect spot. No neighbours in the immediate vicinity. Loads of space.'

In his mind's eye, he pictured Sonja Nordstrøm's wan face. The slow movements of her eyelids. How she had stared blankly into the distance.

The farm was not far from Oslo Gardermoen airport. Soon they turned off the E6 in that direction. Blix put his foot down and overtook all the cars he could. Even though he wasn't using the blue light, most drivers dutifully pulled over on to the hard shoulder.

He rang Abelvik. 'Where are you?' he asked.

'Seven or eight minutes away.'

'OK. We'll be there in five.'

A plane belonging to Norwegian airways was about to take off as Blix and Kovic passed the western runway. Only a few hundred metres further on, he turned off left at a roundabout and accelerated out on to the 120 road. They followed Nannestadveien and stopped at an intersection where a sign indicated Jekkestad. An unmarked car sat there waiting for them with the engine running. Blix nodded to the driver, who was in uniform.

They were surrounded by fields on all sides. One of them was newly mown, while another was green – as if it were springtime. A row of silage bales packed in white plastic was lined up outside one of the farms.

Blix and Kovic stepped out to meet the local officers, and swiftly brought them up to speed on the situation. When Wibe and Abelvik arrived a couple of minutes later, Blix quickly explained what he planned to do.

The tarmac road leading to Jekkestad farm twisted and turned through the landscape. The plan was simple: the other units were to park a short distance away, but move on foot around to the rear of the farmhouse so they had eyes on the whole site. Blix and Kovic would then drive straight into the farmyard and park outside the farmhouse. Permission had been granted for use of weapons.

Before they left the car, Blix took time to fill his lungs with air.

'Nervous?' he asked, glancing across at Kovic.

'Extremely,' she replied.

'Good,' Blix said, putting his hand on the door handle. 'I wouldn't want to work with anyone who isn't nervous in these circumstances.'

Over the police radio they learned that Wibe, Abelvik and the two local officers were in position. Blix and Kovic clambered out and walked across to the big white farmhouse; a red-painted barn stood a short distance away. They saw a tractor parked outside it. A black cat crept through the grass, on the other side of the house. In the sky, birds flew in formation towards some distant destination.

'Stay a bit behind me,' Blix said as he rang the doorbell. They heard a *ding-dong* sound inside.

'There's a white delivery van at the back here,' Wibe reported over the police radio. 'I'll call in the registration number.'

'Copy,' Blix murmured.

He heard no footsteps inside.

'I have a bad feeling about this,' Kovic said. 'Just like before we found Viking Willy.'

Blix also hoped they wouldn't find yet another victim. He rang the doorbell again, holding his finger on the button for a long time before pressing it several times in rapid succession. Then he looked at his watch.

Two minutes to ten.

Still no sounds from inside. Blix made up his mind to give Bergan a call.

Taking out his mobile, he dialled the number. Seconds later he heard a faint, vibrating sound from somewhere inside the house. Blix let it continue to ring and pushed at the door.

It was open.

Blix announced over the police radio: 'We're going in.'

68

Once inside, Blix stopped and listened.

Teisen came flooding back: the silence. The lack of knowledge. The fear of what was ahead. The feeling of time working against him.

'Aren't you going to draw your gun?' Kovic whispered just behind him.

After some hesitation, Blix quietly took out his pistol. Noticed how his muscles immediately tensed. He took a gulp of air. Raised his shoulders and quickly let them drop. He had to get his head straight. Think like a professional – search, evaluate, report, act.

Shoes were scattered all over the hallway floor. Muddy Wellington boots, filthy trainers. The stink of alcohol and stale smoke wafted towards them.

'Bergan?' Blix called out. 'This is the police!'

No answer.

They moved steadily forwards. In the kitchen they found empty beer cans and booze bottles haphazardly strewn across a table; the occasional 1.5-litre soft-drink bottle – some empty, others with a few dregs left. Several pizza boxes were stacked on top of the cooker, the one on top open, with a few crusts and leftovers inside. Snuff pouches. Cigarette ash. A crumpled fag packet.

'Bergan?' Blix shouted again.

Now they heard movements from upstairs. Heavy footfall across the floor.

'Who is it?' they heard a sleepy voice yell.

'It's the police,' Blix repeated.

'The police?'

Blix and Kovic exchanged looks.

'There's no dope here now,' the voice above them groaned. 'I promise.'

'We're armed,' Blix warned. 'Come down and keep your hands where we can see them.'

A number of seconds passed before they heard footsteps on the stairs. A man in his underpants descended with his hands above his head. His belly rolled down towards his crotch, and his hair was tousled and unkempt.

'Bjørn Helge Bergan?' Blix inquired with his gun pointed directly at him.

'Yes. But why ... what...?'

Blix returned his gun to its holster. Kovic followed suit.

'Can you show us your computer equipment?'

'Eh?'

'You've got a computer, I assume? A Mac or something?'

'Yes, yes, of course, but...'

'Just show us it,' Kovic said with her right hand resting on her pistol holster.

'The office is over there,' he said with a nod. 'But what on earth do you want with my computer?'

Blix relayed on the police radio that the situation was under control and for Wibe and Abelvik to come to the farmhouse.

Bergan pointed at a T-shirt hanging over a chair. Kovic nodded. He pulled it on and ushered them into what he had described as an office but looked more like a storeroom. Boxes, bags, a vacuum cleaner, empty beer crates, a few rolled up maps. There was a bookcase with some magazines and a handful of paperbacks. A screen the size of a TV sat on a table beside the window. It was connected to a hard disk tower that sat on the floor beneath the table, along with a printer. Loud-speakers were placed either side of the screen.

'I don't understand why you're so interested in my computer,' Bergan said. 'I only use it for gaming. And shopping on the net and whatever.'

Blix touched the computer mouse. A password dialogue box appeared.

'Can you open it for us?'

'Don't think I really want to.'

Blix shot him an aggressive look. 'Why not?'

They heard a noise at the front door, followed by shoes on the floor and Wibe's voice identifying himself.

'We're in here!' Kovic called out.

'Do you have something to hide?' Blix asked, taking a step closer to Bergan.

'No,' Bergan said. 'But there's nothing on it.'

'We need to see for ourselves.'

Bergan continued to hesitate, but then approached the keyboard and tapped in a lengthy code. The screen burst into life.

Lowering his chin, Bergan cast his eyes down to the floor. 'I'm the only one who lives here,' he said. 'Nobody else uses this computer.'

The screen image that met their gaze was of two naked women. One had her hand over the other's genitals. Blix looked at Bergan long and hard.

'We know you use the dark net a lot,' Blix said. 'Tor.'

'That's not illegal,' Bergan replied.

'No, but right now we're trying to find the place where a web camera showing live images of a kidnapped woman is set up. It looks as if the pictures are being sent from a computer on your property.'

Bergan's mouth dropped open. 'Here?'

'Yes, here.'

Wibe and Abelvik entered the room. Blix turned his head towards them.

'Go through all the rooms,' he said. 'Especially the basement. Search for hidden rooms. If you find nothing in here, then check the barn.'

Wibe and Abelvik were already on the move.

'Well,' Bergan said, his hairline now showing a gleam of perspiration. 'This is absolutely insane. I don't do that sort of thing.'

Blix didn't reply.

Kovic sat down and opened Bergan's system files and checked the folders. Judging by the titles, Bergan had a great deal of pornography. Kovic's fingers raced over the keyboard. She also tapped in the start of the live link address, but the remainder did not appear as an automatic suggestion, so there was no indication that Bergan had opened that address earlier.

'Do you have any other computers?' she asked.

'No, only this one.'

'No tablet of any kind?'

'I have an iPad, but I hardly ever use it.'

Blix studied Bergan, who ran a hand through his dishevelled hair. The feeling grew inside him that they were on yet another wild goose chase. A lengthy one this time.

'What kind of relationship do you have with Walter Georg Dahlmann?'

Bergan stared at them for a few seconds, then his eyes widened and it was obvious to Blix and Kovic that he was at last making the connection between their investigation and the headline news of the last twenty-four hours.

'I haven't seen him since we were at school together. Twenty-five years ago, at least. He's not here, if that's what you think. And what sort of woman is it that—?'

Blix brushed him off with a hand gesture. At the same moment Wibe and Abelvik returned to the room.

'There's nothing here,' they said. 'We're going over to the barn.'

'Be quick about it.'

Kovic tried a few more computer searches, but soon turned to Blix, shaking her head. 'Well, it's possible that something's here, but if there is, he's hidden it well. It demands more skills than I have.'

'Call Krohn,' Blix told her. 'Find out if he can help.'

Bergan protested, but trailed after Blix as he left the house and headed for the barn, Bergan still wearing only a T-shirt and underpants. He did stop to pull on a pair of Wellingtons.

Wibe met Blix at the gaping barn door. Little birds flapped their wings under the rafters in the roof.

'There are definitely no cellars in here,' Wibe said. 'Or a room of any kind. She's not here.'

Blix swore and scanned the perimeter, deep in thought.

He turned round and rushed back to Kovic, finding her sitting with her phone to her ear.

'Is that Krohn?' he asked.

'Yes,' Kovic answered. 'We can't find—'

Blix took the phone from her.

'Do you have the feed open?' he asked.

'Yes. Nordstrøm is awake.'

Blix stretched forwards and yanked the power lead out of the back of Bergan's computer. The screen turned black.

'Do you still see her?' he asked.

'Yes, the screen went black for a fraction of a second, but I still have a picture. What...?'

'Wait,' Blix said as he headed out into the hallway where he'd seen a fuse box. He opened it and flicked off the main fuse. All the lights in the house were extinguished.

'How about now?' Blix asked.

'No change,' Krohn reported. 'What are you up to?'

Blix explained. Krohn sighed.

'She's not there,' he said. 'This is some kind of intelligent mislead.'

'What does that mean?'

'That someone has hacked into the computer where you are now and left behind the details that led us there. We've been duped.'

Blix cursed under his breath and looked again at the time. It was 10.31 a.m.

Bergan came out into the hallway.

'Have you had any strangers out here in the past few weeks?' Blix demanded.

'Strangers? No, I—'

'No computer engineers, repair men, electricians...?'

'No.' He shook his head.

'You haven't had any kind of break-in here either?' Kovic interjected.

'No...' Bergan hesitated a little. It looked as if a vague memory began to stir. 'But I did wonder slightly whether there'd been someone here not so long ago.'

Blix gave Kovic a fleeting look.

'Why was that?'

'It just felt like that one night when I got home from work. That a few things had been moved about.'

'You don't have an alarm system here?'

'No, I've never had any need for one. I don't even lock my door usually; after all, there's never anyone out here. And I don't have much to steal, so it doesn't matter too much.'

'OK,' Blix said, striding back into the office. 'We're taking your computer.'

Bergan protested as Blix began to pull out the cables. Someone had manipulated this computer, and it needed to be checked more carefully; but no matter what Krohn and his team managed to find on it, time was running out. Sonja Nordstrøm could still be anywhere.

69

Emma had been moved from one office to another, and then to a third – as staff had turned up for work and needed their desks. She had no idea whose office she was using right now, but judging by the photos on the desk, it was someone with a wife and three children.

She had left the office door open a crack. Investigators passed by with hurried steps. From time to time she could hear someone shout or run. The entire police station seemed in a state of hectic activity. Dedicated, focused officers all working towards the same goal – finding Sonja Nordstrøm.

Emma contemplated what she was usually occupied with at work. Kasper was right: celebrities were unimportant in the grand scheme of things, even though having dreams might mean a lot to some people. Once this story was done and dusted, she would have a chat with Anita. See if there was any possibility of working on something else at news.no.

There was less than an hour left until noon. Emma checked her emails. Still no messages or fresh demands. Now and again she visited the live link to see what Nordstrøm was doing, but there wasn't much to see. She had done some sit-ups and push-ups around nine o'clock. Just before that she'd received a fresh supply of food and water. She'd yelled and screamed at the person who'd brought it, although he was out of view of the camera, so Emma had no idea whether he'd responded in any way. There was no sound on the feed.

A wild impulse made her call Kasper.

'Well, I never, wonders will never cease!' he said, with a smile in his voice.

'Do you never just say hello to people?' Emma asked.

'Eh?'

'You said that the last time I phoned you as well. About wonders never ceasing.'

'Oh,' he said. 'I see I'm not original enough for your taste.'

Emma laughed this off. 'How are things?' she asked, without specifying whether she meant with him personally or with his work.

'Fine, thanks,' Kasper replied. 'I'm just a little confused.'

'Confused, how?'

'Well, I felt that you and I maybe ... had something. But when I tried to explore that a bit further, you ... backed off. Completely. It was just pretty unexpected. And confusing.'

Emma knew what she ought to say, but couldn't bring herself to do it.

'Gothenburg's not home,' was all she said. 'It's easier to let go a little there.'

'So what you're saying is that the girl I met in Sweden doesn't make an appearance in Norway?'

Emma did not answer.

'Then I hope you'll pay a visit to Denmark soon.'

Emma laughed. It was good to laugh again – it had been a long time.

'I'm a bit stuck on this Jeppe Sørensen story,' she said. 'I can't understand why Dahlmann would pick one of his victims in Denmark and bring him back to Norway.'

Kasper hesitated for a few seconds before agreeing that the Danish footballer was certainly the odd one out in the series of victims.

'Have the Danish police or you Danish journalists looked into his Norwegian connections at all?'

'The police are probably working on that, on both the Norwegian and Danish sides,' Kasper told her. 'We had two hits on Dahlmann in our text archives, but they were from the old case when he killed his ex-girlfriend and her new guy. He's a maniac who's been banged up in jail for the past few years. I can't imagine that he and Jeppe knew each other.'

'It could be through another Norwegian,' Emma said. 'A mutual acquaintance.'

Kasper paused for a moment again before agreeing.

'Maybe his girlfriend would know,' Emma suggested.

'Yes, of course.'

She could hear that she'd given Kasper the spark of an idea.

'Let me check that out,' he said. 'But only if you promise to answer my messages, or even just do something as simple as have a cup of coffee with me before I go home to Denmark. That would be nice.'

Emma considered this for a moment or two.

'Yes, it would,' she replied, uncertain whether he would hear the reservation in her voice.

'I'll ring you soon,' he said.

Emma thanked him for his help and hung up. She sat staring into space for a few minutes, overwhelmed by a feeling of restlessness. She hated waiting, hated not knowing. Kasper might well discover something, but she couldn't just sit still without taking any action.

She opened some of the Danish web pages she was familiar with. Skimmed quickly through some of the countless articles about the Danish footballer's death, in pursuit of any tiny detail the Norwegian media outlets hadn't reported. But she found nothing of interest.

She decided to check Kasper's coverage of Jeppe Sørensen, so she typed both their names into a search engine. It returned a massive number of hits, and she could not be bothered going through them all, since the articles generated by the Ritzau agency always ended up in lots of different newspapers. Emma contented herself with noting that Kasper had done a thorough job.

She was about to wrap up her Internet search when a link from the *Dagbladet Holstebro-Struer* newspaper attracted her attention. One of the articles seemed to be about the area Jeppe Sørensen grew up in. It focused on the fact that several members of the football team he'd played in when growing up had gone on to do remarkably well for themselves. What caught her eye, though, was Kasper Bjerringbo's name; but he wasn't mentioned as the author of the report.

In the photo accompanying the article, five of Sørensen's teammates were circled in red. One of them was a member of parliament. Another was a high flyer in the financial world and had apartments in both Manhattan and Tokyo. But her eye lingered on the boy kneeling beside Jeppe Sørensen, an arm around him. Even though the picture was years old, it was easy to recognise Kasper Bjerringbo's face.

It gave a description of his journalistic career, and said that within the Ritzau system he was known as 'the journalist who didn't just cover the news but created it himself.'

A cold shudder shook Emma's body.

She sat up straight. There was nothing wrong with being an old friend of a murder victim. Certainly not.

But why hadn't Kasper mentioned it?

70

By 11.14 a.m., Blix and Kovic were back at their desks on the sixth floor of the police station.

'What was it Dahlmann did in Afghanistan again?' Kovic asked.

'Don't recall the details,' Blix replied as he collapsed into his office chair. 'But he wasn't an ICT expert, at any rate.'

All around them was frantic hustle and bustle. Everyone was either on the phone or engrossed in case material. Many were out and about, checking tip-offs. One of the screens was connected to the live images of Sonja Nordstrøm. She sat with her back to the wall with her knees pulled up.

Blix ran his hand over his head, searching though his memories, thoughts that had churned over and over in the past few hours and days, but there were no new threads for him to catch hold of.

'It's not too late,' Kovic told him. 'We can still post the link.'

'Fosse will never go along with that,' Blix said. 'Nor the chief of police.'

'Couldn't we set up a false web page or something?' she suggested. 'One that *looks* as if we've posted it?'

'I'm sure we could,' Blix said. 'But he'll see through that very easily.'

'How?'

Blix turned to face her. 'If the feed was real, posting the link would make the Internet explode. The newspapers would latch on to it, and there would almost certainly be extra news bulletins. If we post a false link, none of those things would happen, and the guy behind all this would realise something's wrong...'

'It would buy us some time.'

'No more than ten minutes, though. In any case, we won't make it. There's too little time.'

Kovic disappeared into the ladies' toilets. Blix followed her with his eyes before standing up and moving off to look for Emma. He found her in an office with the name 'Bjarne Brogeland' on the door.

'You're still here, then,' Blix said.

Emma put down her tablet but said nothing. He saw her cheeks were glowing.

'We didn't find her,' Blix told her.

It looked as if Emma had something she wanted to say, but she changed her mind.

'At least you didn't give him the finale he wanted,' she said in the end.

'No,' Blix said. 'Maybe not.'

'So what do you do now?'

Blix had asked himself the same question. 'We plod on,' he answered. 'We may end up being too late to find Nordstrøm, but at least we'll find Dahlmann or whoever's behind all this.'

A frown appeared on Emma's forehead. 'Or the person behind it?' she asked. 'Do you no longer believe it's Dahlmann, then?'

Blix swallowed noisily, wondering whether he should explain that it was far from certain that Dahlmann was acting alone. But before he managed to say anything, they heard shouts from the main office.

Blix rushed out into the corridor, with Emma following in his wake.

'What's going on?' he asked once he reached the others in the investigation team. Abelvik pointed at the screen image of Sonja Nordstrøm.

'The clock has gone,' she said.

Fosse gave Blix a stern look before shifting his gaze to Emma. A comment was about to emerge from his lips, but the next minute everyone's eyes were drawn back to the screen. It had gone totally black.

'What's happening?' Fosse asked. 'Did we lose the connection?'

No one had an answer. The screen remained black. Then another clock appeared on the screen: it read 10.00.

'Ten minutes,' Blix said softly, glancing at his own watch. It was ten to twelve.

Then the clock began to tick.

09.59 ... 09.58 ... 09.57...

'Oh shit,' Kovic said.

For the next few seconds, everyone stood rooted to the spot.

'What the hell do we do?' Wibe asked.

No one replied. They just stared at the seconds, which had never passed more quickly. Soon there were nine minutes left. Then eight.

'I can't bear to look,' Abelvik said.

'Me neither,' another investigator chimed in, but none of them made a move.

Seven minutes became six. Five.

Then a fresh image of Nordstrøm appeared. A still image this time. The same photo that Soleane Publishing had used on the dust cover of *Forever Number One*: Nordstrøm with her arms in the air as she passed a finishing tape in first place.

Four minutes.

'What do you think is going on?' Abelvik said, almost in a whisper.

'When the countdown is over, he'll show us another picture of Nordstrøm,' Wibe said. 'Dead.'

No one commented on this bit of speculation. Soon the clock was down to three minutes. Blix couldn't stand still. He looked at Emma. Kovic.

Two minutes.

'Can't we just post that fucking link?' Abelvik said, standing beside Fosse.

He did not respond. Just stared at the screen.

A minute and a half.

Every second closer to zero felt like sharp blows to Blix's body.

One minute.

More people had gathered. Blix gazed at Fosse. The superintendent had dark perspiration marks beneath his arms.

Forty-five seconds.

Someone upset a cup on Kovic's desk and coffee spilled all over the desktop. Blix didn't see who it was, but heard the offending person groan and apologise. Kovic said it was all right.

Thirty seconds.

Wibe coughed into his armpit. Abelvik held her hand over her mouth. Fifteen seconds.

It was as if all the sound, all the air, had been sucked out of the room. Ten seconds became five.

Four.

Three.

Two.

One.

Then the countdown was over. The clock showed 0.00. The investigators all looked at one another. 'Nothing's happening,' Wibe said.

Then the clock vanished.

Instead a strapline appeared beneath the photograph of the athletics star.

SONJA NORDSTRØM (1968–2018)

The text remained there for perhaps half a minute. Then both photo and text disappeared. In their place was merely a black screen. The connection to the feed also seemed to be broken.

'We've killed her,' Abelvik said. 'We've fucking killed her.'

71

For the next few minutes no one said a word. They all stared blankly into thin air. Then they walked, one by one, to their desks.

It was as silent as a church in the open-plan office. Emma had never participated in team sports, but she could imagine it must be like gathering in the changing room after losing an important match. But this time it had been a life-or-death showdown; the feeling of emptiness was not mere disappointment.

Those who dared to make conversation did so in whispers. The phone rang, it was answered immediately, with a 'wait a minute'. Then whoever it was disappeared out of the office and continued their conversation elsewhere.

Gard Fosse headed in the direction of his own office. Blix slumped into a chair. Emma could see how exhausted he was. His head was bowed. He seemed totally drained of energy.

Emma longed for a shower and her own bed. But she had a job to do. What had happened in the last twenty-four hours was red-hot news.

'You know I'll have to write about this?'

Blix lifted his head to face her.

'I'd rather you didn't,' he said. 'It will simply put more pressure on us, and hassle from the media, relatives, everyone. It will hold us back. Make it even more difficult to bring all this to an end.'

'I know that,' Emma said. 'But I've no choice. Anita has phoned me four times in the past hour. She's wondering what on earth I'm doing. This is a huge development in what may be the biggest news story we've had in Norway for years. I'll lose my job if Anita finds out I've been right in the centre of events again without telling her about it. As far as she's concerned, that may be a bigger crime than not writing about it.'

Blix lowered his eyes again. It looked as if he appreciated her dilemma.

'We need to keep your computer here for a while longer,' he said finally.

'That doesn't matter. We have others at work.'

Sighing, he repeatedly rubbed his hands over his face.

As Emma headed for the door, Blix called after her:

'I don't want you to be on your own,' he said.

'I'll let you know if he contacts me again,' she told him. 'Even though there's scarcely any reason for him to do that now.'

'He could—'

'And if he does,' Emma interrupted, 'I'll let you know. At once.'

Blix seemed to take a few moments to think this over.

'I want you to take a security alarm,' he said, getting to his feet.

Emma looked at him. 'A personal safety alarm, you mean?'

'Call it whatever you like.'

Emma was not keen on the idea. 'Isn't that a bit over the top?' she said. 'Nordstrøm is probably dead. It's surely only a matter of time before Dahlmann dumps her body somewhere. It's over and done with, isn't it? All he'll do now is make the most of number two – whoever that might be.'

'We don't know that,' Blix said. 'And we're not sure it's Dahlmann we're looking for either.'

He gave her an earnest look.

'Dahlmann might be a pawn too, just like you,' he went on. 'We don't know who's behind all this, and as long as we don't, I'm not taking any chances.'

Emma bit her lower lip.

'It's been a long day,' he went on. 'A long night. Can't you just do as I ask? It's not as if you'll be going around with a fucking medallion round your neck.'

A discouraged expression had appeared in his eyes, one that Emma had not seen before. And his voice was more assertive than she had previously experienced.

'Most people just wear it on their wrist, like a watch,' he added, more gently.

Emma hoisted her shoulders before dropping them slowly. 'OK,' she said. 'If you insist.'

'I do,' he said, giving her a smile.

'Is this an official police theory, by the way?' she asked.

'What?'

'That there may be a previously unknown perpetrator?'

'No,' Blix replied, with a sigh. 'It's *my* theory, and no, you can't quote me on it.'

72

The autumn wind had picked up again. Leaves whirled up from the dry pavements. People walked to and fro, and there was constant traffic on the roads. Everything was as before. Just not.

Emma clambered into a taxi and asked to be driven to the news.no office. She thought the driver gave the alarm a strange look when he turned round to take her credit card. It made her feel like a victim, and she didn't want that, so she took it off and put it in her bag. If a dangerous situation arose, it would be close at hand all the same.

As she let herself into the building, someone called out behind her: 'Wait!'

Henrik Wollan ran up to her, caught the door and held it open as she stepped inside. 'Where have you been?' he asked, as his gaze took in her crumpled clothes. The same ones as yesterday. Emma had hoped to avoid this, but now that he was here, she would have to involve him.

'I'll explain up in Anita's office,' she said, letting him lead the way up the stairs.

Anita ushered them in and Emma spent the next few minutes explaining what had happened in the past twelve hours or so.

'So Dahlmann has sent *you* pictures of Sonja Nordstrøm?' Wollan asked. He was standing at Anita's coffee machine picking out a capsule.

'I don't know if it was Dahlmann,' Emma replied, thinking of what Blix had said about another, unknown perpetrator. 'But they were live video images.'

Anita leaned forwards over her desk. 'Can we see them?' she asked, making an energetic hand movement, as if to prise Emma's laptop out of her bag.

'The link's dead now,' Emma explained.

'The police killed her,' Wollan concluded, firing up his laptop. 'Tell me you at least took a screen shot.'

Emma shook her head.

'He sent me a still picture as well,' she explained as the coffee machine buzzed. 'But the police still have my laptop. I can't access my emails from my phone now either. It's possible the police have removed them from the server.'

'So you don't actually have anything to back up your story?' Wollan said, bringing the coffee cup over to his seat.

'No physical proof. But Gard Fosse can't refuse to answer specific questions. And since he knows I was there, he has no other choice than to confirm it. If he doesn't, he'll be lying.'

'I'll call Weedon,' Anita said. 'Find out if he can retrieve your emails.'

'Who's Weedon?' Emma queried.

'The computer guy we use,' Anita said, turning to face Wollan. 'We'll take a two-pronged approach. First we'll report that the perpetrator has contacted one of our journalists with photos of Sonja Nordstrøm in captivity. Then, once the police have confirmed that, a story about the kidnapper's demands, the police's handling of the case and Sonja Nordstrøm's uncertain fate. Start by ringing Gard Fosse.'

'Do I have to do everything all of a sudden?' Wollan objected.

'Emma's by-line can't go on this,' Anita said.

'Why not?'

'Because this time Emma herself is part of the story.'

73

Emma leaned her back against the door of her flat and dropped her bag on the floor. She felt bone weary in a way she'd never experienced before.

She stood there for almost a full minute before kicking off her shoes and hanging up her jacket. The rest of her clothes she stripped off on the way to her bedroom. She could allow herself to relax now, she thought, and she took off her wig before crawling into bed.

When she awoke four hours later, she lay contemplating the ceiling for a while, before reaching out for her mobile phone attached to its charger on the bedside table. A message from Blix, wondering whether she'd got home safe and sound. An unanswered call from her sister. That was all. The call had been followed by a text message in which she asked if Emma would spend Saturday evening with her and Martine and stay overnight.

She wasn't sure she wanted to do that, so instead of responding she ventured on to the Internet and saw that Wollan had still not posted anything about Sonja Nordstrøm. Maybe Gard Fosse had made himself uncontactable.

She checked the other online newspapers but none had any news about the case to report.

Emma lingered in bed with the phone in her hand. After she'd answered Blix, she decided to send a text to Kasper.

Any feedback from your Danish sources about Jeppe Sørensen's Norwegian friends?

It pinged back shortly afterwards.

Nothing so far. It's the weekend, you know. My sources are taking time off.

She weighed up whether to confront him about his silence on his childhood relationship with Jeppe Sørensen. But that would reveal that she'd searched for his name.

She swung her feet out of bed, headed for the bathroom and got straight into the shower. Closed her eyes and leaned back into the hot spray. She stood where she was for a long time before turning off the water, drying herself and wandering out into the kitchen wrapped in nothing but a towel.

The fridge was almost empty. She didn't like the idea of all the people she'd have to mix with if she went out shopping. Instead she sent a message to her sister, writing that she would be over at eight o'clock.

Just as Emma was about to call for a taxi, a message from Anita appeared: *Out now.*

Emma checked news.no. The font used in the headline was larger than she could ever remember seeing before, and she felt instant distaste for reading about herself as part of a news story, even though she was not named. Gard Fosse was tight-lipped, pointing out that a press statement would be issued in the course of the evening.

The phone began to ring almost as soon as she'd finished reading. It didn't require much imagination for her press colleagues to work out which of the news.no journalists might have been contacted by the person who had abducted Sonja Nordstrøm.

She let the calls divert to voicemail, eventually switching off the sound and vibration functions, but the disturbance nevertheless meant it was half past eight before Emma arrived at her sister's. Martine had already gone to bed, worn out after a long day at a water park out in Asker.

'I didn't say anything about you coming,' her sister explained. 'It can be a nice surprise for her when she sees you in the morning.'

Irene served the rest of the lasagne that she and Martine had eaten. Afterwards she opened a bottle of red wine.

Emma told her about the uproar of the last twenty-four hours. Her sister listened wide-eyed, then got up to make sure the main door of the flat was locked, before checking on Martine.

They sat in the living room edgily zapping between TV channels.

'Go back,' Emma said.

Irene did as she was asked. It was an edited transmission of the events of the last twenty-four hours on *Worthy Winner*. The three remaining contestants were seated around a table.

'That's Alex Blix's daughter,' Emma said, pointing at the screen. 'The guy who shot dad.'

Irene didn't comment. Emma replenished their glasses.

'I'm supposed to be covering the semi-final tomorrow,' she added, feeling how strange it would be to return to that type of journalism.

'Can't someone else do it?' Irene asked.

'There aren't many of us,' Emma replied. 'It depends what else is on the go.'

They watched to the end of the programme, then changed to a music channel.

'There's something I thought I should speak to you about,' Emma said after a pause.

Her sister waited for her to continue. Emma moved her wine glass slightly further across the table in front of her.

'I think Martine may have the same hair disorder as me,' she went on.

Irene glanced up at her sister before lowering her eyes.

'I found a few clumps of her hair in my bed last time she stayed the night with me,' Emma explained.

Irene said nothing. Not for a long time.

'You didn't mention it to me,' Emma said. 'Or maybe you didn't know about it?'

Irene quickly lifted her gaze. 'Don't you think I've noticed it?'

Emma splayed out her hands. Her sister's eyes glittered with embarrassment.

Her voice was angry when she continued: 'I just wanted Martine to live as normal a life as possible for as long as possible. Is that so odd, do you think?'

'No,' Emma said, making small circular motions with her red wine glass. 'It's not.'

Neither of them spoke for a while.

'How old were you when it started?' Irene asked in a conciliatory tone.

Emma hesitated. 'Some time in my teenage years,' Emma said. 'Thirteen or fourteen or thereabouts.'

'That was when you ... changed as well.'

Emma knew what her sister was referring to. For a period Emma had felt as if the whole world was against her. That everything was unfair.

'You only saw half of that,' she said. 'You saw me going to a lot of parties and coming home late and so on, but you didn't see all the other stuff.'

'What do you mean?' Irene stared at her.

Emma hesitated again before continuing: 'I ... harmed myself, among other things. I didn't cut myself, because I didn't want to end up with sores and that kind of thing. I didn't want other people to see them. I just needed to feel the pain. And when I'd managed that, I did all I could to deaden it. I drank. On my own, too. From the age of fifteen. I either helped myself to some of Grandpa's booze, or I got people to buy it for me.'

'Where did you get the money for that?'

Emma stared intently down into her wine glass. 'I stole it,' she said, shamefaced. 'The money, that is.'

'Emma...'

'From Grandma.'

She held her glass and swirled the wine round and round. Took a swig. 'I did a lot of fucking dreadful things that I'm not proud of. It's actually a wonder everything didn't go to hell in a handcart.'

They sat for a while in silence.

'Do you still think life's unfair?' Irene eventually asked.

Emma gave some thought to her answer.

'I try not to think too much about it. It doesn't help. The hair problem is something I just have to live with. After all, there are worse things.'

'But you *don't* do that, Emma. You don't live with it. Not really.'

'What do you mean?' Emma looked up at her sister.

'You've just put a lid on it. You've never been open about it, for instance, not to anyone apart from me. That's not the same as living with it.'

'I've no need to share my illness with the outside world. Everything doesn't have to be paraded in public. I've chosen to deal with it in that way. And it's my choice, no one else's.'

They drank up the rest of their wine.

'Of course, you can decide for yourself,' Irene said after a while. 'But if Martine has the same condition as you, I'd like her to have a positive role model. Someone who knows what problems she'll face in the years ahead, and who can give her advice about how to tackle them. I don't want her to harm herself, the way you did, and I don't want her to hide herself away either.'

'I don't hide myself away.'

'No?'

Irene put down her glass. 'How many boyfriends have you had in the past few years, Emma? How many of them have you dared to spend the night with? How many have you allowed to stay the night at your place?'

Emma gave no answer, quite simply because she had no good answer to give.

'How many have been permitted to see who you really are?'

74

Blix couldn't recollect the last time he'd spent the night at the police station, but at some point around the crack of dawn he'd let himself into a conference room and slept on a mat from the gym, with a blanket pulled over him. The wee small hours spent poring over the case files had failed to yield anything useful, apart from an even stronger conviction that Dahlmann was not operating alone.

Stiff after several hours on the hard mat, he got to his feet and took a shower, found a clean T-shirt in the cupboard, and headed into the main office for a coffee. The office was empty, so he took the opportunity to have a look at the news before clicking on to the *Worthy Winner* pages.

The three remaining contestants sat in the kitchen, tucking into an omelette. Apparently Jonas Sakshaug, the chef, had whisked it up for breakfast. Iselin could barely boil an egg.

Blix took the liberty of turning up the volume to hear them complaining about having woken early. He was looking forward to the whole reality show being over, but did hope that Iselin would get one of the final two places, now that she had come so far. What the actual final would comprise was top secret, but the producer, Petter Due-Eriksen, had promised viewers something out of the ordinary. Something no one had ever seen before in the context of a reality show. But first there was the semi-final.

A sudden thought made him sit bolt upright.

Three had to be reduced to two.

Two.

A number still missing from the perpetrator's calculations.

In many ways a reality show was the perfect scenario, Blix thought – and he was as excited as he was scared by the idea that had seized him. A reality-show participant would certainly fit the bill for a perpetrator who consciously pursued celebrities. And now that he had not managed to broadcast to the public live coverage of Sonja Nordstrøm…

Blix stood up.

Three contestants were left. Three who had to become two.

Toralf Schanke.

Jonas Sakshaug.

And Iselin.

The thought made him ill, and he had to pay a visit to the toilet to splash cold water on his face. The first investigators had appeared by the time he came back. As soon as Gard Fosse arrived, Blix requested a meeting to present his theory.

'The fact that three have to become two doesn't give it a direct connection to the number two,' Abelvik objected. 'It's the person who loses in the final who becomes number two.'

'In a sense,' Blix agreed. But he was prepared for this counter-argument. 'But just think about it: it's the perfect arena for someone determined to knock out celebrities. It doesn't necessarily have to be the person who *ends up as* number two who he goes after. The chef, for example, is contestant number two.'

'What do you mean?' Fosse demanded.

'There were originally ten participants on the show,' Kovic explained. 'They were each issued with a number when it all kicked off.'

'What number does your daughter have?' Pia Nøkleby asked.

'Three,' Blix replied. 'So you see there are loads of opportunities here for a perpetrator with our man's profile. He has several options that would fit into his "project", if I can call it that. The one who *becomes* number two, or *has* the number two, are only two of them. He could also make up his mind to go for *two* of the contestants, for instance. Then it would be a double murder. He hasn't done that before. It would also be something of a statement – taking the lives of two of the finalists on live television.'

The mere thought made Blix's stomach churn.

'I hear what you say, Alexander, but I'm not sure you're looking at the potential threat here in an entirely objective way,' Fosse said. 'Given that Iselin is in the midst of it all.'

'That may be, but it's a solid theory all the same.'

Kovic nodded in agreement.

'There's a little more than nine hours until the semi-final,' Blix went on. 'A lot could happen in that time, but if we don't make a dent in what we're working on in the course of the morning, then we ought to decide whether we should approach the production company and the TV channel, and persuade them to postpone the semi-final.'

'They'll never go along with that,' Wibe said, unscrewing a cola bottle. 'There's far too much money and prestige involved.'

'They won't have any choice if we put our foot down,' Blix said.

'How many does the studio seat?' Fosse asked.

'Three hundred,' Blix answered. 'At least.'

'We couldn't check every single one as they enter,' Wibe commented. 'We'd have to go through all their belongings.'

Blix eyeballed everyone around the table. He still didn't have the support he'd been hoping for.

Fosse broke in: 'There's still plenty of time,' he said, making eye contact with Blix. 'See that the broadcast goes out with the highest possible level of security. Until then, we'll chase up all the leads we can.' He stood up, signalling that the meeting was over.

Blix needed a breath of fresh air so he went up to the canteen, which was deserted, it being Sunday, and walked out on to the terrace. There, he filled his lungs and let his eyes feast on the city below as he exhaled again. He repeated the action three times before taking out his phone and calling Merete.

'Hello,' she said. Her voice was gentler than usual. 'How are you doing?'

He heard her move into another room and close the door. She had to be at her boyfriend's house in Holmenkollen.

'You know,' Blix said. 'There's a lot on at work. Especially now.'

'You're working on the countdown case,' she concluded.

'A lot of us are involved in it,' Blix answered.

A tentative silence ensued, as if both were waiting for the other to speak.

'Are you thinking of going to the live transmission tonight?' he asked in the end.

'Yes,' she said. 'Of course I am, it's the semi-final – I've been at all the broadcasts so far. Why were you wondering about it? Aren't you coming?'

'I...' Blix had no idea how to express himself in words that would avoid terrifying Merete. In fact he'd called to ask her not to attend, but he realised that wouldn't work. 'I will, yes, of course,' he finally said. 'How ... do you think it will go?'

'Well, when she's come as far as this, anything could happen,' Merete said.

That was exactly what Blix was afraid of.

75

Towards the top of the slight incline Emma stood up on the pedals, trying to raise her pulse even further. In addition to the physical benefits, she found cycling therapeutic. It was always so much easier to think when she was on the move. When she didn't consciously intend to think over something, the thoughts just came by themselves, when she least expected it.

After the night at her sister's she'd eaten breakfast with Martine and returned home, intending to do some work from her sofa, but she'd found it difficult to collect her thoughts. She knew a hard training session would sharpen her up for the editorial meeting later that day.

Her body hadn't had enough rest, though, and she tired much faster than usual. By the time she passed the car park at Bjerke, she was breathing heavily. She braked and dropped her left foot to the tarmac. As she waited for her lungs to recover, her thoughts turned to Jessica Flatebø, and how she'd been found in the summer cabin in Nordmarka earlier that week. It felt as if it had taken place in the distant past. New victims had been discovered since, so Emma hadn't had a minute to stop and reflect on Flatebø's murder, but now it struck her that the killer must have had intimate local knowledge to know exactly which cabin would be unoccupied – when, and for how long.

Maybe Dahlmann was holed up somewhere in there, she thought, looking towards the forest.

She knew Wollan was very familiar with Marka. She could discuss it with him. It also gave her an excuse to phone Blix.

She turned the bike around and began to make her way back home, keeping close to a group of three men in identical cycling gear on their way down into the city. Once inside her flat, she took the opportunity to do three sets of pull-ups and push-ups before making for the shower. When she arrived at the editorial offices, she felt fit and fresh. It had been several days since she'd last felt so good.

Henrik Wollan peered up at her with tired eyes from the other side of a computer screen.

'Any news?' she asked.

Wollan shook his head. 'Everyone's waiting for the next move,' he replied. 'The only question is whether there's more to come. Or whether it finishes with Nordstrøm.'

'It's not over yet,' Emma told him. 'There are two numbers missing – two and ten.'

Wollan agreed with her, and for once his tone was not sarcastic.

'Coffee?' she asked, walking towards the coffee machine.

'Yes please,' he replied.

She filled two cups and handed one to Wollan.

'What are you working on?' she asked him, with a nod at his computer.

'A sort of biography of each of the victims,' Wollan said. 'It's something Anita wants,' he added, as if he felt little interest in it himself.

'You know Nordmarka well, don't you?' Emma went on, pointing at a picture of Jessica Flatebø lying on his desk. 'Didn't you invite our class to a cabin somewhere out in Marka a few years ago?'

Wollan sucked some of the foam from the top of his coffee cup. Emma knew the answer, because she recalled all the chat there had been about the outing afterwards. She hadn't gone herself.

Wollan nodded.

'Does your family still have that cabin?'

'Yes,' he said, slightly hesitant.

'Where is it?'

'Near Mylla,' he said.

'Is that far from where Jessica Flatebø was found?'

Wollan shrugged. 'Not very. Why do you ask?'

'I was wondering whether you were familiar with the area where Flatebø was found,' she told him. 'Whether you knew any of the neighbours.'

'I'm afraid I don't,' he replied.

'OK, then,' Emma said and went into a conference room and gave Blix a call.

'What is it?' he asked. 'Has something happened?'

'No,' Emma said, with a smile. 'No fear of that, I'm at work. I just wondered how things were going.'

'There...'

Emma picked up on his hesitation.

'There's nothing new,' he said. For the first time since they'd become acquainted, she was unsure whether he was telling the truth.

'Have you looked into the possibility that the person you're looking for might be hidden away somewhere in Nordmarka?' she asked, and went on to explain her theory that the perpetrator must have local knowledge.

'We've created a list of everyone who owns property there,' Blix answered. 'We have a team working on speaking to every single one of them.'

Emma nodded. Of course this was something the police had looked into.

'Well, I have to go now,' Blix continued. Emma noticed the disquiet in his voice. He seemed nervous or anxious.

'OK,' she said, faltering. 'Sorry for disturbing you.'

76

At 2.00 p.m. Blix locked himself in a vacant interview room to phone Enter Entertainment. He searched through the call list on his mobile and located the number for 'TV-Eckhoff'.

'Yes, hello?'

Blix introduced himself.

'You're Iselin's father,' the other man said.

'That's right. But I'm calling in my capacity as a police officer this time. I was wondering what security measures you've taken in connection with tonight's broadcast?'

There was a moment's silence at the other end.

'Well ... we have our usual security here – guards who watch over the entrances and so forth.'

'You don't check people's bags?'

'No.'

Blix gave this some thought before adding: 'How easy or difficult is it for outsiders to get on to the actual stage – or behind the scenes, even?'

'There's no physical barrier between the audience and the stage,' Eckhoff explained. 'But we do have security guards present. After all, we can't risk just anyone appearing in front of the cameras. To access backstage you need to have your own pass.'

'What about the house itself?' Blix continued. 'Is it possible to get in there somehow?'

'Not for outsiders,' Eckhoff assured him. 'There are two entrances: the security door we use to send in food and other equipment to the contestants, and the stage door that we only use during live broadcasts.'

'And they are locked?'

'They're regulated from the control room,' Eckhoff clarified. 'You can't just pop in or out.'

Blix jotted this down on the notepad in front of him.

'The people working on the production side, have they been security cleared? Have you checked everyone's background?'

'We've checked their references and so on. We haven't run them through criminal records, if that's what you're wondering. We don't have access to them, anyway.'

'Can you send me a list of everyone who works on *Worthy Winner*?'

Silence again.

'Why do you need that?' Eckhoff asked at last.

For a moment Blix considered how he should answer this. 'We're taking special measures, in light of what's happened to other celebrities in Norway recently,' he replied. 'So we're going to need extra manpower in the studios for today's broadcast.'

Eckhoff seemed to consider this for a few moments.

'We mainly use our own staff, but I'll see what I can organise,' he said in the end.

'You'll have to do more than just *see* what you can organise, Eckhoff. This is critical.'

'Yes, yes, OK, I'll get cracking on it. It's just that there are a hundred and one other things to do on a day when we have a live broadcast.'

'I understand that, but the safety of your participants must come before everything else.'

'Yes, yes, of course.'

They hung up. Blix ran his hands over his face. He needed food. He needed sleep. But most of all he needed this case to be wrapped up ASAP so that he could relax in the knowledge that Iselin was out of danger.

Eckhoff's list arrived less than an hour later, and Blix skimmed rapidly through it. There were twenty-five people involved in the actual production unit. He appointed a small group consisting of Kovic, Abelvik and himself to go through all of them, checking them against criminal records, and investigating whether they had any links to Walter Georg Dahlmann or any of the victims. By 6.00 p.m., they had checked the whole list. One cameraman had a previous conviction for violent crime from eight years earlier, but nothing more than that.

Blix took one last look at the list, scanning from top to bottom.

'Hm,' he said. 'Eckhoff didn't include himself.'

Kovic gave him a questioning look.

'Do you think he has anything to hide?'

'It wouldn't surprise me if he has something on his conscience,' Blix said.

He dug out Eckhoff's date of birth and conducted the usual searches. There was nothing in criminal records. A wider search came up with several results in film and actor databases. In a profile photo in skuespiller.no, where Norwegian actors were listed, he had long hair, and reminded Blix of someone famous, but he just couldn't remember who.

He sat back a little and rubbed his face with his hands.

'When do the doors open?' Kovic asked.

'In an hour,' Blix said. 'I'm going up there shortly.'

'I'm coming with you.'

77

Blix was restless; and the closer he drew to TV headquarters, the worse he became. He thought of Iselin. The participants had been completely isolated from the news in recent weeks. They'd had no access to newspapers and had only communicated with viewers via a restricted Facebook page. Unless one of them had informed the participants about Dahlmann or the countdown, they knew nothing about what was going on. Maybe that was just as well.

Outside the entrance to the TV building, crowds were already gathering. Several had homemade placards to cheer on the contestants. Blix couldn't help feeling disappointed that none mentioned Iselin, but he quickly shook that off.

Blix and Kovic approached the public entrance. On Fosse's orders, they were both dressed in uniform. The idea was that a visible police presence might scare off any potential perpetrator. At the same time they couldn't turn up with too many uniformed officers as that would generate panic. Instead they were letting plain clothes police officers monitor most of the crowd without them being aware of it.

Inside, Blix located Even Eckhoff, who referred him on to the producer, Petter Due-Eriksen.

Blix had met him once in connection with the promotion and editorial discussions about the programme concept.

'We have plenty of security,' Due-Eriksen said. 'We don't need any outside help.'

'We're not here to help *you*,' Blix said. 'We're here to keep the spectators and the contestants safe.'

'Believe it or not, officer,' Due-Eriksen replied, looking at his mobile phone at the same time. 'Our staff are more than capable of doing just that. It's why we hire them. I don't want your people to interfere with their work.'

'Believe it or not,' Blix answered straight back, 'I don't need your permission. Just tell them to meet me.'

Due-Eriksen grinned, clearly not impressed, but made a nodding motion with his head and then took them to a meeting room, where he assembled all the guards and a few key players from the production side.

Blix spent ten minutes with them, briefing them on the situation. He made sure he created the impression that all of this was normal procedure in the circumstances and merely a preventive measure.

Blix devoted the next half hour to acquainting himself with the layout of the building. The control room for the online transmission was located beside the stage. Inside, three men and two women followed the twenty-eight cameras that produced the live stream twenty-four hours a day.

Iselin was in the centre of the picture on one of the screens on the wall.

Blix approached one of the staff who had attended the briefing meeting. 'Is it possible to stop the live stream if we need to?' he asked.

The employee, a man in his early twenties, turned to face him. 'The main broadcast is easy to pull the plug on, if anything happens,' he answered. 'It's a slightly more complicated process with all the images that go out on the Internet. We'll manage it, of course, but it takes longer.'

On screen, Iselin walked up to a table and took an apple from a bowl. The camera followed her every move.

'Who controls the cameras?' Blix inquired.

'Most of the cameras are triggered by movement. They automatically follow the contestants when they move. We also have two cameramen behind the one-way mirrors in there.'

He nodded towards a door. Blix crossed over and peered inside. It was a cramped back room with cables snaking over the floor. A man with a camera on his shoulder was filming through a mirror wall into the house. Iselin was laughing at something Toralf said.

Blix put his fingertips on the glass and stood watching her. She was so close he could almost touch her. The fact that he couldn't made him blink rapidly several times. He couldn't recall the last time he'd given her a hug. Or received one.

The cameraman turned towards him. Blix gave him a brief nod, then withdrew and closed the door behind him before moving on. He toured the rest of the studio, speaking to everyone wearing a T-shirt emblazoned with the word *CREW*, in order to gain an impression of who they were, what kind of job they had, and where in the building they would be located during the show.

When it was almost 7.00 p.m., Blix headed for the public entrance. Outside, people huddled together. A loudspeaker played music with a thumping bass to whip up some atmosphere. Two security guards stood on either side of the doorway. Another one stood inside.

The first audience members were asked to empty their pockets. When one of the guards simply gave a quick glance at the contents of one girl's handbag, Blix stopped both her and the guard. 'You have to check it more carefully,' he said.

'Come off it,' the guard said glumly. 'She can't be more than fourteen.' He pointed at the girl beside him.

Blix took a step closer and whispered: 'I don't give a shit. All pockets, bags, rucksacks – you have to go through them all.'

Blix had said precisely this during the briefing. He noticed the guard roll his eyes in disgust, but made no comment. He needed everyone with him on the team.

Even though things progressed slowly at the entrance, it didn't take long for the auditorium to fill up. At the moment it looked as if the audience comprised only family members, enthusiastic fans and the usual spectators; and the guards had come across nothing that could potentially be used as a weapon.

When Merete appeared at the entrance, Blix went over to meet her.

'She's OK,' Blix told the guards. 'I know her.'

The guard he'd reprimanded earlier rolled his eyes again.

'What's up?' Merete asked, looking at his stiffly pressed uniform shirt. 'Are you working? Here?'

'Yes, it...' Blix didn't know what to say.

'Isn't Jan-Arne with you?'

'Jan-Egil,' Merete corrected him. 'No, he couldn't make it tonight. Now tell me what's going on.'

'It's probably nothing,' Blix told her. 'It's just to be on the safe side.'

It took only a second for Merete to understand the connection. Her hand leapt to her mouth.

'It's just a precaution,' he said, trying to allay her fears. 'We have people at TV 2 and NRK as well. And several other places, in fact.'

Merete gulped a couple of times before nodding. Blix escorted her inside, following her to a seat approximately in the middle of the auditorium, where they had a good view over everything that would happen on stage.

78

Anita had reminded Emma that she needed to produce something on the semi-final of *Worthy Winner*, but added that she could just as easily do it from home via the TV broadcast, since she'd been working so much in the past few days. Emma had nothing against turning up at the TV studio, though. She always wrote better pieces when she'd been physically on the spot; and Blix's daughter being one of the three semi-finalists had given her renewed interest in the programme.

It was just gone 7.30 when Emma parked her bike in a side street near the building where *Worthy Winner* was recorded, and stood in the queue to get in. There was no separate press entrance, something that had annoyed several of her colleagues. Emma noticed there were more security guards around than on previous occasions. She also had to hand over her bag to a guard, who looked up at her when he took out the personal alarm to scrutinise it.

'Crazy ex-boyfriend,' Emma said.

The guard replaced the alarm in the bag and nodded as a sign that she was free to enter.

Emma found a seat in the part of the audience cordoned off with red tape and labelled *PRESS*. She wordlessly greeted some of the other journalists who'd turned up. Sat down. Caught sight of Blix down on the floor; he was in uniform and talking to a member of the production team.

As Emma glanced around the studio, she spotted many of the people she'd seen working at the police station at the weekend. A great many, in fact. This made her frown. She tried to catch Blix's eye, but he didn't notice her, he was too preoccupied. She sent him a text message and asked what was going on. Received no reply.

Soon the auditorium was full. Blix had still not taken his seat. Through a microphone, someone in the production team requested the audience's attention for a few minutes. The woman ran over the signals that would be given from the floor to indicate when the audience should cheer and yell at the top of their lungs. They tried it out a couple of times until the woman was satisfied with the level of noise.

Emma looked at the time. 7.57. The air was full of expectation and excitement, buzzing with the general racket of the crowd and their roars of approval. The cheers rose a notch or two when the programme host appeared on stage.

Tore Berg Tollersrud picked up the mic and said hello to the audience. He thanked them for coming and hoped that together they would give a tremendous performance.

Emma was less than keen on his choice of words. It was as if they all had a role to play.

'Are you ready, Totto?'

The voice came from somewhere on the floor, but Emma couldn't see where exactly. The lighting technicians checked that everything functioned as it should. A cameraman slid closer to the sofa where the contestants would sit.

Emma felt a creeping sense of foreboding. Once again she spotted Blix down at the front, scanning the audience with a watchful eye.

As the producer moved centre stage, the studio manager held up a hand. Tollersrud took a deep breath and closed his eyes, appearing to go into some kind of trance. Deep concentration.

Then it dawned on her.

Tore Berg Tollersrud.

Totto.

Emma was on the verge of getting to her feet, on the brink of calling out his nickname.

Originally it had been 'To-To', since both his first name and surname began with 'To'.

Two-Two. The number two, twice.

Then the music struck up on the loudspeaker system.

The transmission had started.

79

So far so good, Blix thought once the first tranche of the programme was over. In the auditorium people had stood up to move their legs a little and stretch their backs. But no one left the studio, or made any sign of wanting to.

Blix had not taken in a single word of what had been said. He'd been busy concentrating intently on every single movement in the auditorium, as well as behind the cameras and under the roof, every place where it might be possible for someone to hide. With a gun, for example. But everything had gone smoothly.

He wheeled around and made eye contact with Iselin. At first he didn't know what to do. Then he smiled and waved, fleetingly, but received only a question mark from her eyes in return. She was wearing jeans, a white top and a knitted woollen cardigan. A pale-pink scarf was wrapped haphazardly around her neck. It was almost as if he didn't recognise her. She seemed different. Larger than life. More grown up, perhaps.

A member of the production team approached her, and with that Iselin's attention turned to something else.

Blix was back in search mode. The auditorium was full of activity. He noticed a hand waving – it was Emma. She clutched her phone in her hand and was pointing at it. Blix took out his and saw that Emma and a few others had sent him text messages.

He found Emma's and opened it.

The presenter's name is Totto. To-To. Two – twice.

Blix raised his gaze and made eye contact with Emma again. Then he looked at Tore Berg Tollersrud, standing behind a curtain drinking a glass of water. Checking his appearance in a mirror.

Kovic approached. 'What is it?' she asked.

Blix told her about the message he'd received from Emma.

'Shit,' Kovic exclaimed. 'Why on earth didn't we think of him?'

'I didn't know that was his nickname,' Blix answered; his heart had picked up its pace. 'We have to get the broadcast stopped somehow. Get him out of here.'

'How do you suggest we should go about that?'

Blix stopped to think, but couldn't come up with a useful solution. Tollersrud was the only person who could present the show. And the channel would never stop a programme that was going out live, unless there was a terrorist attack or something.

Blix looked again at the presenter, searching for signs that he felt unwell – as Calle Seeberg had been before he collapsed. Tollersrud was still standing behind the curtain passing his thumb across his mobile screen. Smiling to himself as if someone had sent him a message making an obscene suggestion.

'Let's go backstage,' Blix said, digging out his temporary pass. 'I want to take a look at his dressing room. The make-up chair and wardrobe. And talk to everyone who's been in contact with him since he arrived.'

'We should speak to him as well,' Kovic interjected.

'We won't manage that before the next commercial break,' Blix said, as they hurried towards the nearest security door.

'As long as he doesn't drop dead before that,' Kovic said behind him.

80

Emma couldn't sit still. In the second commercial break she went to the toilet, mainly to have a chance to move about. She waited in the queue, her head whirling with the idea that the broadcast was a natural target for a killer who yearned for attention. Three people would be whittled down to two.

She looked around, noticing a number of plain-clothes policemen with earplugs in. The perpetrator could be somewhere inside the building. She could have unwittingly walked past him. He could be gazing at her now, for all she knew. The very thought made her shudder.

She heard from the auditorium that the transmission was about to resume so she left the queue and returned to her seat. Tore Berg

Tollersrud was interviewing Toralf Schanke about his relationship with Iselin. It had become a recurring theme; the presenter wanted to know if they'd struck up a relationship.

'It's no secret we find each other attractive,' Schanke admitted.

'But are you in a relationship?' Tollersrud pressed him.

Schanke withheld his answer. He smiled, as if he knew he was about to tell a lie no one would believe. He glanced at Iselin, who rushed to his rescue:

'Say "no comment",' she suggested.

People in the audience laughed.

Tollersrud refused to give up, and turned to Iselin with exactly the same question. Emma could imagine the headlines if the lovebirds confirmed they were in a relationship. 'Found Love in the TV House'. 'Yes, We're in Love'. 'We've Already Won First Prize' – a quote neither of them would really have given directly. This evening in particular Emma hoped she could avoid writing about a sloppy public romance.

Jonas Sakshaug was then asked about some of the dishes he'd served up to the contestants. Emma had already stopped listening when her mobile phone vibrated.

A message from Kasper.

He'd spoken to Jeppe Sørensen's girlfriend who had no idea if he knew many Norwegians. The only one she knew of herself was a Norwegian who'd been treated at the same clinic as Jeppe after a surgical procedure on his cruciate knee ligaments, but she didn't know his name.

Emma replied: *What clinic was that?*

The answer came only a few seconds later.

Athlete's Retreat. Situated a short distance from Copenhagen.

Emma Googled the clinic and found their home page. She knew that such treatment centres never gave out information about their clients, but she decided all the same to send an email explaining who she was and that she was trying to get in touch with a fellow countryman who had been there at the same time as Jeppe. It would make an excellent story, she wrote, obtaining a Norwegian's account of what Jeppe had been like during that post-operative period.

Afterwards she thanked Kasper for his help, then fell deep into thought. She located the screen image she'd stored of Kasper's arm around Jeppe Sørensen's shoulder, from the article in the *Dagbladet Holstebro-Struer* newspaper. In the end she made up her mind to send it to Kasper and at the same time ask why he hadn't mentioned before that the two of them were personal friends.

The longer it took for him to respond, the more uncertain she became that she'd embarrassed him or asked something he found difficult to answer. Then the phone buzzed again.

Funny, I'd forgotten that picture. ☺ *But it was a long time ago, and I don't really like mixing business with pleasure.*

The very next moment, Emma heard a gasp from the audience. She glanced up at once, struggling to see what had happened.

'You heard right,' Tore Berg Tollersrud said on stage. 'The contestants are about to undergo a lie-detector test, here and now, on live TV. Are you ready for it? Iselin, what do you say?'

Iselin struggled for a few seconds in an effort to compose herself.

'Well ...' she began, 'I was more or less prepared for anything when I agreed to take part in this, but ... I hadn't anticipated a lie-detector test, to be honest.'

'What about you, Toralf?'

'I've got nothing to hide,' he said. 'Just don't ask me where my house keys are.'

That made the audience laugh.

The presenter then turned to Jonas Sakshaug.

'I've got loads of secret recipes,' the chef said. 'Just don't ask me to reveal them and I'm sure I'll get through this OK.'

'That sounds fine, then,' Tollersrud said. 'Now, each of our contestants is going to be examined individually by our expert.'

Tollersrud pointed to a man who'd taken his place behind a desk with a computer on it. The man smiled and waved to the audience.

'He'll connect you up to his machine and then I'll ask you some questions to which you have to answer either yes or no.'

He turned from the contestants to the camera.

'And then, as ever, it's up to you at home to vote for whoever you believe to be worthy of a place in the final. I think I can guarantee we're going to uncover a liar or two, maybe even three, here tonight. The question is how fatal that will be for them. It depends on whether their moral compass is good or bad. We'll soon have the answer to that. But first – a short break. Keep your seats, folks, we'll be back in just over four minutes.'

81

As befitted a TV star, Tore Berg Tollersrud was allocated his own dressing room, make-up artist and make-up chair. Blix and Kovic were ushered in by a female member of the production team.

'I have to rush back,' she said. 'We're going straight back on air.'

'Just a very quick question: how many people would you say have been in contact with Tollersrud today?' Blix asked.

'Oh, my goodness,' she said. 'Probably thirty or forty altogether.'

She waited, cooling her heels, as Blix digested this information.

'OK,' he said at last. 'Thanks for your help.'

They went inside the room.

'What are we looking for?' Kovic asked.

'Pills,' Blix said. 'Perhaps the same kind as the ones we found in Calle Seeberg's home.'

They searched the table in front of the mirror. Nothing but make-up and a bottle of water. Blix opened the bottle and sniffed the contents. Kovic checked Tollersrud's jacket pockets. She took out a pack of chewing gum, a tin of snuff, and a pen. A business card for a woman called Jorunn Tangen who worked at Rubicon TV. Blix examined the rubbish bin, empty. Sniffed at all the make-up paraphernalia on the table. There were no strange smells indicating that something extra had been added.

'He's done OK up till now,' Kovic commented as she surveyed the room. 'The presenter, I mean. There's nothing to suggest he's feeling off colour.'

Blix surveyed the small, confined space. So far everything appeared normal.

'Come on,' he said. 'We'll have to grab hold of him at the next commercial break.'

They passed through the building again, until they were just behind the stage, where they were stopped by a man wearing a headset.

'You can't go out there now,' he said, making signs for them to stay quiet.

Blix turned towards a monitor to see what was happening on stage. Toralf Schanke was seated on a chair with cables attached to his head and wrists, and his back to the audience.

Tollersrud asked some preliminary questions that had verifiable answers. Name, age, family relationships. The reliability of the test increased when the answers Schanke gave tallied with reality. Then Tollersrud moved on to more difficult questions.

'Have you ever stolen anything?' he demanded.

Schanke considered this for a moment before replying: 'Yes.'

Several seconds elapsed. On the TV the picture changed to a bald man sitting staring at a computer screen. The seconds ticked by. He lifted his eyes and gave a thumbs-up.

Tollersrud continued: 'Are you and Iselin Skaar in a relationship?'

Schanke smiled and shook his head, as if he'd known this question would come up. The onscreen image shifted to a close-up of Iselin, who was watching with interest. Blix could see that his daughter's neck was flushed.

'No,' Schanke answered.

Once again the focus turned to the man overseeing the lie-detector test. He raised his hand in the air as if he were a Caesar deciding whether a slave in the gladiator's arena should live or die. Then he gave a thumbs-down.

A gasp rippled through the auditorium.

Tollersrud smiled as if he wanted to say: 'We all knew that already.'

The camera focused on Schanke. The studio lights made his forehead glisten.

'Is money more important to you than love?' Tollersrud now wanted to know.

'No,' Schanke replied after taking a few seconds to think about it.

Zoom in on the lie detector man. His hand went up. His thumb went down. Schanke gave a fleeting smile, shamefaced. A swift shot of Iselin showed her disappointment at the result.

Tollersrud asked a few more questions, before saying: 'That's all we have for you, Toralf.'

The lights turned on around him and the audience applauded. Schanke took a deep breath, relieved that it was over.

'How was it?' Tollersrud asked when the applause had died down.

Schanke took off the cables and looked at the presenter. 'Bloody mortifying.'

Tollersrud gave no reply and simply nodded his head. 'When we come back again after the adverts, it'll be Iselin's turn. Stay in your seats, we'll be back soon.'

A large red light disappeared from a lamp behind the stage and Blix told one of the staff that he needed a quick word with Tollersrud.

'That's impossible now,' the man said. 'We're in the middle of a broadcast.'

'It's a commercial break right now,' Blix said. 'It's vital I speak to him before he goes on air again.'

The man seemed about to protest again, but instead agreed to show Blix the way. Soon they were on stage. At first Blix was blinded by all the lights. Then he managed to screw up his eyes and catch sight of the presenter, exchanging a few words with Iselin. The man from the production team approached and interrupted him. For a brief second Blix's eyes met Iselin's. They were wide with astonishment, as if wondering what was going on.

Tollersrud came up to him. 'What is it?' he asked with an edge of annoyance in his tone. 'Why do you have to speak to me right now?'

'It'll only take a minute,' Blix said. 'But it's important. Have you been in contact with anyone today you've not met before?'

'Yes, that happens nearly every day,' Tollersrud replied. 'Why do you ask?'

'We're looking for a man who may have tried to get in touch with you,' Blix said. 'Has anyone unfamiliar approached you today? Given you anything, or touched you in some way?'

Tollersrud didn't seem to understand the question.

'No,' he said after giving this some thought. 'No one.'

'You haven't eaten anything that tasted off? Drunk anything that had a strange taste?'

Tollersrud drew back, looking towards a table with drinks, biscuits and fruit just beyond the stage area.

'No. Good God, no – what *is* all this nonsense?'

Petter Due-Eriksen appeared behind him. 'What's going on?' the producer demanded.

Tollersrud, with a biscuit in his hand, pointed at Blix.

'You'll have to talk about this later,' Due-Eriksen said, nudging Tollersrud in the direction of the stage.

'One minute!' someone shouted from the studio floor.

Blix and Kovic made themselves scarce.

'There's actually a good chance nothing will happen here tonight,' Kovic said when they were alone. 'That the perpetrator has seen us and decided to wait.'

'I've been thinking that too,' Blix said. 'Tollersrud will have to be given protection afterwards, once the transmission is over. He'll have to be followed closely. All the way home.'

82

Emma followed the rest of the broadcast word for word, and tried to note all the questions the contestants were given and what they answered. She imagined dramatising the evening's events for people who hadn't watched the show; she had her laptop on her knee as Tollersrud grilled the contestants one by one.

Iselin had emerged best from the questions so far. She was caught in one lie – that she'd never stolen anything – and abashed, had rushed to confess that yes indeed, she had once taken an illicit sample from the sweetie counter at the Rema 1000 supermarket not so long ago. Before Tollersrud had time to stop her, since only yes or no answers were permissible, the audience around Emma had smiled and nodded; many of them had apparently done exactly the same thing themselves, so the damage was clearly limited. Iselin had also been asked relationship questions, and she'd emerged unscathed from them, unlike Toralf Schanke – as she'd admitted they were in a relationship.

Jonas Sakshaug's turn came next. The chef was not asked any questions about girlfriends, but was caught out in a lie almost at once. When asked if he had ever added an ingredient in a meal to be nasty to the customer, Sakshaug paused for thought. Then Tollersrud elaborated with examples of snot, coffee grains, blood, and cat- or dog-food. Sakshaug answered no. The lie-detector test showed that he had.

The chef squirmed in his seat.

'Is it true you have a contract with a publisher to issue a cookery book?'

Once again Sakshaug paused. Emma knew there had been a lot of discussion of this cookery book on the show. He'd also encouraged viewers to share their best recipes on his Facebook page, promising that the best and most tempting dish would be included in his book. He answered with a hesitant yes.

The lie-detector man gave him a thumbs-down.

Emma looked at the people around her. Several jaws dropped. There and then she realised how this was going to proceed. It was one thing to be caught in a falsehood about pilfering, but another thing entirely to lie about a book contract.

Emma wrote down the rest of the questions and answers, but Sakshaug was now totally deflated. He was slumped in his chair. When the round of questions was over, he shuffled back to the sofa and the other two contestants. The subsequent voting in the next quarter of an hour further demonstrated what they all knew. Toralf and Iselin, the young couple, were through to the final.

Before Tollersrud sent the viewers to another commercial break, he said: 'The contestants have not been made aware, in advance, of any of the challenges they have undergone. And as our producer has said repeatedly in the media in recent weeks, the final game will include something absolutely special. Something never before attempted on live TV. To find out what that is, you'll have to turn on your TV again at 9.40 p.m. Until then – bye, and thanks for watching *Worthy Winner*!'

Emma made use of the intermission to finish writing her article and publish it on the web. She hoped for an opportunity to interview Sakshaug after the show had ended, even though he'd disappeared backstage, completely crushed. It crossed Emma's mind that he might well tell her what a bitter blow it was to be eliminated on the basis of a lie, when the others had lied too. All the same, he would probably gain a real book contract after all.

When the broadcast resumed, the presenter rounded up the young finalists to sit side by side on two chairs.

'Well, then,' he began, 'so we're left with the two of you. Love's young dream.'

Iselin smiled, embarrassed again.

'What do you both think about everything you've been through in the past few weeks? Did you think you'd make it through to the final?'

'Not at all,' Iselin said. 'I thought I'd be one of the very first to be voted out.'

'Do you know what I think?' Tollersrud asked. 'I think the viewers at home have been enthralled by your relationship. So, I don't mean you're not worthy winners – after all you're both here, and you've passed the tests brilliantly – but there's just something about love and beginnings, isn't there? Something beautiful happening right in front of our eyes. I don't think I'm the only one who's been curious about whether something's been going on between you. Actually,' he said, winking at them both, 'it's been pretty obvious to everyone who's been following the show.'

Toralf and Iselin exchanged glances and smiled.

'Isn't it good to be able to come right out with it at last?'

'Yes,' they both agreed in chorus.

Then Tollersrud grew more serious.

'But, my dear contestants, we haven't yet reached our goal. The final remains. And that...'

He paused for effect.

'That starts here right now.'

Toralf and Iselin gave each other a fleeting look.

'In the course of the last ten weeks, we've tried to discover which of the contestants is exactly that, a worthy winner. We've done this by giving them various challenges, both moral and ethical, and then it's been up to you at home to decide which of the contestants have behaved best. It's also been a barometer of what most people attach importance to. Together, we've arrived at a kind of common understanding of what characterises a good person, and these two tremendous, lovely finalists of ours are undeniably excellent examples. I think we, and you, have done a wonderful job. Don't you agree?'

Tollersrud received the applause he requested. The audience clapped and cheered.

'So then, of course, we come to the big question: how do we decide between them?'

Tollersrud stared intently into the camera lens before turning to face Toralf and Iselin.

'That, my dear contestants, is something you're going to have to find out for yourselves.'

The contestants exchanged looks again. Neither of them understood any of this. Tollersrud gave a lopsided grin.

'You heard right. Toralf Schanke and Iselin Skaar, you're going straight back into the House, and in the course of the next twenty-four hours you'll have to reach an agreement about which of you is the more worthy winner.'

Neither of the contestants could utter a word.

'And you're probably wondering how on earth you're going to manage to do this? Well, that's one of the things you're going to have to work out. By talking to each other. Really getting to know each other. By digging down into each other's past. By discussing your dreams for the future. But unlike earlier in the show' – Tollersrud gave a sly smile – 'this isn't a process you viewers will be allowed to witness … not until tomorrow, when we meet again for our live broadcast. Then we'll go through everything the finalists have discussed. For those of you who follow us on the net, we're also going to switch off the mics in the house, to avoid all the excitement being over and done with for those of you who switch on your TVs again tomorrow night at eight o'clock. It will still be possible to watch the contestants via our webcams, but it won't be possible to hear what they're talking about. This, dear contestants and audience, is the ultimate test for our contestants. The lovebirds.'

Everyone in the auditorium and on stage was digesting what was proposed.

Tollersrud now addressed the contestants. 'You aren't allowed to come to any conclusion before the clock has ticked down to zero. Nor are you permitted to agree to share the prize money when you meet again outside, once one of you has been awarded it. It has to be a genuine decision, and it must come from the heart, from you both. And if you don't succeed in arriving at a decision…' once again he waited for a moment; '…then neither of you will be declared the winner. Have you understood your task?'

Both Iselin and Toralf seemed lost for words, but in the end they nodded.

Emma thought it would be fascinating to see how the finalists resolved this dilemma. Not least because they'd also fallen in love in the midst of all this.

83

Blix pursued Tore Berg Tollersrud around the studio, waiting for an opportunity to speak to him in private in order to explain the potential threat. But when he managed to, it didn't seem as if the presenter took it very seriously.

'I expect you to keep a good eye on me,' he barked as he hurried to have his make-up removed.

After Blix had instructed Wibe to arrange continual twenty-four-hour surveillance for Tollersrud, he flopped down into a sofa in reception.

'Shall we go home?' Kovic asked.

'In a minute,' Blix said.

His thoughts alternated between the case he was working on and Iselin – who'd now reached the final. He'd only just managed to take in what was to happen in the next twenty-four hours.

It was one thing to distinguish a murderer from a care worker, for example. Most people would choose the same person if asked to point out which one had the better values or qualities. But how would Iselin and Toralf arrive at some sort of truth about what was worth most – one person's ethics, or the other's? Strictly speaking, it was an impossible task, because if one person gave in and relinquished the victory to the other, then that in itself would demonstrate the magnanimity that would make the loser the moral victor.

His thoughts turned to Teisen. He'd often mulled over whether he'd done the right thing when he'd shot and killed Emma's father. And had Gard Fosse actually taken the correct course of action, by following protocol and waiting for reinforcements? Which of them was the better person in that situation?

Even Eckhoff from the production team arrived with a folder tucked under his arm. 'Do you need me for anything else?'

Blix looked around. 'How many people will stay here overnight?' he asked.

'We've a minimum staff level of four,' Eckhoff explained.

'That's all?'

'Plus a security guard.'

Blix got to his feet. He nodded to Eckhoff as a sign that they were finished.

'I'll drive you home,' Blix said, speaking to Kovic. 'Where do you live?'

'I'll just take a taxi,' she said. 'Or you'll never get home yourself.'

Blix realised he was grateful for the suggestion. 'OK. See you tomorrow.'

Kovic walked out into the night. Blix was left standing with Eckhoff. He felt there was something else he ought to do or reassure himself about, but he could not for the life of him think what that might be.

'So what do you make of the final?' Eckhoff asked. 'Do you think your daughter will win?'

Blix shrugged.

'Well, it'll be all over tomorrow, at any rate,' Eckhoff said. 'That'll actually be something of a relief. It's been a long journey.'

Blix hated it when people used that word in such a context, but he nodded all the same. 'How are things with you?' he asked. 'Do *you* need a lift home?'

'No thanks,' Eckhoff replied. 'My car's in the garage.'

They parted and Blix headed for his car. Before he got in, he cast a backward glance at the TV headquarters. He'd been wrong, and was pleased about that. Nothing had taken place. The question, however, was where and when it was going to happen instead.

*

Emma felt weary. The combination of little sleep and a lot of work in the past week was beginning to tax her energy. Once she'd managed to contact Jonas Sakshaug and persuade him to tell her how disappointed and apologetic he was, she looked forward to going home and getting into bed.

She said goodbye to a *Se og Hør* journalist she knew and scooted round to the rear of the TV building where she'd parked her bike. She hoisted the bag containing her laptop and mobile up on to her shoulder and wrapped her scarf more tightly around her neck. The breath from her mouth formed a frosty mist in the air.

She had parked beside a double gate for vehicles. Several other bikes had been propped up there when Emma had dropped off hers, but now it was the only one left. A lamp above an entrance door close by was the only illumination in the area. She was surrounded by darkness.

She was taking out her keys when she stopped and wheeled around. A voice had called out to her, but she couldn't see where the sound had come from. All she could hear was shoes walking on the tarmac.

Then the person stepped partially out of the gloom.

'Emma.'

It wasn't spoken as a question. More like a declaration. The voice was muffled, indistinct, because of the scarf draped around the lower part of the face. The person also wore a hood that covered the head.

Instinctively she took a few steps back. She glanced around rapidly, looking for some way to escape, but she realised she was alone. There was nowhere to go. The exit gates were shut and the entrance door closed.

The man took a step closer. Emma's hand made its way down into her bag, where she'd stashed her alarm. But before she had even managed to pull it out, he pounced on her. There was a blue flash from an object in his hand.

Her body shook uncontrollably. Her muscles seemed to loosen and she couldn't make them tight again. She made every effort to struggle, trying to force out a scream. But she couldn't produce a single sound.

84

Emma opened her eyes a little, blinking in an effort to see more clearly. Grey walls, harsh light from the ceiling. The outline of a figure stepped in front of her.

'So there's still some life in you.'

A woman's voice.

Emma touched her head in panic – an instinctive response – then tried to haul herself up. The ground was hard and cold. Her body protested.

Swallowing hard, she blinked again as if to make sure she wasn't hallucinating. That it really was Sonja Nordstrøm sitting opposite.

She looked more exhausted than the video footage had shown. Her hair was dirty and unkempt, her cheeks hollow.

'Who are you?' Nordstrøm asked, her voice weak and rasping.

Emma cleared her throat and gave her name and occupation. Her eyes wandered around the room while she explained that she knew who Nordstrøm was and that they'd once met in an interview situation.

She recognised the room from the video broadcast. It had no windows, and only a solitary light bulb hung from the ceiling. A rank smell of faeces surrounded them. So there was no toilet in here, just a bucket placed as far away from Nordstrøm as possible.

They sat sizing each other up for a few seconds. As if they both had questions they wanted answered, but didn't know where to begin.

'How long have I been here?' Emma finally asked.

'A few hours,' Nordstrøm told her, automatically looking down at her arm, even though there was no wristwatch there.

'Do you know where we are?'

Nordstrøm shook her head. 'But we're not in the city, I do know that,' she said. 'It's completely silent. I think we must be on an old farm or something.'

Emma looked around again, but couldn't see her bag. 'What about you?' she asked. 'How long have *you* been here?'

'I've stopped counting the days.'

Silence enveloped them again.

'Is there...?' Nordstrøm looked away for a moment. 'Is anyone asking for me out there?' she asked in the end. 'Are they searching for me?'

The tenderness in her question surprised Emma. In her autobiography, Sonja Nordstrøm had appeared to be a results-oriented machine that had never bothered about other people, or worried whether other people bothered about her. Now Emma registered both loss and longing in her voice.

'Is that what you're wondering?' Emma tried to smile.

'I don't mean most people,' Nordstrøm said. 'I'm thinking of ... my family. Liselotte. My daughter.'

Emma had seen an interview with Nordstrøm's daughter in one of the major newspapers. She hadn't got the impression that the relationship between the two was especially warm or close.

Despite this, Emma said: 'She's very worried about you. Everyone is.'

It looked as if Nordstrøm took this to heart. Appreciated it.

Emma brooded over what time it was and whether anyone *she* knew had begun to feel concern about her. Blix, maybe. With a bit of luck he'd already initiated a search. However, this thought didn't fill Emma with hope. The police had tried to trace Nordstrøm for a week now, and they hadn't come anywhere near finding her.

'I was just about to turn in for the night when the doorbell rang.'

Emma looked at Nordstrøm, who was shaking her head.

'I thought it was Stian.'

'Josefson?' Emma asked. 'The writer?'

'He'd called in earlier that evening,' Nordstrøm said. 'He ... I ... We... ' Once again she stared out into space before continuing: 'But before I could close the door, I was stunned by that ... shock thing.'

Picturing it in her mind's eye, Emma regretted her own hesitation when she saw the man approach her outside TV headquarters. If she'd been quicker, she could have set off her safety alarm.

'Do you know anything about the man who attacked you?' Emma asked. 'Have you seen him since?'

'He comes here with food now and again. And something to drink.'

She pointed at a hatch near the bottom of the door. Reminiscent of a cat flap.

'Does he ever say anything?'

She shook her head.

'So you don't even know if he's Norwegian?'

'No.'

'You've never been given any explanation for why you're here, either?'

Emma was about to add 'and why he hasn't killed you yet', but fortunately managed to bite her tongue. Nordstrøm simply shook her head again.

Emma shifted slightly, aware of how stiff and sore she felt. The floor was concrete, covered in old dust and dirt. And she realised that, despite the circumstances and the dire situation they both found themselves in, she was still working. She pondered whether to tell her about the countdown and all the other victims, but decided there was no reason to cause Nordstrøm more anxiety than necessary.

'Have you tried to escape?' she asked instead.

Nordstrøm sniffed. 'I've tried everything. But the walls are made of concrete and that door there...' She pointed at it. 'At least ten centimetres thick. I've no idea what it's made of, but the material is hard. Oak, maybe. And I don't have anything I could use to knock or hammer with either. Anyway, he's got cameras, so he must be watching all the time.' She nodded at the ceiling.

Emma glanced up. There were two solid smoked-glass globes on the ceiling. She couldn't see the actual cameras, but they were behind them, too high to reach. One of the globes was spattered with grime, either food or something else that Nordstrøm must have thrown up at it.

'But now there are two of us,' she said. 'We'll have to make the most of that.'

Emma could only admire the woman facing her. She hadn't been here for more than a few minutes – in a conscious state at least – and already she was aware of how the walls closed in on her; the smell of faeces and damp; the cold rising from the floor and oozing in through the walls. It all made her desperate to escape.

Sonja Nordstrøm had lived here for a week now, and there was still no sign she had given up. Of course she'd always had her own way of mustering more strength than her opponents – had built a philosophy around it. It was a matter of embracing the pain. Loving it. Never showing your competitors that you're feeling awful, but instead giving them the impression that you have an inexhaustible source of energy.

It was her psychology just as much as her physique that had made her 'forever number one'.

This thought gave Emma hope.

Nordstrøm paced to and fro, as if in a hurry to move from one wall to the other. Emma could see that she was brooding about something.

'We have to catch him off guard somehow,' Nordstrøm said, as much to herself as to Emma. 'Take him by surprise. Find something we can use to injure him.'

All at once she stopped and scrutinised Emma's face.

'What is it?'

'You're wearing earrings. They might be sharp enough.'

Emma touched her ears, but the little studs wouldn't be much use as weapons.

Nordstrøm continued to pace the room restlessly, scratching her head. Emma took off her shoes and felt the soles. Too thin. They wouldn't cause much damage or inflict much pain.

Soon Nordstrøm sat down against the wall again, on the other side of Emma, with her hands around her knees.

'I heard a bang not long ago,' Nordstrøm said. 'Before you came down here.'

'A bang?'

'A shot.'

'From a pistol, do you mean?'

'Yes, or ... a rifle or ... something. I don't know much about guns. Sometimes there are other people here,' she added. 'I've heard voices. Footsteps.'

Nordstrøm lifted her eyes towards the ceiling. Emma wondered what this meant. Whether something might happen soon.

After a long, oppressive silence, Nordstrøm said: 'I've never told my daughter I love her.' She stared vacantly into the distance. 'Not one single time.' Her voice was slow and thoughtful. 'I have a grandchild too, one I've hardly ever met. A boy.'

'What's his name?'

'Simon.'

Emma saw that Nordstrøm's eyes were shining.

'I don't even know if he remembers what I look like. Whether they ever even mention me.'

She was about to add something else, but stopped herself.

'How old is he?' Emma asked, as gently as she could. It seemed as if Nordstrøm was keen to answer, but she contented herself with holding five fingers up in the air.

Emma had more she was desperate to ask about, but saw that Nordstrøm was blinking fiercely and rubbing her hands quickly over her face. Then she raised her eyes to the ceiling – she seemed to be trying to destroy the cameras with her steely glare.

Emma wanted to say something encouraging, something to give Nordstrøm hope that she'd be able to meet her grandchild again, something about there being endless opportunities in the future to tell her daughter that she loved her. But she dropped the idea, unsure if she even believed it herself.

85

Emma was losing her grip on time. She'd no idea whether thirty minutes or two hours had passed. However, it felt as if the walls were creeping ever closer.

All of a sudden she heard footsteps – they sounded as if they were on a nearby staircase. Keys jangling.

Emma struggled to think quickly. If they were to have any chance of catching the kidnapper unawares, they would have to do it fast and hard. But there was nowhere to hide. No doors or cupboards to stand behind. No objects or tools to use as weapons.

The footsteps drew nearer. Emma got ready: she'd pounce on him as soon as the door was open, she'd kick it in, towards him, and then go after his hands. His groin. Attempt to put him out of action.

The key was inserted in the lock. Turned slowly around. First once, then a second time.

'No,' said the voice on the other side of the door. 'I can see what you're doing, Emma.'

She swiftly raised her eyes to the ceiling cameras.

'Step back,' the man said. Had she heard his voice somewhere before?

'Stand against the wall.'

The noises in the lock had stopped. Emma looked at Nordstrøm, who gave her a do-as-he-says nod. Emma backed off, slowly, until she came to a halt at the wall. Put her hands behind her back, reluctant to let their captor see them. Nordstrøm remained seated on the floor with her legs crossed. Hands folded. Her eyes fixed on the door.

Then the key was turned all the way round. A metallic clang struck the walls. The door slid towards them. And then he stood in the doorway, the man who'd sneaked up on Emma behind the TV building in Nydalen.

Was it Dahlmann? She wasn't sure.

He had a hood over his head. A shadow seemed to fall across his face. He held a pistol in one hand.

As he stepped into the room he raised his gun. Pointing first at Emma, and then at Nordstrøm.

And then he pulled the trigger.

86

At the morning meeting Blix had to endure a reprimand from Gard Fosse, who felt that the operation at Enter Entertainment's premises had been unnecessary and used a disproportionate amount of their scarce resources, without producing any results. When Blix argued that it was impossible to know in advance whether or not the killer would try to strike, Fosse insisted the operation had been based on weak evidence rather than robust information.

'Police work isn't a guessing game,' he raged.

Blix and his fellow investigators knew they hadn't had a choice, though. If anything had happened without them trying to prevent or hinder it, the criticism would have been even sharper.

'The CEO of the production company has demanded an explanation,' Fosse continued, tearing a sheet from his notepad. 'I've promised him a meeting at nine o'clock. You can go.'

He placed the paper with the CEO's contact details on the desk and pushed it towards Blix, who flung out his arms in protest – he already had more than enough to deal with.

'It's your mess,' Fosse said, rising from his chair. 'The final show is tonight, and you'll have to try to tell them they've nothing to fear.'

Blix let his chin drop to his chest. He wanted to put up a fight, but was fed up wasting time and energy defending his actions.

'Yesterday's decision was correct,' Kovic said once Fosse had left the room. 'I can come with you.'

Blix was about to object, but then nodded and glanced at the clock. 'I could do with some help. We'll also have to go through yesterday's footage while we're there.'

They went down into the basement car park. Kovic settled behind the steering wheel and they set off.

Blix didn't know whether to be pleased or not. Nothing had happened the previous night. The only explanation was that their presence had prevented an attack. Dahlmann hadn't been there, he was sure of that. But Dahlmann wasn't the man they were looking for. The real perpetrator could have been in the audience or in the general vicinity, which meant that in addition to the footage from the broadcast they would have to look through all the CCTV coverage.

In Nydalen, Kovic swung around the corner at the subway station. At the end of the road they could see the vast studio building and the production bus.

Blix checked the note he'd received from Fosse.

'We're to go in round the back this time,' he said.

Kovic turned into the back entrance. A few cars were parked in reserved spaces, but there were 'no parking' signs in the rest of the area.

'There,' Blix said, indicating a gate for larger vehicles. Kovic squeezed the car through it and stopped, trying to ensure they blocked as little of the gate as possible. Blix produced the 'Police Vehicle in Service' sign and placed it on the front windscreen.

'If you could just move that bike a tad for me, then I won't be in anyone's way,' Kovic suggested, nodding at the side window.

Blix hopped out and skirted around the car. He took hold of the saddle and handlebars, but immediately stopped short. The bicycle was black with narrow tyres and goat-horn handlebars. The word WHITE was embossed in grey script on the carbon frame, and the wheel rims had pink speckles here and there.

Emma's bike was exactly like this. It had been propped up in her hallway when he visited. Maybe she was here to do a write-up on the final?

The cycle was locked so Blix had to lift it aside. At the same time he noticed a bunch of keys on the ground, right beside the back wheel. They were attached to a blue-and-white braid, typical of something a child might make at nursery.

He put the bike down again and picked up the keys. Kovic rolled down the side window.

'What is it?' she asked.

'It's Emma Ramm's bike,' Blix told her. 'Her keys are lying here too.'

'She was here last night,' Kovic said.

Blix took out his phone. 'I haven't heard anything more from her,' he said, searching for Emma's name in his call list. 'She was definitely aware we were involved in an operation here. Strange that she didn't follow it up.'

He tapped in her number and was immediately diverted to voicemail.

'Hm,' he said to himself, looking instead for the news.no number.

Anita Grønvold answered the phone on the third ring.

'Emma's not here,' she said. 'She doesn't often come in, in fact. Have you tried the café, Kalle's Choice?'

'Not yet,' Blix said, disconnecting the call before she asked any more questions.

He tried Emma one more time, but without success; the feeling that something had happened to her grew within him.

'The personal safety alarm,' he said, as much to himself as to Kovic. 'We can check the location of the alarm, can't we?'

He called Krohn and filled him in on the situation. Over the phone he heard fingers clattering over the keyboard.

'Negative,' Krohn said.

'Negative?' Blix reiterated, looking across at Kovic. 'What do you mean?'

'The alarm's not turned on,' Krohn clarified.

'She's switched it off completely, you mean?'

'Yes,' Krohn confirmed. 'Or someone else has done that for her.'

87

Emma put her head in her hands and felt the panic wash over her. She tried to scream, but could barely gasp.

Sonja Nordstrøm collapsed on her side, a big, round hole in her chest. The blood spread out beneath her body as her wide-open eyes stared vacantly into space.

The man lowered his gun and fixed his eyes on Emma. She held out her shaking hands.

'Please,' she begged. 'Don't shoot.' Her voice trembled as she struggled to absorb what had just happened.

She glanced at the man, but her vision seemed clouded by fear. She couldn't make out his features. Was it Dahlmann? She couldn't match the old pictures she'd seen with the man in front of her.

The rancid, metallic smell of blood mixed with the stink of excrement. She staggered, took a step to one side and pleaded, again, for him not to kill her too.

But instead of pointing the gun at her, he said: 'Come with me.'

Emma gulped. The noise of the shot still whistled in her ears. The man gestured with the pistol that she should move.

Slowly she took a step towards him. 'Please,' she said.

The man did not answer.

In her mind's eye she saw Irene, Martine, Grandma. Blix and Kasper also turned up in her thoughts, but Emma blinked and tried to force them away.

'You first,' the man said.

Emma concentrated on her breathing. She filled her lungs with air and tried to gather her strength, her courage.

'Where...?' she stuttered.

'Up.'

He motioned again with the gun, impatient now.

'But...'

The man shook out a wristwatch from inside the sleeve of his hoodie.

'Come on,' he said sharply, taking a step aside to let her pass.

Emma was unsteady on her feet, but she managed to move out of the room and up the steep, squeaky staircase. As she held on to the bannister, she felt she was beginning to regain her composure. She weighed up whether to attempt something – to turn around, kick out, try to hit his head or the pistol she knew was aimed at her back, and then run, as fast as her legs would carry her. But there was too much that could go wrong. The man had his finger on the trigger, and even if she managed to land a blow, it was far from certain that he would lose his grip on the gun.

As she reached the top of the stairs, she saw that she was inside a barn. The daylight dazzled her eyes. The barn door was open. A cold gust blasted at her. The man indicated with the gun that she should go outside. She passed a large, dark-red stain on the concrete floor. It looked like blood or paint, and at once her thoughts turned to what Sonja Nordstrøm had said about a shot being fired.

The man had her walk towards a huge, white-painted house. As she moved across a farmyard, towards the house steps, she looked around. On all sides trees surrounded an expanse of grassy land. It would be useless to shout for help; there were no other houses or people nearby.

'Go inside,' he said.

Emma pushed the door open and entered a wide hallway. The heat from a black tiled stove hit her full force, but she could smell something other than wood burning in there; she didn't know what. Something mouldy or rotten, perhaps.

The hallway led into a more spacious room at the far end. The man grabbed her arm and roughly manoeuvred her in through another door, into an old kitchen.

'What do you want from me?' she asked.

'Sit down,' he said, pointing at a bench on the wall below the window.

Another fit of trembling overwhelmed her, making her dizzy. She had to hold on to the kitchen table for a moment, before squeezing in behind it. The window was speckled with damp patches between the two layers of glass, and she felt a draught leaking in. Outside, the forest was almost touching the house walls.

The man removed a candlestick, a newspaper, a glass and a ballpoint pen from the table. Emma's bag lay on the floor beside the fridge, with her laptop jutting out. The man picked up the bag and placed it on the table before her.

'What is it you want with me?' she asked again.

The man gazed at her for a long time before answering.

'I want you to interview me.'

88

'Interview you?' Emma asked in confusion.

'Isn't that your job?' he asked, pushing the bag nearer. 'The media have been talking and writing about me for days. Speculating about who I am and why I've done what I have. Someone has to write the true story. I've chosen you.'

Emma gulped. Stared at him.

'Take out your laptop.'

The man pulled up a chair and sat facing her, letting the hand with the pistol rest on the table.

Emma drew the bag towards her.

'There's no point looking for your panic alarm,' the man said, as if reading her thoughts. 'I've got it here,' he said, patting his trouser pocket.

Emma met his gaze and slowly took her laptop out of the bag.

Emma had no idea what to do or say. He smiled at her, before checking the time again and telling her to begin.

Emma stared blankly into thin air for a few seconds and then said: 'Do you think ... would it be possible to have a glass of water?'

He looked suspiciously at her.

'I'm thirsty,' she said.

He took several seconds to make up his mind, and then stood up and crossed to the sink. Soon he returned, the gun still in one hand, a glass of water in the other.

Emma tried to give him a grateful smile. Her hand was shaking when she picked up the glass and lifted it to her lips. She spilled some water, and used her hand to wipe it away. She put down the glass.

'Thanks,' she said.

The man gestured at the laptop with the pistol. Emma opened the lid. She had fifty-four per cent battery power left, enough for a couple of hours.

'I need electricity,' she said all the same, pulling a cable from her bag.

The man pointed at a plug point beside the bench. Emma pushed in the plug, connected it to her laptop and opened her word processing program.

'OK,' she said hesitantly, as she moved the cursor to the network icon and clicked. The machine began to search for Wi-Fi networks. 'Maybe we could begin with who you are? What's your name?'

'My name's not important. That'll come to light in the fullness of time.'

No Wi-Fi networks.

She cleared her throat. 'I see,' she said softly. 'Where were you born, then? Where did you grow up?'

'That's of no consequence either.'

'What kind of education did you have?' she asked tentatively. 'Where did you attend school?'

'To hell with that.'

Emma shifted in her seat. 'I have to start somewhere,' she said, glancing up at him. Waiting for him to take the initiative.

He was quiet for a moment. Then he cleared his throat and said: 'When I was younger, I wanted to become a film director. Steven Spielberg, Ingmar Bergman. I was keen to use my talent, and to be recognised for that. For the person I really am.'

'And who are you?' Emma ventured. The man didn't answer.

'Some people achieve positions they don't deserve,' he said instead. 'They become rich and famous without possessing a single talent, other than tits they've paid good money for, or songs someone else has written for them. And at the same time there are talents, geniuses, who are never noticed.'

'Like you?' she asked, typing.

He didn't answer for a moment.

'They never noticed,' he said, his voice angrier. 'They never ... fucking ... noticed.'

'What should they have noticed?' Emma said.

'My talents!' he yelled. 'My genius. But no one cared. No one. And then...' He shook his head.

Emma continued typing as he elaborated on how he'd come to despise people who'd excelled and succeeded while he was left to dream.

'But look at me now,' he said proudly. 'Who are they talking about out there? Who's on everyone's lips? Who are they desperately trying to figure out? Who,' he said, 'are they afraid of?'

He paused briefly.

'I've done them all a favour, you know,' he said.

Emma knew he meant the celebrities he had killed.

'I've given them immortality. Because of me, people will talk about them for years. I've freed them from the miserable lives they were living,' he said breathlessly. 'Take Sonja Nordstrøm, for instance. Who'd won everything it was possible to win, but who never managed to live like a normal person. Who pushed away everyone she loved. Her daughter. Her husband. Her colleagues. Her competitors. Even when she wrote her autobiography, her main concern was to denigrate other people. It says something about the kind of life she led, how incredibly cold she was. I don't think I could come across a lonelier person.'

Emma couldn't figure out how the man felt that killing Nordstrøm could be regarded as a compassionate act. Her typing faltered for a few seconds.

'And Ragnar Ole Theodorsen, who'd spent the past twenty years of his life trying to recreate a hit that consisted of four chords. Four! How difficult can it be?' He raised his voice a notch. 'And Calle Seeberg chipped in by giving talentless people like Theodorsen airtime and an audience. What sort of life was that?'

He gave a loud snort.

'He was in ill health too, you know. Maybe he was keen to prolong his life, but he didn't have the discipline to go through with it.' He shook his head. 'I've seen his training runs, if you can call them that. Calle Seeberg was a feeble person. Losing people like that is no great loss to humanity.'

Emma saw how completely wrapped up he was in his own narrative. No matter what she said, it would never persuade him to examine his own actions in a different light.

'Exactly the same as Jeppe Sørensen. He was already suicidal. He'd given up. I just nudged him over the finishing line.'

He raised his eyes to the left, as if a memory had appeared there.

'Jessica Flatebø, she'd also given up. The poor soul was so sorry for herself over all the hatred aimed at her because she stripped off on TV. No one believed her when she said she wasn't trying to attract attention. Boo hoo.'

Emma gaped at him. What terrified her most was the total lack of regret.

'I knew Jeppe, you know,' the man said in an aside. 'Jeppe was an idiot. A scumbag.' An angry expression came over his face. 'He injured his knee. Same as me. He ... behaved as if his problems were greater than everyone else's. That *he* was greater than everyone else. Just because he was a footballer and had scored a couple of goals for the Danish national team? I've met more than enough people like that in my life.'

He was fuming now.

'Jeppe Sørensen was an arrogant piece of shit.'

Emma wrote as fast as she could, realising that what the man was saying about Jeppe was the first thing he'd let drop that might be used to identify him.

'So you received treatment at the Athlete's Retreat too?' she asked carefully, hoping that Kasper had managed to obtain a list of patients and found the name of the man now sitting opposite her, holding a gun.

His eyes flickered and he swallowed a few times.

'What happened to your knee?' she asked, hoping to distract him from his thoughts.

He shook his head. 'I twisted it,' he said. 'The cruciate ligament tore right off. I got a tidy sum through insurance, fortunately.'

He fell silent, smiling in satisfaction.

'But it happened in Denmark?'

'That makes no odds,' he said, becoming serious again.

Emma let it go. 'Was that when you began to make your plans?' she asked instead. 'While you were recovering from your injury?'

'More or less.' He exhaled audibly, almost a groan. 'Jeppe Sørensen was such a moron, I wanted him to die. And everywhere they were going on about "number seven will never return to the football field". The Danish newspapers were full of it. TV as well. His club decided to retire his shirt number, to honour him. It made me throw up. I could see that fucking number seven all over the place.'

'But he wasn't the first?'

He raised his eyes to meet hers. 'What do you mean?'

'No one starts a countdown with the number seven,' Emma said. 'You normally begin with ten, five or three.'

'He wasn't the first, no, you're right about that.'

He didn't elaborate. Instead he continued talking about himself in grand words and phrases. Emma had changed to noting only key words now. His story described a quest for attention. The murders and the way the countdown was managed were ways to draw the spotlight to him. So he'd picked victims who fitted his overall project: people who either didn't deserve to be celebrities, or who handled their elevated status badly. Emma's part was to tell the world what a genius he really was. 'I've always been left to my own devices,' he said with a trace of bitterness. 'I've always stood in the shadow of others. But not anymore. All I've done up till now, I've done entirely on my own.'

Emma didn't want to ask him anything more, but she had to keep him talking – it seemed to her the only way to stop him hurting her, or to give the police time to find her.

'Can't you tell me something about that?' Emma asked.

The man heaved a loud sigh as he mulled this over.

'I was a wimp as a child. Skinny and delicate. One day I decided to do something about it. To grow big and strong. It requires discipline to do that. Self-discipline and stickability.' He nodded with pleasure.

'What else have you managed to do?' Emma asked.

He glanced at the clock as he answered: 'That's beside the point.'

Emma thought about the countdown, which was now almost complete. Dare she mention it?

'Who is number two?' she asked carefully.

He met her gaze.

'You just killed Sonja Nordstrøm, so I presume you've already killed number two. Who was she? Or he?'

He gave a lopsided smile. 'Have you really not worked it out yet?'

Emma shook her head slightly. He went on smiling, but made no sign of answering.

'Who did you begin with, then?' she asked. 'Who was number ten?'

Something glinted in his eyes. His self-satisfied smile vanished. 'Are you nearly finished?' he asked.

Emma looked at him in bewilderment. After all, they'd only just started. He stood up abruptly and paced around the floor, before standing at the window, staring out.

'That's enough for now,' he said, looking at the time.

'But...'

'You probably need some time to edit and polish the interview,' he said, motioning at her with the pistol. 'So get cracking. I'm running out of time.'

89

At 11.32 a.m., Gard Fosse gave Blix permission to report Emma Ramm missing. Afterwards Blix sat leaning over his desk, studying the picture of her used in the all-points bulletin. There wasn't much more he could do. He and Kovic had been to her door, called into Kalle's Choice and paid a visit to her sister.

Their routine inquiries had not yielded anything substantial. No activity had been noted on her phone or bank account, and none of the hospitals had her name listed as a patient. The personal safety alarm still did not respond when pinged.

Striding across the room, Wibe approached his desk. 'She's working with an interesting guy,' he said.

Blix looked at the papers Wibe held in his hand.

'He turned up on Dahlmann's prison visitors list,' Wibe explained. 'Henrik Wollan. He works for news.no.'

Blix nodded. He was familiar with the name.

'What was he doing visiting Dahlmann in jail?' he asked.

'No idea, but he's the only person on the visitors list who also turns up in our investigation material.'

'How is he part of our investigation?'

'He was at Hvaler when Jeppe Sørensen's body was found. He was first to report on it.'

'He is a journalist, after all,' Kovic commented.

Blix sat back in his chair and stared doubtfully at Wibe.

'All the same, we should have a chat with him,' Wibe countered.

His phone rang. It was Merete. She probably wanted to talk about Iselin and the final episode of *Worthy Winner*. He let it ring out.

'Yes, OK. Will you do that?' he asked.

Wibe nodded. Blix's phone began to ring again. Not Merete this time, but Øyvind Krohn.

'You asked me to track Emma Ramm's personal safety alarm,' Krohn said.

'Yes?'

'It was activated fifteen seconds ago.'

90

Emma was writing.

Trying to write, at least. Trying to believe this was just an ordinary article she was working on, but her fingers were cold and her thoughts far from the words in front of her. It didn't help that the man the piece described was pacing impatiently to and fro across the kitchen floor with a pistol in his hand. Her mind continually returned to the idea that this would be absolutely the last thing she would do in life. She would function as a microphone for him, a killer.

The thought made her feel sick. She tried to think of a way to smuggle information into the text to reveal where she was, and who the man was standing at the kitchen window. But she knew neither his name nor their location. She had no messages to hide.

Emma tried to build up the article in chronological order, focusing on the murder victims. He'd simply pushed Mona Kleven in front of a subway train after sabotaging the CCTV cameras. She'd been given many chances in life, but according to the killer her fame had brought her nothing but sharp elbows she used to push other people aside so that she could get ahead.

She included a digression he'd interjected about how unfair life was. That someone could smoke and drink and live a morally reprehensible life until they were a hundred, while others ate and lived healthily, but nevertheless died before they were thirty. She wove in the preposterous information that someone could win 183 million kroner in the Viking Lottery, while others struggled to balance their books. She described how he'd killed Thor Willy Opsahl by hanging him from a hook in the roof of his garage, and leaving him dangling there while he drove away in the dead man's elegant Audi.

She repeated word for word his contemptuous words about the televangelist, together with his description of how satisfying it had been to see him 'meet his Maker far earlier than he'd ever imagined'.

She refrained from mentioning that the numbers two and ten were missing from his great project.

'You can call me the Stage Master,' he said all of a sudden.

'The Stage Master?' she asked.

'Use it as your headline,' he said, as if he had been considering this for a while. 'That's what I've done – put all this on a public stage.'

Emma did as he requested. She typed the headline and inserted a paragraph to explain the title.

'Don't make it long-winded or elaborate,' he warned her, looking at the clock. 'You'll have to round it off now.'

'What's the hurry?' Emma asked meekly.

'You've got two minutes,' was all he said.

'Two minutes?'

Emma was overwhelmed by panic again. She felt as if she were being strangled. In two minutes he would no longer have any use for her.

She tried to swallow, force back the tears, but she couldn't resist them; she began to sob and shake. When he aggressively told her to quit that, she just began to cry even more.

Emma had thought, and hoped, that she would be able to offer more resistance, to fight him, physically even, but it was as if the muscles in her body failed to obey or even understand what they were supposed to do. Her brain didn't function either; she was unable to think rationally.

'What…?' Her throat was dry. 'What will happen afterwards?' she asked in a quivering voice. 'To me?'

He did not answer. The tears poured from her eyes. He put his hand down into his trouser pocket and took out the panic alarm. Left it on the table in front of her and smiled.

'They'll think you're the one who's set it off,' he said.

Emma looked at him in disbelief. 'Have you switched it on?'

He nodded, still with a smile on his face. Emma couldn't understand any of it; this would summon the police here. Immediately.

'I did it ten minutes ago,' he said, sounding pleased with himself. 'They'll be here in…' he glanced at the clock again '…twenty minutes or so. Maybe a bit more.'

Emma shook her head. She understood nothing of what was going on in this man's head. Unless his plan all along had been to be shot and killed by the police when his work was complete. Then he'd avoid being tried for any of the things he'd done. Or else he had a plan for the police as well when they arrived on the scene.

Twenty minutes, she thought. She must stay alive for twenty minutes.

She looked at the text in front of her. Far from finished.

All at once she closed the screen. Snapped it shut.

'Are you done?' he asked.

'No,' she said.

'But…'

She grabbed the laptop and hit it hard on the table, over and over again, trying to smash the screen. Without an interview he wouldn't achieve what he desired.

It was clear from the panic in his eyes that he understood, and he launched himself at her. Emma shoved the table towards him, but it was big and heavy. She couldn't manage to move it more than a few centimetres, but it was enough to slow him down a bit and provide more room for her own legs, so that she could get to her feet. Then she threw the laptop at the window with all her might.

The laptop bounced back and fell on the floor. It didn't shatter, only cracked. It seemed as intact as ever.

The man leapt around to the other side of the table to retrieve it. Seizing her chance, Emma stormed out into the dark hallway, making for the front door, but before she could reach it he'd caught up with her, jerking her backwards as he grabbed her jacket with one hand and her hair with the other.

The movement made her wig come loose and it slid off in his hand. He was so astonished that he let go of her jacket as well. Emma propelled herself towards the door and tore it open.

She took the steps in two desperate leaps, hungrily devouring the cool air as she ran towards the dense forest.

She hadn't covered much ground when she heard him on the gravel behind her. In blind panic, she ran for all she was worth, but the past twenty-four hours had drained her. He was upon her before she'd reached the trees. He flung her to the ground and pressed her head into the grass.

Emma felt one arm locked in his grip behind her back. He pushed his other arm over against her neck, and she realised he was trying to block an artery. He was strong; she understood now how little chance the others had had. She was trapped; she couldn't fight him.

Without warning he let go.

Then she heard a noise. As if someone was striking sparks. Then came the pain, and her muscles were paralysed. Her eyes saw only darkness.

91

'Let's hope this isn't another false alarm,' Blix said. 'Or some kind of diversionary tactic.'

Kovic looked across at him. They'd left Majorstua behind and were on their way towards Røa.

Motorists dutifully pulled over to let them through. They had soon passed Røa en route to Sørkedalen, where soon the houses were more scattered, farms took over and Nordmarka spread out on the right-hand side. Several patrol cars were in pursuit, but Blix and Kovic led the pack.

'The location's not very far from the cabin where Jessica Flatebø was found,' Kovic remarked – she was moving back and forth from the map displayed on her mobile screen. 'It ... looks like a farm.'

Yet another farm, Blix thought. The sense of being tricked overwhelmed him once again.

'Have we traced the owner?' he asked.

Kovic opened a message from the police operations centre.

'It belonged to a man who died eighteen months ago,' she read out.

'Who owns it now?'

'It looks like a company.'

'OK, so who owns the company?'

Kovic read on a little. 'It doesn't say.'

'No information at all?'

'It says something about a foreign bank, but no name or contact details.'

Shaking his head, Blix kept a tight hold on the steering wheel as he manoeuvred the car on through Sørkedalen. Soon he took a right turn into Zinoberveien and swept past a car park. The tarmac surface gave way to gravel and pebbles. Although Blix had often skied in Nordmarka, he was far from familiar with the terrain. He knew there was a profusion of tracks, rivers and lakes in the area they were traversing now, forests and wilderness where people liked to go hiking at all times of the year. But it was also the perfect place in which to hide from the outside world.

'How long is it since the alarm was activated?'

'Twenty-eight minutes.'

'How long have we left to drive, approximately?'

'We should be at the turnoff any moment.'

Blix dropped his speed. The road had narrowed almost to a single lane.

'It's over there on the right,' Kovic said, pointing at a narrow track curving off from the road. Braking, Blix swung on to it, tall shrubs on either side. Branches lashed and scraped the sides of the car.

'Shit!' Kovic exclaimed, twisting her neck back towards something they'd passed.

'What is it?'

'Didn't you see the camera?'

'What camera?' Blix took his foot off the accelerator and turned his head.

'There was a CCTV camera hanging in one of the trees just after the turnoff,' Kovic told him.

'So he may be watching our approach,' Blix said. 'Bloody hell.'

'Brake,' Kovic said. 'It's just around this bend.'

They drove through a grove of closely packed trees. There was light further ahead. Blix braked even harder and stopped where the trees ended and an extensive grassy area stretched out before them. A white-painted house could be seen in the distance, smoke curling from the chimney. A satellite dish was attached to one wall, and there was a barn, partly hidden by the house.

'How far behind are the others?' Blix asked.

'Four or five minutes, maybe,' Kovic replied.

The car engine was running, but it was making so much noise that Blix switched it off. All at once they were enveloped in total silence.

'There's a light at the window,' Kovic said.

Blix sat studying the house, searching for movement at the windows.

An alarm broke the stillness. Intermittent and piercing, and unmistakeable: a smoke alarm.

Blix and Kovic exchanged looks before turning their eyes back to the house. Something grey billowed up inside one of the windows.

'Damn and blast,' he said, turning the ignition to start the car. 'Call it in!'

Kovic grabbed the police radio while Blix stepped on the gas, making the wheels spin on the gravel. The acceleration whipped them both back.

'We're really exposed!' she yelled. 'He's probably armed. We should wait for backup.'

Blix didn't reply, and they continued heading for the white house. More and more smoke was visible inside the windows, and the alarm continued to screech.

When they reached the farmyard, Blix stood on the brakes and opened the car door before the vehicle had completely stopped. Jumping out, he unholstered his gun and clicked off the safety catch.

'I'm going in,' he said to Kovic, who was still in the car.

'Alex...' she began.

'Stay here and cover the exit. Stay in touch with the centre. I have to see if Emma's in there.'

With a single leap he mounted the steps and tugged at the door. It was open. He pulled it towards him, and the acrid smell of smoke hit him full blast. He took a couple of deep breaths of clean air. And then plunged in.

Inside, he held one hand over his mouth. Coughed once. Shouted Emma's name. No answer.

The hallway was wide with a high ceiling. The floor was covered in solid wooden planks that creaked beneath his feet.

'Emma?!'

Still no answer. But he could hear something else that disturbed him even more.

The crackle of flames, coming in short bursts. The popping of timber as it buckled, the fluttering sound of tongues of flames licking up over a wall or curtain.

It was impossible to hear whether there was anyone else in the house. Footsteps or movements, or even shouts – everything was drowned out by the noise from the fire and the shrieking smoke alarm.

He rounded a corner. With his gun at the ready, he advanced as fast as he dared. His eyes had begun to smart. He coughed again, and put his arm across his face. Reached another open door. But the hallway continued on, and further in, on the floor, outside what he assumed to be a living room, he spotted a motionless pair of feet and trouser legs.

'Emma?!' he shouted again.

Keeping one arm over his mouth, he held his pistol in front of him with the other. Hunkering down to make himself smaller, he moved forwards.

A spurt of flame lit up the room. The legs on the floor must belong to a man. The shoes were large.

Blix came closer.

The man was stretched out on his side. On the floor, beside his right hand, lay a gun. He had a gaping hole in his head. Nonetheless, it was not difficult to see who this was.

Walter Georg Dahlmann.

Further inside the house he heard the pop and crash of a minor explosion. The flames were taking hold of the room. Blix pulled back. He wouldn't be able to remove Dahlmann's body from the house. He had to concentrate on finding Emma. Calling out her name, spluttering and floundering, he tumbled into another room. It was empty, apart from a number of gas bottles propped up against one wall. The stench of propane seeped ominously up from the floorboards.

He lurched back into the hallway; he was starting to feel dizzy now and it was difficult to get his bearings. The smoke stung his eyes. He screwed them shut for a few seconds. When he opened them again, he could make out the main door somewhere ahead of him through the smoke. Using the wall for support, he staggered forwards, coughing profusely, until he was out and could feel the steps beneath his feet.

Kovic charged towards him.

'We need to move back,' he shouted. 'The building could explode.'

Kovic scrambled into the car as Blix stumbled across the farmyard to the forest's edge. Kovic reversed the car all the way back before dashing over to him.

'Are they nearly here?' Blix yelled.

'Yes,' Kovic replied. 'Can't you hear the sirens?'

But Blix still had the noise of the smoke alarms ringing in his ears. He shook his head in an effort to recover his wits.

The next moment, the air ripped apart.

92

The explosion hurled a searing whirlwind towards Kovic and Blix, knocking him over. He staggered to his feet and watched as the fresh oxygen from outdoors made the inferno burn even more strongly. The flames cast orange lights and shadows all around. The smoke changed character and became darker, almost black.

'Dahlmann was in there,' he said. 'He was dead, with a gun beside him.'

Kovic took a few paces towards the blazing house, as if she wanted to come closer to an answer about what had happened.

'Did he take his own life?' she asked, mostly as a deduction. 'Maybe he knew we were closing in on him? That it was all over.'

Blix heard another, smaller explosion in another part of the house. The flames that followed lunged out on one side, like arms and fists, before shooting upwards.

Blix hawked a few times; it felt as if his lungs were full of soot.

'What about Emma?' Kovic asked.

Blix shook his head. 'I don't know,' he answered. 'She might still be in there.'

The first patrol car entered the farmyard and stopped a good distance from the flames. A young police officer approached Kovic and Blix.

'Is the fire brigade far away?' Kovic asked.

The officer glanced back in the direction he had come from. 'Maybe quarter of an hour.'

'Check the barn and the rear of the house,' Blix said, pointing. 'In case there are any more people here.'

Responding with a nod, the policeman raced towards the barn while relaying a message on his handheld radio. The inferno grew even bigger, the flames now bursting through the roof, twisting and twirling as they rose into the sky.

Another patrol car arrived on the scene. Blix directed it towards the other one.

'He must have rigged up the house,' Kovic said. 'To remove every scrap of evidence.'

'Maybe,' Blix replied pensively. 'There were gas canisters in there. But I think we were the ones who set it off.'

'How do you make that out?'

'It all let fly when we turned up, just as we stopped in the stand of trees over there, almost to the exact second. As if we drove over a trip-wire or something.'

'We did pass that camera,' Kovic said.

'Yes,' Blix said. 'And from the very first moment we've been dealing with someone who has planned everything right down to the tiniest detail, and who has carefully laid out the pieces of the puzzle for us and virtually timed both when we should find a victim and when a victim should be killed. This,' he said, pointing at the house, 'falls nicely into place in the series.'

'Do you think Dahlmann could have managed that?' she asked.

Blix had always doubted Dahlmann's abilities. Now he was even less certain of them.

'I just can't accept that he could,' he said. 'Why would he also make himself a victim?'

'And what was Dahlmann known for?' Kovic said. 'He killed *two* people. He was a double murderer. Is *he* number two?'

Blix nodded. There was a good chance that Kovic's reasoning was spot on.

One of the uniformed officers emerged from the barn and sprinted towards them.

'They've found something,' Kovic said.

They went to meet him.

'There's a body in there!' he told them, indicating behind him. 'A woman.'

Blix swore and picked up speed, Kovic following on his heels. The officer led them into a room at the far end of the barn and then down a staircase to a cellar with thick stone walls. Blix paused in the doorway. A bulb hanging from the ceiling was the only source of light. Beside the far wall, Sonja Nordstrøm lay in a pool of coagulated blood.

'She can't have been dead for more than a couple of hours,' the police officer said.

A couple of hours, Blix thought, unable to make this add up. He was missing something.

'Have you searched the rest of the building?' he asked.

'Yes,' was the prompt reply. 'There's no one else here.'

'OK, then,' Blix said. 'This is a crime scene. Seal it off.'

They heard the sound of several sirens grow loud outside. The fire brigade had arrived.

As Blix and Kovic emerged from the barn, the fire fighters were already rolling out huge water hoses.

With a crash, the left gable wall of the house collapsed in a cascade of sparks that the hot air currents tossed back up to the heavens.

The water thundered through the hoses, but the flames grew stronger, as if receiving continual nourishment. The house would be razed to the ground, and it would take hours, if not days, before the burnt-out ruins could be examined and they could search for Emma's remains.

'It's all over, then, isn't it?' Kovic said at Blix's side. 'His number series is complete. Sonja Nordstrøm, forever number one, is dead too.'

Flakes of grey ash drizzled down on them.

'But we still don't have number ten,' Blix reminded her.

'Yes, but it's over and done with now, surely; number ten came first, presumably?'

Blix nodded. 'If Dahlmann was acting on his own.'

'There's really nothing to suggest anything else,' Kovic said. 'I don't think he could face going back to prison. This could have been his plan all along, to make himself part of his grand project.'

'But why drag Emma into it?' Blix protested. 'All Dahlmann's other victims were celebrities, and Emma wasn't.'

Kovic couldn't come up with a good answer. Blix followed the jets of water with his eyes, back to one of the fire engines. He coughed repeatedly once more.

'But he did have problems with celebrities,' Kovic said. 'His girl-friend became famous. That destroyed his life. She found another boyfriend, and no one would believe he had acted in self-defence when he killed them. And when he became a celebrity, after we'd posted him nationwide as a wanted man, he killed something he'd come to despise wholeheartedly. In many ways we've come full circle. And his work is complete.'

Blix hung on Kovic's every word, but still he resisted her argument. Emma's role in all this, and the order of the killings, still troubled him. All the other victims had followed a particular chronology. If Dahlmann, number two, were behind it all, he would have had to kill number one – Sonja Nordstrøm – before he killed himself. It just didn't fit the pattern.

More police cars had arrived now, and Gard Fosse stepped out from one of them.

Blix walked over and explained that Dahlmann's corpse was inside the burning building, and that Sonja Nordstrøm's cadaver had been found in the cellar in the barn.

'And Emma Ramm?'

Blix shook his head as yet another wall caved in, scattering another cloud of sparks. Kovic gave Fosse a condensed version of her personal theory of how Dahlmann had shot Nordstrøm before taking his own life.

'Then it's all at an end,' his boss concluded. 'It all stops here.'

Blix was less sure. He recalled the image of Dahlmann lying on the living-room floor. The position, the amount of blood, and the placing of the gun. Something jarred. He simply couldn't make the details fit a suicide.

'We really have to find out where it all started, before we can be certain it's all over,' he said, setting off towards the car. 'That means we must find number ten.'

93

An hour later they were back at their desks in the police station. Kovic sat beside Blix, poring over a computer log. Nicolai Wibe was on the phone, while Tine Abelvik leafed through a printout of death notices. They were hoovering up all the death notifications they could find that had any connection to the number ten. Blix had told them to think creatively and extensively, and also to contact other police districts in the Østland region.

'Jeppe Sørensen went missing on the twenty-ninth of September,' he said. 'We know Viking Willy, the lottery millionaire, and Mona Kleven, the woman with nine lives, were killed before that, so everything from about the middle of September until the twenty-ninth is relevant. If you can't find anything in that time frame, go even further back.'

The dead person who had been the one to trigger the countdown should also be famous – this was where the snowball had started rolling – so it was likely that this particular victim had some special significance for the killer.

Blix had taken a shower after they'd returned from the burning house in Nordmarka. It was still difficult to breathe normally, but he'd turned a deaf ear to the advice that he ought to consult a doctor.

All the same, he found it difficult to focus. His thoughts centred on Emma. The uncertainty about what had happened to her. The idea that she had been inside the burning house was persistent and unsettling.

He tried to steer his mind back to Iselin. It was only a matter of hours until her sojourn in the house would be over, and he really had to attend the final show.

He opened his browser so he could take a look at her, but instead of logging in, he raised his head. Someone had switched on the overhead TV. Gard Fosse was wrapping up a hastily called press conference. The main message was repeated in a strapline at the foot of the picture. Sonja Nordstrøm had been found dead. With the police closing in on him, the killer had set up a series of explosions and was now presumed to have died in the ensuing fire. Live aerial images from the farm in Nordmarka appeared in one corner of the screen. Smoke was still rising from the ruins.

Blix turned to Kovic. 'We should send Krohn up there,' he said. 'Get him to check the camera beside the track. It must transmit via Wi-Fi. Maybe there are some images on a server or something, so that we can see the comings and goings.'

'You still don't believe Dahlmann was acting alone?'

'I just want absolute certainty,' he replied, getting to his feet. 'And the camera may have triggered the fire in some way.'

Blix couldn't find Krohn in the office, but managed to reach him by phone.

'Can't it wait till tomorrow?' Krohn asked after Blix had explained the situation.

'Only if you don't think there could be data that might be recorded over and deleted,' Blix replied.

Krohn exhaled audibly. 'OK,' he said.

Blix thanked him and headed for the toilet. He rinsed his face with cold water before returning to his desk and tilting his computer screen.

'What did he say?' Kovic asked.

'He'll check it out,' Blix said as he clicked into the *Worthy Winner* website and located the live images from the house; there was no sound now. Iselin was sitting on top of the safe with the prize money locked inside, legs dangling. Toralf Schanke stood facing her. It was impossible to see if they had come any closer to a decision about who should leave as the victor.

Five minutes later, Fosse entered the office, with Pia Nøkleby half a step behind him.

'Let me first thank you all for your efforts,' he began. 'We still have a major task ahead of us. There's a lot to be cleared up, but I've seen how all of you have hammered away, and before we move on to the next phase, you all deserve a bit of R&R with your families.'

Blix shook his head. He was sure that, as far as Fosse was concerned, this wasn't about the health and wellbeing of his investigators; it was more about his fear of an excessive overtime budget.

All around him, computer screens turned black and people began to stream out of the section. Only Kovic remained at her desk.

'I can't go home now,' she said. 'I don't have the peace of mind to do that. There's a number ten somewhere to be found.'

Blix had no plans to head for home either. He had an uncomfortable feeling there was an important connection somewhere that they had overlooked.

94

It was the smell that woke Emma. A sharp, putrid stench that slowly penetrated through her nostrils and up into her brain.

She opened her eyes and blinked.

Opened them wide, smothered a sob.

Her brain took a few seconds to register what her eyes were staring at, a dead woman sitting in a rocking chair, her head dropped on to her chest. A blue rope encircled her neck and her hands were tied behind the chair. Emma took a trembling gasp for air. She hoped the man who stood facing the dead woman had not heard it.

He was muttering something Emma could not quite catch. The elderly woman had undoubtedly been dead for some time. Her skin had shrivelled, and the decomposition process was fairly advanced. That was what Emma could smell.

Emma closed her eyes as the man moved around, unwilling to let him know she was awake. Not yet. A length of fabric was fastened tightly around her mouth. Her arms and legs were also tied snugly to the chair she sat in.

'Do you think I *wanted* to bring her here?' he said. 'I can't go to anyone else in the media. Not now.'

Anger, Emma thought. She had screwed up his plans. 'Yes, I *know* that, Mum,' he said. 'I'll get rid of her afterwards. When it's all over.'

Mum, Emma thought. The dead woman was his mother.

She swallowed something dry and hard in her throat, struggling to gather her thoughts. She must have been brought back to the place where it had all started. To his own mother. She was the one who was number ten.

But why had he murdered her?

I'll get rid of her afterwards. When it's all over.

Fighting a sudden urge to try to free herself, Emma opened her eyes and looked at him – there was no point in pretending any longer. She felt a fierce hatred swell within her. She detested every single tiny centimetre of this man and what he had done. To her, to everyone.

Emma strained at the knots, but they were firmly tied. Underneath them she was already starting to feel pain. A wound in her head throbbed fiercely. A red-hot stinging sensation on her neck. He suddenly turned to face her, and Emma flung curses and shouts of aggression at him, but through the gag they all came out as *mmmm*-sounds.

He smacked his lips, as if to tell her she was behaving stupidly and it was useless to struggle. This didn't stop Emma from tugging and tearing at the knots, but with every exertion the rope just dug deeper into her skin. She would soon start to bleed.

'You want to say something?' he asked.

With difficulty, Emma stopped herself struggling and making a noise.

'Do you want to beg for forgiveness?' he went on, 'Do you regret your behaviour?'

It felt as if the gag was about to strangle her.

'I can take off your gag for a minute, if you want to apologise,' he said. 'And if you can promise me you won't scream. Have you made up your mind to say sorry, Emma?'

She gazed up at him, and received only a look of indifference in return. As if it didn't matter to him what she answered. But she nodded. Anything to get rid of the gag.

He moved so close to her that the fabric of his hoodie touched her nose. It smelled of deep-fried food. She felt his fingers on her neck. The knot gradually loosening. A headache that rapidly eased. Soon she was able to use her tongue to push the cloth all the way out of her mouth. It was easier to breathe.

'Thanks,' she gasped, surprised to find she actually meant it.

He took a step away from her. Contemplated her. Waiting for her to say something.

At first she didn't understand what his expression meant. Then: 'Oh,' she said, moistening her lips. 'Sorry.'

He cast his eyes down. 'For what, then?'

'For ... trying to destroy the laptop. I'll finish writing the article about you. I promise. I'll make sure it gets published, and read.'

He appeared to consider her suggestion. But he didn't answer. Instead he walked across to his mother again. Moved her head a little. Her lower jaw fell open, revealing nicotine-stained teeth. He pushed the jaw closed, but it fell open again.

'How did you kill her?' Emma asked, looking away at the same time.

He gave no response.

'I don't need to write anything about it,' Emma added.

He took two steps back, as if to study his mother. There was a lengthy pause before he said: 'Don't you recognise her?'

He was still standing with his back to Emma now.

'Should I?'

'Maybe you're not old enough,' he said. 'But my mother was an excellent actress at one time. Performed at the National Theatre. Was in a couple of films too.'

He paused again.

'She injured her arm on stage one evening, but didn't go to the doctor's straight away. In fact she left it so long, the operation and the pain she had to suffer gave her an addiction to pills. It's probably twenty years since she performed in her last play.'

He perched on the edge of the table beside his mother. Swept back some of the grey hair that had fallen across her dead eyes.

'I wrote a few stories,' he continued. 'For her. To try to bring the actress in her back to life again. I hoped that she might want to develop the stories further, together with me. Think professionally again. Gradually regain the desire to live, not merely exist, one pill at a time.'

He shook his head.

'Instead she made a fool of me. Who was *I* to believe I could create something? She may have been bitter,' he said. 'That her career was over. Furious at life, perhaps, furious that she had ended up with a son like me.'

He entwined his fingers. 'She never supported me,' he said softly. 'Never helped me. Didn't ever appreciate the things I was good at.'

For a brief second Emma felt a scintilla of sympathy for him. But an attempt to move her hand reminded her that she sat tied to a chair in a dead woman's house, and that she would suffer the same fate if she didn't think of something clever, and fast.

'She didn't have much of a life,' he said. 'So I took it from her. Did her a favour. She's going to be famous again now, after this.'

He smiled, fleetingly, pleased with himself.

'On that subject,' he said, moving from the table, 'I need to get a move on.'

'Where are you going?' Emma asked.

'I'll tell you all of it later,' he replied. 'When I come back. Then you can include it in your article.'

The next minute he was beside her again, forcefully shoving the cloth gag back into her mouth and pulling it tight at the back. Emma tried to protest, to scream, but she couldn't do anything about it. He was too strong. Too determined.

Once he was satisfied, he grabbed a bunch of keys from the table and turned to his mother again.

'I'll be back again in a couple of hours, Mum,' he said. 'You're going to be so proud of me.'

He smiled at her. Smiled at Emma.

Then he turned heel and left.

95

Emma had to rip her gaze away from the dead woman. She tried to move her mouth to loosen the gag, but it was impossible. The same was true of the knots at her hands and feet.

Through the flimsy curtains Emma caught sight of a grand, white house not far off. Neighbours, she thought. People.

Exerting her whole body, she found she was able to jerk herself forwards. It was possible: she managed to shift the chair a centimetre or two, turning in the direction of the window. Emma executed another hop with the chair, forwards again. And another jolt, moving a little closer.

Her body ached, but she had to grin and bear it. Centimetre by centimetre she edged closer to the window. Her efforts were making her hot, and when the first drop of perspiration ran down the side of her head, she stopped for a second, suddenly aware that she was no longer wearing her wig. It made her feel naked. Exposed. But she had no choice but to escape. She pushed the thought of her baldness out of her mind and stretched her legs against the chair to get a better grip. She strained her stomach muscles and jumped another few centimetres towards the window.

The sweat was pouring off her now. Her clothes were sticking to her skin. Eventually she began to get into a rhythm, but her enthusiastic movements almost tipped her over. She stopped and held her breath until the chair was steady again. Then she continued.

A table blocked her route now. Emma hopped as close to it as she could manage, trying to think how she would manage to move it. When she felt the chair make contact with the edge, she tried with all her might to give the table a push.

It did not budge.

She would just have to go on trying. She took a breath and relaxed her muscles a little before contracting them again and making another gargantuan effort – but the table did not give an inch. But this time she didn't stop; she just continued hopping, into the table, time after time after time, and soon she saw that it was moving, ever so slowly. Heartened by her progress, she went on bumping herself and the chair into the table. She was bleeding underneath the knots, and her muscles were screaming in protest, but it didn't matter: it was working – she managed to move the table. Perspiration trickled down into her eyes, but she blinked it away.

Finally she was beside the window. The most important task was still ahead of her. Making contact with someone. She craned her neck, and succeeded in dipping her head under the curtain. The light from outside seemed to hit her in the face.

It was late afternoon.

She saw a light on in an exterior lamp outside the grand, white house, but she could see no movement, outside or inside the small window nearest the driveway.

Emma managed to push her head against the windowpane; it felt cold on her bare scalp. She managed to grunt out a few sounds; they would never be loud enough to alert anyone. She had to attract attention by some other means.

She'd been sitting gazing out of the window for a while when her ears suddenly pricked up. Was that the thrum of an engine? She scanned the scene, and a moment later spotted a car driving up to the house next door.

Emma immediately began to shriek, but the gag muffled the sound. She tried to jiggle the chair closer to the wall and the window, but there was no more space. However, her movements made her head strike the window, making a noise.

That gave her an idea.

She watched the car come to a halt. Heard the engine noise cease.

Emma breathed in with all her might. Shut her eyes. Mustered renewed strength and steeled herself for the pain she knew would follow. It felt as if it was now or never. Life or death.

She opened her eyes and saw a man step out of the car. She had to do it now. She banged her head against the window with all her strength.

No response. He didn't see her. Harder, she said to herself. You have to do it harder. To amplify the noise.

Once again she took a deep breath. Focused on the window. Forgot the pain. Thought of the future, however short or long it may be. That what she was doing here and now might well be the most important thing she would ever do.

Using every scrap of energy she possessed, Emma banged her head on the windowpane again.

Then she did it again.

And again.

She heard a splintering noise and saw that the glass was cracking. She just had to continue, one thump at a time; she didn't stop to see if the man outside had noticed her – she just thumped and thumped and thumped, until all at once the window shattered over her, around her – the crashing sound of breaking glass was ear-splitting, and she screamed behind the gag – from fatigue, joy, and pain.

Shards of glass, sharp as knives, rained down upon her; she could feel them slicing into her skin, and the blood immediately start to drip from her head and throat. But what she clung to, what gave her hope while the colours danced around her, was the wind, cold against her skin. It came from outside.

96

Blix studied the footage of Dahlmann planting the phone belonging to the Danish footballer at the press conference. Krohn had pieced together a sequence in which the double murderer was caught by the cameras outside the police station.

He played the sequence several times. With each repetition, he grew increasingly uncertain about whether it was Dahlmann he had spotted on his way to Pastor Hansteen's house. There and then he had felt confident. He had stopped the subway trains, closed off streets and sent a helicopter into the air to search for a man in a suit that was slightly too small for him. Because there had been something familiar about the man. His build had tallied, but not his stiff gait.

His phone rang. It was an internal number, from the operations centre. The female caller introduced herself as head of operations.

'We have a standing order here that you should be notified of all messages that have any kind of connection to the number ten,' she began. 'At the moment we have a patrol car en route to Drivhusveien number ten in Bryn.'

'What's happening there?' Blix asked.

'A woman who was tied to a chair has managed to use her head to break a window,' the caller explained. 'She's bleeding pretty badly. It was the man in the house next door who called it in.'

'Someone held prisoner?' Blix queried.

'It seems so,' the woman replied.

'Who lives there?'

'We have a Martha Elisabeth Eckhoff listed at that address,' she told him. 'Sixty-seven years of age.'

Blix stood up.

'Repeat that name,' he said.

'Martha Elisabeth Eckhoff. I think she's an old actress or something.'

A distressing thought flashed through Blix's mind.

'Hold the line!' he bellowed as he logged into the *Worthy Winner* page.

'What is it?' Kovic asked.

Blix didn't answer, but clicked through the website to locate the recordings of the tests the contestants had been subjected to.

'Hidden camera,' he said, pointing at the film showing the contestants' reactions when they found their 500-kroner notes.

On screen, the farmer parked his red Nissan. Even Eckhoff entered the picture, dropped a 500-kroner bill and walked off.

'He's limping,' Blix said, to himself just as much as to Kovic. He still had the head of operations on the phone. 'Check whether she has a son called Even,' he told her, looking at the time. 'Pronto!'

He heard the sound of a keyboard tapping at the other end. Blix pulled on his jacket while he waited. Kovic stared at him in anticipation.

'Looks like it, yes,' the head of operations answered. 'Even Eckhoff, born thirty-first of January nineteen eighty-seven; mother – Martha Elisabeth Eckhoff; father – Erling Sebastian.'

It all added up. The studios in Nydalen and Emma's bike left there after the broadcast. Now Blix remembered who Eckhoff had reminded him of.

'The estate agent guy,' he said. 'He walked the same way. He had a limp too.'

Blix didn't take time to explain, but asked the head of operations to keep them posted about what they found at Drivhusveien ten. Then he tilted the computer screen showing the *Worthy Winner* web page so that Kovic could see it.

At the top of the page, a clock was ticking.

WILL THEY AGREE? was written underneath, on a sign bearing a picture of Iselin and Toralf – staring at each other as if engaged in a duel that was a matter of life or death. The clock continued to tick. It was one hour and fourteen minutes until the countdown would be over.

'In a countdown,' Blix said, looking at Kovic while struggling to hide how afraid he now felt, 'do you end with one, or do you end with zero?'

'Zero,' Kovic said. 'Zero is also a number.'

Spot on, Blix thought.

The clock always ticked right down to zero.

97

'Tell me what you're thinking,' Kovic said as Blix heaved himself into the driving seat.

'Even Eckhoff,' Blix replied, turning the ignition. 'He's trying to trick us, the way he's tricked us all along.'

'How?'

'Dahlmann was number two,' he explained as the engine fired up. 'The double murderer. The chronology and the countdown fit. He was just a useful idiot Eckhoff used until his turn came. He must have been at the farm, which is why no one could track him down. Eckhoff hired him to do minor tasks here and there, such as delivering an envelope to Radio 4 and planting a phone on the floor at a press conference. And then he was killed when the time was right, once Pastor Hansteen was dead and Eckhoff had no further use for him.'

'What else?'

'The final show,' Blix answered through compressed lips. '*Worthy Winner*. Eckhoff has been in the wings the entire time. He's prepared something for number zero as well.'

'Shouldn't we speak to Fosse about this?'

'To hell with Fosse,' Blix said, thumping the steering wheel impatiently as he waited for the garage door to slide open. 'Phone the operations centre and tell them we're on our way to Nydalen. Ask them to send backup.'

Kovic made the call, gave a brief summary, then listened for a moment.

'They've broken into number ten Drivhusveien,' she told him. 'Martha Elisabeth Eckhoff is dead. She's sitting there tied to a chair. Emma's there too.'

Blix glanced across at Kovic. She put her finger into her ear to hear better.

'They're on the way to hospital with her now,' she told him.

He was relieved that Emma was safe. At the same time, she impressed him. Breaking a window with your head showed great single-mindedness.

The sound of their siren reverberated off the buildings flanking the road. Vehicles moved aside to let them pass.

'What will we do when we get there?' Kovic asked.

'Find Eckhoff,' Blix replied. 'Stop whatever he's planning to do.'

Blix checked the dashboard clock. The transmission had begun. He realised he should've been there already. A few things had got in the way, he thought grimly. He tried to put himself in Eckhoff's mind, imagining what might be about to happen. His whole plan had been rigged up like a countdown. In the TV studios, the clock was still ticking down to zero – to the selection of a 'worthy winner'.

When they arrived at the vast studio building, there was nothing to suggest anything untoward was about to occur. A man stood outside smoking, a woman tugged impatiently at the lead of a dog sniffing around one of the lampposts. Blix turned off the blue light and siren, and manoeuvred the car into the smoking area beside the main entrance. The man standing there looked at them inquisitively as he stubbed out his cigarette.

Blix checked his gun before holstering it to his hip, so that it was hidden beneath his jacket.

Then they marched in.

An enormous TV screen on the wall in reception was showing live images from the studio. Iselin and Toralf were seated on the sofa on stage chatting to the presenter.

One of the security guards Blix had spoken to the previous day got to his feet on the other side of the counter.

'What's up?' he asked.

'Even Eckhoff?' Blix inquired. 'Is he here today?'

'I saw him a minute ago,' the guard replied, nodding. 'He's probably backstage.'

'I need a pass,' Blix said.

Making no objection, the guard pulled out a drawer and took out a card marked *Visitor*.

'Are you any closer to reaching a decision?' Tore Berg Tollersrud asked on the TV screen, glancing at the clock. 'In twenty-eight minutes we must have an answer.'

Blix took the pass and let himself into a corridor.

'Stay here,' he told Kovic who was standing behind him. 'Wait for our backup.'

He used the pass again to open a side door leading into the studio, then fumbled his way through a dark curtain and peered inside. The stage was fifteen metres away from him. On the floor between the stage and the audience, four cameras were set up.

He scrutinised them before letting his eyes rove across the audience. He could see Merete and Jan-Egil, but saw nothing of Eckhoff.

His gaze moved on up to the roof. Under the ceiling, spotlights in various sizes and colours were rigged up. There were ladders and cable ducts, which meant someone could be up there, but the lighting made it difficult to see clearly.

Blix moved from the side door out into the corridor and found his way backstage. Several members of the production team were huddled around screens showing live images of what was taking place on the other side. The voices from the stage and the sound of the audience's reactions were muffled and not completely in sync with the pictures on the screen.

'You've been living in the house for ten weeks now,' Tollersrud said. 'The safe containing the prize money has been in there with you the entire time. One million kroner.'

A woman wearing a headset nodded at Blix and smiled in recognition.

'Have you seen Even Eckhoff?' he asked her.

The woman looked around, as if Eckhoff should really have been in the room with them. Then she shook her head and turned back to the screen.

Blix walked on into the area behind the stage.

'The safe has a coded lock,' he heard Tollersrud explain. 'Have you never been tempted to try to open it?'

'Jonas did,' Toralf answered, referring to the contestant who'd been eliminated in the previous show.

This comment provoked a ripple of laughter in the auditorium. Blix investigated a cubicle, where he found a number of coffee pots and plates of biscuits.

Tollersrud held up an envelope.

'Inside this are the four digits needed to unlock the safe. You can take it with you, go back into the house and open the safe. But don't forget: only one of you gets to take the million kroner out with you.'

Music and applause filled the air as the presenter announced that there were twenty-five minutes left until time was up.

Blix proceeded out into the corridor again to check the make-up room, then followed a spiral staircase up to a large break room. Two security guards were seated there. On a large TV screen, he saw Iselin open the envelope containing the code for the safe.

'Three-two-one-zero,' she read out, with a chuckle.

The camera located her mother in the audience. Merete laughed and clutched Jan-Egil's hand beside her. The picture shifted to Toralf, who was keying in the code.

Blix's phone rang. Gard Fosse's name appeared on the display. Blix dismissed the call and tapped in Kovic's number as he approached the guards.

'Have you seen Even Eckhoff?' he asked.

One of the security guards half turned towards him and shook his head.

Kovic answered.

'Has backup arrived yet?' Blix demanded. 'We need more feet on the ground.'

'One patrol car has turned up,' she replied. 'The emergency squad are apparently three minutes away.'

'Didn't he say we had twenty-five minutes left?' Iselin said on screen.

Blix could hear that she was confused, and there was apprehension in her voice. He pivoted around to the TV monitor. Saw the camera zoom in on the contents of the safe.

There was no money inside.

Instead he could see some red flashing lights: they were numbers on a clock. And it was ticking down from three minutes and twenty-one seconds.

Blix used his free hand to grab on to a nearby chair for support.

Something surged inside him.

'Fuck,' Blix swore into his phone. 'Eckhoff has planted a bomb in the TV building. We've got three minutes before it goes off!'

98

Blix charged down the spiral staircase, along the corridor and into the studio. There was a crackling sound coming from the studio manager's headset, but neither he nor the camera operators seemed to have understood the situation. Tollersrud was still on stage. A monitor showed a close-up of the contents of the safe. The device ticking down. 02.56 nudged towards 02.55. It was possible to see the leads protruding from four bulky, grey packages.

Some of the spectators in the front rows were scrambling out of their seats now. Blix spotted a fire alarm, rushed over to it and smashed the glass so that bells began to ring. The image on the monitor went black. Someone shouted that there was a bomb. It took only a few seconds for panic to begin to spread. A cameraman dashed to the exit, with another close on his heels. Members of the audience clambered over the rows of seats, pushing and shoving. Shouting, screaming.

Blix bounded on to the stage and darted toward the house entrance. The sliding doors had no handles, so he tried to push them aside. They would not budge. He cast around for some kind of tool.

Looking around he saw the studio was still full of people. Kovic and four uniformed officers were fighting their way through the stream of fleeing spectators. The producer, Petter Due-Eriksen, was with them.

On the screen, which had turned black, a message appeared stating that the transmission would be 'back shortly'. Two smaller screens still showed pictures from the interior of the House. One camera seemed to be fixed on the clock. 02.39, 02.38. The other screen automatically shadowed the movements of the contestants. Iselin and Toralf were standing at the security doors, the other exit from the House. But they were also shut.

'What's happening?' Due-Eriksen asked.

'Even Eckhoff,' Blix said with no further explanation. 'Open the doors!'

'They're electronically controlled,' Due-Eriksen told him. 'They shouldn't be locked, just shut.'

Due-Eriksen tried to push the doors open while one of the uniformed police officers applied all his weight to the other section of the door, but to no avail.

Blix grabbed hold of another policeman's shoulder. 'Battering ram!' he roared.

The policeman passed on the message. The emergency squad responded that they were less than a minute away with all the necessary equipment.

The on-screen clock had counted down to 02.09. The seconds were ticking far too fast.

'Is there another way in?' asked the officer who'd tried to open the doors.

'The security doors,' Due-Eriksen replied, and disappeared with him.

The remaining police officers continued to work on the sliding doors. One of them had found a hammer he used to batter the hinges. The other had picked up a metal bar.

Iselin and Toralf were making their way back through the house. The cameras followed them, and a moment later they heard knocking from inside. The TV pictures showed that Toralf was using his fists.

Blix was at a loss. He was about to draw his gun and shoot at the hinges when the emergency squad arrived, dressed in dark jumpsuits and balaclavas, armed with machine pistols. Two of them carried a battering ram between them. Heavy boots clattered across the TV studio floor.

They leapt on to the stage without a word. Blix pointed at the sliding doors, and urged them to be as fast as possible. The men took up position. Two of them lifted the battering ram and let it smack against the doors. The timber splintered, the doors were dislodged, but did not give way.

Blix kept an eye on the screen showing pictures from inside. Iselin and Toralf had moved back a little. The battering ram struck again, but not with enough force. Iselin took a step back, turned around and disappeared out of view. The camera tracked Toralf as he stepped towards the sliding doors and pulled at some loose beading.

'Where did she go?' asked Kovic.

The camera beside them now displayed 01.24. Still time, Blix thought in panic, as the battering ram broke through. Then the back of Iselin's head appeared, obscuring the camera angle.

'She's closing the door of the safe,' Kovic said.

Blix nodded, pleased at her presence of mind. This would reduce the effect of the explosion.

'Everybody out!' the leader of the emergency squad ordered.

Toralf was hauled out through the shattered door. Due-Eriksen was already heading for the exit, along with the uniformed police officers.

'What about the bomb?' Kovic asked.

The emergency squad officer shook his head.

'Too little time,' he said before repeating the command to his crew: 'Everybody out!'

Blix forced his way through to the opening.

'Iselin!' he yelled.

He hunkered down and squeezed through. Called out again.

'Blix!' Kovic shouted at him.

'You get out!' he roared back.

'The security doors!' Kovic told him, pointing at the two screens relaying images from inside the house.

Blix was unable to see what she was talking about. He turned, peered through the opening and saw on the screen that the security doors were open.

'Eckhoff,' Kovic gasped. 'He went inside.'

Blix wheeled around again and drew his gun.

99

Someone had turned off the fire alarm. A weird silence enveloped Blix. He held his pistol out in front of him, in his right hand, using his left hand to support it. He tried to recall the TV images he had seen over the weeks to find his bearings in the house, then moving forwards with practised movements.

He first caught sight of them in one of the huge one-way mirrors on the wall. Eckhoff stood waiting with Iselin in front of him. He was pressing a pistol to her temple and had the other hand tight around her torso.

He had already also spotted Blix.

'Come out!' he commanded.

Blix filled his lungs and tried to gain control over his own breathing. He looked around the corner. Avoiding eye contact with Iselin, he focused on Eckhoff and the sight on the barrel of his own pistol.

'Release her!' he ordered.

Eckhoff smiled. 'We're still on air,' he said, gesturing towards one of the fixed cameras streaming live on the Internet.

'Let her go!' Blix yelled.

Eckhoff took two steps back, hauling Iselin with him, shrinking behind her body. Blix was four metres away now. Iselin was pale. Her lips were quivering. Tears filled her eyes.

Blix had Eckhoff's left eye in his line of sight, just above Iselin's shoulder. His gaze was steady, as if he felt no doubt or remorse.

'What's it been like, watching your daughter become more and more famous in here?' Eckhoff asked, blinking away a bead of perspiration.

Blix didn't reply, but took a step closer to increase the size of the target.

Eckhoff motioned again towards the camera. 'You know, Blix, you're going to be a celebrity yourself now?'

Blix didn't reply. His pistol barrel had begun to tremble. He had held his aim for too long. Tensed muscles and frayed nerves. The red dot was dancing around the sight. He was suddenly back in Teisen nineteen years earlier. The picture of Emma and her father clamoured for space in his thoughts. It was as if a fog had descended over his eyes, blurring what was happening in front of him.

'It'll soon be over,' Eckhoff said.

Blix felt the pulse throb in his neck. He took a deep breath and held it in.

'How long do we have left?' Eckhoff continued, kicking the closed safe.

The slight movement made the sight slip across to Iselin's forehead. Blix breathed out again. Adjusted.

'Ten seconds?' Eckhoff suggested.

Blix curled his finger around the trigger. Focused his mind, his body, his emotions.

Eckhoff's voice changed into a slow echo: 'Nine seconds? Or eight?' He smiled.

Blix held his breath again.

And fired.

The shot penetrated Eckhoff's left eye, knocking him back in a cloud of blood. Before he hit the floor, Blix had fired two more shots into his chest.

The shower of blood splashed over Iselin, covering the left side of her face. Sobbing uncontrollably, she was about to collapse. But Blix rushed forwards, grabbed her in his arms and dragged her towards the front exit. He pushed her in front of him, out through the splintered door, then pulled her across the stage and towards the public entrance. Counting to himself.

Four, three, two.

Iselin tripped on a step beside him. Blix hauled her up, and pulled her out into the corridor.

Then came the explosion.

A resounding boom that made everything shake.

Blix flung himself over his daughter and used his arms to protect his own head. The door behind them was blown open. A cloud of dust scudded out. Objects clattered down from the walls and ceiling. Tinkling glass all around. The lights went out and an alarm began to wail.

Blix scrambled to his knees and checked Iselin in the dim light.

'Are you OK?'

She coughed, but then nodded and clutched him tightly. Blix helped her up and supported her with his body as they moved towards the exit.

The doors were thrown open and four firemen hauled them out, shoving them further into the chaos outside.

And then Kovic was beside them, holding people off and waving to an ambulance.

Merete broke through the barrier the police were struggling to set up, and rushed towards them. Iselin let go of Blix and threw her arms around her mother's neck.

Leaning forwards, Blix rested his hands on his knees. Took a deep breath and closed his eyes.

It was over, he thought.

At last it was over.

100

Blix was ushered through the hospital corridors, and ended up in a waiting area for patients and relatives. He recognised Irene Ramm. She introduced him to her daughter, Martine, who smiled shyly, but took Blix's hand when he held it out to her.

A short distance away, a man with curly hair and glasses stood up. 'Kasper Bjerringbo,' he said. 'I ... I'm a friend of Emma's.'

Blix shook his hand too, before turning to a woman he recognised from the news. Anita Grønvold, Emma's boss at news.no. She also got to her feet and shook his hand.

'Have you been in to see her?' he asked, glancing towards the nearest ward.

'Not yet,' Irene answered. 'She's sleeping. The doctor wanted us to wait until she woke.'

They passed the time by watching the news bulletins on a big TV screen. Recent mobile videos of the explosion appeared, together with interviews with people who'd been in the audience – former contestants, and employees who'd worked on the last broadcast. Petter

Due-Eriksen had to give a comment, and Gard Fosse issued a statement in which he emphasised the fact that the police had prevented a far more serious incident, thanks to their speedy and competent action.

The perpetrator was now identified as Even Eckhoff, and snippets about his life were now being broadcast. A camera team was outside his mother's house, but details of how Emma had shattered the windowpane to call for help had not yet hit the headlines.

Just before midnight, a doctor allowed them to go in. Emma blinked sleepily, but watched them as they entered. A machine made a peeping sound. A monitor showed her pulse rate as fifty-eight. One by one they gathered around her bed.

It was Martine who spoke first: 'You don't have any hair anymore.'

Emma looked at her. Smiled lamely, before turning her gaze to Irene. Then Kasper.

'I haven't had any hair for years, sweetheart,' she said to her niece. 'But I've got a lovely bandage, don't you think?'

Emma lifted her hand and touched her head. Martine crawled up on to the bed.

'The doctor told me what happened,' Emma said, her eyes now on Blix. 'That you shot him.'

Taking a step forwards, Blix nodded.

'He made me interview him,' Emma said, turning to Anita now. 'I didn't manage to finish editing it.' A twitch contorted her face.

'You mustn't think about work now,' Irene told her. 'You just have to relax and get better.'

Emma gave her sister a fleeting smile.

'But not for too long,' Grønvold interjected, before winking at Emma and starting to cough.

Martine put a hand on Emma's head.

'Careful,' Irene said behind her.

'I can't feel anything, anyway,' Emma said. 'It's fine.'

Martine carefully caressed the shiny part of her skull that wasn't covered by bandage.

'It's smooth,' she said.

'Yes, it is,' Emma replied.

'It looks a bit strange,' Martine added.

Emma shot a look at her sister again, before saying: 'You get used to it. I think it looks pretty cool, in fact.'

Kasper began to say something, but had to clear his throat first.

'You do,' he said. 'You look...' it seemed as if he didn't know how to continue the sentence '...even better than before,' he rounded off.

Emma smiled. Her lips were dry.

'But will your hair never grow again?' Martine asked her.

Emma slowly shook her head. 'No it won't, honey bunch. But it doesn't matter. To be honest, it's absolutely fine.'

EPILOGUE

In the weeks that followed, it was difficult for Blix to do his job. Everyone he phoned and met wanted to talk about what had happened. Every day he was contacted by journalists, ostensibly asking about another case he was working on, but actually wanting an interview about the countdown murders. These varied from profiles of him as an investigator and a person, and what his life had been like since the Teisen tragedy, to probing questions about the actual homicides, what his experience of them had been and the pursuit of the killer, day by day. Members of the force's senior management wanted Blix to agree to these interviews, keen for the force to appear in the best possible light. 'We have a unique opportunity here now,' Gard Fosse had said. '*You* have a unique opportunity.'

They had called from TV stations in Norway, Sweden and Denmark, wanting him to take part in the typical Friday evening chat shows. They were happy to conduct these interviews anywhere at all, and at any time that suited, if only they could get him in front of a microphone and camera.

Blix had turned them all down. He'd had more than enough attention to last him a lifetime.

Around Christmas, things began to calm down. Blix had signed up to work over the Christmas and New Year holidays and took on extra shifts so that others in the section could spend time with family and friends.

'To tell the truth I'm perfectly happy to be working,' Kovic said when Blix asked how she felt about working on New Year's Eve. It usually fell to newcomers to take on the less popular shifts.

'And I knew well in advance,' she went on. 'Anyway there's always so much hassle at New Year's Eve. So much unnecessary drama. All my newly single girlfriends start to whinge about the start of the New Year, then try to steal someone else's guy when they've had a couple of glasses too many. I prefer to spend my evening with crooks!'

'You've worked too long with me,' Blix said. 'Look out, or you'll become an old sourpuss too.'

Kovic smiled.

New Year's Eve was an occasion like no other on the streets of Oslo. Even though there were regulations about where setting off fireworks was permitted, there were always a few people who fired off rockets where they shouldn't, and there were always more fights than usual. In the hours leading up to midnight, Blix and Kovic had to don their uniforms, to help ensure a visible police presence in the city.

The streets were covered in slush, as the recent snowfall had been replaced by rain. They manoeuvred their way around the biggest puddles and stopped from time to time to watch the occasional rocket soar into the misty sky.

When they reached the cathedral, Blix's phone rang. It was ten minutes to midnight.

His face brightened. 'Hello, my best girl,' he said – he had never stopped calling Iselin that.

'Hi, Dad,' she shouted – Blix could hear a din in the background. The sound of music, partying, people yelling and laughing. 'I just wanted to wish you a Happy New Year now, before it gets impossible to phone anyone later. The phone network will break down completely, as usual, once the clocks strike twelve.'

'That's nice,' Blix said – he had to swallow a couple of times. Iselin had called him increasingly often recently, just to find out how he was, or to have a little chat.

'Where are you?' he asked, even though he knew her plans for the evening.

'With some friends in Grünerløkka.'

He could tell by her voice that she'd been drinking, but her diction was still clear.

'Is it all going with a swing?' he asked.

They'd talked a great deal about what had happened in the *Worthy Winner* house. Iselin had spent hours with a psychologist, sometimes together with Blix. Processing it all had been difficult because she'd become such a public face; everyone she met wanted to talk to her about what had occurred. Her being at a party was a good sign.

'It's going pretty well,' she finally answered, but Blix could hear some reservation in her voice. Rockets exploded above him. Blix had to put a finger in his ear.

'What is it?' he asked.

'Nothing,' she replied at first.

Then: 'It's just ... it's not long now until people start counting down to midnight. I...'

Blix could hear someone shout in the background.

'I'm just dreading it a little.'

'I can understand that.'

They turned into Karl Johans gate. At the end, in the distance, the yellow glow of the palace façade. 'Do you want me to stay on the line while you all count down?' he asked.

'No, not at all,' she said. 'It'll be fine.' Then she added: 'I think.'

Blix's heart was warmed by her words. He wondered whether they should make tracks for Birkelunden, where he expected Iselin's friends would come out to see the colours in the sky, but there wasn't time; he wouldn't make it.

'He's gone,' he said instead. 'Eckhoff's no longer around. He can't hurt you any longer.'

'I know that,' she replied. 'But what if there are other madmen about?'

Blix understood her anxiety. 'If you're scared, stay inside,' he said. 'OK? Don't venture out.'

Iselin didn't answer immediately.

'But that's a bit dreary, too. And then I'd be letting that idiot control me. I don't want that to happen.'

Blix gave a smile.

They were approaching the outdoor ice rink at Spikersuppa. Crackles and bangs were exploding everywhere.

'It's getting a bit difficult to hear you now,' Blix said. 'I need to pay attention to what's going on round about me too.'

'OK. Happy New Year, Dad.'

'Happy New Year, my best girl.'

And they rang off.

Blix looked across at Kovic. She was smiling, but she said nothing.

They walked down to the City Hall at Rådhusplassen, where a teeming crowd of people had assembled. Many of them had their eyes glued to a raft out in the harbour basin, from which Oslo City Council set off rockets every year. The show began at midnight on the dot. Blix looked at his watch. It was one minute to.

Around them were throngs of happy people, who were singing, hugging one another, smoking and drinking. Usually the police came down hard on drinking in the streets, but it was a hopeless battle on a night like this.

Kovic and Blix stopped to observe the chaos around them.

'New year, new opportunities,' Kovic commented.

'New cases as well,' Blix replied.

Nearby, someone turned on a megaphone and announced that there were thirty seconds to midnight. Everyone was encouraged to join in the countdown.

Kovic and Blix looked at each other, both with their own private thoughts.

The people joined in: 'TEN, NINE, EIGHT, SEVEN, SIX, FIVE, FOUR, THREE, TWO, ONE...'

Then came the explosion.

ACKNOWLEDGMENTS

Thomas: So Jørn, apparently we have to write some acknowledgements for our book.

Jørn: Ack—?

Thomas: Acknowledgements.

Jørn: What is that?

Thomas: It's that thing at the end where we say our thanks.

Jørn: Ah. Thanks for what, exactly?

Thomas: Help, I suppose. Support. Guidance. Wisdom.

Jørn: I see. I don't really do that kind of thing. I've never done it with my books.

Thomas: Me neither. Well. Not until I signed with Orenda Books, that is.

(beat)

(sighs)

(beat)

Jørn: I really don't know what to say.

Thomas: You don't have anyone you want to thank?

Jørn: I can thank YOU, perhaps.

Thomas: Well, thanks, partner, that goes both ways, but I really don't think that's what they're after.

Jørn: Oh. Right.

(beat)

(sighs)

(beat)

Jørn: I can thank my dog.

Thomas: Your dog?

Jørn: Yes, I take my dog Theodor for a walk every morning. He helps me think. Come up with ideas.

Thomas: I'm sure Theodor will appreciate your mentioning him.

Jørn: Don't you have a son named Theodor?

Thomas: I do. I'll be sure to mention *him*.

Jørn: Did he help you out during the writing of this book?

Thomas: Not really.

Jørn: So why thank him, then?

Thomas: Good question. I don't know.

(beat)

(sighs)

(beat)

Thomas: I'm going to thank my family in general.

Jørn: Why?

Thomas: Why not?

Jørn: I suppose they're instrumental in allowing us to do what we do.

Thomas: That's what I thought as well. Plus, they're nice people.

Jørn: Mine, too.

Thomas: Glad to hear it.

(beat)

(sighs)

(beat)

Jørn: You have a son called Theodor ... that's funny.

Thomas: I really don't think so.

Jørn: How old are your kids now?

Thomas: I have no idea.

(beat)

(sighs)

(beat)

Thomas: Shall we thank our publisher, maybe?

Jørn: I'M our publisher.

Thomas: I know that, Jørn. In Norway you are. Thanks, by the way.

Jørn: You're welcome.

Thomas: This is for the UK and the world market.

Jørn: Ah yes. Sorry.

Thomas: We must say thanks to Karen and West.

Jørn: West?

Thomas: WEST CAMEL, our editor.

Jørn: Oh. Right. Is that his real name?

Thomas: I don't think so, but he has edited our book, and he has given us a really hard time about it, too.

Jørn: I remember. You want to thank him for *that*?

Thomas: No, but he did a heck of a lot to make the book what it turned out to be. You and I couldn't have done that, us being Norwegian and all.

Jørn: I suppose you're right.

Thomas: Neither could our translator, Anne Bruce.

Jørn: Because she's Norwegian, too?

Thomas: No, Jørn, she lives on a Scottish island.

Jørn: Oh, wow.

Thomas: I know.

(beat)

Jørn: So why couldn't she...

Thomas: She's a translator, Jørn, not an editor.

Jørn: Right.

Thomas: And West did some polishing of her words.

Jørn: *Our* words.

Thomas: Yes, but she translated them.

Jørn: Right. Thanks to Anne, then.

Thomas: Yes. Thanks to Anne.

(beat)

(sighs)

(beat)

Thomas: We mustn't forget Karen.

Jørn: Right. Karen.

(beat)

Thomas: You know who Karen is, don't you?

Jørn: Duh. Karen is Karen. Karen Sullivan. Queen Orenda.

Thomas: Yes. The mother of dragons.

Jørn: Hm?

Thomas: Don't tell me you haven't watched *Game of Thrones*?

Jørn: I watch crime shows, Thomas. *Bosch* and *Criminal Minds* and, ahem, my own TV show.

Thomas: Never mind, then.

Jørn: It's called *Wisting*.

Thomas: I know, Jørn. You should thank *him*.

Jørn: Funny. But Karen. Yes. Of course. We owe Karen a lot.

Thomas: We do. Without Karen there would be no book.

Jørn: Karen really is quite something.

Thomas: She really is. She's a power house. And a brilliant publisher.

Jørn: You've known her for quite a while, haven't you?

Thomas: I have. I'm co-leader.

Jørn: You're...?

Thomas: I'm ... never mind. It's a long story.

Jørn: I don't mind long stories.

Thomas: I know you don't, but this isn't a story, Jørn, we're acknowledging people. And dogs, apparently.

Jørn: I love my dog.

Thomas: I know you do.

Jørn: And I love writing books.

Thomas: You should thank yourself, then.

Jørn: We can do that?

Thomas: Not really.

Jørn: So why...? Never mind.

(beat)

(sighs)

(beat)

Thomas: So that's it?

(beat)

(sighs)

(beat)

Jørn: I think so.

Thomas: I can't believe you wanted to thank your dog.

Jørn: I can't believe your son is called Theodor.

Thomas: No one calls their dog Theodor.

Jørn: Well, I do.

Thomas: I know. Now the whole world will know, too.

Jørn: I love my dog.

Thomas: I know you do.